THE BEND

MYTHIC WILD WEST
Book 1

J.H. Kimbrell

DEDICATIONS

To my sweet mother, Patricia Kimbrell.

To Johanna Fally, my bestie overseas, without whose insistence that we explore the American Southwest years ago, this book and series would not exist.

To Phoebe Juel and Serafina Baldacchino, and Jan Robnett for all of your love and years of support.

To Jackie Northesk, who asks me often if I've been writing, and sometimes that's just what I need.

And to my patient beta brigade: Catherine Yvonne King, Dana Gorbet, Juliana Ferguson, Tammy Holt, Tara Cornet, Jennifer Lee Crow-Cassady, and Leisa Stamey.

MICA BEND, ARIZONA TERRITORY

October, 1888

CHAPTER ONE

A distant thundering rose on the scrubby plains surrounding Mica Bend, pushed back by the clutch of steep mountains to the south, appropriately named the Arduous Range. It swelled from rumble to roar until it reached a crescendo. A coarse whistle blared out a warning note and held it like the worst opera singer in Arizona Territory.

"Here it comes," Silas LeBlanc commented at the noise of the train. "And…"

The crescendo peaked at the point where the great iron horse would have stopped at a depot that now sat defunct less than a half-mile outside the town's main thoroughfare. The train thundered on, though, with one last screaming whistle blow before quickly fading into the distance going west.

"… there it goes," he finished, his voice bearing a particular flavor of southern drawl.

The roar reduced again to rumble, then hum, then faded altogether.

Hiram Wells sat kicked back on a bench outside the Orleans Palace Saloon, hat tipped over his eyes to rest them for a moment against the early October sun that had begun its western decline. He grunted back at Silas, in no need of a reminder. It had only been a few months since the Southern Pacific Railroad determined that Mica Bend was not worth stopping for. The engine could make it easily between Benson and San Simon to water up, not far apart at all by rail, and too few people got on or off at the Bend anymore. Not enough silver came out of the mines now, but plenty of mercury remained in its place. Stopping and starting again was a whole lot of effort for a beast designed to deliver people or

1

freight fast and efficiently, and a town with not enough of either was a waste of time.

Only an outgoing mail catcher bag was snatched on the way through, while an incoming mailbag was kicked out into the dust. Right about now, Mr. Fraleigh was picking up the arriving bag and galloping back to the mercantile, where he also managed the postal counter and telegraph. Caleb and Ellie, Hiram's two younger children, would no doubt be accosting him shortly to see what had arrived.

"Ah, well, Benson still has a depot," he replied from under his hat.

"Yes, but I surely do miss the convenience," Silas replied. Hiram heard a familiar slide of fabric as his friend produced a flask, the twist of a cap, and then a long swig and gulp before the southerner took a breath. They would bide their time like this often on the saloon's front benches. Mica Bend had not seen much excitement since Wyatt Earp and Doc Holiday had paused there on their way through to New Mexico on their now-famous vendetta ride. That was six years ago. Except for a tiny occurrence, nothing else too lively had happened since, which suited Hiram fine.

They spent a moment longer in companionable silence with barely any foot or hoof traffic in the thoroughfare. Hiram listened to his chestnut gelding, Teddy, snuffling in the shade at the end of the saloon walk next to a trough. A desert wren trilled happily somewhere on the top edge of the false front on the clothing shop across the way. From under his brim, his gaze followed his outstretched legs in worn dungarees down to his boots crossed at the ankles. A bark scorpion, slender and less than two inches long, crawled around the edge of his cocked-back heel, its tail dragging lazily in a lack of aggression. What it was doing out roaming in the last half of the day was anyone's guess, but Hiram kept an eye on it to make sure it didn't decide to go exploring up under his trouser leg. The hiss of a striking match sounded, followed by the brief waft of sweet tobacco rolling past as Silas lit up a cheroot.

"I'm thinking about moving the Palace to Phoenix," Silas mused, clearly to fill the silence.

"You say that every day," Hiram countered. "As if Phoenix needs more saloons." The scorpion settled under the lean-to of his heel, figuring that must be the perfect shady spot to wait out the rest of the day. *I still see you*, Hiram thought as its tail remained visible. One carefree move, and he could crush it.

"There's talk the legislature is making it the new capital soon."

"Legislature can't make up their minds."

"Bet they could use more lawmen up there."

"Bet they could use a lot of things."

"Oh, now that's just denial, H," Silas replied. "You only wish this place could be as stimulating as it used to be. Time to move on to greener pastures."

Hiram tilted back his hat and finally looked up, his friend's figure coming into view leaning in the open doorway of the currently empty saloon. Despite the lack of patrons, Silas still dressed immaculately in a black suit and silk burgundy vest, crisp white shirt and tie with a derby hat nudged slightly to the side on a head of coarse light brown hair always kept close-cropped. A descendant of French creoles, he had freckled olive skin and full lips, a combination that confounded some women while others flocked to the exotic appeal. Not that Silas had much of a flock now like he used to, but he still had Izabel, his one remaining saloon girl, a pretty, Mexican woman who was now essentially the queen of the Palace. His fashion sense had forever dubbed him the Chinese laundry's number one customer, but Hiram estimated that it wouldn't be long before the southerner would be cleaning his shirts himself.

"Denial? Another year or two, Phoenix might just be ashes as well."

"You're funny," Silas said dryly and narrowed his jade eyes—his most exotic feature of all—and took a long drag on the cheroot.

"Besides, where you going to get the money to start up again anywhere else? You aren't going to have any takers on this place."

Silas coughed. "Alright, that is enough reality for me today."

Hiram finally cracked a wry grin.

The peace was interrupted by the higher pitch of a boy's voice shouting at the top of its lungs, *"Papa!"*

Hiram sighed and gently gave the lethargic scorpion a nudge with his sole until it dropped down through a small knothole in the boardwalk. Then, with another grunt, he sat up and repositioned his hat. "That was fast," he commented.

Silas winked as he exhaled two narrow columns of smoke from his nose.

From up the thoroughfare, Hiram's two youngest children came running from the direction of Fraleigh's Mercantile four blocks down, their pale hair haloed in the afternoon light. Twelve-year-old Caleb was in the lead on his ever-sprouting legs, and six-year-old Ellie trailed behind with a ratty doll clutched in the crook of her arm, a faded pink ribbon holding her flaxen hair out of her face.

"Papa!" Caleb wailed again when he wasn't too far from the steps, loud enough to stir Hiram's previously quiet horse to grumble and pin his ears back.

"Voice down, boy, dang," Hiram said as the kid stomped onto the boardwalk, holding a parcel that was torn open and waving a letter at his father. His knees and front of his shirt were red with dust indicating he'd fallen, with a belly flop for good measure, in his charge from the postal counter—if poor old Mr. Fraleigh had even made it that far with the mailbag.

"Afternoon, young man," Silas greeted him.

"Afternoon, Uncle Silas," Caleb replied while thrusting the letter at Hiram. "Uncle James sent more stories, an' a letter for you."

Hiram took the letter and tore it open, squinted to read his brother's somewhat frilly handwriting. Within his periphery, he kept some attention on his children riffling eagerly through the remaining parcel and withdrawing a series of pamphlets on newsprint.

"Quit crowdin' me, Ellie!"

"What chaptews he send?" Ellie's higher-pitched voice blared back excitedly. She was still working on her pronunciation of hard *Rs*, *ERs*, and *Ls*, so words like *chapters* came out more like *chaptews*, but her clarity and intention were not a problem to translate at all.

"Back off!"

"Wemme seeee!"

As Hiram read his own mail, the lines in his face must have deepened without him knowing, but Silas picked up on it immediately.

"He still beckoning to you with that typesetter position?"

"Yes," Hiram said.

"You look like you swallowed a bad clam."

While Caleb continued to flip through his pamphlets—elbowing his sister away and spinning to keep her smaller hands from grabbing and tearing them—Hiram fought to give full attention to his brother's compelling argument for why he should leave Mica Bend and bring the children to Philadelphia. James ran the lucrative print house where he and Hiram had grown up helping their father typeset newspapers. For various reasons, a young Hiram had never been satisfied with that life and thus eventually struck out on his own.

The letter inquired if, perhaps, the adult Hiram might consider the safety and security of relatives and a sustainable job. The splinters in the Wells family could be reunited into a more prominent supportive clan again if only Hiram could pull himself away from the Bend. *A fresh start*, it promised. *Stability for the children*, it insisted. *Haven't you put yourself through enough in that dust bin?* it asked.

Hiram lowered the letter and folded it, resisting the urge to crumple it completely. His brother meant well but still managed to churn the slightest undercurrent of anger. He shoved the letter inside his vest against his damp shirt, where the paper would soon be sweat-stained.

"He didn't put in chapter nine, but here's ten and eleven," Caleb lamented.

"Awwww," Ellie echoed him. "We won't know how Henwy saves Victowia fwom those giant monstew bats."

"I'm sure you can fill in the blanks," Hiram muttered as he forced himself into a stand. Twin lances of pain gripped his lower back to either side of his spine. By some miracle, he managed not to wince. "Where's your sister?" he asked when he'd made it to his feet with dignity.

"'Prolly in the barn with Jesse," Caleb snickered.

Hiram gave him a light swat on the back of his angelic head for the improper suggestion. "Go find her and get to any homework you have." Before his only son could object, he snatched the clutch of pamphlets away by virtue of much longer arms than Ellie's. "I'll take those until later."

"Papa!" the boy objected. "Give 'em back!"

"Yeah, give 'em back!"

"That was quite an echo," Silas remarked with a cringe.

"I'm not playing," Hiram said firmly as he held the pamphlets out of the boy's reach, perfect hostages in his almighty grip. "You both get home to your homework and chores. You can have these after. Now, get."

Caleb's head dropped in defeat, but he nodded and turned to trod down the boardwalk steps. Ellie followed him with her doll clutched tighter—if it had been a puppy, she would have strangled it by now with that hold—but a few paces off, she turned back around, and the perfect image of innocence transformed into a scathing glare at her father. If not for the adorable purse of her bottom lip, Hiram might have thought his youngest child suddenly demon possessed. His brows shot up as he gave her his best, *I'm-gonna-count-to-five-and-you-better-get-moving* face. She spun and followed her brother.

"And find your sister!" he shouted after them.

Just off Hiram's shoulder, Silas chuckled.

"It isn't funny. You see what kind of respect I get."

"You lack their mother's more subtle influence, H, that's all."

Hiram stared down at the collection in his hands, temper melting as he thought of how his Rachel would have handled things with a soft voice and little effort. Silas was not wrong.

"What are those things anyway?" Silas asked, indicating the pamphlets. "Caleb's been eating them up like candy for weeks now."

The cover on the top pamphlet was a block print of a man in a wing-like black cape looming over a woman draped across a chaise lounge. The title, rendered in stylized letters of a dripping design, read TALES OF THE VAMPIRE, LORD COVINGTON: A ROMANCE OF INTRIGUE AND HORROR, CHAPTER 11. Overall, the publication was five pages, printed front and back, placed in order and folded together down the middle with no binding, adding up to roughly nine pages of chapter plus the cover sheet.

"They're penny dreadfuls. James got the idea when he traveled to England years ago with our father, but I guess they've caught on here. Decided to try it out himself selling a chapter at a time, mostly a bunch of silly horrid tales and nonsense. He's been trying them out on my kids as if he hasn't got kids of his own."

Silas' eyes remained on the cover, his demeanor softening in the pregnant pause that followed Hiram's complaining. "They don't sound any different from those dime novels we used to read and trade back and forth, and we were far older than Caleb and Ellie." When Hiram failed to come up with a viable argument, he continued, "Speaking as a friend, H, it might not be a bad idea for you to take James up on that offer."

"Hell, he'll have me putting together this same shit he's sending Caleb."

"Oh, come now, the boy's just bored. What else is there for a young man to do around here? Hmm?"

There was nothing subtle in the question, just as there was nothing subtle about Silas' talk of moving to Phoenix. There truly was *nothing* to do around here anymore, and Hiram had no idea to save his life what he might do about that.

Then Silas pushed it just a little further, adding, "What about Lucinda?"

Hiram took a deep breath to keep from snapping at his friend but, again, Silas was not wrong. His oldest child was sixteen now, sunny-haired and dark-eyed like her late mother and eager to see a world beyond Mica Bend. It wouldn't be very long before she started rebelling, and Hiram braced for the war that was sure to give his heart and temperament a good challenge. He would cross that bridge, he determined, when he came to it.

"I mean, really," Silas continued, not realizing how much Hiram was ready to let the discussion go, "it wouldn't kill you to consider going, especially with that back of yours. Oh, yes, I saw you get up in pain. Don't deny it. Did you know the Hansons out on Pit Creek have picked up and left? They're well ahead of the rest of us stragglers."

Hiram readjusted his stance, ignoring the comment about his back. "You mean Zachary packed up and piled out just like that with Cassie?"

"That's what Terry Wilkes said," Silas clarified. "He went out there yesterday to pay back a few dollars he owed Zack, found the house empty."

"Huh." Hiram scratched the dark stubble on his chin. "Isn't like Zach to leave without collecting a debt, even a small one. Think I'll ride out there and take a look before supper."

"What about your guest?" Silas asked.

"Oh, he'll keep for a bit longer."

Silas produced and consulted a pocket watch then looked toward the sun and its angle on the horizon. "You've got two, maybe three hours of light left."

"That'll do. Hey, if you see Nathan, tell him where I went."

Silas nodded, "Yessir, Marshal."

Hiram glanced down at the tin star pinned to his linen duster and adjusted the collar to make it more visible. If he was to make it to Pit Creek and back before dark, he didn't have time to track down his deputy, who was still on afternoon patrol, and tell him.

After giving his back a little twist to loosen the muscles up, he headed down the steps and over to the trough where he unhitched Teddy and checked the saddle straps and the water level in his canteen.

"H," Silas said to call back his attention and nodded toward the thoroughfare. "Looks like you've got company."

Hiram looked up to see a man in perhaps his early thirties riding toward him on a dappled gray mare.

The stranger, bundled in a dusty buckskin coat, fastened with big buckles across his chest, sported a wide-brimmed hat, eyes hidden behind a pair of dark, smoked amber spectacles. A Winchester rifle sat holstered next to his saddlebags and a thick bed role, all of it indicating that he had been on the road for days and probably slept under the stars. "You Marshal Wells?" he asked. "A Mr. Fraleigh down the street said I'd find you here."

"Yeah? How can I help you?"

"I understand you have something of mine in your jail?" He sounded as if he were summoning the greatest of patience.

He cocked a brow. "What is that?"

"My brother."

This was news of the highest for Hiram. "Really? You're Seth Raines' brother?" At first glance, the newcomer burrowed a place in the marshal's memory, every detail from the dark brows visible above the spectacles to the slant of his cheeks and a small scar on his chin, the scraggly hint of a mustache over his upper lip. Even the pink velvet on the end of the horse's nose had a place. Only the man's eyes remained to be marked down, and Hiram figured that would happen soon enough.

"Yes, Sir. Name's Ben Raines."

"Well, then I guess you want to see him."

"I'd appreciate that, Sir. Thank you."

Polite, Hiram thought. *The responsible one?* That was the general read he got from the stranger. "He's sleeping off an afternoon bender."

"I'm not at all surprised. If you've got a moment, I'll take him off your hands."

"That will be my pleasure." The jail was opposite the direction he needed to go for the Hanson farm, but he was grateful for this particular delay. "This way, Mr. Raines, let's get you reunited with your brother."

Ben Raines nodded and waited on his horse.

That was when the town's doctor-cum-pastor, Norman Becker, rounded the corner at the back of the alley between the saloon and the Raskin Hotel next door. Becker froze for an awkward moment when his eyes met the marshal's.

They *both* froze. Hiram briefly wondered why the old man was coming the back way around as if he were trying to sneak into the saloon. Then He moved Teddy out of the way so Becker could pass.

The pastor looked more grizzled than usual. He clutched the handle of his worn leather Gladstone bag in one hand, but the closer he came, the more apparent the white collar showed around his neck, even if it was yellowed from sweat and dust. His black shirt and jacket had both long since faded, not taken care of nearly as much as Silas took care of his clothes. Becker was in his early sixties with a full head of hair that framed his face in gray-streaked brown frizz. Large watery gray eyes and the heavy white mustache under his nose emphasized a hangdog look.

"Marshal," he greeted with wariness in his voice. His eyes darted curiously toward the newcomer.

Hiram didn't give so much as a nod of greeting.

"Pastor Becker!" Silas called from the boardwalk, clearly trying to lighten the tense atmosphere that tended to descend when the two crossed paths. "What can I do for you this afternoon? The usual?"

Becker kept going, clearly trying not to mind Hiram any longer than necessary, and then stepped onto the boardwalk. "Whatever it takes," he said.

"Whatever it takes!" Silas echoed enthusiastically and gestured him on through the batwing doors. He then gave Hiram one more look, a glance at Ben Raines, then back again. "Be careful."

Hiram only nodded back. *I will.*

The younger Raines had arrived almost two years ago and been generally respectable to those who met him. A prospector for the Perseverance Mine who at first rented a room at the Grand Saloon, the man had not blazed into town like he had any agenda other than honest work, but he seemed jumpy at times, always looking over his shoulder and only occasionally partook of the Grand's lousy whiskey.

Then the Grand had closed early in the slump, and Raines drifted. He never camped in Wagon Town but usually somewhere out on the edge of the Arduous Range, where he kept prospecting for a bonanza of his own. Then he had fallen into a pattern of drunk and disorderly conduct at the Palace.

His arrests, however, were primarily based on his insistence on carrying a single action Colt Army revolver *while* drunk and disorderly. He was younger than Hiram—late twenties at a guess—too young to have fought in the war, but something haunted him, and Hiram knew when to leave well enough alone about a man's past. He had confiscated the gun several times, examined and seen that it had never been converted from a cap and ball percussion cylinder to cartridge as many were now. Raines packed all six chambers but, as with percussion cylinders, could rest the hammer between caps and not risk firing unintentionally.

He also had nightmares.

While at his desk, Hiram often found his attention called to a disturbance in whichever cell Raines occupied at the time. There might be a murmur or a quiet choking noise that turned into a shout as Raines snapped awake like something bit him. Sometimes there was no build-up at all, just a simple startle into consciousness and a long moment of quietly regaining composure on the bunk.

Today, Hiram opened the Venetian blinds on the big front window, flooding the room with perfectly angled sunlight, and approached the cell with his body half turned so that Ben Raines, who had been standing back watching, remained within his periphery. During the ride up the thoroughfare, the newcomer had mentioned that he was older than his brother by five years. He had not seen Seth in at least three years since some family disagreement had taken place, so he had no idea what kind of reaction he would get when his brother saw him now.

Hiram could sympathize with that. He didn't know how he would react were his own brother to show up suddenly. He hadn't seen James since Caleb was four, and Ellie had never met him at all.

He jiggled the key in the cell lock on the right side. The damn thing always stuck, and neither marshal nor deputy had gotten around to having it greased. Beyond the bars, he could see the young man lying face up—Hiram had left him lying belly down as a precaution—in a frayed undershirt and dungarees, one leg stretched on the bunk, the other bent and a boot firmly planted on the floor. Long, unkempt dark hair spilled away from a face that twisted ever so slightly as if in pain or fear.

Yep, Hiram thought, *more nightmares in there*. Right as the lock finally gave and the key turned with a loud *screeeeeech*, the prisoner's body jerked, and his eyes snapped open. While the younger Raines stared at the ceiling for a long moment collecting himself, Hiram turned back to Ben. "He's all yours," he said and stepped aside.

Ben unbuckled the heavy buckskin coat, removed his spectacles, tucked them into a pocket inside, and then stepped closer. His eyes, it turned out, were a deep nut brown like his brother's, and the family resemblance came into full perspective in facial shape, cheek angle, and brows. Both had scant mustache or beard growth; both were somewhat olive-skinned and dark-haired though Seth clearly hadn't cut his in years, and Ben was neatly clipped in the back with full, sweeping bangs around his forehead.

"You let anyone into this town anymore, don't you, Marshal?" Seth spoke up, his voice a rasp from booze, sleep, and maybe a little stomach acid in his throat. "Thought you were more cautious than that."

"My judgment's been slipping since I let you in, Raines," Hiram replied.

While Ben stepped into the cell to retrieve his brother, Hiram went to the safe that sat against the wall behind his desk and unlocked it to take out the Colt Army. The gun was nestled in a holster on its gun belt along with a custom pouch that held additional paper cartridges and rounds. He slid the gun from its holster and took an indulgent last look at it while quietly listening in on the reunion.

"God, it gets worse every time I see you," Ben said. "This your permanent residence?"

"Ha," Seth replied dryly and burped. "Yeah, what would Mama say?"

"Mama's the reason I'm here." Ben helped his brother sit up, though Seth flopped around like a rag doll just to be a difficult ass about it. "Oh damn… that breath, brother. Blow a buzzard off a shit wagon."

"'S jus' whiskey."

"Time for food and maybe a bucket of cold water."

"Pump's around the side," Hiram piped up helpfully. "Well water's nice and cold."

"Fuck you, Marshal," Seth grumbled.

With great effort, Ben got an arm woven under Seth's shoulder, pulled him to his feet, and steered him toward the cell door. The threat of a cold dousing, however, must have driven new life into the younger brother. Seth pulled away, got his balance, and proceeded to walk out of the cell on his own. He headed straight for the door on a mission to either flee from his unexpected visitor or to puke.

Hiram stepped up to Ben and handed him the gun belt. "I'll leave this in your hands. You be the judge when he's ready to have it back."

"Thank you kindly, Sir. Guess I better catch up with him before he finds another bottle to crawl into."

J.H. Kimbrell

CHAPTER TWO

There was a smooth, pale leg under those skirts somewhere, but Jesse Warren was not having any luck getting to it. He only wanted to caress Lucinda's knee, but she was in a flighty mood today and kept squirming as he lay beside her in the hay of the rearmost stall in the Wells' barn where excess hay bales were stored, creating a platform off the ground even if it was on the scratchy side. Lucinda's horse, Remington, nibbled quietly on some grain in the next stall over.

But the horse was the last thing on Jesse's mind as he dropped light kisses on Lucinda's neck to the lobe of her ear. He nuzzled her golden wheat hair, which bore the fading tang of a vinegar wash, and beneath that, a scent that was distinctly Lucinda that drove him crazy. He had no intentions of taking her womanhood—her father was far too keen for Jesse to take a chance like that and thus have the marshal's Peacemaker shoved in some part he didn't want it shoved in—but he did want a good feel under those skirts, and that wouldn't hurt anything. He wanted most for her to relax. He wanted to hear her sigh pleasurably and have her kiss him back.

Today was not to be that day.

Her prattle had begun with a complaint about a pesky coyote that she had been chasing away for weeks as it kept coming back to try to dig into the chicken coop that she'd helped her mother erect a couple of years ago. The flock had been a hobby for mother and daughter as much as it had been a source of food for the whole family. Some of the older hens they'd raised were still alive and thriving with several generations of descendants and a huge, majestic rooster who ruled the roost with the most impressive spurs Jesse had ever seen. Now that her mother had passed, Lucinda had become especially protective of the hens, the rooster, and all their chickabiddies, only choosing the most ill-tempered ones for the supper pot. Now the coyote had her so worried that she was losing sleep over it. No other creature had been so aggressive as *that* creature.

Jesse sympathized to a point. A chicken's life was the last thing that might have him tossing in his bunk all night. A typical day for him involved helping his coworkers wrestle down and brand livestock and even longer days and nights driving to pasture and shepherding, so his only priority off duty was rest, relaxation, and courting Lucinda Wells.

"I want so much to leave," she murmured. "If Papa would only…" But then she went quieter as she clearly knew all too well, and so did Jesse, why her father had stalled any discussions of the future and potentially leaving Mica Bend for greener towns.

"But then, how would you take your mama's chickens?" Jesse asked, smiling down at her, and thinking the question clever until she looked at him as if he had sprouted another head.

"That's what cages and a wagon are for. The chickens didn't get here on their own to begin with." At long last, there was a smile in her eyes. Jesse shelved his attempts at shenanigans to see *that*. The deep brown surrounded by fans of lighter lashes rendered him speechless. Blonde hair and brown eyes did not commonly turn up together, and they were perfectly balanced in Lucinda Wells. She'd inherited those features from her mama, and Jesse had always noticed how large it made her eyes seem. He was thoroughly enjoying the view of those eyes when a question came out of her mouth that halted his progress like a stubbed toe. "Would you go with me, Jesse? If Papa actually *did* take us elsewhere, would you go, too?"

"I, uh…" he stalled.

"I mean, if he would let you, that is. Would you want to go with us?" She blinked slowly, softly. "With me?"

"Uh…"

"Like San Francisco, maybe? Some place more civilized."

"You're just dreamin', Lucinda. Your daddy ain't gonna take you anywhere." Didn't take a second for him to realize he'd messed up. He swore to himself as he watched her eyes darken, brows furrowing deeply.

"Of course, I'm dreaming, Jesse!" she snapped, and the heels of her hands shoved into his chest right at the nervy junctions with his shoulders. The minor discomfort effectively pushed him to roll away from her and, skirt layers ruffling, she scooted to the foot of the hay platform and scrambled to her feet, dusting off in the main pathway through the barn. "Dreaming is about all I've got around here in this cactus pit."

"Hey, it ain't that bad." He tried not to raise his voice. "It's quiet here. I like it, even if there's nothing especially going on." He stood, dusting off, and looked down at her determined, pretty face, heart-shaped and lightly freckled. "I'm just saying—" he attempted to walk back what exactly he'd said, "—that your daddy clearly ain't plannin' on goin' anywhere *soon*."

"I wasn't asking about *your thoughts* on Papa's plans," she replied.

"Then what were you asking?"

She huffed an irritated breath and shook her head at him. "I was asking if you would follow me anywhere, Jesse."

Jesse couldn't conceive of going *anywhere* else *anytime* soon for *any* reason. "Lucinda," he tried to reason, "I thought you was just playin' there. Look, I've got a good job. Even if this town dries up, it won't matter to Bryce Tucker. His ranch holds its own. I'm not sayin' I wouldn't go with you elsewhere, but we could still make a nice life in Benson, don't you think?"

"Oh, *come on*, Jesse, you're just a peon to Tucker. He can replace you quick as lightning."

He cringed at that implication. "But there will always be other ranch jobs." Of that, he was sure.

Another huff. "Fine," she said with a deeper tone of surrender and pushed past him toward the barn entrance. "Well, I'm not waiting around for you to get your nose kicked in branding cows."

"Now that ain't fair," he insisted, going after her.

The barn, corral, and the chicken coop that kept Lucinda up at night, were situated behind the Wells' home, which was right beside the main road that led directly into town by another half mile. Lucinda stormed past the corral, where Jesse's horse, Peso, watched her head toward the house's back door. Jesse knew that if he didn't catch up with her, there would be a door slamming in his face.

"Wait up! Lucinda…"

But then she did. Jesse thought maybe he'd been forgiven until he heard the same noises that had gotten her attention. She turned her head toward the stretch of road visible from here, where a series of oaks created a corridor of shade. There came the sound of multiple hooves tramping and wheels grinding before out of that shade slipped a massive, covered freight wagon pulled by a team of six stocky draft horses whose powerful muscles rippled in the afternoon sun. The high flat sides of the wagon were painted black with garish red and gold lettering sweeping across them dramatically. The style was so fancy Jesse struggled to read it on his first look over.

The Chamberlain Players.

Behind the freight wagon came the smaller shape of a coach, painted as black as the behemoth that preceded it, and a team of six Saddlebreds that were all pure black, gleaming like onyx as they marched proudly. The coach they pulled appeared to be completely windowless, and its sides were painted with the same showy red and gold signage as the freighter.

Lucinda's mood immediately lifted, and she picked up her pace, running to the other side of the house to apprehend the freighter.

"Lucinda!" Jesse called and hurried after.

She rushed out through the garden gate and jogged slightly alongside the wagon until she caught up to the front and called up to the driver, a man in perhaps his late twenties who was dressed in a double-breasted black long coat of a foreign design belted at the waist. Tall black boots showed where his feet propped on the rest. Long, flame-red hair spilled out from under the hat that shaded his eyes.

"Sir!" Lucinda called. "Hello!"

"Hello, young lady!" he answered. Jesse thought he heard something of a brogue in the voice.

"Is your troupe stopping in Mica Bend?"

"We are indeed! Eh, in fact, might you guide us to the…" he freed one hand from the reins to unbutton one side of his coat and withdrew a letter that he thumbed open and eyed. "The Simpson Boarding House?" The wagon eased to a slower roll.

"Of course. It's two miles out on the other side of town." Lucinda absently made hand gestures. "There's a private path that forks off from the road to the right. There's a signpost. You can't miss it."

"Thank you most kindly, Miss. I hope we see you at the opera house. We've got Shakespearian performances of the highest order, best talent you'll ever see come through." He picked up the pace again.

"Yes!" she all but cried, "Yes, I'll be there!" She stopped keeping pace and turned excitedly to give Jesse a brilliant smile, bouncing ever so sweetly on the balls of her feet as the big wagon passed and, in its wake, came the coach. The driver, also a young man in his twenties, was dressed in the same coat style as the one ahead, but his hair was short and dark, his face less friendly. He offered no words but touched the brim of his hat toward her as he guided the coach on past.

"Players, Jesse!" she squealed with the coach's passage. "And they're performing Shakespeare on our stage!"

"Well, there's your civilization," Jesse remarked.

She nodded enthusiastic agreement to that.

Then, for lack of any good sense, Jesse messed up again. "Don't know who the hell would want to play here anymore, though."

"You just get," she scolded him. "You can just go take your supper at the Raskin, Jesse Warren."

"What?" he demanded. "What'd I say?"

The miners' camp, sprawled around Mica Bend's northwestern entry, had once been a sea of tents flapping in the dry breezes that trapped grit in every seam and infiltrated corners or buried stakes from view. A shady grove of cottonwoods had made life there a little more bearable for its inhabitants over the years. In the Bend's heyday, the camp had been a cheerful place with the miners and their families arranging their tents in a circle around a central fire pit in which the women cooked or sewed while their husbands prospected. In the evenings, there was sometimes music if someone happened to have an instrument and the skill to play it. Children ran amid the alleys formed between the tents, the occasional scream rising from a scorpion sting or a rattler spotting. A circle of wagons, cooperatively arranged through the grove, had formed something of an outer wall with a corral at the back and the main entrance where the camp faced the road, thus creating a sense of added security within the camp. The arrangement had earned it the name Wagon Town by the more settled inhabitants of the Bend.

Frank Evans had camped there plenty of times when he had to lay low. He could keep his head down, grow a beard if he needed to, and no one was the wiser. After all, he'd ridden with the Jack Taylor gang off and on over the last three years and managed to keep his name from being attached to them. Taylor was rotting in a Mexican prison now, and all the other members had been picked off by Cochise County Sheriff John Slaughter. The last of them, Federico—who was both an idiot and a weasel—had been captured and hanged in August, but Frank suspected that his own name had finally come up before Federico's demise. Maybe the saphead had hoped to cut a deal by naming unknown associate members of the gang. That would be just like him, but at least it still didn't spare him from garglin' on a rope.

The whispers that he might finally be a wanted man reached Frank a week ago in Phoenix, so he had decided to get out of that more populated town and either head south into Mexico or as far east as possible. However, he was not going to cut down through the lowest border of Cochise County and tempt fate by passing too close to Sheriff Slaughter. The man seemed to have eyes and ears everywhere.

It didn't help that Frank's baby brother, Harlan, was in tow.

His mama would kill him if anything happened to Harlan. Frank, however, was more concerned about acquiring horses and funds and getting the hell to Mexico. He would put Harlan on a train back to Kansas if he could, but cooperation of that sort was not forthcoming. Harlan wanted to learn *things*, and he'd bound himself to Frank's every step. So, Frank had headed to Mica Bend, which was nearly skin and bones as far as towns went, where there was a bend in the railroad and patches of ground were scaled with sheets of mica that shimmered with the angle of the sun.

They were currently sitting outside the tent Frank had pitched within the shade of Wagon Town, but their arrival had been a rude awakening. The wagon wall had whittled down to only five wagons, and the corral was empty. It seemed some of the families had been selling off their horses to replace the depletion of silver and thus stranding themselves here. Frank had hoped to help himself and Harlan to two of those horses, but with that plan a bust, all they could do was hunker down until Frank came up with a new plan. Maybe the place didn't provide the kind of camouflage it used to, but the brothers had gone unnoticed by the deputy marshal who had passed by on patrol earlier, so Frank felt fairly relaxed. He listened to the fire crackle while his brother fumbled with a soup pot, the only cooking utensil they had left.

"Watch it, Harlan, don't spill our supper!" he hissed.

"Ain't spillin' nothin'," the younger Evans answered and glared. He was eighteen, well over a decade younger than Frank, and had never finished school or stayed with any trade for very long. Their mother had sent him west to join Frank and hopefully learn something that would gain him employment, a home, a wife.

Mama had no idea of the things Frank was teaching Harlan. When Frank sent home funds to support her and his other siblings, he never reported where they came from for obvious reasons.

"So, how far you think we need to go around before we can go meet us some pretty señoritas?"

Frank gave the side-eye to his kid brother, who stirred the pot and grinned wickedly. "Y'ain't touchin' no señoritas til you can shoot the broad side of a barn."

"Well, I cain't practice on any barns 'round here," Harlan griped. "When we gettin' out of this pisshole?"

"Soon."

"Why're we waitin'? Bank here's still got money in it. Least enough to get us somewhere. Come on, let's try it!"

"Keep your voice down," Frank hissed, glancing at the nearest neighboring tent. Fortunately, a tent over from that, a young woman sat rocking a baby. The child—Frank had no idea if it was a boy or girl—had been screaming off and on all day, with its exasperated and bedraggled mother making multiple apologies to the camp's scattered remnants that it was teething. While Frank daydreamed about what it might be like to commit infanticide, he reminded himself that the screaming was a worthy distraction from his presence in the camp. When he was sure no one had heard Harlan's loud mouth, he said gruffly, "Bank here ain't got shit." Stealthy reconnoitering had told him that. "Besides," he added, "you ain't got any idea of the finesse it takes to rob a bank, and we ain't got horses."

Frank was considering how to get horses and staring through a part in the cottonwoods toward the main road when he saw them coming. The six substantial draft horses were pulling the largest freight wagon he'd ever seen, black-painted with showy lettering on the side. It came around the far bend first and down the lane, followed by an equally painted black coach. Immediately he got up and made a hurried creep to the edge of the grove for a better look, aware that Harlan scurried up to his side the way he'd always done since they were kids.

"The Chamberlain Players," Frank read. They watched as the hulking vehicle drove by, not sure if the driver, sitting high at the front, had noticed them. Then came the lighter clop of smaller hooves and four black horses pulling the coach, which was decorated to match its predecessor. Now *those* horses, Frank thought, were worth stealing. Smaller, easier to mount in a hurry, and speedier than those hauling the freighter. "We'll be keepin' an eye on that," he said. Glancing back, he found Harlan blinking stupidly at him.

"Why?"

"Why'd you *think?*" He gave Harlan a hard slap on the side of the arm. "Like I said, bank here ain't worth a hit. Everyone's done withdrawn what funds they have, but I guaran-damn-tee ya, they're itchin' for some entertainment. Ladies'll come out with their purses, and ranch hands'll be ready to find some way to spend their wages somewhere other than the saloon. That's a whole lot richer pot than the bank."

Harlan still blinked at him, then finally got the message and chuckled. Frank gave him another slap on the arm to herd him away from their vantage point and back to the camp and their waiting supper, but before he turned, he swore the man driving the coach saw him.

Dark eyes barely hidden under a wide-brimmed black hat appeared to shift in his direction within the tree line, hold for mere seconds, and then angle back toward the road. Frank wasn't sure why, but it gave him a weird chill. Likely the guy didn't have a clue who he was and, for the most part, seemed focused on just getting his passengers to their destination.

Frank proceeded to get his little brother back to their tent and the soup that was probably about to burn. But there was something about that coachman's gaze that lingered with him, and, for a while, it overpowered any thoughts of holdups, horse thieving, or killing crying babies.

The sun had settled lower than Hiram would have liked by the time he reined in his horse at the farm just near the long-dead mesquite tree on which Zach had hung his landmark sign that read: HANSON in flecked letters. He'd had to stop on the road a couple times to get out of the saddle and stretch his back which ached far too frequently these days. Still, even with the pain and running late, Hiram relished the wide-open sky and the cloud-patched wash of peach and gold tones forming in the west, while the moon, creeping toward full, hung over the darkening east. If he didn't make it back to town by dark, at least there was enough moonlight, and the roads in and out of Mica Bend were easy to see pounded out in the dust and lined with scrub, barrel cacti and mounds of prickly pear. Even on a moonless night, with the starlight above, the sandy landscape still reflected enough that a lost man could find his way, and if he didn't go by the ruts in the road, he could locate and use the railway as a compass.

Hiram dismounted and paused at the bare and worn mesquite signpost, listening for any signs of life at all, such as chickens clucking or cowbells clanking as the herd came in from the fence line some hundred yards out from the barn, but there was eerily *nothing*. As Terry Wilkes had reported to Silas, it appeared that Zach had indeed up and departed without a word to the town. To simply pick up and go was no possibility for even the smallest farm. The necessities for self-sustainability were not something one could pack up and haul out without a few complications and a swell of gossip.

Zach likely would have sold his tiny herd, and his chickens, to Bryce Tucker, whose ranch sprawled further to the southwest between Mica Bend and Benson. Hiram would have heard about that via Jesse Warren, the young ranch hand who was currently wooing his daughter. Jesse would have commented while in the Orleans Palace, and then the whole town would have known, and then Zach would have been besieged with queries about his plans. That was how things worked in the Bend, especially since the only remaining reporter, Jack Newsom, had shut down his press and moved to Tucson a year ago.

It all made no sense, and the lack of cow and chicken noises aside, the place was overall *too* quiet. There should be other sounds at this close to dusk, whether birds calling out somewhere in the scrub or insects buzzing their last as the day came to an end and the autumn season crept in. It made Hiram's skin prickle under his clothes as he guided Teddy past the sign and into the main yard where the barn and corral stood a little distance out to his left, and the house stood to his right. A few paces out from the corral stood the lean-to that Hiram had helped Zach build a couple of years ago to shelter his firewood.

Teddy grumbled, and his ears pinned back slightly, a horse sign that Hiram did not take lightly.

"Easy," he whispered to the gelding and slowly led Teddy to the house, where he tethered him to the porch railing.

From there, he stepped up onto the porch, where the clomp of his boots seemed intrusive and loud. He tried the front door, found it locked, and stepped to the side to peer through the window into the house's front parlor. Like many homes in and around Mica Bend—and even some of the businesses—it was a prefabricated structure much like Hiram's own house. The catalog-ordered kits had been shipped in from the likes of *Lyman Bridges of Chicago* and other lumber suppliers during the same silver and copper boom that had conceived Tombstone and Bisbee and dozens of other mining camps in the region. He removed his Stetson to get his eyes up closer to the panes and squinted to focus on the darker area within. Enough light still fell into the parlor for him to make out some remaining furniture covered in dust cloths in the shape of a sofa and the boxiness of a long sideboard. Well, that looked to be in order. Maybe Zach and Cassandra were planning to come back for it.

Hell, maybe Zack decided it was no one's damned business what he planned.

Hiram stepped back, pausing as his gaze adjusted, blurring away the contents of the parlor and now refocusing on the reflection staring back at him, shaded under the porch but still clear enough to make out details. A few crows' feet branched out from his light blue eyes, though the lines were not as deep or as plentiful as he felt like they should be, and three days' worth of dark stubble gave his already sharp chin a black outline that fell just shy of harsh. He would shave again in another day or two because the discomfort of the dust catching in it bothered the hell out of him. His hair, however, was a longish mess of light brown waves currently ringed at the crown by the impression his hat left. Rachel had always cut his hair for him, but now he'd let it go since her scissors last touched it some nine months ago. Before she…

Hiram looked away from his reflection, his throat growing tight before he put his hat back on and strode quickly off the porch, getting back on track. He threw another glance around the yard and proceeded to walk toward the barn. A breeze stirred as he went, whipping the length of his duster and sending a surge of fine grit across the yard around the corral. It was surprisingly chilling and carried with it a smell of char, faint but still pungent. He might attribute it to October's arrival, but a wind *this* frigid was a season too early.

Then, in an instant, the breeze tapered off, the smell fading with it. If something had been burned nearby recently, there was no telling where the odor had drifted from. Out there, on the plain amid the scrub and cacti, were many dips and washes, indentions in which Zach, or anyone, might safely burn some rubbish. More likely, it came from a camp set up somewhere further down the road. Finding the exact spot this evening, whether camp or wash, was not an option.

Hiram continued to the barn and walked its perimeter, pausing around the back where Zach usually kept his buckboard wagon under a shed roof built out from the rear of the barn where he could chain one of the wheels to a post. The buckboard was gone, that being Zach and Cassandra's primary means of transportation. Between the missing wagon and the covered furniture, Hiram understood why Terry Wilkes assumed they'd moved on.

And it was time for him to get back to town himself.

Coming around the barn from the back, completing an entire perimeter walk, he looked back to the house where Teddy remained tethered to the porch. Just past the corral, he froze as he recalled something.

Between the house and the barn ran a tunnel. Seven years ago, upon the news of Apache leader Geronimo's flight from the San Carlos reservation, just north in Gila County, with a gathering of over seven hundred Apache warriors, Zach had grown concerned over renewed attacks on white settlers. Although Geronimo and his followers fled into Mexico, Zach, experienced in copper mine construction, decided to dig the tunnel for an emergency hiding place or escape route. The endeavor took him the better part of three years. Most everyone in the Bend figured that by that point, Zach was no longer afraid of Geronimo or any other such hostile; he just wanted to finish that damned tunnel on principle.

They also agreed that Cassandra Hanson must be something of a saint.

Upon being finished, it was a perfectly stable tunnel with good strong posts and lagging to support the sides and ceiling and impressively wide enough that two people could walk through it next to each other and their shoulders wouldn't touch. The area that stopped under the kitchen in the house ended up being used as a root cellar, while the other end terminated with a ladder up through a trap door in the barn floor.

Hiram had seen the tunnel only once when it was brand new, and Zach was proud to show it off. Thinking about that tunnel, Hiram felt the doubt creep back. Zach had put a lot of sweat into this property over the years, so it was still hard to imagine him simply leaving it without a word.

Taking a breath, he decided on one last look before he retired back to town and supper. Then he would swing by the saloon again to see how the evening was going there.

The corral gate creaked with an ear-grating pitch as he swung it open and went to the barn, flung open those doors, and looked upon nothing more than a scattering of deep hay rushes in three empty stables. Thin streams of dimming golden light fell between the planks of the barn's western wall. The trap door for the tunnel lay directly ahead, and—Hiram raised a brow—the handle was *exposed.*

The rushes were scattered away from it when usually they'd be intentionally raked over it, along with a thin layer of dirt. With no reason for anyone to go down there much, it had remained that way for some time and well concealed, but now the iron handle was visible.

Maybe Zach had retrieved something from down there before he departed?

"Well, shit," Hiram muttered. It would be remiss of him not to take a look. *All right, do it, H*, he told himself. The voice in his head uncannily resembled Silas' and the gentler mocking tones the southerner was known to employ. There was probably no one or *thing* down there, but so as not to be unprepared, he reached across his belt and drew the Colt Peacemaker he'd carried for most of a decade now. Nerves crawled in his belly and chest as he bent down and gripped the handle, then he hoisted up the door in a rush, breathing through the intense shot of pain that clenched his lower back. A gust of more cool air came out of the opening, and dust motes and bits of hay swirled up and then descended. Once the door was up and he used his entire body as a prop, the pain ebbed slightly. Hiram looked down into nothing more than a dark pit, barely making out the foot of the ladder. "Hello?" he called. "Anyone down there?"

No one here but us snakes, the Silas voice answered in his head.

Hiram stared and listened. From below came only silence and the scent of raw earth, mustier than usual. The monsoon season had been particularly aggressive, so plenty of moisture had probably remained trapped down there since the last rain. He glanced around the barn, offhandedly looking for a lantern. *No lantern?* Good, because he didn't want to go down there, and it would be idiotic to go without some light or by himself.

To hell with that.

He gritted his teeth at his twinging back and eased the door back down before he let the handle go and dropped it the rest of the way into place with a clap that made him wince. The slam pushed out one last gust that stirred the rushes back further. Feeling like a fool, he holstered the Colt and shook off the last of the prickles. He'd disturbed the peace, such as it was, enough. So far, it did seem that the residents of the Hanson farm had quit the place. Though the quietude and cool wind were eerie, they were not evidence that anything unnatural had happened to Zach and his wife.

With that, he turned on his heel and headed out of the barn, closed the doors behind him, and returned to his horse.

The gelding was watching him with ears cocked forward, curious and alert. "Ready to head back?" Hiram said. "Me, too." He untethered and led Teddy around the side of the house to a water pump and trough. Might as well take advantage of Zach's abandoned resources. He pumped fresh water into the trough and guided Teddy's head toward it only to feel a pull on the reins as the horse refused to drink, issuing a grumble, and backing up.

"True what they say about leading a horse to water, huh? It's a decent ride back, you know?"

Teddy replied by pulling back, his hooves lifting a little higher, stamping out renewed agitation.

"*Shhh,*" Hiram quickly soothed. "*Shhhhh-shhhh-shhh.*"

Then something rattled and banged from the barnyard, jolting Hiram where he stood and causing Teddy to utter a slight squeal. Pulling the reins, he guided Teddy back around the house and saw that one of the barn doors had been flung open by the breeze.

Breathing a sigh of relief, he chastised himself for having not closed the doors well enough. "See? Just a barn door." He took a moment longer to keep soothing Teddy, rubbing the blaze up his nose and blowing soft hushes into his velvety nostrils, and decided not to bother with the door again. When he was sure his horse was calm enough, he finally mounted up again and turned to ride back toward town, only to pause one more time before exiting to the main road.

In the old worn-down mesquite tree signpost, there sat an owl. A strange creature, unlike like any Hiram had ever seen before, perhaps migrating through from somewhere.

"Huh," he muttered.

It looked much like a screech owl with the harsh lines that looked like brows dipping down the middle of its face and the ear-like points of feathers on the top sides of its head, but it was significantly larger than a screech owl. Most of its feathers were solid dark with few spots or bars, and its eyes appeared to be nothing but oil-black orbs in the dimming light.

The bird gave what sounded like a warning screech but inclined its head, appearing to observe him curiously. Hiram, tired of winding himself up over every little noise, every breeze, every inch the sun dropped below the horizon, *and* every bird, greeted it by giving a nod and touching the brim of his hat.

"Evening," he said.

The owl twittered slightly before launching and flying off, carrying the silence with it.

Hiram marveled for a moment at nature's engineering. Then he finally heeled his horse on and rode in the direction of the rising moon.

CHAPTER THREE

The Widow Oliver—*Maria*, she preferred to be called—lamented, as she walked home, that she'd spent much of the day chastising Caleb Wells and his little sister Ellie for not sitting still. Then, to her added frustration, she'd had to chase them down to hand them the books they'd left at their desks. They were far more interested in making a beeline for the post office counter in the mercantile than anything. Maria felt she had a deeper understanding of all the Wells children. With their mother gone, they were temporarily lost, each grieving in their own way, struggling to focus on getting on with life. Their older sister, Lucinda, had completed her schooling two years ago and been interested in taking up teaching, but any instruction Maria had given her to help nurture that goal had been abandoned months ago. Now, Lucinda had mostly assumed the household and social responsibilities of her mother. Meanwhile, their father did his best to balance family with work, but the scales tended to tip toward work as they always had.

She understood this too well, given her own husband's death seven years ago. Richard had run the assayer's office near Wagon Town since the birth of Mica Bend. They had met and married in Carson City just before the discovery of silver along the San Pedro River valley, and with that came the rise of Tombstone—*dreadful name*, Maria still thought— and before anyone knew it, one camp after another sprouted up.

The Perseverance vein lay at the foot of the Arduous Mountains south of Mica Bend. One Dafyd Jones had located it. A Welshman with plenty of mining experience, he had a particular nose for silver. Jones immediately filed his claim and invited several assayers to the site, Richard among them. Richard saw such promise in the place that he decided to stay and established himself before Maria finally came to join him. They lived in an apartment above the office, for his convenience, and did very well on what he made both working for Jones and freelancing to other prospectors. She was soon thrilled to open a school for the camp's children. The couple began to discuss building a house, having a child of their own, and renting out the apartment to some other newcomer.

But overnight, it seemed, their fortune was ripped out from under them, and Maria was left alone and lost. She would never forget that day and how she stood before her class of then thirty students, children of all ages whose parents ran the businesses that lined the main thoroughfare, as well as children from Wagon Town. In her memory, the vision remained of the school door cracking open, casting in a sharp line of daylight before it widened to reveal Marshal Hiram Wells' silhouette with his hat and duster. Usually, he had a languidness about him, but that day he carried himself rigidly.

"Miz Oliver," his voice echoed across time. *"You may want to dismiss the class. I need to speak with you."*

The following vision was Richard lying on a table in the rectory at the back of the church, which also served as Pastor Becker's clinic.

His pale skin. God, his pale skin, splotched and purple around his eyes. A gaping wound, coated with dirt, distorted the side of his head. She had just seen him alive and vibrant that morning, handsome as always in his suit as he headed downstairs to the office.

Marshal Wells had found him while on patrol, tipped off by a group of coyotes pacing along the rim of a crooked gulch that ran along the southern outskirts of town. Miners and anyone else going out to Perseverance had to step precariously down into it, cross, and go up again. They'd stamped out pathways into the embankments to get pack mules up and down. Then every monsoon season, the paths washed away a little, grew steeper and more jagged, and proposals for a bridge had never come to fruition, hindered by some excuse from Mayor Watkins and the town council.

It looked like a bad fall, a tragic slip that resulted in Richard tipping headfirst into the gulch and hitting his head upon a rock. His assayer's kit lay spilled open, contents dashed around him. Yes, it *looked* like a tragic slip, but the marshal felt something did not add up. Because Pastor Becker had peculiar and morbid expertise examining the dead, he had been called out to look at the scene. There was something suspicious about Richard's fall, all right, he said. The rock did not have enough blood on it, but given the face-down angle of his body, it should be drenched along with the ground around it. The purplish hues around his eyes and on his cheeks had been what remained of his blood settling. But as for where the rest went, that had nothing to do with a *fall* into *that* gulch. Those stains would be discovered elsewhere.

It would be only a week before Marshal Wells uncovered the truth behind Richard's murder, and for that, Maria remained forever grateful for his diligence.

The explanation had left her with a storm of sickening emotions, resenting her husband's killers, resenting her husband for bringing them to the Bend in the first place. Richard had been approached by three miners attempting to high-grade silver ore from Perseverance right under Jones' nose, and they needed an assayer's help to process the stolen ore and sell it to the smelter. Richard, however, had taken the moral high ground, but before he could report them to Jones, he was found dead at the bottom of the gulch.

During his investigation, Wells had kept Maria protectively in the dark until the men were arrested. Then she learned everything. Both she and Dafyd Jones pressed their different degrees of charges, and then they witnessed the men's hangings together at the gallows on the other end of town behind the jail. Maria had never felt so empty than at that moment.

"If you need anything, let me know," Jones said. His eyes were kind when he said it.

But now Jones had gone, moved on to more fertile ground. When the Perseverance vein played out, he left a skeleton crew to keep chipping at it, and Maria, still in her twenties, became known as the Widow Oliver. She still grieved, years later, felt it aging her. She hadn't the means to pick up and leave, and even if she did, she couldn't leave her class. Though now it had dwindled to only twelve children, she couldn't find it in her heart to leave them, not until the town breathed its last and she was forced to move on.

The Wells children, in particular, added to that weight. Their restless behavior today aside, they still had her sympathies and empathy. Losing someone in this town, especially now, went beyond heartbreaking. Their mother, whom Maria had also come to call a friend over the years, had been a supportive angel. She had once confessed to Maria that she worried about her husband in his job. He was good at it. Too good. That would surely, eventually, draw bad elements because Hiram had the kind of grit that caused the Earp brothers' gang wars in Tombstone that had forever rippled across the county. But Maria couldn't appreciate that gumption more after all the time the marshal had put in to solve Richard's murder.

All these thoughts and recollections, inspired purely by those three sad children, clouded her sense of time on her walk. Suddenly, she found herself home, staring at the assayer's office and beyond it, another twenty or so yards out, the shadowy grove where Wagon Town still hung on for its own dear life. It wasn't much more than a handful of straggling prospectors now, all hoping to find the new vein that would rekindle a boom in the Bend. From here, she could see about three little campfires flickering within the grove. Further down the road stood the outline of the Wells house and its small farm against the deep gold horizon. Some of the windows flickered with light, and she thought she glimpsed the figure of Marshal Wells riding in before the movement veered off the road and appeared to meld with the landscape. A cold wind stirred, sweeping a cloud of dust across her path. She lifted a corner of her shawl over her nose and mouth to block it out, squinted to keep it out of her eyes. With that, she turned back to her abode, face away from the wind.

The office windows were dark, reflecting the mixed hues of twilight. For a while, after Richard's death, she'd rented the office to a new assayer, supplementing her income, but he had recently moved on, leaving the entire building quiet and her pockets a little emptier. Every step, every creak in the wood seemed so much louder now as she climbed the outside steps to the second story. An insect suddenly trilled loudly somewhere down below in the dark, and she welcomed the noise because it was a piece of life, no matter how tiny.

She arrived later than usual, having dined in the Raskin Hotel kitchen in exchange for after-school tutoring of John Raskin's eight-year-old son, Toby. Directly above, a rim of clouds caught the moonlight and glowed like the silver that once enriched the Bend. On the top landing, she presented her key to unlock the door and had just cracked it open when the wind picked up, and she thought she heard the soft beat of wings or a rustling of fabric, and then a voice spoke just behind her.

"Why so sad?"

It was male, deep but with a gentle lilt that seemed intended not to startle her. Regardless, tingles ran under her skin, down her arms, and up the sides of her cheeks. She spun to look up into the half-illuminated face of the visitor and wondered how he'd followed her up the steps without being heard. She'd sworn no one else was in the street with her on this end of town.

"I, uhm... who?" she stammered. He was no townsperson that she knew, and she knew virtually every resident on some level. "Who are you?"

With the darkness of the apartment behind her and only the moon and some ambient light from the town, she still only saw half of the face, angular, haloed by pale hair that flitted with the breeze. The intense eye staring back at her from the visible side was light gray, washed clean of color, a white void that pulled her attention in.

"Again," he said. "*Why* so sad?"

"I am alone," she answered, the words tumbling out of her mouth before she could stop them.

"Is that so?" The corner of full lips turned up. "Why is a pretty thing like you alone?"

"My husband died." Her voice sounded hollow now, distant. A strange tension rose in her that she was saying too much but *God, she wanted to talk* to this stranger.

He gave a soft *tsk*. "What a pity for him. What was his name?"

"Richard," she whispered.

"Richard, hmmm. Such a common, boring name. I've known many Richards."

What offense she felt at this comment barely held. It drifted quickly from her mind as the man stepped closer.

"But what if I could help you see your beloved Richard again. You'd like that, wouldn't you?"

She nodded vacantly, reason slipping as to how this might be possible. Yes, that was what she wanted most of all. She barely felt his hand sweep up under her chin, grasp and angle her head up, her glazed eyes looking at that beautiful night sky and its budding stars. He stepped up against her more directly, his free arm wrapping around her waist to cinch her closer, and she briefly caught a scent like dried leaves and earth on him. Then the view of the sky shuttered as he swept her backward into the complete darkness of the apartment.

She distantly heard a board creak under her before excruciating pain consumed the entire front and side of her neck, like a trap clamping over her windpipe and the space beneath her ear. It dug in ferociously, tore, shook, gnawed. Her breath stopped almost immediately, preventing any scream.

Not that she *would* have screamed.

Beyond the blackness above her, the pain, the taste of blood bubbling up onto her tongue, she smiled weakly as she thought she heard her husband's voice whisper to her.

"Come here, sweetheart."

Hiram basked in the smell of the house every evening as Lucinda's cooking skills, trained by her mother, took center stage, and reminded him of happier times.

They sat in the kitchen around a big serving bowl of chicken and dumplings with a side of buttered turnips, a small, dried fruit pie waiting by to be divvied up for dessert. Caleb and Ellie were on one side of the long table, Lucinda on the other, positioned to quickly get up and tend to the fire or replenish the serving bowl. Hiram sat at the end, spoon dipped into his bowl, staring at the empty chair across from him. There was a plate and utensils set there, too, placed by Lucinda because she couldn't bear the thought of leaving that end of the table empty, and neither could Hiram.

"Well, that should be enough for lunch tomorrow," Lucinda said as she closed the cooking pot for the final time that evening. "Beans tomorrow night."

"Eww," Ellie groaned.

"Is it not good, Papa?" His eldest's voice reached through to him, and Hiram looked down to realize his hand had gone slack, about to let his spoon slip into the bowl of gravy, bready clumps, and chicken.

"Oh, yeah," he murmured and straightened up in his chair all the better to engage with his children. "It's wonderful, honey."

"Can we have ow chaptews back now?" Ellie asked.

Hiram eyed the chunks of turnip huddled to the side of her bowl as if they were trying to hide just below the rim. "If you eat your turnips." The sour look on her face was worth it as she took one slow bite. Maybe he'd relieve her of her misery. Turnips weren't his favorite either, even if they were cooked perfectly the way Rachel would have done.

Caleb, meanwhile, had finished and was staring at the fruit pie.

"Homework is done?"

"Yessir," the boy replied. "Just some reading."

"Papa," Lucinda said and cleared her throat. "An acting troupe just arrived. They're going to play at the opera house. May I go to one of their shows? It's Shakespeare," she added as if that piece of information proved the troupe any less bawdy than the last one that came through.

This news brought a brief look of shock to his face as he'd have never expected entertainers of any kind to find interest in the Bend again, and then Hiram sighed. One thing Silas was right about, the kids needed entertainment, whether in horrid pulp tales or actors making asses of themselves on stage. "Sure."

"Can I go, too?" Ellie asked.

"Little old for Shakespeare, aren't you?" Hiram shot her a wink. He was enjoying her bright little smile, the happy bob of her head, when Lucinda pointedly ruined the moment.

"Oh, she should definitely go. It'll be good culture for her."

Hiram suppressed a snort and stirred his dumplings before he glanced at his boy child, who was crossing his eyes at his sisters, particularly Lucinda, while he sucked in his cheeks and made fish lips. "Caleb," he chastised softly. "Face'll stick that way."

The warning had little effect other than to make Ellie giggle, music to the ears. Hiram sighed again and went back to his meal.

After supper, Hiram typically went back by the saloon. Nathan was probably there by now, and the Palace was as much a debriefing office as the jail these days.

Plus, it came with the added benefit of a drink.

First, however, he always saw his children off to bed. Lucinda would stay up a little later watching the house, working on her embroidery in the front parlor, but Caleb and Ellie were already in their room upstairs.

Hiram climbed the narrow stairwell and, at the landing, turned into the corridor that divided the two smallest bedrooms in the house. Lucinda's was on the right, and Caleb and Ellie's shared room on the left. Straight ahead, tucked into a cubby of space between the rooms, was a curtain that hid a commode stand.

The light of an oil lamp flickered through the crack on the left side door. Caleb's voice raised within, reaping the rewards of the returned pamphlets that Hiram wished he could burn. But that would only provoke rebellion that he was not ready to deal with. Funny how he could walk up to a drunk ruffian stirring trouble in the middle of town and hoist them into a cell to sleep it off with no qualms, but he couldn't stand up to his children very well. That had been Rachel's job.

He slowed as he approached the door, enjoying not the ridiculous story but the sound of his son's voice delivering it with acted gusto.

"...it was with great pain to his heart that Henry raised the blade. His hands shook. Sweat beaded on his brow, icy against the chilled night air. He took one more look..."

Oh yes, they had to deal with those giant monster bats, Hiram thought, recalling Ellie's great worry over some missing chapter or other. He reduced his walk to a creep and peered through the crack, which perfectly framed a view of both brother and little sister situated for the night. Caleb was propped up at the head of his bed with the oil lamp drawn as close as possible on the side table, while Ellie hunkered down under her blankets and held her doll tight. How she even slept after these bedtime stories, Hiram could only wonder.

"Children are more resilient than you might think," Rachel had told him once when Caleb was himself Ellie's age and had discovered a rattler coiled in front of the outhouse door. Rather than fetch either parent, the boy had marched right into the barn and up to the wall where Hiram hung tools, retrieved an ax, and promptly chopped the snake's head in two as clean as you please. While both parents had been concerned that the thing might have managed to strike out in defense before that lucky fatal blow, Caleb had remained eerily cool about it all.

"Kiw'd it," he said. He'd had the same speech issues then as Ellie had now.

"Yeah, killed it good," Hiram remarked while still feeling a little sick in his chest. He was about to unleash a rant on why Caleb was to always come to him first before trying such a thing again when Rachel calmed him.

"H," she said, laying a hand on his arm right as he raised a finger to shake at his son, "we chose to live here with these dangers. At least he knows how to deal with them. Don't be angry about that. Besides," she added with a little knowing smirk, "he's like his father."

On that note, Hiram lowered his finger, examined the twitching remains of the now cleft-headed snake, and revised his rant down to a simple request instead. Caleb gave him a clipped but proud nod and was allowed to go back to his play.

Outside the bedroom door now, Hiram smiled at the memory. So maybe Ellie was, like her brother, more prepared for the horrid tales than most adults would expect. He listened a moment longer, trying not to roll his eyes at the lousy narrative.

"For a moment," Caleb continued, "he saw Victoria's face as she had been before, his beautiful golden-haired wife, but now what lay before him - this was not Victoria. This was a stranger, a fiend in her body. No, Victoria was dead."

"Awwww," Ellie murmured in mourning for the late and lovely Victoria.

"Bracing himself, Henry brought the blade down on her neck, cleaved her head from her shoulders, and set her spirit free. Blood drenched the floor of the musty crypt—" A page rustled as it was turned.

Hiram took the pause as his signal to get in there and end the madness now. "And to be continued," he said as he pushed the door open.

Caleb looked up at him, face golden in the lamp light, large blue eyes wide with surprise at his father's entrance. "But we're at the good part."

"Well," Hiram reasoned, "the sooner you go to bed, the sooner tomorrow will come, and you can finish it."

Caleb gave him a dubious look to that logic but then nodded, folded the pamphlet shut, and placed it on the bedside table.

"Good man," Hiram said. "Now I expect to see that light go out when I get to the head of the steps, understood?"

"Yessir," Caleb replied, but he seemed satisfied to have finally gotten to read a little more of the tragic adventures of Henry and Victoria that his uncle had cooked up. He scooted under the covers with no further ado, and Hiram helped him situate them before kissing his forehead.

"Goodnight, son."

"Goodnight, Papa." If Caleb said any prayers, he kept them silent. Hiram didn't know, and he had not enforced any rule on the matter since Rachel's passing.

On the other hand, Ellie was a staunch supplicant and already had her little hands folded under her chin. "Now I way me down to sweep, I pway the wowd my souw to keep. God bwess my papa and brothew and sistew, and pwease tew Mama that we wove hew. Amen."

Every night, precious though it was, it stung to hear it. Hiram sat on the side of the bed to push the covers up to his daughter's chin and found her eyes studying him.

"Papa, how come you don't say pwayews anymow?"

He blinked, stumped that she had noticed, but she was too young for talk about how a man might struggle with his beliefs, how he might suddenly find God to be either a cruel bastard or a myth altogether. His chest tightened deep inside, like a fist clenching, as he summoned an answer, keeping himself together. "It's nothing, Sweet Pea. You just keep saying 'em for the both of us, all right?"

She made a purposeful clipped nod to that. They gave each other a peck on the cheek, and he saw that she was situated before he stood and went to step out of the room. He took one more look back at them from the hallway and then closed the door to the same width as before. The stairwell was aglow from another lamp down below, and when he looked back, he was relieved to see the light in the children's room go dark as Caleb kept his word..

CHAPTER FOUR

After tucking in his youngers and then kissing his oldest on the forehead, Hiram lifted his hat and duster back off the hook by the door and took his horse into town on a road rendered in frost by the moonlight. If you looked out into the surrounding desert, the shadowed shapes of the scrub, cholla, barrel cacti, and the occasional saguaro were all highlighted in the same frosted effect. But to stare at the shadows beneath this veil meant to wrangle with the eerie notion that one of the shadows might suddenly move. A coyote, perhaps, or something *else*. Above this panorama of phantoms stood the small mountain range that had once given up its hoard but, in return, had taken countless lives as payment. To think about that made a man's spine tingle and his mind wander to how many ghosts might be out there trapped in that nacreous landscape. Hiram didn't believe in ghosts, but he still rode at a decent clip to beat the penetrating chill as desert nights were frigid in any season.

At the edge of town, past the old mining camp, assayer's office, Grain Exchange, and the now out-of-business Grand Saloon, he homed in on several dots of soft orange glow. By this time of night, kerosene lanterns had been hung over the boardwalks along the Orleans Palace and the Raskin, both of which were centrally located on the thoroughfare.

When Silas first arrived in Mica Bend some ten years ago, he'd erected the Palace on funds acquired from boxing matches—mostly his own and a few fixed ones at that—and other gambling ventures and invited Hiram to join him as half owner. Hiram had, at that time, gone back to Pennsylvania after he and Rachel had their second child and worked for

Seneca Oil in Titusville. The job was miserable, and he missed the open ranges and drier climate he'd experienced on prior adventures, so he took Silas up on his offer. After the family had settled in, it was soon discovered, on the Palace's rowdier nights, that Hiram made a better bouncer than he did a business owner. While Silas tended the bar and his ladies entertained, Hiram kept busy tamping the noise down just so and made sure any guns present stayed in their holsters. Somehow this had catapulted him into law enforcement. He'd won the appointment of marshal from the town council, and his focus turned as he proved he could keep the peace about town as well as he did in the saloon. Then his first significant case had been the murder of Mr. Richard Oliver, Mica Bend's original primary assayer. Solving that one had secured his elections thereafter. Since business at the Palace had boomed, Silas was able to buy out Hiram's share, but the place became the favored meeting hole over the small office in the jail at the southeastern end of town.

There were only four other horses at the hitching post outside the Palace. One of them belonged to his deputy, and one was the now-familiar dappled gray mare, and two were gorgeous black Saddlebreds that he didn't recognize at all. As always, he steered Teddy to the corner and used the railing for his hitch. He'd always done this, and every local knew it. They also knew Teddy was off-limits to anyone but his owner—or those with special permission from said owner (family, for instance)—and that included petting or bribing with treats.

Hiram shook his head as he paused before the steps, next to which a hole had been knocked in the cover panel that usually kept the boardwalk looking neat and helped to—though not always—keep out critters that might find the underneath to be a nice burrow. A few days ago, Silas' Saddlebred stud, appropriately named Arsenic (or *Arse* as he was more often and appropriately called), had seen fit to get uppity and kick a broad hole in the wood, demonstrating how degraded it was. It was Hiram's duty, as town marshal, to keep the saloon keeper informed that he should have the hole repaired. As a friend, he'd likely let it slide indefinitely.

A moment later, he flung open the bat-wing doors into the establishment and observed the room as he walked toward the massive bar to the left where Silas was tending. The place was well lit by a circular chandelier in the center and oil lamps in mirrored sconces attached to the balcony supports. Steps at the far front of the bar led up to the balcony that framed the room. Opposite the bar, on the main floor, the underside of the balcony created shadowed nooks where the tables were reserved for poker.

The balcony accessed four rooms in which Silas once kept several ladies of the night. All but Izabel had left, and she was nowhere in sight. At one time, the place would have been a den of activity no matter the day of the week, but now only a couple nights were busy, those usually being pay days for Bryce Tucker's ranch hands, and even they didn't stay very long since there were no women left in whose arms they could sleep off their booze. Hiram slept up there occasionally now because his bed at home was uncomfortable in its emptiness.

The lack of horses outside was no indication of how many patrons might be inside. Many townsfolk simply walked in. John Raskin had come over from his hotel and was situated at a table with Mr. Fraleigh. Those two were a common enough sight. At the bar, Nathan hunched over a half-drained mug of beer at the end closest to Hiram's entrance while Pastor Becker was at the other, isolated over a whiskey tumbler, his Gladstone on the counter next to him. Given the man had been there since before the sun went down, there was no telling how much his glass had been refilled.

As Hiram approached Nathan, his eyes darted to the other occupied tables. Two newcomers—presumably the owners of the black horses—sat with Mayor Watkins. They were both young men in dust-patched black coats that were almost uniform in appearance but unbuttoned and pushed unceremoniously back from their chests, revealing sweat-stained white shirts and dusty creases. In front of the one with long red hair sat a beer mug and a black hat with a broad brim. His companion, sporting short dark hair, had also removed his hat, which matched the other one, and propped it over the back of his chair. If he didn't know any better, Hiram would have taken them for some kind of traveling preachers in those getups. Mayor Watkins, who, like Silas, always dressed well, was engaged in chatting them up as he smoked a cigar.

At the other table, some fifteen feet away and closer to a poker nook at the front, sat the Raines brothers with their heads inclined. Their voices hissed with quiet tension at each other, and Seth's jaw looked tight, angry. Whatever had them going, it was between them, and Hiram left it that way. Seth looked to have cleaned up some, though his long hair was still on the greasy side. Ben had removed his buckskin coat to relax with his sleeves rolled up and his vest unbuttoned.

Eyes primarily on Watkins and his guests, Hiram leaned against the bar and asked his deputy quietly, "Patrol go well?"

"As well as can be expected. Silas already told me about the Raines brothers 'n that you let Seth out this afternoon. Looks like they're stayin' at the Raskin for the night then movin' on in the mornin'. Passed that bunch there as they came into town." The young negro nodded over his shoulder at the table of interest where Watkins' voice could be heard rising and falling.

"Bunch?"

"They're with an acting troupe that just arrived," Silas answered as he came up. He was out of his jacket now, sleeves rolled up, an oiled leather apron protecting his clothing and a bar rag slung over his shoulder. He absently sat down a bottle of whiskey and a shot glass behind the main counter.

"Ah, right." Hiram recalled Lucinda's news and enthusiasm over supper. "Heard enough about that already."

Silas grinned but didn't inquire how the marshal had come by the information. "What can I get you?"

"Coffee," Hiram said, knowing Silas kept some brew warm most hours.

"The usual then." Silas went down the bar and disappeared into the back room.

"He says you went out to the Hanson farm to check it out," Nathan said as he took a swig from his mug.

Hiram reached over the bar and retrieved the shot glass and bottle that Silas *just happened* to leave. He poured the shot and put the bottle back. "Yeah, like Terry Wilkes said, it's just an empty house. They left some furniture in there covered up, but Zach's buckboard is gone. Still, it doesn't sound like him to leave without telling anyone. Especially if someone owed him money."

"Well, some of these folks get an opportunity to get out and fast, they'll take it."

"True. So, tell me about this bunch of actors. Lucinda was all talk at dinner."

Nathan gestured over his shoulder again. "Those two drove in a private coach and a freighter. Haven't seen the troupe yet, but they're staying at the Simpson house while they're here. Apparently, Watkins made the arrangement. That's why he's over there looking so pleased with himself." Nathan nodded toward the table where Raskin and Fraleigh were hunkered and speaking with lowered voices. "Mr. Raskin's got his hackles up that they stayed at Miz Simpson's place rather than his hotel here in town. Guess that was part of the deal they made with our illustrious mayor."

"I understand they perform Shakespeare," Silas rejoined as he arrived with a steaming mug.

"I heard," Hiram said. Then he added with false drama, "Alas." He threw back the shot and plunked the glass down hard on the counter, took a sharp breath as the whiskey cleared the day's dust from his throat. He savored the lingering smoky taste and then switched out for the coffee only to take a sip and cringe, nearly spitting it out. He forced it down with a bitter gulp. "This is your chicory," he griped.

"Indeed," Silas said. "So sorry to disappoint you, but the Arbuckles' is getting low, and I've been forced to blend, just like we do it back home." He seemed all the more amused as Hiram smacked his tongue against the roof of his mouth.

"Here, gimme that back." Hiram retrieved the shot glass and the bottle without any resistance. "Jesus Christ, Silas. Warn me next time." As he poured, his gaze drifted too far down to the other end of the bar where Pastor Becker sat hunched, propped on one elbow, sweaty red forehead pressed to the back of one hand which still held the empty tumbler. "He's been here all this time?" He immediately regretted asking.

"He's had enough, too. Be nice of you to escort him back to the church, Marshal," Silas said with smug relish.

Hiram tossed back his next shot much faster than the first. "Shit."

If only the suggestion were not so true. Becker looked well and good corned, and that ended a relaxing night far more than Silas' chicory. He pushed away from the bar, feeling his deputy's and his best friend's eyes on him as he started toward Becker.

"Marshal!" Watkin's voice called sharply to him, and that was worse than Silas being right.

This time he said it under his breath. *"Shit."* Now deputy and bartender had to be grinning ear to ear at his additional discomfort. "Yes, Mayor Sir," he said as he turned toward the summons.

"Come over here, please, meet a couple of our guests."

Hiram wove toward the table and stood looking down at the two. The redhead regarded him with a friendlier manner than his companion.

"This is our Marshal Wells," Watkins said to the men. Then to Hiram, "This here's Jasper O'Brian." He indicated the man in question, the one with long red hair spilling over his shoulders, pale skin with a smattering of freckles.

"Mr. O'Brian," Hiram said and thrust out his hand, and the younger man took it in a firm grip.

"And this is Morgan Reed," Watkins finished. "They're part of The Chamberlain Players that just came to town."

"Right," Hiram tried, to no avail, to sound enthusiastic. He shook Reed's hand and found it just as strong. "My daughter is mightily ready to see some Shakespeare."

"Oh, would that be the young lady that greeted us on our way in?" O'Brian asked.

Hiram detected a brogue, but there was a leer of sorts in O'Brian's green eyes that he didn't care for. He chose not to reply and thus confirm anything and then looked at Morgan Reed, who seemed busier studying what was left of his beer.

Watkins noticed this right off. "Ah, you're almost done. Silas! Another round over here, please!"

Hiram knew the sharp smell of horse manure even when it didn't come from a horse. The mayor must have something in mind regarding the troupe, but Hiram knew he would hear about it all later. The mission to rescue Pastor Becker from his woes suddenly seemed ideal. "Well," he said to dismiss himself, "I've got to take care of something here. I'm sure I'll speak more with you gentlemen soon."

Watkins lifted a finger, started to add something, but that was when Hiram overheard Seth Raines growl out some insult—at whom it was aimed, he did not know—from only a few tables over.

"Pieces of shit."

To this, Ben Raines said something softer but just loud enough that Hiram caught some of it. *"Venunurtal galmedvandrux, brother."*

Whoa, wait. Hiram turned to look at them, wondering what the hell language *that* was, and he'd overheard quite a few in his travels. It sounded rather melodic, the tone implying that Ben was attempting to diffuse his brother's temper. Also strange, Hiram thought, that he had not picked up on any kind of foreign accent in their everyday English. If anything, the brothers both had a soft western twang, but even that was hardly noticeable.

"Vangraf veun druxmedgis gedgrafgis gondruxvanmedurvagrafgal," Ben said, commanding mouthfuls of long, strange words in that calm voice.

Seth responded in the same language, louder, angrier, but Hiram couldn't keep up with it. Then he suddenly stood up, his chair shooting back behind him, legs scraping over the floor, and his hands braced on the sides of the table. "Then when *will* we get involved?" he spat.

Immediately Silas' arm shot out as he pointed across the room. "Seth Raines, don't you dare flip over another table, boy!" When Silas dropped his casual tone down into that forceful boom, even Hiram would not have argued with him.

Hiram turned toward the two, gesturing for calm with his left hand out while his right tensed at his side. "What's the problem over here, gentlemen?" he asked while observing that Seth did not have his gun belt on. Likely, Ben had stashed it for safekeeping. His hand relaxed a little.

Seth took a deep breath, nostrils flaring wide, before letting it out, and then he shook his head. "Sorry, Marshal." His eyes narrowed and cut right to the table with Watkins and his guests, paused, then made a sweep across the entire room before coming back around to his brother.

Ben stared up at him with an expression that said patiently, *Are you finished?* Hiram did not have to hear that in any language to understand it.

With that, Seth turned and stomped out of the place, shoving the batwing doors outward with a force that left them flapping in his wake.

Ben stood, grabbed his coat from the adjacent chair, and fished in his pocket before slapping two Morgan silver dollars on the table, far more than the cost of two beers. Hiram looked at the gleaming silver disks, recognized them for the apologetic currency they were. "Please excuse us, Marshal, and have a good night." Then the older Raines followed his brother out the door. Somewhere, a few paces out in the street, their voices sounded off at each other again before fading out.

"It's time for that young man to leave town," Watkins announced, his snappish, authoritative tone nothing but show where Hiram was concerned.

"I don't think he'll be a problem much longer," the marshal replied, eyes still on the doors as the flapping slowed to a stop. Satisfied that the brothers were keeping their confrontation private, he felt his shoulders uncoil, turned, and resumed his mission. He approached the inebriated pastor and reached up to take the tumbler out of his hand before it fell out. He sat it firmly on the counter in Silas' direction, where it was quickly whisked away.

"All right, Becker, that's your limit. You shouldn't be seen like this in public anyway."

Becker's head nearly dropped as his hand prop gave way with the sudden movement. He looked up, blinking, and Hiram imagined he probably saw double. He started to take Becker's elbow and hoist him off the stool.

"Do not manhandle me, Marshal," he objected. "I've made four house calls and delivered a stillborn child today. I'm entitled to unwind accordingly." Becker's English was excellent but laced with the remnants of a German accent and the occasional simple word. It could be faint at times, but right now, it was more pronounced if a little slurred.

Hiram quickly recalled that there was only one woman in the town who was known to be *that* pregnant. "Maddie Krane?"

Becker almost tipped off the stool as he tried to get his footing. "Ja."

"I'm sorry to hear that."

Maddie Krane's husband, Ronald, was the town's sole remaining bank owner, who had been struggling since so many citizens had removed their funds, while others had cashed in investments and moved on. It had left the couple struggling, especially with the baby on the way.

Hiram reckoned he'd go by the Krane home tomorrow and give his condolences. That was what Rachel would want him to do even as he found the thought of it personally painful. Adding this to his new list of things to do, he returned attention to his current task.

"Looks like you've unwound in spades, Pastor," he said and glanced over at Watkins and his guests.

The mayor was too busy with some diatribe about the life of the town, that the players need not be concerned about having a decent audience, and he wanted the two men to deliver that message to their troupe leader. The man could spin excuses with the greatest of skills.

But it was how his gaze met Jasper O'Brian's that stood out most to Hiram. The redhead, and his companion, were watching him coolly, looking right past the chattering Watkins with such intensity. Or was it Becker that they were staring at? What was so interesting about a drunk physician was beyond Hiram. Then O'Brian gave a subtle eye roll, and Hiram interpreted that to mean both were trying not to glaze over while listening to Watkins. They'd been driving teams all day, from the sound of it. Could they not enjoy their beers in peace?

Hiram felt sorry for them but left them to their fate as he took on his. He gripped Becker's shoulders and pulled him up straight. "Come on, Norman, time to get you back to church."

"Whoa!" the pastor objected. "Wait!" He grabbed for his Gladstone bag, wavered, took a breath, and steadied himself, his face turning all but green as he managed to burp rather than puke.

Hiram gritted his teeth and leaned close, whispered gruffly. "Could you at least *act* like the goddamned man of the cloth, or doctor, or whatever it is you claim to be?"

"But I…" Becker's pewter eyes turned toward Hiram, hopeless at first, and then some tiny piece of dignity crept in. The hangdog look lifted slightly. He straightened himself, clutched his bag tighter, and wrenched his shoulders from Hiram's grip. "I said," he repeated, "I will not be manhandled."

Hiram held up his hands in mock surrender and then gestured toward the doors. "Well then, after you."

*
**

Becker was not a drunk.

This Hiram knew and, given his own past, he was the last man who should be pointing fingers when it came to self-anesthetizing.

But after a tough day, the pastor was known to spend an evening at the Palace having one too many. Hiram took the Gladstone bag off his hands and had him hold onto Teddy's saddle horn as they walked, slow and steady, toward the southeastern end of town, past the jail and the mayor's office. Teddy grumbled about it a little, but as long as the clinging load didn't try to climb on, all was well.

"Breathe," Hiram kept instructing Becker, hoping the brisk night air would revive his charge further.

Another watery burp answered him, but nothing else was said between them.

Hiram had borrowed a lantern off the boardwalk and held it out with his free hand, creating a bobbing circle of light before them. They made their way toward the Lutheran church, a typical long boxy structure with a steeple at the front, white paint sand-scoured, that sat somewhat on its own at the lower bend out of town. It had been the first Protestant establishment here.

The far older Spanish mission stood behind the schoolhouse across the thoroughfare on the south side. The Catholic chapel and a small parsonage were all that remained of the mission and were run by Father Ramirez, who liked to bicker over which path was correct. His views, however, did not stop him from coming to Becker's clinic for any ailments or simple visits. It had once been amusing to see priest and pastor debate with each other at one of the front tables in the saloon or the hotel restaurant, but now Hiram was happy not to encounter either of them at all.

Other than these centers of faith, Methodist circuit ministers had also come through and held gatherings in some homes or the shade of Wagon Town, but Hiram hadn't heard of any such recent visit. He had not been to church in months, choosing to spend his Sundays in the saloon or catching up on home repairs, and Becker had not been invited to dinner at the Wells house either.

He took Becker around the back to the rectory, which doubled as the clinic. The back door faced the little cemetery, fenced in with a giant oak at its southern end. Hiram felt his chest tighten, his lower back tense and send a zing of pain through his core as he fumbled with the lantern and the medical bag while prying Becker's hand from the saddle horn. Teddy grumbled, as he was wont to do, but stayed put near the corner of the building while Hiram guided Becker to the rectory steps.

"Come on." He tried to kick one of Becker's feet upward onto a step and take some of the load off himself before his lower back revolted. Becker groaned miserably, and Hiram thought maybe he should bend the pastor over and try to force him to puke if that would help. Then Becker seemed to get his bearing on his own, snatched his Gladstone away, and climbed the steps in what had to be a force of drunken will, opened the door, and let himself in.

Hiram followed with the lantern and held it aloft to cast light around the room that was both residence and office. There were two cots, one on each side, with an examination table in the center. A counter covered with other medical accouterments, vials, jars, and cabinets of gauze and antiseptics filled the opposite wall, a small desk situated near the back door while another door adjacent led into the sanctuary. The space under the counter had been utilized for makeshift bookshelves that were crammed with old volumes.

The air carried an undertone of old sweat slightly overpowered by the fragrance of dried herbs hanging from the ceiling. While Becker had plenty of common medicines on hand, everything from Dover's powder to quinine and laudanum, he relied as much on the herbs he'd grown in a plot next to the cemetery on the other side of the oak. Each plant was placed carefully to suit its needs for sunlight or shade, water, sand, or richer soil. Now and then, he requested cow chips from some of the ranch hands who would bring him buckets full to fertilize certain beds that didn't usually care for the Arizona climate. His presence as both preacher and doctor had meant Mica Bend never acquired a drugstore as everyone came to him. He was meticulous in his care of each herb, cautious with his choices to prescribe more traditional medications.

Well, at least most of the time.

Hiram sniffed irreverently at the fleeting thought, sat the lantern down on the center table, and guided Becker to one of the cots. The older man immediately collapsed, falling onto his back, eyes rolling as he groaned again.

"On your belly, Norman," Hiram said. When there was no immediate response, he raised his voice. "*Norman.* Get on your belly, so you don't end up gargling your upchuck."

If there was upchuck coming that was, but Hiram would be damned if he'd spend the night on the other cot just to wake up to that extra lousy smell. With a heave and a grunt, he got Becker to roll over, his face on the edge of the cot, and decided that was sufficient.

"…'m sorry, Hiram," Becker suddenly mumbled, drool gleaming on his pursed lips, eyes still closed. "She was so beautiful… beautiful soul… 'm so sorry…"

Hiram tried not to sneer. Looking at the man made his stomach sour.

The pastor began to snore, his face reddened on its high points, deeply shadowed in the lines around his mouth and eyes.

Hiram stepped back, looked around the room. A hurricane lamp sat on the counter, well out of reach of any flailing arms should Becker awaken and move about in the wee hours. Hiram patted his vest pocket and found, next to his watch, the little silverplate match safe he always carried, a long-ago gift from Rachel so that he "could always illuminate his way." He withdrew a match, struck it, lit the lamp, and turned the wick down to a gentle glow, enough of a night light that the pastor could find his way around.

Briefly, his gaze swept across the counter, over jars with familiar labels, the brass gleam of a microscope, around to the room again, the door into the sanctuary, the opposing cots that looked shoddy and uncomfortable, the little desk by the door where Becker wrote up his diagnoses or prepared his sermons. All he could think was how grateful he was that Rachel had not died in this stinking room but in the comfort of home.

Then he shut that thought from his mind, locked tight before he grew angry, before he decided to extinguish the lamp and let Becker fumble around in the dark, shitting himself or puking or whatever came of this current bender.

"Good night, Norman," he said flatly, then he grabbed the lantern and quickly made his departure.

CHAPTER FIVE

It wasn't every school day that Lucinda gave her siblings a ride up the thoroughfare, but today was one such day since they'd gotten out of the house a little late. She had planned on going for a morning ride and already had Remington saddled up, so off they all went. Riding sidesaddle with two passengers was awkward but not impossible. Caleb was directly behind her, with Ellie clinging on behind him.

Mica Bend stirred with the usual signs of life, starting with the aroma of bacon cooking on a fire in Wagon Town as the Wells children clomped by and then scattered distant voices as a few folks came and went from the Raskin Hotel ahead. From their mount, all three called out their daily greetings as they passed shop keepers opening. Mr. Fraleigh, outside his mercantile, gave a tip of his hat, and Mr. Wilkes at his barbershop offered a fond hello. He, at least, had a few clients lined up for a shave, and Miz Elliot was heading into the shoemaker and repair next door.

Already her father's horse, Teddy, was tethered at the corner of the Orleans Palace next to the hotel. Every morning he had coffee there before going to his office at the jail up the street, and then he would head out to either patrol or attend some menial duty like tax collections or picking up odd bits of trash.

The morning sparkled with dew collected on the patches of grass that had taken root along the edges of the boardwalks and top edges of troughs, the dust in the air tamped down at least until said dew lifted. The October sky deepened from a paler blue in the east to a more periwinkle color in the west, and Lucinda basked in it. Then the corner of her brother's McGuffey's Reader, fattened by those ridiculous story pamphlets hidden between its pages, dug into her back.

"I swear, Caleb, must you stuff your schoolbooks with that nonsense? You won't get away with reading them in class."

Caleb ignored the complaint and suddenly blared out behind her ear, "Good morning, Father Ramirez!"

Lucinda winced and elbowed her brother in the ribs.

"Jesis, Caweb." Ellie's speech was especially lazy this morning.

"Don't swear, Ellie," Lucinda corrected her.

Ahead of them, the old priest hustled along on the left, going in the opposite direction, no doubt eager to get to a plate of biscuits at the Raskin. His long black cassock swished over the ground at his feet, his portly belly bobbing. "Good morning, children!" he called back before he disappeared from her periphery.

Then Lucinda brought her horse to a near standstill. Welcome new sounds arose around the middle of town as they started to pass the standalone structure of the opera house, Mica Bend's crowning glory with its brick structure, exterior columns, and extra tall front that made two stories look like three. Inside, it accommodated box and balcony seating and served as a public house for town meetings. So few acts had been enticed to perform there lately, though, so it was little wonder she'd gotten excited to see the Chamberlain Players arrive yesterday afternoon. She'd felt like she was welcoming a band of heroes come to save the town from a long and arduous cultural drought. Speaking of which, the hulk of the black freight wagon, with its elaborate signage, sat just within the shade of the building on its northwestern side. The front double doors stood open, and out poured the industrious zip of saws and the bang of hammers. Lucinda's heart skipped happily at the idea of a night out to see the lights flickering warmly on the stage, the glitter of the crystal chandelier that hung from the ceiling.

"Come on. We're late." Caleb goosed back.

"We are not." Lucinda nudged Remington back into a walk, still staring into the gaping shadow of the open doors.

On the next lot up on the right stood the bank, currently closed, and then Bixby Brothers' Carpentry which used to focus on signage, but caskets had become their primary business. Their latest choices were lined up out front, prompting Lucinda to look away and pay more attention to the next lot on the right where the school stood at the bend toward the southeast going out of town, across from the mayor's office and the jail.

To her surprise, the students stood scattered around aimlessly. Some sat on the steps, and others paced when they usually would be filing inside already. As she reined Remington closer, it became clear that the doors were locked, and there was no sign of Miz Oliver waiting for the moment to ring the bell out front.

"What's going on?" Caleb asked over her shoulder.

"I'm not sure." Lucinda brought her horse to a stop. There was an order to dismounting as she kicked her leg over the upper horn and dropped to the ground before turning to help Ellie down first, then Caleb helped himself.

"Whewe's Miz Owivew?" the youngest Wells asked and started ahead as Lucinda went to tether Remington in the shade on the northwestern side of the building where two other horses stood. She came back around the corner to find Caleb hugging his book as he spoke with Toby Raskin.

"She helped me last night," Toby was saying. "Came and had dinner, too."

"She's not here?" Lucinda asked.

Heads shook, and shoulders shrugged.

"She'll be along soon, I'm sure." It occurred to her that she and her siblings had not encountered the teacher on the way in as they often did. Miz Oliver would walk beside them for a spell some mornings, chatting pleasantly. Lucinda retraced this morning's ride in her mind, wondering if there was something she'd overlooked when she spotted her father across the broadest section of the thoroughfare arriving at the jail with a packet under one arm and Nathan catching up with him. "Papa!" she called and waved until she caught his attention.

From this distance, she could see that he had an exchange with Nathan and handed him the packet before the deputy nodded dismounted to head into the jail. Papa turned and rode across the street, frowned as he drew closer and saw that something had to be off for twelve school children to be milling around aimlessly.

"Why aren't you in class yet?"

"Miz Oliver ain't come yet," Toby offered.

"Can I come over and stay at the jail?" Caleb blurted out.

"Now, hang on just a moment," Papa said and angled his hat against the sun. "How long have you all been waiting?"

Billy Wayne spoke up louder than necessary. "A whole hour!"

A few nods confirmed the claim.

"Somehow, I doubt that," Papa muttered. "Alright, everyone, wait right here."

"Cain't we jus' go home?" Jamie Garret asked.

"No, you stay," he pointed at the ten-year-old. "No one goes anywhere until I check on your teacher."

Lucinda nodded and huffed a stray strand of hair from her face. "Want me to go with you, Papa?"

"No, just wait with the kids. I'll be back." He immediately reined Teddy around and bolted up the street at a full run, heading to check the apartment above the assayer's office.

At times like this, Lucinda noticed how the love in her father's eyes was still there but distant, tamped back by the call of work. She watched him disappear down the thoroughfare, little puffs of dust kicking up in Teddy's wake. A long wait later, and there was still no word. Everyone had begun to gather near the horses to stay in the shade. Jamie and Caleb played with a grasshopper, teasing it from behind with a twig to see how far it would spring, while Ellie paced, bored out of her mind and getting fidgety.

"Oh, for heaven's sake," Lucinda finally swore and unwound Remington's tether from the hitch. "I'm going to see for myself."

"I wanna go!" Ellie demanded.

"No," Lucinda snapped, "you and Caleb go over and sit with Nathan, stay in sight of the school. Papa won't get mad if he comes back and you're at least *there*." This unofficial permission from their big sister prompted both younger siblings to perk up. Caleb abandoned the hapless grasshopper to whatever fate Jamie had in store for it, and in seconds he was running, with Ellie on his heels, across the thoroughfare, nearly plowing over Mayor Watkins, who had to take a quick step back.

"Caleb, watch out for other people, you little cretin!" Lucinda shouted.

Watkins looked none too pleased but adjusted his jacket and hat and proceeded toward the jail. *Oh, Lord, he's heading for Papa's office, too,* Lucinda thought as she guided Remington to the school steps and used them to hoist herself onto his back. She steered the gelding around and up the street in a steady trot. She was almost to the assayer's office when she saw her father returning, his eyes shaded under his hat, but by the tight lines around his mouth, she could tell he wasn't happy about something.

"Papa?"

"Told you to stay at the school with the others." He reined up beside her but then his eyes softened. "Miz Oliver isn't at home. No one else has seen her this morning, either."

"Oh no, do you think something has happened?"

He looked back toward the office and the steps that ran up the side of the building to the apartment. "I'll discuss it with Nathan. Just go on about your day. I'll send the kids home. No use having them lolling about a locked school."

Lucinda suppressed a smile as a thought occurred to her. "All right. Caleb and Ellie are already at the jail waiting for you. I think Mayor Watkins is sniffing for you, too."

"Thanks for the warning." With that, he winked at her, gave Teddy a heel, and they dashed back off down the street.

Lucinda turned her horse back around as well, her attention shifting from the diminishing figure of her father on his horse to the dip back from the street where the opera house stood.

Moments later, she stepped into the open doorway and blinked to adjust her vision from the brilliance of morning to the dull, dark gray inside. Only a series of kerosene lanterns along the stage illuminated the place and made partial silhouettes of the men working. She recognized one of them, who was currently hammering something on the floor. His long red hair gave him away, and she recalled his pleasant smile, his greeting from the seat of the freight wagon.

"Hello?" she called as she dared a step forward that took her underneath the center balcony that faced the stage directly. She came out from under it to the open view of the cathedral ceiling where the chandelier hung between the rows of box seats on the next floor. The crystals caught remnants of warmer stage light and cool blue light from the open doors. A miasma of dust hung in the air and layered the floor. Racks of folding chairs aligned the walls, ready to be taken out and arranged for the main floor audience.

"Hello, young lady!" the redhead called back to her as he stood, hammer in hand, and stepped closer. "Good to see you again." He now wore a dusty shirt and trousers rather than the heavy uniform coat and hat, and sweat gleamed on his brow.

"Good heavens, how do you see in here to work? Lucinda Wells, by the way."

He gave her a gentle handshake and a courtly bow that almost made her blush. "Jasper O'Brian," he replied. "Well, the play is at night, you see? So, we put the set together based on the lighting we'll have for the performance."

"That makes sense." She looked down at the prop he'd been working on, a large flat cut-out board with a tree painted on it. Jasper had been hammering it to a stand.

His dark-haired companion gave her a courteous nod. "Morgan Reed," he introduced himself quietly, then picked up the tree and moved it onto the stage where a similar prop had already been set up. He adjusted it and looked back to Jasper, who gave him gestures for placement. A little to the right. No, back a little. There. Ominous shadows of tree branches appeared to sprout against the rear curtain, which was a rich green, and suddenly a plain old stage became a forest.

"I *do* see," she said and smiled as fresh excitement rose in her. "Oh, this is so wonderful. What is the performance?"

Jasper opened his mouth, but then an entirely new voice answered.

"A Midsummer Night's Dream." Young and male, it came from one of the side doors to the backstage, which led down to the extensive basement level. Called *the vaults*, part of the space was directly under the stage, convenient for costuming and makeup, while the rest was divided into sections for prop storage.

There, framed by darkness, his face and shirt just within the glow of the stage, stood the most beautiful young man she thought she'd ever seen. Jasper and his coworker forgotten, Lucinda moved closer for a better look.

Sporting a cravat and silk vest that would have made her Uncle Silas swoon, the newcomer appeared not much more than Jesse's age, but unlike Jesse, he was far more refined. Soft brown hair spilled around a perfectly symmetrical face, his skin uniform and smooth as alabaster where Jesse already had sun lines from his work. Green eyes of a lovely creamy jade hue examined her, then creased ever so slightly around the edges as his full lips curled into a smile.

Lucinda wished she felt ashamed to be already comparing the two, but she didn't. Where Jesse made appearances on weekends, sometimes after a stop by the bathhouse but more often dusty and smelling faintly of manure, this handsome figure looked indescribably clean and ethereal, taller and leaner, too. "Oh, hello," she said and was immediately annoyed by the rising tremble in her voice. She cleared her throat. Winced. So much for feminine grace.

"May I help you?" he asked. There was an accent. English, she thought, though very faint.

Again, she tried not to stumble all over herself, to keep it together. "I saw the troupe wagons come in yesterday, and well, I just wanted to extend a fond welcome. I'm Lucinda Wells. My father's the town marshal." That, at least, sounded more business-oriented, like she was an ambassador delivering an official greeting on behalf of one of the town's most known families.

"Well then, the honor is mine, Miss Wells." To her surprise, he reached out and took her hand, kissed the back so delicately as if brushing with a feather.

It was not, however, the back of her hand that tingled, but something else that forced the heat of a blush into her cheeks. Lucinda managed to suppress a gasp but almost forgot to lower her hand when he let it go.

"I'm August Chandler. That is… August, please. Not Gus, though. I hate Gus."

"Lucinda, please," she said, happy to find a common thread. "But not Lucy. I hate Lucy." To hear him chuckle sincerely, richly, made her feel far too accomplished. "So, the play is A Midsummer Night's Dream?"

"Yes."

"And you will be performing which character?"

"Lysander." He took a dramatic bow. "At your service. Though we are a small troupe, so we all juggle several roles, including Jasper and Morgan over there." He nodded toward the two working men who were assembling another tree on the stage. Soon the forest would be complete. "Unfortunately, we must abridge the performance slightly. It's mostly the highlights, but the story will be intact. Are you," he began as if treading carefully, "interested in an acting career, Lucinda?"

The idea of it flooded her with romantic notions: getting to travel from town to town, to see the world, to capture the energy of an audience dressed in its finest, to study and deliver Shakespeare on the one hand and Henrik Ibsen on the other while in the most beautiful of costumes. What would her mother have thought of such aspirations?

"Ibsen?" August asked.

"What?" Lucinda said and blinked. She didn't realize she'd said the name out loud. Maybe she had mumbled. *Oh, dear, please say I didn't mumble.*

That would be more unbecoming than she could bear.

"You enjoy Ibsen?" He did not seem deterred in the least.

She nodded enthusiastically. "Yes, quite." In truth, she only knew a fraction of the man's work translated poorly into English from Norwegian. Miz Oliver had fondly noted her interest in literature and drama and, despite her having finished schooling, still lent her several scripts to read, among them *Peer Gynt*.

"Quite rare." His head tilted, spilling loose a long lock over one cheek that he quickly swept back. "Ibsen is perhaps a tad elevated for what our audiences usually wish to see in towns such as this. Yes? Where are we, again?"

The tone of humor in his voice kept the comment from sounding too snobby, but it wasn't any less accurate. No one in Mica Bend would be remotely interested in the bizarre but philosophic fairy tale nature of Peer Gynt, not even her little brother, despite his nose being so buried in pulp tales all the time. "Mica Bend," she said. "Everyone just calls it the *Bend*."

"But in San Francisco…" he suggested.

"It would be a smash," Lucinda concluded, smile renewed.

"Well, some of my colleagues and I are rehearsing downstairs. I must get back to it. Please promise me you will be here Friday night for the performance."

"I wouldn't miss it for the world, August. I will help spread the word. If you have fliers to pass out, let me know. Anything I can do to help."

He dipped into another bow. "Gratitude. I will look for you in the audience. Good day, milady Lucinda." Without a sound, he melded back into the darkness of the small corridor behind him. Lucinda resisted the urge to step into the doorway, to seek one more glimpse of him. But he had rehearsals to do, and she didn't want to be as a pesky fly disturbing him or the rest of the troupe. Hopefully, she would meet them Friday night as well. As with all performances in the past, there would be an after-party, and she was looking forward to asking the other actors about their lives and careers.

She turned from the dark frame of the doorway, realized that all hammering and sawing had ceased, and that Jasper and Morgan were watching her from the stage. There was something dark in their eyes, a look of disapproval, maybe? Perhaps they saw August as wasting time when he should be rehearsing. That had to be it.

"Friday then," she said, offering them a generous smile. They only nodded back before she hastened out of the building, swallowed hard as she stepped into daylight that stung her eyes and made her dizzy. Or, she realized, it was not the sun but the sensation that burned between her legs. Frightening. Thrilling. Delicious.

In a rush, she grabbed Remington's reins and led him as she hurried up a block and around the corner of the clothing boutique into the alleyway next to the shoe shop. There she positioned the horse between her and the thoroughfare, creating an adequate blind as she leaned back against the wall of the boutique and doubled over, shoved an elbow into her skirts as if to staunch a cramp, but it was no cramp that troubled her, and all she could think about was seeing the gorgeous Mr. August Chandler again as soon as possible.

Milady Lucinda. His voice rang so clearly in her mind, left her hoping that he was as thrilled to meet her as she was him, and with that, she giggled giddily and straightened herself back up.

Milady Lucinda.

*
**

Norman Becker awakened to the vague memory of Hiram Wells unceremoniously flopping him onto his cot in the clinic and telling him *very* loudly not to sleep on his back. The reason for that logic became immediately apparent when Becker noted the sour smell of whiskey and bile and hoped the marshal had departed well before his prediction came true. He now lay waiting, not moving lest his head explode and his stomach revolt with dry heaves.

He drifted in and out for a moment from darkness to alertness. Blessed darkness to acrid reek, darkness to painful, lancing light, darkness to the smell of… biscuits and butter?"

"Oh Lord," he grumbled as his stomach lurched.

"Good morning, Norman," Father Javier Ramirez said as he sat a little covered basket down on the examination table in the middle of the room. "John Raskin told me you might be a little under the weather." For a briefness, he was little more than a black blur until his cassock came into focus. He had removed his hat and placed it on the end of the table.

"That's Pastor Norman to you, Ramirez." However, he did need food, and biscuits from the Raskin kitchen were an excellent place to start. With some effort, he pushed himself up into a sit and then sprawled back against the wall.

His counterpart of the cloth puttered around the room, got the fire in the potbelly stove started. "You stay still. I'll heat water. I suspect you'd like for me to make some of that headache tea of yours."

"Willow bark's over there," Becker said, waving a slack hand toward the spread of apothecary on the counter.

Ramirez got to work, and soon the soothing crackle of a fire roared in the stove, and the iron kettle began to rumble. An outside observer might easily realize this was not the first interaction of this sort. He readily followed instructions to crumble the willow bark into a strainer along with a bit of dried lemon leaf to help take the bitterness off. While the tea steeped, he prepared a biscuit and handed it to Becker.

"Thank you. Starch is good for absorbing bile."

"Norman, it's too early for one of your over-explanations."

Becker nodded. Admittedly, he tended to get carried away in a natural inclination to explain things and educate people. His library, stuffed into shelving wherever he could find it under the counter, comprised volumes on medicine, history, and folklore, much of it in German and derived from his father's collection. Perhaps he felt a need to translate it constantly.

After Becker had nibbled his biscuit and a teacup was settled into his hands, Ramirez sat down next to him, carefully avoiding the regurgitated whiskey on the floor. Becker would clean it up later, but for now, they both tolerated the smell while he recovered.

"So, John told me that Maddie Krane's baby was stillborn," Ramirez explained the reason for his presence, "and that's why you decided to crawl into a bottle last night."

Becker took several long gulps of tea to speed its effects to his aching head. "Ja." He had to take another long moment to get his thoughts around it, to not feel sick at his stomach again as he relived the moment the child arrived. "I don't understand it, Javier," he said weakly. "Two days ago, that baby was kicking furiously, almost broke his mother's ribs. Maddie was so happy, so excited. But then yesterday…"

"Not breeched then?"

"Not at all. Came out headfirst. Smoothest extraction I've ever performed, but then there was no cry." He had absently opened one hand out before him as if holding that cold, still babe now. There had been blood on his fingers, but not enough to indicate a complication. It was, in all practical sense, a perfect delivery.

But there was no cry.

No first breath exploding in a rail against the emergence from the warmth of the womb into the startling light of the world.

He'd held the infant upside down by the ankles, smacked its back repeatedly to no effect, and then, upon having to admit it was a stillbirth to the mother, Maddie started screaming. Her husband, Ronald, had tried to calm her as tears coursed his own face. Becker, numb as he tried to explain it to himself, left the bereaved parents and wandered into the hallway, fell against the wall and slid down where he bowed his head and prayed because it was all he had left in him at that moment.

Ronald demanded answers. Of course, he did. What father wouldn't? But Becker had none. Much as he disliked administering laudanum, he'd had to give some to Maddie to calm her, and then he examined the little corpse, prodded its middle to feel out organs which were right where they belonged. Felt of the damp little head, which was perfectly formed, the fontanels in the skull no wider than they should be or damaged. In the end, Ronald took the tiny body, wrapped it up, and said he would take care of burial arrangements.

"That baby should have *lived*, Javier," he rasped. "It should have been crying its lungs out and ready to latch onto Maddie's tit like a leech. I just don't understand it."

Ramirez looked out into the room, reflective and quiet, then crossed himself. "The Lord giveth," he murmured and shook his head sadly. "I'm sorry, old friend. It sounds like there was nothing you could do."

"Ja, it just happened." Becker drank the rest of the tea to treat a suddenly dry throat. "Sometimes things just… happen. So…" he cleared his throat, adjusted his habitual speech for emphasis. "Yes, I climbed into a bottle and curled up nice and warm."

Because all I could think about was holding that cold, dead child.

"And the marshal brought you home last night?"

"Begrudgingly." With the mention of that encounter, Becker couldn't help but liken yesterday's loss to none other than that of Rachel Wells. She'd been pregnant with her and Hiram's fourth child by almost three months, long enough that the couple had begun to start speaking of it outside the family to friends other than Becker. Then her health had taken a dramatic downward turn with symptoms of headaches, vomiting, no appetite. She might have survived the typhoid that raged in her body, but it was the miscarriage of the child that took her life. That night would live on in Becker's memory for years, and he knew it was fastened deep into Hiram's, where it had been festering for months. The man put up a decent front, but his refusal to talk civilly to Becker or even come to church revealed far more.

He hates me, Becker thought. *He has every right to hate me.*

With the fluctuating thoughts between the dead Krane child and Hiram Wells' grief, Becker felt hot tears well up and hang suspended on the limbo of his lashes. He would forever feel that he'd failed that family, and to his eternal shame, it had not only been Rachel Wells and her child that had died that night but the last shred of her husband's faith.

Now he felt he'd failed another family, and he didn't even know how.

CHAPTER SIX

The morning was proving far too interesting for Hiram's taste. After he'd found no sign of the town's schoolteacher at her apartment over the assayer's office, he then had an entirely different encounter with the Raines brothers as he was passing the livery.

Ben Raines was already on his horse, aimed to get well and good out of town. The smoked spectacles were settled back in place over his eyes, his buckskin coat buckled across his chest again, and the Winchester ready in its saddle holster.

"Heading out then?" Hiram wasn't looking for conversation so much as a bit of closure on the matter as he paused Teddy next to the gray.

"Such as it is. My brother is in no hurry, as you can see." He gave a slight toss of his head. Seth was still out front of the livery's open doors inspecting the saddle mounted on a chestnut gelding similar to Teddy. "Thanks for keeping an eye on him 'n not bein' too troubled by his antics."

"I've dealt with far worse. Well, good luck to you." He touched the brim of his hat.

"Same, Marshal." Ben tapped his brim, and Hiram moved on to the brother of the moment.

Seth had just worked his way around to the other side of the horse, head down and face hidden under his well-worn Stetson as he adjusted the stirrups.

"Seth," Hiram said, drawing his attention.

The young, troubled face looked up at him, brown eyes catching sunlight under the brim. The man's eyes had always looked deceptively innocent to Hiram, but all sense of that had long gone out the window from the moment he'd spent his first night in a cell. To be honest, Hiram wasn't clear that Raines had really started any of the brawls he'd gotten into, but he sure did finish them. Some of the Bend's known ruffians had probably expected an easy target, just from looking at those eyes, and got more than they bargained for.

"Marshal." He looked down again, finished cinching, and came around the horse into full view. Though he was in a long linen duster for the road, it was pushed back from his side, rendering obvious the Colt Army now back on his hip and tied down to his thigh. Its pouch of paper cartridges was slightly visible under the yellowed material.

"I guess this means I don't have to worry about you gracing my jail ever again?"

Seth pulled on a pair of gloves, his mouth set in a grim rictus. "I like you, Marshal Wells, so I'm gonna say this, and you'd do well to listen." He lifted his head and walked over to look straight up at Hiram. Teddy, surprisingly, was calm with the sudden closure of distance, his ears relaxed. "Get out of this town. I know it's complicated for you after your wife and all, but just go. Take your family, encourage anyone else you can to get out of here."

Hiram stared at first, barely aware of how his brow had drawn in at the slightest mention of Rachel. "You know it isn't that easy for these people to just up and go."

"I'm not talkin' about the slump, Marshal. It's something else." The seriousness in his tone made Hiram's arms prickle.

"Seth," Ben Raines called over his shoulder. "Let the man get back to his job."

"What is it then?" Hiram asked.

"I hope it's nothing. I hope I'm wrong." He turned and went to his horse, gripped the horn, positioned his foot in the stirrup, and hoisted himself into the saddle with ease. "Don't think about it too long. Just go." He took the reins in hand and, with a click and a heel, steered the horse forward to line up with his brother's.

Hiram shifted Teddy's position sideways so he could watch them proceed up the last block of the thoroughfare, past the mercantile on their right and the closed Grand Saloon and the Grain Exchange. Just past the assayer's office, they kicked their mounts into a run, leaving little trails of dust. It was then that Hiram wished he'd asked what language that was they had been speaking last night, but no matter. They were gone, and it sounded like Seth Raines' departure couldn't be more permanent.

"Hell of a thing to say," he muttered and heeled Teddy on, soon to run into Lucinda, who had yet another warning for him.

If Watkins was looking for him, Hiram felt like he'd dodged a bullet when he got to the office and jail in relative peace. After another serving of Silas' chicory blend, he required *real* coffee before dealing with any bureaucratic nonsense.

He removed his hat and duster to hang by the door, head aching a little as he looked around the room. Firstly, to his disappointment, his deputy had not started a fresh pot yet. Secondly, his desk and Nathan's faced each other, each with a chair placed at one end, and each chair was filled with one of his kids. Ellie sat at the end of his desk, knees tucked against her chest, playing with a lock of her hair, trying to braid when she was probably tangling it more than anything. Caleb had the other chair, facing Nathan's desk and happily reading the pulp pages wedged into his schoolbook.

"You took those to school?" he asked accusatively.

Caleb looked up with wide eyes, cornflower blue and innocent, and blatantly lied. "No."

Hiram could feel Nathan smirking as he sat leafing through the latest packet of wanted ads to come in from the U.S. Marshals. "Move over there next to your sister," he said flatly. Given current matters, he'd have to address being lied to later.

Caleb scrambled out of the chair and heaved it closer to Ellie.

Hiram propped against his deputy's desk and leaned over to say quietly, "Maria Oliver is not in her apartment. No one's seen her since last night before she walked home from the hotel kitchen after tutoring Toby Raskin. The apartment was unlocked, but it didn't look disturbed."

Nathan's dark brow knitted, and he looked up at his boss with concern. "You don't think she left?"

"Not without saying something to somebody. Maria wasn't like the Hansons. She couldn't just pack up and get out of here without notice, she didn't even have a horse. Besides, she was here last night, so if she did have the means to leave, it would have been this morning, and somebody would have seen something."

"I'll take the morning patrol and keep asking around."

Hiram nodded, stared for a moment of grim thought.

"What?" Nathan said. "You've got one of *those* looks."

"What look?"

"One of those *Marshal Wells* looks. When you're thinkin' too hard for your own good."

"Oh, nothing, just thinking about something Seth Raines said before he hit the road."

"And you're going to listen to something the town brawler said?"

Hiram shook his head and looked down at the papers scattered in front of his deputy. "So, what do we have?"

Nathan shoved one of them aside. "Jacob Conner. We got a telegram on him a while back. Caught in Bisbee and hanged already. This one, too." He discarded one Marlon Jakes. "Caught in Phoenix last week."

"Great, every town around us is up to date, and we just get the runoff." He snatched the useless posters and balled them up. "And that one?"

Nathan held up the final. "Frank Evans. Looks like a mean cuss, I s'pose. Says here he's suspected of running with the Jack Taylor gang."

"What? Thought Sheriff Slaughter nailed the last of them in August." Hiram went over to the little pot belly stove in the front corner, opened the door, stuffed the wads of paper in, and added a couple of pieces of wood. He'd damned well have his coffee one way or the other. If there was any left in the little rickety cabinet by the stove.

"This may be old, too, but we should hang onto it."

"Sure, I'll put it on the wall." In his periphery, he caught that Ellie had gone over to one of the empty cells at the back of the room and was swinging on the unlocked door. "Hey! Ellie, get down from there."

"I'm bowed," she whined.

"Bo*rrrr*ed," he corrected her. "Of course, you are. You're not in school where you should be."

"Schoow is bowing, too." She kept swinging and gave him the same dirty look he'd gotten yesterday after confiscating Caleb's pulp.

Caleb was merrily reading said pulp now, but at least it kept him quiet.

The throbbing in his head elevated a little more. Hiram struck a match to get the stove going. While the fire began to pick up, he grabbed the percolator, still full of muck from yesterday morning. "Gimme that," he said to Nathan and took the last ad, stared at Frank Evans' face, memorizing every detail instantly.

He visualized what the drawing would look like as a photograph, from the crooked nose to the heavy brow. In his mind, little details filled in, such as how the facial muscles moved, what the man's teeth looked like given the way his lips were set thin and slightly drawn in, what his mustache would look like trimmed in different ways, and how it would affect the appearance of his face. This visualization method had come in handy in his career, and it had never failed him except when he was surrounded by too many distractions like his daughter still swinging on a cell door. "Ellie!" he raised his voice again. "I said get down!"

Then with the percolator in one hand and the wanted ad in the other, he stepped outside and looked to the far side of the thoroughfare just slightly adjacent where the schoolhouse stood empty, its students now dispersed. Then he swore under his breath to see Lucinda's warning finally coming to fruition.

Strolling toward him was Watkins, coming from upper town, back straight as if he had an arrow up his ass, black cane in hand, derby hat situated just so on hair meticulously coiffed with pomade. "Ah, Hiram, *there* you are." A waft of too much cologne thickened the air around him.

"Mayor." Hiram sat the percolator down on the bench seat below the office window.

"Good morning. I wish to speak with you about our guests." He stepped up onto the boardwalk.

"Guests?" Hiram turned to the side of the door, where a display frame hung on the wall. Its glass opened so he could slide the wanted poster in next to a few older ones that had long since faded in the display, but to his knowledge, they were criminals who had not yet been apprehended, at least not by anyone in Cochise County.

"The Chamberlain Players, of course. I had to pull quite a few strings to get them to come here."

"I'm sure you did."

"They'll be staying two weeks, putting on a play each Friday night. I've even had the town council put aside funds to supply tickets gratis for those who may not afford them. We'll hold a drawing for them this week at Fraleigh's store."

"How generous."

"Now listen, I want you to make sure the town is at its most polished. Pick up every single scrap of trash you see, make sure all the troughs stay full and clean."

"I already do that, Titus," he said as he closed the case back up and took one more look at the newly added face.

"Their safety is also important, so I trust you'll keep your eye out for any bad elements, like that Seth Raines."

"I do that, too." He retrieved the percolator. "And that Seth Raines was never a problem. What is the big deal here?"

Watkins ran a finger along the edge of a neatly trimmed mustache. "The deal is to raise the morale of our town, send out a message that Mica Bend is not on the downswing. We are still strong, and there is no reason why we can't recover. That's why it's important to fill as many seats as possible any way we can." He presented the silver ball end of the cane as if shaking a finger for emphasis. "There's more silver out there, Hiram, but we just need to have the patience and determination to find it. That crew Mr. Jones' left behind has found new ore."

"Really?" He heard plenty of whispers in his line of work but not a single one lately about new ore. "Enough to bring Jones back here and reinvest his precious time and money? Enough for him to provide new jobs for the Wagon Towners?" Hiram stepped off the boardwalk and around the corner between his building and Watkins' office, where they shared the water pump. He dumped the used coffee grinds out of the filter and pumped enough water to clean it out before adding fresh to the pot.

Never to leave the marshal a moment of peace, Watkins followed. "Maybe. We haven't heard from Mr. Jones in some time, but it won't be long before he'll be sending in a new assayer, hmm? I'm sure of it."

"Whatever you say. Now, if you'll pardon me, I need my brew, and then I need to look for Maria Oliver."

"The Widow Oliver? My goodness, what is wrong?"

"Oh, I see you didn't notice that she failed to come into work today." He gestured across the street at the shut-up school. And then, right on the heels of that concern, he remembered that he needed to drop by the Krane house and give Maddie Krane condolences on the loss of her baby. A fresh curse tightened his lips, but he kept it quiet from Watkin's ears. "So, don't worry about the trash, Titus," he said as he quickly stomped back toward the office door. "I'll take it out as always."

*
**

Hearing Mayor Watkins' voice outside made Nathan wince for the marshal's sake. Neither of them cared for the man, who was more prone to pomp than duty. He got up from his seat and went to stoke the fire Hiram had started, hopefully getting it hot enough that the man could have his coffee quickly. As he stoked, he cocked an ear toward the window, caught mention of the acting troupe, the stream of aspirations to keep the town motivated until more silver presented itself. Over their voices, he heard the cell door screech as Ellie continued to swing, and finally, it was Caleb who reined in his sister.

"Ellie, come here. Papa's not gonna tell you a third time."

It worked a charm as she hopped down, scrambled over to her brother, and climbed onto his lap. For six, she was petite, blond like her mother and siblings, though she and Caleb had both inherited Hiram's eyes, and Lucinda had Rachel's. Her size let her fit perfectly on Caleb's knee, where she twiddled with the same long tangle of hair and looked at the pamphlet in his hands.

Caleb began to read to her at a soft murmur, not quite loud enough for Nathan to make out, but now that the chaos was tamed, the deputy got up and went to lock the cell door in place before it served as a carnival ride again. Because the floor had a subtle sag, both cells tended to swing wide open automatically, and only locking them alleviated that. He tried to hear more of the conversation outside without being too obvious, but he knew Hiram would fill him in if it were important.

Nathan was twenty-six or twenty-seven. He wasn't sure. The son of emancipated slaves, he had been given no certainty of his actual age, just that he was born in the spring in Alabama and his parents had set out for the West to start over. While they'd made it to San Jose and stayed, when he came of age, he felt drawn back inland to work on the ranches in Arizona. He loved the landscape for some reason, the scatterings of saguaro cacti reaching like multi-fingered hands toward a sky that looked like the dome of Heaven, especially when it was dusted at night with more stars than a man could count.

Eventually, he'd found his way to Bryce Tucker's ranch between Mica Bend and Benson, but when a disagreement with one of the other hands began to escalate, he looked for new work. Luckily the town marshal in the Bend needed a deputy, and that had stuck for now. He hoped it would stick for a long time. He enjoyed working with Hiram, watching and wondering how the man's mind worked, and he enjoyed the kids, too, when they were behaving. In recent times, there was a fifty-fifty chance of them behaving or acting out. Grief, he knew, had many faces. How Hiram was working through his was particularly hard to decipher.

"So, what ya'll readin' over there?" he finally asked now that his ears were spared the creak of metal hinges and thirty-seven pounds of rambunctious child.

"Tales of the Vampyre," Caleb announced.

"Lowd Covington," Ellie chimed in.

"*Lord,*" Caleb corrected her.

"Huh," Nathan said. "I ain't never heard of that. Whatever happened to stories about gunslingers?" He picked up a broom and swept some foot debris from around the benches by the window.

Caleb shrugged. "I guess they're kinda passé now."

The deputy looked up at them, broom paused. "Well, ain't that something."

Ellie imitated her brother by shrugging, too.

CHAPTER SEVEN

The last thing Jesse needed was to glance up from his task trussing a seven-month-old calf's feet to find Lucinda sitting on her horse at the corral fence. She was in one of her prettiest dresses, blue with a trim of white ruffle across her bust, sitting up perfectly straight in her sidesaddle with a parasol held aloof to shade her eyes. For seconds his hold loosened hazardously, and the calf started to writhe. His section of rope slid through his glove only by a few inches but enough to nearly get him kicked to the inside of his thigh.

"Whoa!" His coworker, Amon Yount, all but threw himself on the calf's back end, grabbed the rope and jerked it hard, effectively cinching all four hooves back together.

Jesse snapped from his distraction and bore down with his own weight while Georgie McCorkle hurried in with the brand. The calf bellowed as the brand hissed, and the air filled with the odor of burning hair and hide. Both young men eased the ropes and then scrambled to their feet. The calf followed suit, bucked its back hooves before trotting off as it was turned back into the bigger corral by two other hands. Georgie plunged the brand back into the fire barrel to prepare for the next calf.

"Sorry about that." Jesse wiped his sleeve across his brow under the brim of his hat, felt a paste of sweat and grit scour his skin, and took a breath, deflated to think that he smelled of cow piss. "Damn."

"Uh oh," Amon said when he saw what had drawn the younger hand's attention. "Whatever she's gotta say, you better get over there and hear it before we do the next'un."

Jesse nodded as he wandered to the fence, looked up at the vision before him and smiled while considering that he shouldn't get too close. Her skirts, raised by her left knee slung over the saddle's upper horn, trailed down in a rather regal curtain of linen that had probably seen fresher days, but it was still lovely. Her hair was pulled up into a loose bun with delicate tresses dangling around her ears and forehead.

"Well, ain't this a pleasure." He hoped she wasn't looking for him to go riding with her. He had to work, didn't have the town marshal for a daddy to take care of him, and he hadn't gone into ranch work to lollygag while his fellows sat in the saddle wearing out their butt bones over a herd. "What's the occasion?"

"Just taking a ride and decided to come out to see you."

"Yeah? Why?" His tone was far more nonchalant than he intended.

Her soft golden brows furrowed; dark eyes narrowed with insult.

"Sorry, I stink to high heaven." If only she'd come out at any other time. "You sure look pretty." Her dress almost matched the October sky, the parasol a lacy cloud over her head.

"Well," she began. "So, you know the acting troupe that came to town yesterday? The Chamberlain Players?"

"Vaguely," he teased. Truthfully, he couldn't forget after the way the sight of the freighter and coach had lit up her face.

"Well, they're putting on *A Midsummer Night's Dream* on Friday night. Are you free to escort me?"

It was a request that he'd been expecting as he couldn't imagine her family was that interested, least of all her father, who would likely have to work security for the production. *He'll hate that,* Jesse thought. So, if she wanted an escort, here he was. But something in her voice niggled at him. A little bit of craftiness. A razor's edge on which he would surely slip and have his ass handed to him if he said no.

"Uh, sure."

A chorus of whoops rose behind him, and Jesse turned to find his coworkers, every last one of them covered in dust from their hats to the hems of their dungarees, all smelling just like him, conglomerated to watch the exchange with glee. Amon, foremost, grinned from ear to ear but gave him a gesture that was clearly intended to be a rescue.

Get back to work, loverboy.

"Well, I best… ya know…" he stepped back, gestured at the other men. "Calves ain't gonna brand themselves."

"All right then," she said, "good day."

"G'day." He kept an eye on her while stumbling blindly toward the other hands. She turned her horse around and set out at a light trot, a skilled rider in her own right with one knee kicked over the upper horn of the sidesaddle while the other thigh was wedged under the lower one for stability. In many ways, Jesse thought it was a gutsier way to ride than straddled just because it looked so lopsided, but it was graceful, and he savored the sight of her narrow waist, held up so straight and proud. But now that he saw both sides of Remington as he bore his mistress away, the alteration to the saddle showed. On the other side—the side that had been hidden from his view while she towered over him from outside the corral—a shortened 12-gauge lever-action shotgun was sheathed for quick access and defense. That, Jesse knew, was an adjustment made by her daddy, who had taught her well how to use it.

"That lil girl's got you roped!" Amon laughed as Jesse finally swung his focus around and straightened his stride. "Careful you don't hang yerself on it," he added more seriously.

"Shaddup, Amon." To his relief, the jeers kept to a minimum, and quickly all were back to work, the picture of Lucinda Wells emblazoned in all their minds.

Afternoon patrol usually constituted a good time to wind down, even while Hiram's senses were perked up, listening for rattlers along the path, scanning the chaparral for movement that belonged to something larger than a hare or a bird. Once outside the town, the stillness soothed him along with the gleam of sun on the western faces of the Arduous Mountains and especially their palace-like columns that all but turned to gold.

All his menial tasks were done, every nagging little request Mayor Watkins made was addressed. He had stopped by the opera house where he spoke briefly with Jasper O'Brian and Morgan Reed. They had erected quite an elaborate stage and were getting ready to go out to distribute promotional fliers, but he'd still not met the rest of the troupe. Strange, but not a concern. He'd paid a consoling visit to the Kranes, who were understandably despondent from their loss, and then everyone else he needed to see for one reason or another. Utmost, he had asked the same questions repeatedly regarding the Bend's missing schoolteacher, and he still had nothing. A more thorough look through her apartment rendered no clues. Having no idea of the inventory of her possessions, he could not say if anything was missing, but the place *felt* untouched. There was a small collection of jewelry in her dresser, clothes, books, a teapot still full of cold tea next to an empty cup and saucer, but Maria Oliver herself remained absent, and a new concern weighed on his mind.

Hiram had one more place to look for her, and he'd put it off by completely circling the town up through the livery and Chinese laundry and down through the small neighborhood on the south side, then up and down the thoroughfare twice. Now, as he paused to watch dust devils whirl at the base of the mountains near the Perseverance mine, he heard hooves of a single horse rumbling up behind him. He twisted in the saddle to look at the rear view of the Bend's southern line of buildings and the little blocks of homes scattered around them. Their western walls were all dashed in the same golden light that graced the mountains. Growing with the closing distance, Silas was riding out on Arsenic, the stud prancing proudly along the more beaten trail through the scrub.

Hiram felt an aching relief and waited until his best friend had reined up beside him with a hushed, *"Whoa!"*

Silas kept Arsenic, who had a biting habit, positioned slightly forward, head out of the vicinity where he could attempt to take a hunk out of Teddy. "After you rode past the Palace for the third time, I figured you might be signaling a need for company."

Hiram's head bobbed absently.

"You still haven't located the Widow Oliver," Silas confirmed.

"Maria," Hiram emphasized, "and no, I haven't. There's no trace of her at all." He looked out upon a landscape that appeared to be a flat stretch of scrub and cacti from this distance and angle. "Except maybe over there," he said.

"Want me to ride with you?"

He nodded, and they set off, winding their horses toward the very place where, seven years ago, Hiram had picked up his first murder case.

There had been a pack of coyotes practically swarming one area along the edge of the hazardous gulch that wasn't visible unless you were right upon it. They had scattered in every direction as he galloped boldly up to the edge. One jumped into the gulch and scrambled up the other side, sliding, leaping, and clawing until it reached the top and disappeared into the scrub. Then Hiram looked down into the treacherous gap at what had captured their grim attentions. The sight of Richard Oliver's body had taken a moment for him to register.

The soles of the man's shoes were up, and his head was down, body draped like a rag doll against the jagged slope. His assayer's kit was busted open, its contents scattered around him in a glittering fan of broken vials and tools.

Now Hiram steered Teddy as close as he dared and dismounted, walked to the edge of the gulch, lowered himself into a crouch, took a deep breath, and looked down at the very same spot. He let the breath out with relief. "We all know Maria's not exactly been happy here," he explained quietly. "She's good with all the kids, been very patient, and a good teacher, but I thought maybe…"

Silas dismounted and steered his horse to a tumbleweed that was still rooted. He left Arsenic there to munch on the last of its dying leaves and came to squat next to Hiram. "You thought maybe she'd finally decided to follow Richard down there."

"But if she isn't here, then where is she?" Hiram looked up, scanned the horizon again. "I'm at a loss."

"You and Nathan can only do so much out here in this kind of country, H," Silas reminded him. "Honestly, I've never understood how any lawman can deal with it. It's all thorns and bristles and sand in everything."

That roused a bittersweet chuckle. Times like this, he appreciated how consoling Silas' drawl could be. A welcome crisp breeze whispered around them as Hiram continued to look out, feeling helpless to the force of the landscape. Then on the wind, he thought he smelled something else, something recent that he'd detected before.

"You smell that?"

Silas sniffed. "Smells like an old campfire, maybe?"

"Yeah, like char. I got a whiff of something similar out at the Hanson farm yesterday, but there's something else in it." Hiram drew in a long breath through his nose. "Something rotten."

"Something always smells rotten out here. Observe." Silas gestured to a distant expanse of sky where the shades of several vultures circled, ink dashes against blue and rose wash. "Could be anything, a dead deer or coyote."

"Could be Maria Oliver." Immediately he rose from his crouch, gritting his teeth as his arthritic back once more reminded him that he spent too much time in the saddle, and turned to hoist himself back into the punishing seat. "I'm checking it out."

"Wonderful." Silas rose and went to grab Arsenic's reins. "Now I'm sorry I said anything."

They followed the line of the gulch, weaving tediously around the scrub, until the rut grew shallow, less rocky, and finally turned into nothing by a sandy wash. After well over a mile, it seemed they were getting no closer to the source of what had captured the vultures' attention. The scent of something burnt grew heavier along with that undercurrent of death, cloying for long moments before being swept away on a swelling fall breeze, rendering it impossible to determine from which direction it came. Hiram, normally quiet and focused on such a patrol, began to grumble about the ride and how the landscape, and the winged shadows whirling above it, slipped further and further away as if teasing him.

But he could not, in any good conscience, focus elsewhere. People did not fade into the black for no reason. Maria Oliver was out there somewhere. He was sure of it as he watched those vultures circle and a slight chill slithered down his spine with the next cool breeze that carried that faint smell of char. Then he recalled, for some unknown reason, Seth Raines' warning that he should take his family and leave town, and that chill reached through his skin and into his bones.

CHAPTER EIGHT

As with all life, the days moved on, and no sign of Maria Oliver surfaced. After chasing circles of vultures proved fruitless, the town held a council meeting outside the mayor's office since the opera house was occupied. Three sparse search parties dispersed with Hiram leading the first, Nathan the second, and Silas volunteered to lead the third. Still, after almost an entire day of circling the sprawling land, the mine, and the base of the Arduous range, they all came back empty-handed. Cranky and tired, a few men complained of scorpion stings, saddle-sore asses, and skinned elbows from sliding out on the more treacherous terrain when they got on foot.

None were more cranky and tired than Hiram.

After all searches were given up, evening prayer vigils were held, one in each church, and he attended the one at the old Spanish mission chapel only for the sake of respect, but he did not actually bow his head or pray so much as numbly sit through it. At a dead-end, the case nagged him, and all he could do, in the end, was temporarily have a bolt put on Maria Oliver's apartment to keep anyone from helping themselves to her things.

By the end of the week, Miz Raskin had volunteered to open the school and do her best to keep the Bend's children face down in their readers. Hiram had never heard so much complaining, which escalated Thursday afternoon when he learned that she had taken away Caleb's pulp stories with no sign of giving them back.

He wished he cared, but when Thursday's train blasted through, a new packet of penny dreadfuls dropped from Philadelphia, and all was right in the world of Caleb Wells. They arrived with another letter from Hiram's brother, this one less ham-handed about how he thought Hiram should bring the family "home" and more about how he hoped the kids were enjoying the stories. Wouldn't it be nice if they took an interest in journalism or some other form of writing? Printing presses, with all their rapid advancements, were a very noble line of work. If he'd been face to face with James, it would have taken all of Hiram's will not to punch his brother.

By Friday, he was in his own special hell, corralled into helping Watkins distribute more fliers for the Chamberlain Players' performance even though Lucinda had already done her part on that front. She had been beside herself all week about it. Then at dinner one evening, she let it slip that she'd already met a young actor in the troupe whom she was eager to see put *his* talents to work on stage.

"When did this happen?" Hiram asked over a plate of bread, gravy, and eggs growing cold because he'd been too exhausted to eat.

Lucinda's brown eyes beamed, reminding him too much of her mother. "Oh, the morning Miz Oliver went missing." She at least had the decency to pause and walk back her flippancy. "I mean, all I did was stop by the opera house to offer a welcome from our family to theirs."

Hiram, having already caught the "actor" and "he" in her comments, pointedly asked her who was escorting her on opening night. When she answered that it was Jesse—of course, it was *Jesse*, but Hiram was trying to make a point that was lost on the girl—he thought he smelled the distinct aroma of teenage shenanigans. But who was he to think he could address it properly? That had been Rachel's department, and she had been good at it. He reminded himself that Lucinda had not only lost a mother but her greatest confidante and counselor in the whole damned town and right when she needed that most.

Further, Silas had been right about him.

Lacking any sense of subtlety in dealing with such matters, Hiram shied readily away from filling his wife's former role. If he was honest with himself, he secretly enjoyed seeing his little girl's giddiness and did not want to shatter that with reprimands over feminine guile.

So, Friday evening, as dusk fell, he visited the bathhouse and barbershop then returned home to get dressed up at the vanity in the master bedroom downstairs. Going one better, he managed to harness the ornery bastard that had been growing in him all week over *everything*. The man in the mirror looked a little neater with his face bare of shadow and hair smoothed back, if still on the long side. He'd donned his best black trousers and silk vest and traded the linen duster for his long wool coat. His every day worn Stetson remained on the hook by the front door and a crisper one, reserved for nice occasions, sat waiting on the corner of the vanity. His boots, however, remained informal because he only had one good broken-in pair. His last touches were to transfer his pocket watch and match safe to his vest and pin his badge onto the coat's bulkier collar and buckle on his gun belt, feeling the weight of the Peacemaker settle into familiar place.

He stared at a framed tintype of Rachel on the vanity. It was an older picture, taken after Lucinda had been born, but it had been Hiram's favorite, gazing back at him with the faintest of enigmatic smiles. Maybe it was the little bit of distance in her eyes that gave him enough strength to leave it displayed while he'd stashed away her other pictures. Under the light of the oil lamp, her expression appeared to shift ever so slightly at him, but what it was trying to say remained a mystery.

Across the top of the frame hung a silver chain with a delicate cross pendant on it that draped down and laid against the glass under her face. It was the only piece of jewelry Rachel had owned other than her wedding ring, which had been buried with her. That it was a cross was purely ignored, tolerated because he could not bring himself to put it away yet either. Swallowing a hard lump, he tore his gaze away from hers, grabbed his hat from the vanity, turned down the lamp, and went to go buck up for a tedious night.

Then in the front parlor, his heart nearly broke all over again.

Lucinda stood before him in her finest pale pink satin dress, her waist cinched tiny and her bosom swelling slightly out the top amid a piping of lace. He wondered, with dread, when his daughter had developed a bosom. Her lower curves were accentuated by a graduation of ruffles with a bustle in the back. Hiram took a breath and recalled the afternoon last fall when his wife and older daughter had spent many hours in the boutique because it was time Lucinda had at least one formal dress in her closet. Her shining hair was pinned up with spiraling tresses meticulously separated to frame her face. The gold chain and petite locket, which he and Rachel had given her on her fourteenth birthday, graced her slender neck.

Ellie stood beside her, in a little pink linen dress, petting the satin and grinning, clearly getting ideas of her own that already raised new dread in her gaping father.

"You look beautiful, honey," Hiram finally said without choking. He completely forgot, for an instant, that she was likely playing a game of besting one suitor against another.

"What about me!" Ellie demanded.

"You look like that rag doll you carry," Caleb griped as he came into the room.

Hiram snapped from his fatherly stupor and shot him a warning glare. Then he sized Caleb up as well. The boy looked only slightly more polished than usual in his Sunday trousers and a wool jacket. He had, of all things, his McGuffey's Reader tucked under one arm.

"Why are you taking that with you?" Hiram asked.

"I thought I'd catch up on homework. I don't want to see no stupid play."

"Caleb—" Lucinda started to chastise him.

"No," Hiram intervened for her, "you want to read your penny dreadfuls. I know they're hidden in there. That's why Miz Raskin confiscated those others, isn't it?"

"No."

"Stop lying, Caleb. You've been taking them to school hidden in your book. It's a great scheme, boy. I get it. They fit in there perfectly, but you need to let 'em rest." The hangdog look Caleb tried to pull twinged the nerves in Hiram's back along with his patience. The ornery bastard was about to rise again. "Leave the book, *now*."

"It's rude, Caleb," Lucinda said more gently.

"You're just going to have to sit and twiddle your thumbs," Hiram added.

Caleb looked from one to the other, betrayal at his sister, wilting before his father. "Yessir," he finally replied and stomped over to leave the reader on the parlor sideboard.

Satisfied, Hiram settled his fine hat on his head and went to the door. "All right, I guess I'll see you there."

"Yes, Papa," Lucinda said.

"Yes, Papa," Ellie echoed her.

Outside, the sky had turned muddy, but plenty of evening light defined the road going past his house, while less than a quarter mile up, he could see a campfire burning within the cottonwood borders of Wagon Town. Beyond that, the diminishing dots of lantern lights hung down the thoroughfare for as far as the eye could see from this position. Teddy, saddled and ready to go at the fence post, perked up to the sound of footsteps that also made Hiram turn.

Jesse was just approaching from around the side of the house. He was as polished up as one of Bryce Tucker's ranch hands could get, and Hiram couldn't help but feel a little sympathy for him. "Oh, hey, Marshal Wells, I just put Peso in the corral. Guess I'll walk Lucinda into town."

"You'll have to. She's too fancied up to ride." He almost wished he'd stayed in the house longer to see the kid's reaction. "Caleb and Ellie will be with you, too," he added as he mounted up, sorry to disappoint him. His youngest children seemed to like Jesse, which made them perfect chaperons as far as he was concerned. "I've got to make rounds. Do not let Caleb come out of that house with his schoolbook under his arm."

Jesse's brow furrowed in confusion at the order. "Uh, yessir?"

With that, Hiram reined around and steered his horse on.

The opera house was surprisingly fuller than Hiram had expected, and for a moment, he thought maybe Watkins, for all his blather, was onto something about lifting Mica Bend's morale. There were six buckboards and a carriage lined up out front, and the hitching posts were packed with horses that he imagined were commiserating with each other in their boredom. Grady Cox, a retired old prospector who took any work he could get now, had been hired to watch them. The tall windows of the place, having been closed from the inside by heavy drapes all week, were now aglow from within, the warmth contrasting against the chill of the autumn night.

After the play started, Hiram drifted in and out of the building through the main doors as quietly as possible, checking on the audience, most of them in the rows of folding seats on the main floor. Their heads and shoulders were dark silhouettes against the brightly lit stage that was impressive to say the least, in its creation of Shakespeare's colorful fairy forest outside Athens, Greece. He knew that Silas, who could be just enough of a snob about cultural affairs, would be in a box seat on the balcony along with Izabel, and so would Watkins, among others.

On the stage, Jasper O'Brian and Morgan Reed made appearances. Two young women joined them, along with a green-eyed golden boy whom he assumed was the subject of Lucinda's recent infatuation. He noted how elaborate the costumes from the garb of the young human couples to the gossamer wings of the fairies, which he knew must be thrilling his younger daughter to bits. For such a small troupe, the production was impressive indeed, somehow working smoothly even as they hustled to juggle roles and costumes.

However, as was typical, he found he could only digest so much of it. He was on the job, and that excused him to step back outside and resume patrolling, watching, listening, whatever the hell Watkins wanted him to do this night. Up the street from the direction of the jail, Nathan's figure on his horse appeared trotting back from making another general pass. He bled into clearer view as he came within a shaft of light from one of the big windows.

"Never would'a thought we had this many people still around," the young deputy said as he dismounted and led his horse up to the hitch.

"Still sparse, compared to three years ago," Hiram said, recalling a time when the opera house audience had sprawled out into the streets, once for a variety show with Eddie Foy, who had hit every boomtown in the territory, and again for a performance of *The Pirates of Penzance*. Nathan had not lived in the Bend or worked with him that long, so he had no basis for comparison. Hiram looked across the thoroughfare at the Orleans Palace.

Silas had closed and locked up to attend the play and was likely to linger for the after-party. When that was over, he would return to the Palace to catch the runoff of late drinkers. Other attendees, like Bryce Tucker, would probably stay at the hotel tonight, gifting the Raskins with some much-needed business.

A crisp breeze gusted down the street and slipped up inside the sleeves of Hiram's coat, raising the hairs on his arms under his shirt. "Cold tonight," he commented. "Why don't you go on in and try to enjoy the show a bit? I'll keep a lookout here a while."

"You sure?"

It escaped him that he didn't answer the question, but he'd no idea how to tell Nathan that something felt wrong about that breeze. He wasn't sure why. It wasn't pushing in a storm. There were no thunderheads over the mountains. In fact, there were not *any* clouds visible in the sparkling sky with its moon now past full. Were every lantern on the boardwalks to go out, everything would appear outlined in silver, and the thoroughfare would remain illuminated. He listened to Nathan's steps crunch softly away and stood observing.

Beyond the voices contained within the opera house, he heard a subtle creak of wood. It came from somewhere down the side street between the opera house and the clothing boutique next door. The imposing black freighter the troupe had hauled in was parked there, close to the wall, and Hiram knew that there was a rear service door on the other side of it within convenient access of the freighter's back gate. The stocky draft horses that towed it had been moved to the barn at the Simpson house outside town where the troupe was boarding. From his prior rounds, he knew that the coach and six black Saddlebreds were parked on the other side of the building. Horses and coach faced out into the main thoroughfare, ready to leave with its passengers once this long night of entertaining and celebrating was over.

After a moment, the noise repeated. Likely it was just the freighter creaking with the persistent breeze, but he decided to check into it. Readjusting his coat against the chill, he walked down the side street, around the freighter, and there found the service door. Steps led up to a landing. He smelled lingering cigarette smoke and deduced that one of the troupe had just been out here on a break.

It occurred to Hiram that he could use the back way to get a look at the front of the audience. He eased up the steps, trying not to stomp too heavily, and opened the door into the deepest part of the backstage area divided off by layers of backdrop curtains employed for different settings. At the very back, clothing racks and standing blinds were set up for quick costume changes. By now, these were well in disarray from said speedy changes with multiple costume pieces slung over the blinds and racks.

The curtain in current use was softly illuminated from the other side with the silhouettes of the forest props cast upon it and lending an eeriness to the backstage. A male voice rose in a sing-song pattern, and Hiram recognized it by its brogue.

"The ousel cock so black of hue, with orange-tawny bill, the throstle with his note so true, the wren with little quill."

Hiram raised a brow. Jasper O'Brian was *not* a bad singer.

A woman's softer lilt answered him. *"What angel wakes me from my flowery bed?"*

The audience came to life with a roar of laughter that ebbed and flowed and rose again. Hiram wondered what he'd missed that was not in the dialogue. Still minding his steps, he approached the side corridor closest to him, where a velveteen curtain covered the western stage entrance. None of the actors were here, so he assumed the next entry must be from the other side. Good, at least that meant he wasn't interrupting. He only had to nudge the curtain an inch to see well enough.

From this angle, he could get a good look at the audience, but first, he took a gander at the stage from the side, watched an attractive young lady, dressed in a glittering white, gauzy gown as Titania, queen of the fairies. She was in the process of sitting up from a fluffy pile of fake flowers, stretching lazily as petals dripped away from her sensuous arms. In the stage light, she glowed unnaturally, fitting for her character, and it wasn't just the dress but her skin that was so luminous.

Hovering over her, Jasper wore the awkwardly huge paper mâché head of a donkey.

So, that was what had set everyone off. Hiram remembered the cast list now and that Jasper had been saddled with the role of the imbecile *Bottom* along with two other parts. The donkey head would at least make that character change a little easier.

O'Brian's body language alone was decently hilarious as he found just enough pause in the laughter to dive back into his lines. *'The finch, the sparrow and the lark, the plain-song cuckoo gray…"*

Hiram angled his gaze around and off the stage into the audience. There were at least forty people on the main floor, their faces gradually fading into the shadows under the rear balcony where he knew Nathan was lurking. It did look like most who lived within the town, and the outlying homes, were here, all but the handful of Chinamen who ran the laundry back next to the blacksmith. Their numbers had decreased significantly along with the departure of Jones and his miners.

On the balcony, as expected, he spotted Silas, who was sitting next to Izabel. Both were glowing from laughter, smiling at each other, and then looking back to the stage expectantly for more. To see his friend enjoying himself gave Hiram a little piece of joy.

Bryce Tucker sat in one of the boxes on the adjacent balcony. He was a tall, jowly man with a generous mustache. Next to him sat his wife, Maeve, whose mouth always reminded Hiram of a horse's sphincter with its constant look of distaste.

Then his gaze roamed over to the next box and Watkins with his entourage, Joseph Briggs, Paul Granning—the two of them and Watkins all that remained of the town council—and their wives. He didn't delay on them, instead dropping his gaze straight down to locate his children.

Apparently, Lucinda's new connections had afforded her front-row seats. She had Caleb and Ellie on one side, Jesse on the other. All were laughing except Caleb, who was doing exactly what his father had told him to do: twiddling his thumbs.

Despite himself, he felt a smile tug at the corners of his lips. He'd hoped Caleb would be pleasantly surprised and enjoy the play, but it appeared the kid was just determined to keep a pout on for principle's sake. Ellie, meanwhile, had been won over by the magical fairies on stage, and whether she could follow the plot or not didn't matter. Even from here, he could see how her eyes lit up with wonder, and then there was Lucinda with her mother's dark mahogany eyes.

The girls laughed harder as the scene unfolded, but Hiram was no longer paying the play any attention. The voices echoed away to nothing in his ears. He felt his chest stir at this vision of his children, so happy, almost like things had never changed. Before he realized it, he'd raised his free hand, pressed fingers to his lips to prevent himself from gasping too loud, and his eyes blurred briefly. He gave himself a moment, then swallowed down a hard lump to banish the flood. He couldn't stand here dumbstruck like this all night, so he blinked to clear his vision, lowered his hand, and proceeded to scan the rest of the audience that was visible from this angle.

Next to Lucinda, Jesse looked like he was trying to keep up. This, too, was worth a chuckle, but mostly, what Hiram noticed, was that the young ranch hand kept looking at Lucinda. The stage lights caught in his eyes, revealing a different kind of enchantment to what the entertainers brought. Hiram dared take it for an actual look of love because he recognized it, the same sipid gleam he'd cast many times at Rachel. Lucinda, however, was more riveted by the stage, oblivious to the admiration angled her way from the next seat over.

That poor kid, Hiram thought, but he'd be lying to himself if he didn't admit it was both sweet and amusing in one. Jesse did not yet know that, at least from now until next weekend, he had some steep competition.

He moved down the line, past the Raskins, past Terry Wilkes. Down from them sat a few of Jesse's fellow ranch hands, like Amon Yount, who were especially whooping it up. That whole lot was the most likely to get liquored up after the show, and Hiram was already braced for that.

A row up from the ranch hands was Mr. Fraleigh with his tired eyes and the fretful Miz Elliot. Even Ronald and Maddie Krane had made it, both in need of some escape since they had buried their child two days ago. The Kranes did not laugh as hard as their neighbors, but they were not exactly fighting the urge. He still felt considerable pain for them and their loss.

So many faces he knew, so many lives he'd become entangled with and cared about. It made him ache to think they might all have to move on, that the Bend was in its end days and soon would blow away with that uncanny wind that had seized him outside. He glossed across Pastor Becker, who was sitting next to Father Ramirez a row back from the kids, and then just down from them, his gaze froze.

Hiram's stomach and heart merged with a punch that caused him to step back, his reverie broken, his hand letting go of the curtain.

"Can I help you?" A male voice, firm and collected, startled him, and he all but spun and stumbled, managed to regain his balance without flailing.

Instantly he thrust a single finger to his lips in a *shhhhh* gesture, corrected his stance and indicated the badge on his coat. "I'm Marshal Hiram Wells," he whispered. Only then did he get a better look at the newcomer and, stunned, found himself confronted by the most beautiful *man* he had ever seen.

The stranger's presence towered as much as the physical features of his height and broad shoulders covered in a green velvet cloak. Gold grease paint highlighted strong cheekbones that angled toward a square, clean-shaven ax of a jawline that could probably actually cut wood. His pale gray eyes and brow line were heavily defined for the stage, while his long blond hair, teased into a lion's mane of a style, was adorned with a crown of ivy and antlers. Steadily he returned the examination with a wolfish tilt of his head.

Hiram leaned in closer to keep his voice down but still be heard as the audience roared to life again. "You're this gang's Oberon, I take it?"

"What gave me away?" He spoke with some of the smoothest sarcasm Hiram had ever heard, too, almost on par with Silas when he was in a mood. The gaze dropped and narrowed more intensely on Hiram's badge.

"Micajah Edwards," Hiram replied.

"How did you know?"

"I read the playbill. My daughter's been waving it in my face all week.

Just a moment," Hiram said and quickly turned back to the curtain, peeked out to make sure he'd seen whom he thought he'd seen.

Sure enough, no further back than three rows, in clear eyeshot, fully illuminated by the reflected stage light was a face he'd examined days ago on a wanted ad. Frank Evans sat next to a man who was the younger spit and image of him but with a scraggly beard instead of a mustache. "Kid brother, maybe?" Hiram muttered to himself. He watched them lean closer, share some exchange, then go back to laughing at the comedy on stage.

Jasper and his ass head were a hit.

But what to do about Frank Evans and his companion?

He let the curtain go and eased back. If Evans had ridden with the Jack Taylor gang as the U.S. Marshals suspected, then he could be a very dangerous man, prone to spook. From the stage, it was impossible to tell if either of the two was armed. They had dusters on, which could hide anything, including gun belts. The next question was why Evans would even be *here*, risking discovery at a public event that had become so high profile thanks to Watkins. For now, everyone was distracted by the play, but what about the after-party? Maybe Evans was planning to slip off and into the night directly after the show? No, that did not feel right at all.

Maybe…

Hiram suddenly recalled the chain and locket on his daughter's neck. It was small, delicate, the front of the locket adorned with a seed pearl because when Lucinda was born, her doting parents referred to her as their little pearl for years. It wasn't much, but it was genuine gold.

Upon that thought, everything else *shiny* he'd seen in that audience flashed before him. Bryce Tucker's fingers were riddled in gold rings because the rancher liked to show off his well-being when he came to town for any reason, let alone a night at the opera house, and his wife was no less boastful with her glittering gem necklace that was not mere paste. Father Ramirez always had on his gold ecclesiastical ring.

How many others were in the audience wearing their best baubles tonight? Silas was, of course. He had a gold chain that never left his neck, and Izabel had her own jewelry that was not exactly low-end. While other pieces might be costume and worthless, there was still enough of value scattered amidst the crowd, not to mention wallets and handbags that might not be carrying much other than whiskey money, but lump it all together, it would get a wanted man anywhere out of the territory he wanted to go and out of law's reach.

"Excuse me, *Marshal,*" the man behind him interrupted his thoughts. "Your presence backstage is amusing, but I *am* to go on soon."

"I'm sorry, Mr. Edwards," Hiram said, "I believe we have a situation here."

"Do you now?" His full lips drew back into a devious smile. He didn't know that Hiram was tamping down a growing panic at the sight of his children sitting two rows up and just down from a wanted criminal. "Tell me about this situation. Maybe I can help."

CHAPTER NINE

He had a careful process to follow in *situations*. The threat had been identified—*step one*. He'd evaluated it—*step two*—with considerations of the crowd, location, and what he did not know so far about his suspects. Namely, were they packing guns, and were they going to leave or linger?

By the time of the after-party, it appeared they were going to linger, but he'd already made some preparations—*step three*—for that scenario. He had also dropped a few whispers in select ears to assure calmness prevailed should the situation escalate. Hopefully, it would not. The only ears he had not managed to connect with were those of his children, who had momentarily disappeared amongst the excitement of the play's conclusion. This little matter was the only hole in his preventive measures, and it had the heaviest effect on his mood. Under his coat and shirt, the nerves that had originally clenched at the tickle of cold air now hummed steadily, rendering him fully aware of the shape of his skin, his muscles and bones.

Hiram removed his hat—he could not have the brim affecting his range of vision—and found a place to stash it. He took off his badge, slid the tin shield with its cut-out star into his coat pocket, and positioned Nathan just outside the main doors with a street howitzer before he went off to pretend to socialize and play nice with the crowd.

Once the lights were raised with the central crystal chandelier burning at its most brilliant, the opera house floors were opened for folks to roam freely with a small bar serving wine and champagne. The main doors remained open, allowing in some of the cool night air to temper the heat of so many bodies in one place and multiple lamps burning. To keep his

Peacemaker out of sight, he remained in his heavy coat, beginning to hate every minute of it as sweat beaded on his brow.

The gaiety had now become a mere illusion to him as he slipped through the chattering crowd, overheard commentary on how wonderful the performance, how beautiful the props and costumes. For a briefness, he kept an eye on Frank Evans and his companion, who tended to drift in and out from under the balconies where the light was dimmest. They kept on the move, disappearing here, reappearing there until he suddenly could not find them at all.

Come on, he thought. *Just leave already and prove me wrong.* He would feel *so* much better if he could catch them in the street.

When at last one group of patrons parted to clear his view, he finally found Lucinda at the front of the stage, Jesse all but hanging protectively on her shoulder. Caleb and Ellie were both wearing thin and had taken seats beside each other, leaning back with knees drawn to their chests at the foot of the platform. The magic of the evening was rapidly evaporating, and it was especially late for them. Hiram relished the idea of having to scoop up Ellie and carry her home with her heavy little head notched in his shoulder, but that was a dream for an entirely different night.

Lucinda and Jesse were in a circle of three completed with August Chandler, the actor who played Lysander. He wore the costume of a frilled, white shirt and trousers, his stage makeup still perfectly intact, not a drop of sweat on his forehead. Hiram headed toward them, looked up at the balcony where Silas stood against the ornate banister gazing back down at him. They nodded curtly to each other, and then he noted Bryce Tucker still in his box, enjoying a glass of champagne while his puckered wife was elsewhere. Hiram made brief eye contact with the wealthy rancher and proceeded toward the kids.

Clustered near them, a circle of Mica Bend's ladies, including Martha Raskin, praised Micajah Edwards, who still wore his elaborate Oberon costume. They devoured his charm, smiled dreamily as he regaled them with tales of his travels and performances.

Upon the stage, where the donkey head now sat abandoned, Nora Long, the actress who had played both Hermia and Titania, was encircled by her new fans, including Amon, who was doing all he could to keep his fellows elbowed back from her. The young woman, still in her gossamer dress and wings, smiled coyly at their affections and probably sowed more than a bit of discord between them.

Out near the entry, Morgan and Jasper were also singled out for discussion, though their gatherings were much smaller, and soon Morgan stepped away to go smoke. Of the entire troupe, he had proved the quietest and most reserved, which explained why he was more of a technical man backstage. He'd filled in one role and then disappeared completely to tend props and curtains.

The final member of the troupe, Genevieve Blakely, had filled the roles of Hippolyta and Helena. A red-headed beauty in an elaborate tunic and breastplate, she had attracted a circle of men at the bar where she waved about a flute of champagne as she spoke.

Hiram began to wonder who would be getting lucky tonight and who would be getting slapped by his wife.

"A man shouldn't be that pretty," Jesse's disgusted voice jarred him from the thought.

"Yes, well, tell that to them," Hiram whispered back and nodded casually toward Edwards and his gushing followers. "I've honestly never seen this many pretty people in one place at the same time. Whole town is horned up." His attempt at humor went ignored. Then upon looking at the kid, he realized that Jesse's eyes were not fastened on Edwards but on August Chandler. They blazed dark with jealousy as Lucinda lavished one compliment after another on the actor.

"Oh, you were wonderful, and I can't imagine how you all change costumes so fast or shift from one role into another. So well done. *So... So...* well done."

"It's all carefully orchestrated," August explained. "The trick is not to make too much noise backstage."

"And the way you alternated roles? Pure brilliance. That cannot be easy. I did notice you've compiled some of the characters." Lucinda's hand rose and she fingered delicately at the tiny locket, calling attention to her slender neck. August's soft brown eyelashes lowered to watch, and he appeared to draw a longing breath. "Robin Starveling and Tom Snout, for example. Your abridged version gave some of their lines to Bottom or Quince!"

"You noticed that?" August's brows rose in amazement.

"I did indeed! But it was meticulously re-crafted. I commend you."

"I need a drink," Jesse suddenly growled, spun, and practically flung himself away from them, not that Lucinda noticed. "When's Silas openin' up the Palace again?"

"Whoa." Hiram caught his arm, drew him back, leaned in and whispered, "Hold on there, cowboy. Something may be going down here, and I need you to take Lucinda home."

Jesse drew back, frowning at the request. "What? What's about to go—"

Hiram started to shut him up before he announced it to everyone in hearing range when Miz Raskin, having detached herself from Edwards' doting harem, suddenly appeared between the two and did all of the damage herself.

"Marshal!" she said with glee, cheeks rosy from too much champagne. "Oh, I'm so glad you made it tonight. I have something for you."

Hiram cringed, and his eyes darted to try once more to find Frank Evans and his pal, hoping they hadn't heard the loud greeting wherever they were. "Yes, ma'am?"

She raised a small, beaded handbag and unclipped the top to draw out a fold of familiar pamphlets. "I took these from Caleb yesterday at school, but I felt it best to return them to you instead of him. We mustn't reward idleness, after all." She giggled. "Hmmm?"

Hiram noted how they had been folded to fit into her purse. Caleb wouldn't be happy about that, but they seemed to have a little extra wear and tear. "Miz Raskin, did *you* read these?"

"I shall neither confirm nor deny." She giggled again as if the horrid tales contained something more suggestive.

Caleb noticed what was happening and scrambled to his feet, pushing himself between Lucinda and August Chandler, drawing a rebuke from his sister while the pretty actor looked much put out. "Hey, can I have 'em, Papa?"

Ellie stirred in his wake, got to her feet, and shoved between Lucinda and her new suitor.

The last thing Hiram needed was another distracted kid. All he wanted was for Jesse to calmly and purposely escort Lucinda and her siblings out the door and home if he could get his eldest to curb her infatuation. "No." He shoved the pamphlets into his coat pocket next to his badge. "You'll get these later."

"Please!"

"Excuse me, Miz Raskin." Hiram pulled his boy aside and leaned forward to say calmly, "You'll get them back tonight, I promise. I need you to help Jesse round up your sisters and get them home."

"*Why?*" this came out dripping with gall.

Hiram opened his mouth while his mind scrambled for an easy explanation that didn't involve a wanted criminal and possible accomplice in their midst. Causing panic would get him nowhere. It was at that very moment, just as Ellie scrambled up to his side, that all hell broke loose.

A gunshot pierced the crowd noise, followed by the shatter of glass as the bullet struck a piece of crystal in the chandelier. Gasps and outcries rose sharply around the room and then dropped into silence as everyone recovered and turned to look for the source.

Damn, Hiram thought and shoved Ellie backward into her brother's arms. Despite his efforts to blend in and play ignorant while still searching out Frank Evans, he'd become too overwhelmed. The man was already close, and he had a Colt Peacemaker of his own aimed right at Hiram's head. Hiram immediately raised his hands.

"Yep, that's it, boy," Evans spat, "get yer hands up. So, *Marshal*, is it? Where's yer badge?"

"In my pocket," Hiram replied calmly.

"Well, just leave it there. Yer gun?"

Hiram leaned his left hip out slightly so that his coat fell away, revealing the outward jut of the grip since he preferred a cross-over draw.

Evans chuckled. "Nice." He stepped in quickly, the end of his Peacemaker pressing up under Hiram's chin as he used his free hand to pull the marshal's gun from its holster and confiscate it. "Harlan!" he yelled.

The young man scrambled into view from somewhere off to his right, breathing heavily with excitement, a bag gripped in his hand. "Yeah, Frank!" he cheered to find something finally happening. "Let's do it!"

"All right, folks!" Frank announced then. "Fun's over! Take off yer jewels, take out yer money. I don't care if it's real or fake or if ya only got a penny on ya!" When there was a stunned pause, he looked around, and then his voice dropped a near octave into a harsh roar. "Do it *fuckin'* now!" He spun Hiram's gun in his hand, snapped it into a secure grip, and held it out to point from one frightened face to another. Then, just to prove his point, he sighted in on one of the guests who still absently held up a champagne flute. He fired, the glass shattered, and more startled cries went up. The glass had been in the hand of Maddie Krane, who started gasping in spasms, frozen in place with fear. Blood ran from a cut in the side of her hand. Hiram caught sight of her husband, who was also frozen and helpless to do anything.

Nearby, the fiery-haired Genevieve Blakely looked sharply toward the troupe's head actor as if to tell him to do something. Micajah Edwards only appeared to shrug at her, the gesture subtle, not enough movement to set Evans off.

Hiram's eyes tracked all of this while he remained perfectly still, arms held up like a cactus, and as such, he grew pricklier and angrier by the second. So, Evans had shown off that he was ambidextrous with a pair of revolvers, but Maddie Krane was the last person in the room who needed that kind of scare and stress. He slanted his gaze steeply to his left to check on Lucinda, who had stepped backward until the edge of the stage stopped her.

Caleb pulled Ellie back a relatively safe distance. She wept profusely, face red and screwed up with fear. "Shhhhh," Caleb said, gripping her tighter all the while staring at his father's life in peril.

"Now put yer stuff in the sack my brother's bringin' 'round!" Frank shouted, his breath rank in Hiram's face.

When everyone remained too fixated in fear, it was Micajah Edwards' honeyed voice that spoke up. "Do what he says. We do not want any bloodshed. Your belongings are replaceable, but your lives—" he paused there, voice taking on a low, breathy rasp, "—are not."

"Yeah, listen to yer fairy king!" Evans laughed. "Do it!" A wave of movement surged through the room. Earrings and necklaces were removed, wallets and money clips pulled from pockets. "You, Padre! Get that ring off!"

Father Ramirez was shaking too hard to get his ecclesiastical ring off of his chubby finger.

Hiram looked up during this minute pause and noted Silas at the banister above, Izabel beside him though his arm was thrust out protectively in front of her. She crossed herself to see the priest being threatened.

"Come on, Javier, do it," Becker's voice said anxiously from somewhere out of Hiram's range of sight.

"I don't give a shit if yer a holy man!" Frank shifted sideways while still keeping his gun under Hiram's chin. He drew Hiram's pistol up and swung. There was a crack as he backhanded the little old priest, who immediately spat out blood. Father Ramirez took in a sharp breath and trembled as he finally fumbled the ring off, no doubt leaving his finger to grow black and blue.

As the open sack hurriedly passed around and goods dropped into it, Evans angled the extra gun up at the balcony. "Ya'll up there, drop yer goods down here, now! Hurry, or I'll be painting yer faces with yer marshal's brains!"

That was when Hiram heard four guns cocking, cylinders rotating into place with the most satisfying series of clicks, from above and along the banister.

"Not if we take you first," Silas's voice replied with such coolness it made Hiram proud.

He watched Frank Evans' face shift from twisted fury to startled at this new development.

"What?" Hiram asked without a hitch. "You thought I'd be the only one here with a gun?" He looked Evans straight in the eyes, realized for the most fleeting of moments that he had not been as spot on with visualizing the features from the wanted ad. Evans had a scar on his left temple that was omitted from the sketch.

Among those, besides Nathan, whom he had informed earlier that they had a criminal in their midst were Silas, Bryce Tucker, and two of Tucker's security hires. They all carried a small arsenal under their coats, and Silas always had a Derringer hidden in his boot.

"I swear I'll end you, Marshal." His lips curled back from gritted yellow teeth.

"But they'll still end you, so we'll be even, won't we?" Although the gun under his chin jammed upwards a little more, he barely reacted. He saw the panic truly rise in Evans with the realization that he was trying to glare down someone who did not care if he lived or died. The only thing Hiram cared about was that his children were safe. He didn't think of the trauma they might suffer upon seeing him murdered here tonight, but he took comfort in the absolute *fact* that Silas and company would put so many holes in Evans that *pincushion* would be an understatement.

The man shook now, his smelly breath gusting faster, and he yelled at his brother, "Harlan, goddamnit! Get a move on!"

"So, you ran with Jack Taylor, huh?" Hiram said, his voice reducing to a low growl. "That means you took part in some pretty successful holdups, including a train robbery. Impressive. Gave you balls but no brains, didn't it, Frank? You don't have Taylor or his gang now, or you might have pulled this off, but you bit off more than you can chew here. You scramble on out now, and you might live to try this shit again."

The next few seconds felt like time slowed. Hiram held his ground, gun or no gun planted under his face; if Evans pulled that trigger, at least he'd forever be haunted by the intense eyes of the man he killed. The dam broke when Evans, in a coordinated series of abrupt and desperate moves, shoved his first captive back and lunged to his left, going for his second past Jesse and August.

Then he made the mistake that would seal his fate.

He grabbed Lucinda by the arm, but in the process, dropped his gun, and it clattered off somewhere amidst the bottom edge of the stage.

Jesse started to reach out, shouting, "Don't touch her!" but Evans backhanded him as he had Father Ramirez and sent him spinning.

"Jesse!" Lucinda cried as she was dragged into Evans' arms and spun around to face out, presented as a human shield, and the gun placed against the side of her head was Hiram's own.

The marshal caught his breath now, new rage bursting up to pound in his temples. "Evans, don't you fucking dare."

"You just get away now," the wanted man growled. "Get away… Harlan!"

The younger Evans scurried to his brother's side. "Yeah, Frank, we've got a bunch'a stuff." He waved the bag, demonstrating its weight in heisted jewelry and coin.

"We're going now. I'm gonna walk this pretty filly to the doors, and yer not gonna stop me." In a burst of stumbling movement, he pulled her with him, her pale pink skirts whispering over the floor and nearly tripping her. The crowd parted quickly to let him through while Lucinda quivered, her eyes brimming with tears. Her mouth formed *Papa*, but she thankfully didn't say it out loud because Evans did not need to know how much leverage he had acquired.

Hiram gave them a space of perhaps ten feet and then began to stalk lividly closer only to have Evans stop, jam the gun harder against Lucinda's temple. He froze as she winced then burst into tears.

"Heh, she sure does smell good," Evans said and pushed his luck harder. "I may just have to take her with me. Eh?" He stuck out a slathering tongue and licked Lucinda's cheek, leaving a long slug trail from her soft jawline up to her temple, where the barrel of the gun remained a critical threat.

"Hey, Frank, way's clear!" kid brother called as he started for the door.

Beyond the two and their hostage, Hiram saw Nathan peer around the door on the left, the shotgun held at the ready. Hiram shook his head slightly in warning; he didn't want Evans to get any more wound up once he saw the deputy. Either way, the street howitzer was useless in a situation like this. With Evans' and Lucinda's heads so close together, the scatter would get both of them.

Then, how Micajah Edwards was suddenly at his side, Hiram didn't know. He didn't hear the actor approaching, but then the blood roaring in his ears may have drowned that out. All he knew was the presence suddenly there, a shape of green in his periphery, but he didn't take his eyes off the man holding his daughter captive.

"Please, we never wanted anyone to get hurt here tonight," Edwards said in that eerily fearless voice of his. "Look, you want jewelry? Here…" A second later, a hand stretched out and offered a gold pocket watch, let it drop and swing gently on the chain. "It's worth a lot. You can add it to the bag, but just let the girl go." Hiram appreciated the gesture, but it did nothing to bring him down from the near mania spinning in his head at how far the situation had played out.

"Harlan, grab a couple of horses," Evans said, and his eyes remained on Micajah Edwards. "Time to burn the breeze."

"Yeah, Frank… yeah…" The boy hurried out of the building, disappearing off somewhere toward the hitching post. A second later, a yelp sounded along with a tumbling noise. "Shit!" Harlan's voice carried. Then another yelp and another tumble.

If his blood weren't boiling, Hiram would have been amused. His expectations of a reaction from the older Evans were, however, disappointed.

Frank did not react at all. He stared with a bizarre vacancy for a long moment at Edwards, suddenly oblivious that an expensive pocket watch was dangling before him for the taking or that his brother had just discovered that stealing a horse was not so simple. Then suddenly, he snapped to. His eyes widened with a look that Hiram could only define as terror. Where it came from, he didn't know, but it rippled in the way he took a sharp hiss of breath and shoved Lucinda away. She stumbled into Hiram's arms, sobbing, while Frank turned and bolted out of sight. Evans' frantic steps carried, stamping the dry ground, horses grumbling at his passage.

"Marshal!" Jesse's voice called.

In one smooth action, Hiram eased Lucinda off onto Nathan, who lowered the shotgun to embrace and coo at her that she was safe now. He turned to see the young ranch hand hurrying toward him, wading past the other patrons, the grip of the other Peacemaker turned out, ready to fit into Hiram's hand. He took it, checked the hammer, and spun it around, aiming the grip out like the head of a hammer. Then he walked outside to see that young Harlan was laid out on the ground after a second attempt to climb onto one of the horses, only to discover the saddle loosened. The older Evans was scrambling toward Teddy, the one horse that had his saddle cinched on properly.

Hiram paused.

Evans attempted to climb on, but Teddy was having none of it. The gelding reared high, violent in the way his body twisted. He squealed toward the sky as he threw the interloper off with extreme prejudice. Frank Evans hit the ground on his ass, the gun flying from his hand. He was trying to sit up, gritting his teeth in pain as he searched for his wits, and Hiram chose that moment to storm forward. In the wake of the horse's hooves stomping away, he dropped into a kneel alongside the downed man as he swept the grip forward and pistol-whipped Frank Evans across the face.

"You can hold me hostage all you like, but that's my daughter, you sonofabitch!"

*
**

Hiram almost expected Watkins to fire him that night, but then there would have been no one but Nathan to haul the Evans brothers down to the jail. While the opera house patrons attempted to cool down from so much fear and excitement, Watkins tailed him across and up the street as he and Nathan focused purely on delivering their charges to the lockup.

"I can't believe you didn't tell me your plans!" he ranted, cane shaking like the finger of an angry schoolmarm. "You told Silas, even *Tucker*, but you didn't stop to think that the mayor should be informed?"

"The mayor wasn't armed, and the fewer people knew, the better." Hiram had Frank Evans shackled at the wrists and gripped by the back of his grimy shirt as he forced the woozy, pistol-whipped man across the thoroughfare. He had his own Peacemaker back in his hand where it belonged, and Evans' gun was now resting temporarily in the holster. Nathan was close behind with Harlan. They'd left their horses at the opera house because Hiram feared he'd have ended up dragging Evans viciously across the street rather than leading. Hell, he might have kept dragging him around the jail to the gallows and taken matters into his own hands for the second time that night.

"But you even told Mr. Edwards. You don't even *know* him."

"Well, I had to explain what I was doing backstage. The dude has a pretty cool head on his shoulders." Hiram left it at that. He dumped his prisoner against the boardwalk support in front of the office and fumbled for the keys in his other coat pocket. Nathan gave Harlan Evans a hard shove and put him on the ground next to his brother before assuming a stance with the shotgun.

"Well, the next time you decide on some other such deviltry to deal with a known criminal, you *tell* me."

"Titus, I suggest you get back there and keep smoothing things over before the town's *morale* suffers." Hiram opened the door and looked back at the disgruntled mayor. He almost said, *I don't need any more of your shit*, but walked it back and chose to convey perspective. "I'm tired. I just had a gun under my chin and my daughter crying in front of me with a gun to her head."

That drove the point home and probably secured his job if Watkins *had* been considering dismissal. Watkins opened his mouth, had no words, and finally nodded. "Very well, but we'll be reviewing this matter tomorrow."

"Looking forward to it." Hiram watched him turn to go, then stepped inside, groped in his pockets for other items, withdrew his badge and Caleb's now well-creased pamphlets, and tossed them absently onto his desk. He patted down to find, in his vest, the match safe next to his pocket watch. He withdrew a match and lit the hurricane lamps on both desks. With the room now lit, he and Nathan quickly hauled their catch inside.

Each brother was patted down and checked thoroughly for anything hidden on his person that might aid an escape and then given his own cell. Hiram even took their boots which he left with their smelly coats piled outside the cells. Then he watched Frank Evans drag himself onto the plain bunk in the cell and flop against the wall, shadowed face staring back at him.

Hiram held up the Peacemaker. "Where'd you get this, Frank? Stolen?"

The man spat, leaving a trail of blood down his chin that gleamed from out of his shadowed nook.

"Will be interesting what Sheriff Slaughter has to say about all of this," Hiram pressed. "You get this off that deputy of his that Taylor's last rats killed in Contention City two months ago?"

Evans buckled down and looked like he was not going to say anything more, especially after the name of Slaughter had come up.

Hiram took that as positive an answer as any. He went over to the safe and opened it, then opened the cylinder on the gun and emptied it of its remaining four cartridges that he placed on the shelf with it along with the belt. On second thought, he withdrew one—just one—bullet out and then shut and locked the safe. He lifted his Peacemaker, opened the loading gate, rolled the cylinder to the empty chamber, and replaced the cartridge Evans had fired.

Then he went back to the desk, took out a sheet of note paper, and scrawled a message on it that he would have telegraphed to the county sheriff's office in Tombstone. Then things were going to get more interesting.

"Guess we better get back to the party, then," Nathan suggested. "See how everyone is doing for ourselves."

Hiram nodded, eyes still on the man in the cell while steady anger still burned behind them.

"Yer daughter sure is pretty," Evans dirty voice grated out. Although the man's mouth was not visible, Hiram could hear the slimy grin in his tone, the attempt to rile him up.

It was all Hiram could do not to shoot him through the bars. He braced himself and replied, "Yes, she is. And you're still one ugly cunt."

CHAPTER TEN

There were people he expected not to see upon returning. The Kranes had departed the opera house, and so had Norman Becker and Father Ramirez (likely the padre was getting his bruised mouth examined in Becker's clinic right now).

He had not expected to enter again to an explosion of claps and cheers from those who had not been spooked away by the holdup. The applause rooted him to the spot. He gaped into the main hall, and anger turned to utter discomfort. He'd felt better with Evans' gun under his chin than being applauded.

"Look, he's blushing," Silas teased as he appeared from out of nowhere.

Izabel was on his arm, smiling seductively, a glint of wine still on her lips. "That was amazing," she said. "I couldn't believe you did not flinch with that bastardo in your face." Though almost as petite as Lucinda and just as feminine, Izabel had a way with words and no fear of using them occasionally. He had not had a chance to compliment her earlier on her attire. The deep burgundy silk dress suited her coffee skin, and her hair, usually a curly black mess, had been piled into a bun from which curls were selectively allowed loose. Hiram liked her, especially since his long friendship with Silas was one of those that female companions learned to tolerate, and Izabel handled it well. He appreciated most that she had remained with Silas so long into Mica Bend's silver drought when the other Palace girls had left. Now she was practically his common-law wife, and Hiram suspected that should the time come that the saloon folded, they would happily leave town together.

"I almost flinched at his breath," he said to a round of chuckles, and then it seemed everyone came at him when all he wanted to do was find Lucinda. Though there were only perhaps ten in all, it felt like a thousand smiling faces swarmed him, the effect dizzying, reminding him that he was coming down off of a powerful rush that had not been an enjoyable one.

"Wouldn't have been the way I'd have handled it," Bryce Tucker said with a wink.

"I swear I would have soiled myself…"

"Can't believe two criminals had the nerve to sit right here, and…"

"We sure haven't seen excitement like that in a while…"

"Most brave of you, Marshal," Mr. Fraleigh said.

Fraleigh being one of the people Hiram wanted to see, he leaned closer to lower his voice and slipped the note to him. "If you would, Mr. Fraleigh, telegraph this message to Sheriff Slaughter. Tonight, if possible, but tomorrow morning early should be fine."

"Yessir," the little man replied. "Happy to."

Amid the handshakes, thank yous, pats on the back, and more comments about how he hadn't flinched, he tried to peer past them until, finally, he glimpsed the ruffles of a soft pink dress. He tore himself away, hurried toward it to find his daughter sitting in one of the folding chairs near the stage, head bowed as she dabbed her face with a handkerchief. Kneeling before her, tending to her with a tender gleam in his eyes, was August Chandler.

"Oh, meant to tell you," Silas explained, following him. "The loot the brothers collected has been distributed seamlessly back to its owners. Jesse walked Caleb and Ellie home after all of the excitement. So, they're fine. Lucinda wanted to wait for you."

"Thank you," Hiram whispered.

She looked up at his approach, automatically reached out to him, and Hiram—seeing, for a blurry briefness, only a scared little girl—pulled her to her feet and into a bear hug. Her soft head fit perfectly beneath his chin to banish the lingering sensation of a gun barrel. "Honey, I'm so sorry."

"Wasn't your fault, Papa," she whispered, and he heard a sniffle burrowed deep against his coat.

August had risen and was keeping back, giving them space, as did Silas and Izabel.

Hiram found himself rocking slightly. He continued to hold her while he looked back up at Silas. "Where's Watkins?" He had noticed a distinct lack of the annoying man's presence when he'd expected to be accosted yet again.

"Gone off to pout, I suppose," Silas replied and then explained that Watkins had barely gotten into a speech attempting to spin the fault on Hiram before the troupe, and most of the patrons, intervened with a fit of boos and hisses. Shamed into silence, he had slipped away somewhere. "Maybe he'll turn up at the Palace momentarily to drown away his embarrassment. Ah, here we are." He gestured to his right and smiled proudly. "And now you must meet your new fans, H."

At last, father and daughter separated, and Lucinda dabbed at her face again, under her eyes, and returned to August's side. Hiram noted their hands almost touching, the back of her slender finger arching slightly toward the boy's much larger hand. It looked like a lean, strong hand, even if said boy was ridiculously pretty. Then he followed Silas' gesture.

Micajah Edwards stood in the center room, now out of costume, makeup removed, and garbed in a crisp black suit, hair combed out straight and flaxen, dripping over shoulders that formed the top of a perfectly V-shaped figure. He was still as imposing as he'd been in character as Oberon and still just as unnervingly beautiful. His complexion, perfect in its almost waxy uniformity, did not need grease paint or eyeliner to highlight its allure, and the townswomen in the hall still ogled him. The rest of the troupe, also now changed into more casual clothing, had assembled around him, including Jasper and Morgan. With them gathered in one group, it was clear that Edwards was their leader and probably managed everything from booking the troupe to payouts.

"I'm at a loss of words how impressed I am, Marshal Wells," the tall actor said as he reached out and pumped Hiram's hand up and down. "That is the first time we have ever performed only to be entertained in return. I was stunned how you did not flinch. We all thought you were about to die of lead poisoning."

"Let's be clear." Hiram prickled all over again. "I wouldn't call my daughter being taken hostage *entertainment*."

Edwards raised his chin, clearly taken aback by the marshal's directness, but the point got across perfectly. Then he nodded and dipped his head with such chivalry it was impossible to stay irritated with him. "Of course. My apologies."

"There's that word, *flinch*." Silas attempted to lighten the mood again as he clamped a hand down on Hiram's shoulder. "Our Marshal Wells simply does not do that."

"How did you recognize that man out in the audience with the lights so dim?" Edwards asked. "And what criminal actually looks like his wanted sketch?"

Hiram let Silas keep answering for him. "Oh, he can tell what they look like. He *never* forgets a name or face, and he never backs down."

"Indeed?" Edwards looked particularly amused.

"You should have seen the time he sassed Wyatt Earp."

"Silas—"

"Six years ago. Earp and Holiday were on their vendetta run heading into New Mexico. So, they came prancing into Mica Bend with their posse like they owned the thoroughfare. Expecting asylum, I guess. The whole town clenched up tighter than a hummingbird's tweet, and Hiram here... he just strolls up to Earp and says—" Silas lowered his voice into a raspy mockery of his friend. "*'Condolences on your brother, but no one here wants the hornet's nest you've stirred, Earp. I don't care which star you're wearing now. You can water your horses, but damned if you're staying here one minute longer.'*" He looked at Hiram intentionally wide-eyed for approval. "Did I tell it right?"

"I don't sound like that." Hiram felt the tension finally begin to uncoil. He thought of how he had been standing in the opera house's open doors, watching his child cry in the arms of a wanted man, who was holding a gun to her head as he grossly licked her face (for that alone Hiram could have immediately held a hanging). Then another man, a stranger, gently attempted to intervene in a non-threatening way. "You tried to help my daughter," he said, looking at Edwards. "You offered that watch. I don't know what made Frank Evans let her go and bolt, but what you did... I appreciate it."

"I was just doing anything I thought might calm the storm. That watch isn't as valuable as I claimed. I was bluffing."

"That so? You did it well, Mr. Edwards."

"Please, everyone that knows me calls me Cage," he replied, gesturing to the troupe around him before thrusting out his hand for another comradely shake. "I would very much like for you to do the same."

By the time festivities at the opera house subsided just before midnight and moved over to the Palace, he felt like he could lay down on the tracks and not hear the train coming. That was saying something considering what a light sleeper he'd become over the last few months.

He had first put Lucinda in Teddy's saddle, led the two home, and checked on his other children. They were snug in their beds, and Jesse had helped himself to the sofa in the front parlor, where he had slumped back with his legs stretched out over the floor. The kid was dead to the world, his neck cocked so awkwardly sideways that he would probably have a crick in the morning. Lucinda barely noticed him there, despite the loud snore that told Hiram the kid was still alive, as she said good night and kissed her papa on the cheek.

Hiram had looked sympathetically at the young ranch hand and left him to whatever happy dreams might be swirling in his head, not about to drive him out and make him ride back to his bunk this late. He had appreciated Jesse's quick recovery during the opera house crisis and how he'd retrieved Evans' gun and delivered it straight into Hiram's hand with such perfect coordination. Hopefully, his daughter would reevaluate how it had all happened and discover the same appreciation, but for the rest of tonight, she deserved not to have to think about much at all.

After he saw the last of a soft pink ruffle disappear up the stairwell, fatigue did not stop him from steering right back to the saloon, which was barely populated by now. Nathan stayed briefly and then bid everyone a good night to go to his one-room crib at the north back of town with an agreement to meet Hiram at the office by eight in the morning. Of Tucker's ranch hands, only three remained. Amon Yount was missing along with Charlie Preston. Among the three present, cheers and jeers went around that those two were getting lucky.

Of the troupe, only Cage Edwards had come to visit, and when the man of the hour arrived, he requested to start an ongoing tab for himself and Hiram and ordered rounds of something from the top shelf. That happened to be a bottle of Kentucky mash that Silas usually guarded fiercely. Given the recent events, the saloon keeper acquiesced readily and placed two crystal tumblers before his guests of honor.

"How did you two meet?" Cage asked as he ran a finger around the rim of his glass, making it ring softly.

"New Orleans," they answered simultaneously, the chorus thrown out of perfect synchronization by Silas' Louisiana drawl over Hiram's Eastern Pennsylvanian.

"That is to say, my hometown," Silas amended. "I was on my way out, driven by a certain angry plantation owner who accused me of stealing his daughter's virtue."

"*Did* you steal it?" Cage smirked as if fishing for juicy gossip.

"No, the damage had long been done." Silas gestured at Hiram. "I was about to be lynched and dumped in the Mississippi, and this young man here rides in like my white knight with a machete."

"Horse *shit*," Hiram interrupted and finished his tumbler before he thought about it. "He dandered up a member of the Klan with that mouth of his."

Silas feigned offense with a gasp and added another round to Hiram's glass.

"A machete?" Cage's brows raised.

"He didn't have his Peacekeeper then," Silas rejoined. "All right, so I might have angered some malcontent in a gaming den hidden on the plantation grounds. H happened to be watching and took my side, and he *did* have a machete strapped to his thigh."

Cage blinked and shook his head, keeping up. "Why did you have a machete strapped to your thigh?"

"Job," Hiram explained. "I cleared brush on the same plantation where Silas dipped his wick." He hated telling this story to anyone else. The truth was far more complicated and hung muddied somewhere between Silas' version and the one Hiram would never forget despite the passage of time. "He might have been a pain in everyone's ass, but he didn't deserve what they were dealing."

"So here we are, one great escape and a million adventures later," Silas concluded before his best friend kept glaring at him.

"Marvelous," Cage said, looking from one to the other and covered his mouth as he yawned. "Now, I am afraid that I must turn in before Miz Simpson gives up and locks me out of the boarding house."

Silas chuckled. "She *will* do that."

"Indeed. I bid you goodnight, gentlemen. It has been a pleasure." He turned and strolled through the batwing doors and into the night.

"How is he getting back to the Simpson House?" Silas watched after him. "He doesn't have the coach or a horse. You think it's safe for him?"

Given Cage's height and the width of his shoulders that dropped down to that narrow waist, Hiram was sure there was some considerable muscle under that fine black suit, and he wondered how an actor sustained it. The man might seem a dandy at first, but he looked like he could take care of himself for the two-mile walk in the moonlight. "He'll be fine." He turned back to the bar. "Another, please."

"Well, since it *is* on *him*," Silas said as he poured. "Looks like you've made a new friend."

Hiram sipped. Smooth though the mash was, the after bite roughened his already tired voice but loosened his restraint. "Jealous?"

"*Shiiiit,*" Silas drew out. "At most, I have a comrade in rescue. First you save me, then him and his whole damn show, you've always been such a big hero."

Hiram gave him a steady look, both of them aware of how untrue that was.

Then Silas somewhat deflated as he noticed the tumbler next to Hiram's. "He barely touched his. Who wastes good booze like that, anyway?"

Hiram confiscated the remaining glass and lined it up with his own. "No, he didn't touch it at all."

"There you go with that noticing *everything*, again." Then to Hiram's ultimate dread, he sobered from all humor and leaned closer. An intensity coalesced in his jade eyes before he asked far too seriously, "So how are you doing after what happened tonight?"

Hiram paused with his glass halfway to his lips. If he knew Silas, the man had been waiting for the right private moment to ask that. "Other than wanting to murder Frank Evans six ways to Sunday?" He gulped the last down and picked up Cage's glass.

The harsh words did not affect Silas. "I assure you most of the town wishes that." He retrieved the first glass and put it behind the bar. "I know you, H. You've got nerves and balls to match. Always have. But the way you were doing, I swear for a minute there…" He swallowed, lowered his voice. "You had me scared that you were *trying* to *get* Frank Evans to *kill* you."

Hiram tossed back the last of the mash and gulped hard, almost coughed as it hit his throat, and then there it was, the pleasant buzz he'd been waiting for. "Wasn't anything, Silas," he gruffed. "I knew Evans for a yellow belly the moment I saw him. I was bluffing." He sat the empty glass down harder than intended. "I'm good as gravy."

"Good bluff." Silas stared in feigned wonder. "And now, Marshal Wells, I'm cutting you off."

Hiram nodded, "Yeah, guess I better get down the road." He could hear the slur in his voice.

"Are you sure you shouldn't just stay here? You're more than a tad tangled."

"No, m'good." Hiram slid from his stool and pulled his dignity together. "I'll see you tomorrow."

"All right. Well then, I need to attend to my lady love," Silas said. Then, as was his skill, he dropped his tone but raised his volume, "All right, gentlemen, your room's ready upstairs. Time to go."

"But we wanted another round," one of them objected.

"Bar's closed!" And when Silas made up his mind, that was it for everyone.

A moment later, Hiram stood on the boardwalk outside, listening to the bolts slide in the heavy security doors now shut behind the batwings. The window on one side went dimmer as the saloon's owner went around inside turning down the lamps. There were a few scuffling steps as the patrons herded themselves up the stairs, and then the lights on the other side gradually dimmed. Hiram looked out on the lonely street and then Teddy standing at the corner, head lowered in partial slumber.

To sleep perchance to dream, he thought. *Who in Shakespeare said that?* He'd only heard the phrase and been informed of its author, but he'd neither seen nor read the play to which it belonged. Well, he was sure Lucinda would educate him later if he asked. He stepped down off the platform and went to retrieve his horse, awkwardly hauled himself into the saddle, and trotted out into the middle of the empty thoroughfare, still bathed in moonlight though some shadows had grown longer. He paused and drew a deep breath. The frigid air snapped in his lungs, waking him up just enough, and he exhaled a white cloud. Just as he got ready to toss the reins and head for home, a thought struck him that he could not ignore.

He'd left not only his badge but Caleb's story pamphlets at the jail on the desk, and that began to nag at him. His son had witnessed the entire ordeal, had seen his father standing with a gun barrel pressed under his chin as if it was nothing, and it just now occurred to Hiram that that could be as bad as Lucinda's experience. He hoped that Ellie was simply too young to wholly understand everything that had happened, other than that it scared her, and that could be relieved with a little careful love and care.

On that note, he spun Teddy around, much to the gelding's irritation, and trotted toward the jail. After hauling in the Evanses and going back to the opera house, he had not even seen Caleb awake, just a glimpse of him asleep in his bed, yet he'd promised to give the stories back *tonight,* and he always kept his promises.

As he neared the jail, his horse snorted and spooked slightly, causing Hiram to whisper, "Easy… shhhhh…." The reason behind the sudden upset rose in the far distance on the howls of coyotes, mournful and blood-curdling. They weren't much of a threat way out there near the mountains, but all the same, Hiram figured on getting into the office, grabbing the pamphlets and his badge, and getting out quickly. He needed sleep, and soon.

He tethered the irked Teddy and hurried to the door, but inside found that the ambient moonlight had dropped considerably, and he could barely see anything. He sought out his match safe and struck a match, then used the flame to find the lamp on his desk, lit it and turned up the flame just enough that he could get a glance at the two sleeping men in the cells. As before, they were mostly shadowed, two lumps against the rear wall, slumped on their bunks. They were quiet.

Too quiet.

"You boys alright?" he asked, not that their wellbeing was of any concern. There was no answer, but he thought he saw one of them stir, breathe heavily and roll over.

Satisfied that his prisoners were still secured and had not been up roaming their cells looking for a means to escape in the dark, he returned attention to the desk, grabbed the pamphlets and badge, and slid them back into his coat pocket. He reached up to lower the flame on the lamp and was overcome with a sinking sensation. It didn't drop him quite to his knees, but he felt like he'd almost nodded off on his feet.

He reached for the edge of the desk to steady himself and found in a blink that he was back on his horse, under the moon and stars and facing the other end of town toward home.

Teddy stood in the middle of the thoroughfare, not far from the Palace boardwalk, waiting for him to decide to move forward.

"What the—?" he twisted in the saddle, looked up and down the street. Not a soul in sight, and the coyotes in the distance had gone completely quiet. The Bend slept from one end to the other, and he alone floated in the center of its emptiness.

Was he *that* tired? Had he drunk *that* much sour mash?

He couldn't remember if he'd even turned down the wick on the lamp or locked the jail door as he left. It was like one of those moments when he became lost in thought while riding and, next thing he knew, had cleared several miles without noticing the passage of time. Only, he'd had no thoughts at all to get lost in. He could not even retrace his steps in his head, go back to the door, back to the desk. It was all a frightening blank. He shoved a hand into his pocket and found the pamphlets and badge there, ran his thumb over the edge of the tin shield, so yes, he *had* retrieved them.

But then what happened?

He was normally so confident of every step he took, every observation he made, but for a moment to be missing entirely from his memory was unheard of even after some of his worst benders. The foreign sensation of panic rose in him, quashed these last seven months by a million doors slammed inside him to keep from falling completely into the helplessness he'd felt the night Rachel screamed and writhed in agony while blood began to bloom upon the bed beneath her. His anguish had clawed at him until he was raw inside, and his body could move, but his soul could not, cauterized into a special limbo where he tolerated the pain but didn't break from it.

It was from out of that limbo that he'd looked Frank Evans in the eyes just hours ago and did not flinch, because any other way would unbind the helplessness again. Now hot tears threatened to rise, and he swore he could see the steam trailing away on the night, crackling like the heaving puffs of his breath. He needed to find a means to anchor himself quickly, needed to embrace oblivion in sleep. Leaning forward—his stomach lurched as he clumsily rammed it into the saddle horn—he kicked a leg over, slid to the ground onto both feet without incident, and then turned and stumbled toward the dark saloon, leaving Teddy where he was. He half-stepped, half-crawled onto the boardwalk and flung the batwing doors out of the way, fell against the security doors behind them, and banged hard on one of the decorative panels with the flat of a hand.

"Silas!" he tried to shout, but only a grating whisper surfaced. He banged harder and clawed to hold himself upright before he slid down onto his knees into a crumbling mess. How long this went on, he was not sure. Probably only minutes, but it felt like hours creeping by with excruciating slowness. Then a ghosting of warm light moved past the window to his left, and a click and squeak sounded as the bolt slid on the other side and one door opened.

Silas stood there in his trousers, a worried look on his face. He held up a candlestick that burned like a beacon for Hiram's sanity to take refuge.

"H?" he whispered.

"I wasn't bluffing," Hiram admitted. "I wasn't bluffing at all."

CHAPTER ELEVEN

Sunlight flicked at him through a sheer curtain waving on a morning breeze.

He stared up at the familiar, tooled plaster ceiling for a long time as he sprawled comfortably in the same bed he always sprawled in when he couldn't face staying in the one at home. The mattress on that bed had been replaced, but some nights he awoke and swore he smelled warm blood, and then he would find himself here, but never had he delivered himself with the kind of noise he'd made last night. He recalled banging on the saloon door, which may have disturbed a few folks sleeping in the Raskin, but at least that was all they'd probably heard. How he'd come to do such a thing was blessedly vague now, pushed into a safe corner by the deepest sleep he'd experienced in months. His stomach was a little sour, but he was surprised that he didn't have a boomer of a headache.

He felt surprisingly *good*.

Even better when he caught the aroma of hot coffee. Pure, unadulterated *coffee*.

"So, the dead do rise," a woman's voice purred with a Hispanic accent.

He lifted his head and focused on Izabel, draped in a burgundy satin robe that scarcely covered her shapely breasts. She was so used to roaming the upper saloon in skimpy clothing, and Silas had not enforced any rules to the contrary even now that they were essentially a couple. Her hair was down in its usual curly mess but failed to conceal his love bites riddling her neck, and she smelled of sex.

All of this Hiram was used to, his focus primarily on the mug in her hand. "Good morning," he said and, with a few grunts and back twinge, pushed himself up into a sit. All clothing but his undershirt and trousers had been removed, placed neatly on a valet hook on the far wall. His boots sat beneath, and his gun belt rested in the nearest chair. "Is that what I think it is?"

"Si," she replied as she brought the mug over and handed it to him.

He took it with graciousness. "It's just Arbuckles'? No chicory?"

"No chicory." She smiled and sat on the edge of the bed, seduction built into her every move. "That came in this week. He ordered it especially for you."

Hiram closed his eyes, sniffed the steam rising from the top, and sipped the brew. Then something else occurred to him, a flash of his poor confused horse standing in the middle of the street as he'd charged at the saloon doors. "Teddy?" he asked.

"Silas took him to the livery last night after you disturbed the peace."

He started to grin about that but then realized she was deadly serious. "Where's Silas?"

"Gone to Benson again to pick up stock for the bar. He'll be back late this afternoon."

Hiram nodded, sipped some more. Given that the train ignored the Bend now, Silas was more than mildly inconvenienced like the other business owners. "So, he ordered this especially for me?"

"What is the saying? The squeaky wheel gets oiled?" She adjusted her robe before it fell too loose. "You are a squeaky wheel, Wells."

"Great," he muttered. "Always wanted to be a squeaky wheel."

"He would do anything for you, you know?" she said soberly. "Even stay here in this fading town until you decide to get off of your *ass* and go, too."

Only slightly perturbed, he finished a swig on the mug. "What're you talking about? He's been gabbing about moving to Phoenix now for weeks."

"It won't happen without you."

This conversation was making him uncomfortable all over again. He took another gulp. "Well, guess I better get to work."

"You scared him last night, just like you scared your kids. Don't do it again."

Ah, so that was it. He resettled. "Look, Iz, I was just doing my job the only way I could figure in that situation. I didn't want people to panic. That would have complicated things far more than—"

"He won't go anywhere until he knows you will be all right."

While he recognized her good intentions—and had to oblige that they *were* for Silas' sake—he wasn't in the mood for tough love this early. Wait, how *early* was it, anyway? That sunlight through the curtain seemed awfully high. "What time is it?" he interjected. His pocket watch was way over there in his hanging vest.

"At least eight-thirty."

"Damn." He coughed, turned up the mug, and swallowed down the last of the coffee. The heat soothed his throat, and he ignored Izabel's irritation as he plopped the mug back into her little hands and pushed himself up off the bed. "I need to meet Nathan at the jail and check on the brothers."

She stood and shook a finger at him. "This conversation is not over, jackass."

"Right now, it is." He shrugged into his shirt, buttoned up, and slipped on his vest. "I have to check on my kids, too. *Shit*—" So much to do. The list started compiling in his mind.

In one final non-stop flow of motion, he slid on his boots, buckled on his gun belt, grabbed and tossed his coat over his shoulder, and made a beeline for the door.

And found her draping herself in his way, filling the opening in as much as she could, one hand on her hip and one on the frame, flaunting those assets as well as her sass. "We are going to have this talk whether you like it or not."

"You know I've got a bad man sitting in my jail right now thinking dirty thoughts about my daughter, and it's all I can do not to take his head off, right?"

Seeing that she would get nowhere, Izabel surrendered. "Fine."

He dropped a kiss on her forehead before she moved out of his way. "Thanks for the coffee, Iz." She managed to track around with his departure and pop him squarely on the ass before he scrambled off fast enough.

The security doors were still closed downstairs, and he had to slide the bolt open to let himself out. The thoroughfare was quiet, but then it was a Saturday morning after an entertainment event that had nearly turned into a tragedy. Most of the remaining townsfolk had probably elected to stay in for a while and enjoy their own coffee. Even Watkins was not out and about complicating the lives of everyone around him.

Hiram closed his eyes to briefly bask in the peace, took a deep breath, savored the morning air.

"Papa!" Caleb's voice hollered from not far away.

Thank goodness. His eyes snapped open, and he looked to see his son and younger daughter running toward him. He hurried down the saloon steps and planted his feet just in time for Ellie to slam into him, little arms wrapping as far around his hips as they could go. His hand immediately cupped her head as her face buried itself in his lower belly, his thumb caressing the silkiness of a flaxen lock.

Caleb at least slowed down so that he didn't barrel over his father and sister. He stopped short, stared as if he didn't know what to do next.

"Hey," Hiram said more softly to both. "Sorry I didn't make it home."

Caleb gawked for a moment, then found his tongue. "It was a long night. Figured you'd end up sleepin' at Uncle Silas'." Spoken with all the wisdom a twelve-year-old could muster.

"How's Lucinda?"

"Fine, I think. Jesse looked after her a little, then headed back to the ranch. She's workin' on the chicken coop like she does."

Of course, Hiram thought. When Lucinda was stressed about something, she turned to tending the chickens she and her mother had bred together. It was a whole lot healthier than drinking too many rounds of Silas' sour mash. He would leave her to it for now but check in on her as soon as possible. First, to get breakfast to go and head straight to the jail to check on his guests, then, pending all was fine there and Nathan could sit with them a while, he'd check with Mr. Fraleigh on the status of the telegram to Sheriff Slaughter. Besides his elder daughter, he'd also run checks on various others around town, like the Kranes, whom he felt needed it.

"Come on," he said and peeled Ellie loose. "Let's go get some biscuits and bacon."

They waited outside the hotel kitchen while Miz Raskin filled his order. Hiram was highly aware that he still sported his finest suit, coat, and hat, all but announcing to everyone that he had not slept at home. Beside him, Ellie fidgeted, and Caleb leaned against the wall, arms crossed, calmer than he'd been in a while, and then it occurred to Hiram that he'd overlooked something. Something important, the whole reason he'd dropped in on the jail one more time last night before…

Before what, exactly? A breakdown, a bizarre moment of panic?

Only Silas and perhaps Izabel witnessed it that he knew of, so he quickly shifted course. He shoved a hand into his pocket and pulled out the penny dreadfuls that by now had seen too much wear.

"I did intend to give these to you last night," he said as he handed them to Caleb. "I'm sorry, son. I didn't mean to keep them."

"You didn't mean for a lot to happen, Papa," Caleb said quietly and took them. For a moment, Hiram expected a complaint at the state they were in, and he'd prepared an argument that Caleb could always press them out in his McGuffey's Reader all over again. Instead, the eyes that lifted and looked at him were no longer as youthful, tainted by an experience that had robbed the boy of just a little more of his innocent view of the world and rendered dreadful pulp tales irrelevant. "Maybe they… Maybe they ain't all that great, after all. Kind of silly, like you been sayin'."

Taken aback, Hiram uttered, "No, Caleb."

"I wanna go see Mama," Ellie said pleadingly, pulling on his coat.

"Oh, alright." He took her little hand before she could swing on him as she liked to do the cell doors at the jail. "It'll have to be this evening, though, Sweet Pea. Papa's got a lot to do today."

She nodded with her lower lip pursed.

"Here you are, Marshal," Miz Raskin said, appearing in the doorway with a neat white kerchief bundled up. The inviting smells of freshly baked biscuits and crispy bacon wafted from it. "It's on the house today." She winked at him. "Unfortunately, that's the last of them for now, so count yourself lucky."

"Oh, why is that?"

"We're out of milk," she lamented. "All the milk John picked up for the baking has already soured. What's in them in your hand is all that was still good."

"Really?"

"I guess you haven't heard it's been a problem everywhere for almost a week now. We sent word around several of the farms to see if we could get more, and they all said they couldn't supply any."

"Huh."

"It goes sour soon as any of the cows are milked, made Rand Henke's son quite sick. Oh dear, I hope it isn't some illness with the livestock."

She touched flour-dusted fingers to her rosy cheeks and then turned and went back into the kitchen. "I hope the beef isn't going bad, too," she could be heard lamenting.

"Have a good day, Miz Raskin," he tried to call after her. Though he found her story odd, soured milk was the least of his worries right now and a matter for a veterinarian, not a lawman.

As Hiram passed back through the dining room with his children, he noticed only Bryce Tucker and his wife were having breakfast. The two men nodded respectfully to each other, and then the Wells family proceeded out onto the street. Nathan should have been at the jail long before now. Hiram was surprised that his deputy had not come out to hunt him down and inquire why he was so late on such a crucial morning.

"Are we feeding them, too?" Caleb asked coolly as he walked, hands shoved into his pockets, the pamphlets tucked dismissively under one arm.

"They don't desewv bweakfast," Ellie backed him up.

"Bad guys gotta eat, too," Hiram said as he stepped up to the door only to find it locked.

"Papa, will you get any reward money?" Caleb asked, stepping to the side where he stared at the wanted poster of Frank Evans still pinned behind the display glass outside.

"Don't know, I still need to hear back from Sheriff Slaughter." He fumbled into his opposing coat pocket, thinking, *Where the hell is Nathan?* He produced the key for the jail and turned it in the lock. As he was putting it back into his pocket and juggling the kerchief, Caleb pushed past him and held the door. "Thanks, son," he said as he started forward and lifted his head.

Only a few steps ahead of him, Caleb had frozen stiff as he stared past the desks and toward the cells.

The odor of sweaty clothing was overpowered by that of blood and shit permeating the room, and Hiram almost gagged as he looked over his son's shoulder, taking in the entire scene in seconds.

In the cells, the bodies of Frank Evans and his brother Harlan each lay in a heap on the floor. That was realization one, but number two was that their heads were removed and laying feet away from torn neck stumps that trailed shreds of red muscle and upper sections of spine that hung loosened like beads on a broken necklace. Number three was that there were gaping holes in their upper stomachs, and number four was that two dark lumps were laying near each body—*hearts*. While there was some blood on the floor and the remains of their persons, there should have been so much more. Still, there was enough to cause the entire jailhouse and office to reek.

Realization number four was that Ellie was about to ram her way through the door next to him. The bundle of biscuits fell to the floor as Hiram's hand swept down, spread wide, and instantly covered her entire face, the center of his palm firmly over her eyes so that he felt her lashes fluttering against the skin.

"Hey! Lemme in!" she objected.

"Caleb, take your sister and get out of here," Hiram said, maintaining as much calm as possible. When the boy remained in shock, he couldn't help but raise his voice. "Caleb!"

"Yessir," his son said even as his breath began to quicken, the horror before him sinking in. He turned a pale face set with blue saucer eyes upon his father.

Hiram struggled as his youngest tried to pry his hand free. "Go find Nathan," he said. "Find him and send him over, but do not breathe a word about this. Not a word. You hear me?" He finally shoved Ellie out the door and shuffled back and forth to keep her from plowing her way inside. If the situation were different, it would have been downright funny.

"Go!" he shouted again at Caleb, almost cringing at the force in his voice.

Caleb finally gathered his wits and nodded, turned away, and hurried to wrangle his little sister back onto the street.

"Hey! Wha's in thewe?" her voice rose, objecting. "I wanna see!"

Hiram kicked the door closed behind them and watched through the glass as his son herded the tiny spitfire away. Then he finally stepped forward to take the entire scene in full.

"Fuuuuuck me," he whispered and tried not to vomit.

And all this time, he'd thought last night's events had been the worst.

It had taken Becker far too long to fall asleep as he came down from the fear that had gripped him for those few minutes that felt like hours. When it was over, he'd immediately taken Father Ramirez with him back to the clinic and there put three stitches in his friend's cheek where that maniac Frank Evans had struck him with Hiram Wells' gun. He and the little padre had then each had a small dose of whiskey from the emergency bottle he kept in his apothecary. He watched Ramirez fall peacefully asleep on the patient cot on the other side of the room, but in his cot, he struggled.

Visions kept repeating in his mind of Hiram Wells with a gun rammed firmly up under his chin while he refused to back down. Now Becker kept asking himself if the man had turned suicidal because that was how it looked, never mind that all three of Wells' children were witnessing their father tempting fate. That was traumatizing enough whether or not it ended with his brains on the balcony banister above. While everyone else in the opera house had readily applauded the maneuver as heroic, Becker saw only the desperate actions of a lost soul, and it made him ache all over again inside.

When his concerns finally exhausted him, he dropped off quickly only to be awakened with a start by a loud knocking on the clinic door. His once best clothing felt like a rumpled mess wrapped around his body, the creases in his armpits and his neck against his shirt collar sticky with sweat. He pried himself off the cot and stood on wobbly legs, realizing that sunlight now poured through the window over his slanted desk. A scribbled note lay there. He blinked, rubbed his eyes, and went to look at it.

Went to repent, it read. *Thank you.* Becker snapped his head around to finally notice that Ramirez was no longer on the other cot. At some point after dawn, the priest had removed himself and could not resist leaving a typical Ramirez joke behind over spending the night in a Protestant establishment. Well, he could stow that nonsense because Becker would be dropping in at the mission chapel later to check on him and ensure that the cut wasn't showing signs of infection.

Then the knocking started up again, and Becker remembered why he'd crawled from his cot in the first place.

"Pastor Becker!" Nathan Ramsay's voice called. "You in there?"

In two steps, he reached for the door and pulled it open, startling the young black man who looked up at him with disturbingly serious eyes. For a second, his stomach sank as he expected to hear the worst. Had Hiram Wells done something even more horrid last night? Something to his person from which there was no return?

"Nathan, what's wrong?" he asked.

"Something's happened," Nathan said, words that again tripped Becker's nerves. Then he completed his statement, and Becker felt lightheaded with relief. "Marshal Wells needs your assistance at the jail."

CHAPTER TWELVE

By the time Nathan returned with Becker on his heels, curious as an old hound, Hiram had meticulously closed the Venetian blinds on the window just enough to keep prying eyes out but let enough light. The glare on the glass from outside would also help. After the two men were inside, he closed and locked the door.

Becker sniffed the air thoroughly before his nose wrinkled up, his eye on the doorknob as if he might bolt. "Nathan said the Evans brothers are dead. What happened?"

"He warn you how?"

"I suspect it wasn't natural causes. You finally shoot them, Marshal?" This was spoken with such bone dryness that Hiram couldn't tell if it was supposed to be humorous or not.

"*No,*" he responded a little more defensively than intended.

"So, what happened?"

"See for yourself. *Wait.* Just know I didn't do this. I came in this morning with my kids. We were even bringing them some biscuits from the Raskin."

He closed his eyes and pinched the bridge of his nose, feeling that panic stirring within. If he didn't watch himself, he'd start rambling aimlessly. It didn't help that he'd had some kind of blackout last night while in this very building. But if he'd had something to do with it, there would have been blood all over him. He would have *known* it was him. Hell, even if he'd tried to rinse off blood, plenty would have remained on his sleeves, and the icy water from the pump would have jarred him out of whatever stupor had overcome him. All of that had spun through his mind before Nathan arrived. He could at least explain that much away. Furthermore, he had not touched *anything* or unlocked the cells for a closer look at the bodies.

He took a breath, dealing with the disgusting stink in the air, and looked at his deputy. "Nathan, watch the front?"

"Yessir." He assumed a place at the window where he could peer between the blinds.

Becker looked Hiram up and down, one brow perfectly arched in discrimination. "Did you sleep in those clothes?"

"No." He winced, looked down at his good vest and trousers, the sleeves on his best shirt rolled up. He'd removed his coat and hat and hung them by the door as usual. "Yes," he owned up. "I ended up staying at the Palace." He decided not to mention that he'd come back here for a moment last night only to retrieve his son's pulp pages. That would complicate the narrative right now. "Just look at the bodies, but don't say you weren't warned."

"Oh, the smell is warning enough." Becker turned and finally took in the scene. Then his face went from a screwed up, braced expression to something Hiram could not read at all. The muscles relaxed into a blank canvas painted in the middle with that sizeable white mustache. His watery gray eyes darted from one cell and its expired occupant to the other. Finally, slowly, his brows drew together, and that was something Hiram could translate a little bit. As had been the case with Richard Oliver's body being found in the gulch years ago, Becker shifted from doctor and preacher to investigator with surprising readiness. Fascination consumed him as he stared for a moment longer, evaluating his task.

Hiram did not like calling the man in, but there was a specialty there that had been helpful before.

Becker removed a mostly unused pencil from the pocket of his coat before he draped it over one of the desk chairs. Then he rolled up his sleeves. "Open the cells," he said, "and hand me that lamp."

Hiram did so, then gave him space to move back and forth from one cell to the other. He watched Becker squat down and hover the lamp over each Evans brother. Over each head. Over each neck stump and the mess trailing from it. Over each pulpy heart that appeared to have been thrown aside like rubbish. The light cast over the gleaming red of exposed and torn flesh, caught the cloudy blue of Frank Evans' open eyes that looked like they may have been frozen in terror at the moment of death. The dead man's mouth gaped as if he'd started to scream, while his younger brother's face had a more blissful, dumbfounded look on it.

Becker straightened and craned his chin steeply, raised the lamp as he looked straight up at the ceiling, then back down again. The pool of light caught on the now dried, crystalline residue of a puddle of piss around the lower region of Frank's torso. He daintily prodded at each heart with the end of the pencil, turned the crushed organ over with a *plop* to see both sides, arranged the splay of arteries still attached. Squishes and meaty slips sounded as he turned full attention to the bodies and poked at them, slid the pencil inside the holes in their upper stomachs just below the junction of the ribs, confirming that it went in at an upward angle under and into the chest cavity.

After what felt an agonizingly long wait, Becker finally spoke up. "It's strange enough there's so little blood. It should be all over the place, even on the ceiling. Those hearts should have leaked it out around them, too. Some has escaped through the cracks in the floor, of course, but there should be whole *ponds* around these bodies. It would also be impossible for any killer to avoid leaving footprints in it."

Hiram had already made this deduction to remove himself as a suspect, but he felt far better having someone else confirm it. This was not like the case of Richard Oliver, who was murdered and bled out before his body was moved and dumped into the gulch to look like an accident. The Evans brothers had not been taken from the jail, killed, then put back in their cells. There would have still been blood trails, whether in small drips or smears in other areas of the jail.

"Someone came in through either the front or back door," he said, "got into each cell separately, killed each brother… separately… because that's the only way it could have been done, right? Then they locked up on their way out? Why the hell lock back up again? It would have taken reversed lock picking to do that. I had the front door and cell keys on me, and the back door only has an inside bolt. I always take the keys with me when I've got someone in the lockup."

Then something else occurred to him. He walked over to the safe and dialed it open to find Frank Evans' gun on the shelf right where he'd left it along with the three remaining bullets.

"Think there could've been a third accomplice?" Nathan asked from his watch post. "Someone who wanted to silence 'em?"

121

Hiram gave it a moment's thought. "Maybe, but if he could break in that way, he might as well free them. This looks like some kind of angry vendetta."

On that note, he found Becker staring at him, the light of the lamp in his hand cast on one side of his face and emphasized a look of intense scrutiny. "I know someone who would have it out for them," he said pointedly.

"Fuck you, Pastor," Hiram snapped before he could control it.

"Hey now," Nathan's calm voice cut through his boss' fleeting rage. "Ain't no way anyone would believe you could do something like this, Marshal."

"I was not *accusing* anyone," Becker clarified, "just pointing out the awkwardness of the situation after last night's events."

He has no idea, Hiram thought and put a damper on himself before his nerves betrayed him again.

Becker rose from his crouch, stepped out of the cell, brought the lamp back to the desk, and set it down. "I would support that disgruntled accomplice theory except that I cannot tell how these injuries were inflicted without closer examination."

"Of course, you can tell. Someone cut off their heads, stabbed them through the stomach to get up in there and cut out their hearts."

"That's not what I mean, Marshal. Not just stabbed or cut," Becker corrected him. "*Tore* out their hearts."

"What do you mean?" Hiram said, wanting to understand how a poke with a pencil could deduce so much already.

"These hearts are a mess but not from being cut out. Cuts are neat, but these are ripped up." Becker gestured him back into the cell, bringing the lamp along again, and both men crouched around Frank Evans, leaving his little brother in peace for the time being. Nathan kept glancing at them, raising his head to try to see around, to listen in. Becker held up the pencil and handed its clean end to Hiram. "Take it, just slide it up in there slowly."

"Alright." Hiram did as instructed, winced at the sound of the wet slide, felt sick as the wooden rod slipped readily in. The cavity was so wide that he could stir it around.

"See, that's no mere stab wound. Muscles close back in around a knife. Those in there are torn wide open. You feel that to the side and the other?"

"Yeah?" Hiram suppressed a gag reflex, swallowed hard.

"You're past the stomach and liver. They've been shoved aside or to the back. To either side of the ribs, there're the lungs, but you get to the middle of them…"

"And there's where the heart normally goes," Hiram gasped and absently prodded deeper, finding the pencil's tip came up against the vacancy in the middle of all the other organs that Becker described. If he pushed the rod in any further, he'd lose it. It was disgusting but powerfully fascinating, too. "Are you saying something as broad as a forearm and hand made this hole?"

"I'm not saying anything yet."

He drew the pencil out and stared at streaks of blackened blood on its shaft. "Is that color normal?"

"No, it's not," Becker said. "As I said, I'll need to conduct an autopsy. Also…" His open hand hovered over Evans' head then pointed to the shreds of skin and muscle that had once connected his neck to his shoulders. "These decapitations are not from any cut. The skin and muscles are torn in such a way as to suggest…" His brow furrowed again.

"Well, get on with it," Hiram urged him.

"Their heads were *twisted* off, Marshal. The heart removal is baffling enough, but the heads are something that would take a lot of strength. Humanly impossible if you ask me. Think about it. An animal like a wolf can drag a rotting deer carcass by the head, and the neck won't release. Muscles, bones, tendons are strong connectors well after death. It's the same with a man as it is a deer. It takes gnawing, twisting, ripping."

"You've got a disturbing way of thinking, Becker," Hiram said. He stood and took a long, deep breath. "And what about all the blood? Where'd it go?"

"That…" Becker shook a finger absently at the air, staring in thought for a long moment. "That I can't explain. Just let me examine them in better light. If we can get them over to the clinic, I can do that."

"This rate, blood or no blood," Nathan said, "we are as much suspect."

"Yeah," Hiram muttered. *Especially me.* "All right," he concluded as new theories formed in his thoughts. They were all over the place, too many grasping for that one cohesive, believable explanation that was not soon coming. "For whatever reason, whoever did this might still be around and might even be baiting us." *Baiting me.* It all felt too personal.

Why else leave the Evanses in the jail to be discovered like this? "I don't want to spook what's left of the town, not after last night."

"Hell, you're lucky the town ain't gathered 'round for a hangin' already," Nathan said. "With all of those witnesses, no judge would call you in for leavin' out the trial."

"Details, Nathan," Hiram sighed patiently.

"Right, jus' sayin'."

"Damn, I already sent a telegram to Tombstone about the arrest last night. Sheriff Slaughter should be responding any time now." Any number of things might happen then. Slaughter might send a posse up to Mica Bend, or he might ask Hiram to deliver the package himself. The *package* that should be two perfectly healthy, whole, and *living* individuals.

"He's pretty reasonable though, ain't he?" Nathan asked. "He ain't gonna think you had something to do with this." Something caught his attention, and he looked back out through the blinds. "Heads up, here comes Watkins. You've got about thirty paces."

"Shit," Hiram hissed. "He can't see this. He'll just hamper our investigation."

"But you gotta throw him a bone," Nathan warned. "He's gettin' closer."

Hiram looked pointedly at Becker.

"I *won't* say anything," the pastor insisted and took back the gore-smeared pencil with carefully pinched fingers.

"Twenty paces," Nathan counted down. "Oh, wait, Terry Wilkes just intercepted him."

Hiram threw up his hands. "All right, I'll stall him. You two figure out how to get them over to the church.

"I'll get my buckboard," Nathan volunteered. "We can take 'em out the back door once you distract the mayor."

"Good, that works." Then a new thought occurred to him, and Hiram's chest grew heavy. "Damn it. Caleb saw them. My kid saw *this*."

"He's on the move again," Nathan announced

"Then get out there," Becker said. "Take care of Watkins and then take care of Caleb. That boy needs his father."

"Ten paces," Nathan warned.

Hiram nodded vacantly, thoughts still a consuming whirl in his head. At that very moment, a loud sputter sounded from the lower end of Frank Evans' body as a postmortem fart released and filled the immediate space with a stench far worse than the first. *"Oh my God,"* he gasped.

Nathan pulled a face and dragged his neckerchief up over his nose and mouth.

Becker, not quite as fazed by the behavior of corpses, decided that was a good time to be clever. "Ah. You *see*, Marshal, you *are* still capable of invoking the Almighty."

When Hiram stepped outside, hat in place and coat over his arm, he held onto the doorknob until he felt the vibration and click as Nathan turned the lock back over from the inside for good measure. He was just in time as Watkins was about to step up onto the boardwalk, his black cane poised in dandy perfection.

"Marshal, I thought you might like to debrief me on the situation, now that things are much calmer," he said curtly.

"Mayor," Hiram replied, touched the brim of his hat, and proceeded to shrug into his coat. "Well, we have a new situation. The prisoners are very sick this morning."

"Sick? Good heavens, with what?"

Death, he felt like saying. *They're sick from death*. He elected to fine-tune the story so that it was more of a fib than an outright lie. "We don't know. I hope they didn't spread it around the opera house, but the doc's in there with them now. We figure it's best to quarantine the jail for the time being. You shouldn't go in there. Smells horrible."

Watkins took an impressive step back and remained off the boardwalk. "It's not... it's not cholera, is it?"

Given how worried the very idea seemed for the mayor, Hiram ran with that. He pursed his lips in feigned thought, fingered his chin. "I don't know. Pastor Becker will report when he knows something, but probably best to stay away from him, too."

"Yes, makes sense. And you? You were directly in Frank Evans' face last night. Are you sure you're well?"

"So far, I feel fine, but yeah, best to keep a distance from me, too. Just in case." A strangely satisfying pleasure bubbled up in him to be able to say that and have Watkins agree with him. "Don't say anything to anyone yet. It could be nothing, so we don't want a panic."

"But if it *is* cholera, we must consider setting up a quarantine ward."

Hiram nodded along, keeping that idea kindled. "It is far too soon to say. Frank Evans had the back door trots pretty badly last night, though, so..."

Watkins' face screwed up to that. He was at a clear loss, all but tripping over his own feet.

Hiram had never known the mayor was so frightened of the disease. There had to be some old and probably terrible reason for that, but he didn't have the time to care. All he knew was that every time he took a step forward, Watkins took one back. Hiram smiled inside and exploited that just a little more by laying a hand over his lower belly and wincing as if he'd just had an intestinal cramp. "Ow."

"What? What ow?"

"Oh, nothing. Probably the biscuits from the Raskin. Now, I need to check on my children. Caleb and Ellie were with me when we discovered the Evanses this morning." Not that Watkins ever went near his children, but now he would keep further away, at least for now. "Try not to worry too much, Titus," he added. "We're all in good hands with the doc." That came out with a little too much acid.

"Yes," Watkins agreed. "Yes, we are."

"Now, if you'll excuse me. I have things to do, and I don't want to get in Becker's way."

"Right." He gave a jittery nod and turned to walk toward his office while Hiram headed northwestward back toward home.

As he walked, his thoughts blackened by the second. What if the killer *was* still in town? Did he have it out for anyone else? That seemed unlikely. The Evanses felt like a very specific target, bringing him back to Nathan's theory of a vendetta, especially given the brutality of the murders. Still, that did not help him relax or feel that the citizens of the Bend were any safer. His previous search for the town's missing schoolteacher surfaced in his thoughts, and he wondered if it could somehow be connected. Unlikely, given how different the cases. They were over a week apart, and while one was a disappearance, the other was a total punch in the face.

He had just gotten Teddy out of the livery, mounted up, and was trotting past the mercantile when old Fraleigh happened to come out and wave him down. "Mr. Fraleigh, yessir?" he called out and steered his horse closer.

Fraleigh, wiry and small, had always seemed older than he probably was with his chalk-white hair and spectacles. Utmost, he was a patient man, and given how he'd been harassed by Caleb and Ellie over the mail for weeks now, Hiram couldn't appreciate that enough. "Marshal, we have a problem. I sent your message out to Tombstone last night. Figured I might as well. Didn't get a confirmation, so I tried again this morning."

"Oh?" Hiram saw that Fraleigh had the same slip of paper in his hands that he'd written the message on last night. If Slaughter hadn't gotten word on Frank Evans' capture, then it bought a little more time to make sure the story was straight, or hopefully, time enough to *solve* how two prisoners had been brutally murdered while secured in *locked* cells in a *locked* building. The matter of their blood being missing seemed like more of a technicality. "Huh, well…"

"Well," Fraleigh continued, sounding troubled, "see, I just ran some tests, sent out codes to Benson and San Simon. I'm not getting any responses back."

"You mean the lines out of here are down in both directions?" That changed everything all over again.

"Appears so," Fraleigh said.

"This just keeps getting better and better," Hiram grumbled under his breath.

"Sir?"

"Nothing, just…" He sighed and gave a conflicted blessing. "Keep trying then," he said. "Keep running tests. Let me know if you get a response."

On the map, Tombstone, Benson, and San Simon all formed a long, acute triangle with Mica Bend almost in the middle along its top line. If none of those three were getting a signal, then the Bend was essentially cut off from everything around it. Only the train connected the towns along its route, and that was of little use now. Thus, he could only hope that a telegrapher in one of those towns, or others along the same wire routes, would notice soon enough that their own messages were not being confirmed. Until about a decade ago, it had been common for the Apache and other Indians to damage the lines, and some farm families cut down the poles to use them for building or firewood, but those concerns had, for the most part, faded with time. Once a problem was identified, a Signal Corps crew would scout along the lines looking for the area of the interruption, which at best would be found within a day and repaired.

Hiram hoped a day was all he needed.

Fraleigh nodded and held up Hiram's leaf of paper again with purpose. "I shall do that."

"Thank you." Hiram started to face the street again.

"And Marshal?" Fraleigh added.

He withheld from tossing the reins a moment, looked back at the little man.

"No one blames you for anything that happened last night," he said. "You did what you had to do. Heck, if I'd known about those boys being there, I'd have panicked, probably made it more dangerous."

The platitude did some good for Hiram's mood. "Thank you, Mr. Fraleigh," he repeated, then he reined Teddy on for home. He paused again as he rode past Wagon Town and looked through the opening in the cottonwood grove that served as a natural gateway. He could see only two covered wagons on the far side of the circle when there had been as many as five a week ago. There was still a tent or two, and he could see the scant flicker of a campfire. Wood smoke billowed gently through the trees, illuminated by rays of sunlight. He thought he could hear a woman crying deep in there, from inside one of the tents. Regrettably enough, the inhabitants of the mini village had always been so transient he had never had a chance to get to know too many of them. Only their names and faces remained embedded in his memory if he had officially met them. A handful of independent prospectors, like Seth Raines, had stayed to stubbornly try to find another vein out around the Arduous range, but if he were to guess from this view, they were rapidly giving up. It appeared some may have hauled out this morning after word of the holdup at the opera house got out to those who had not attended.

Could Maria Oliver have just given up, too? Rather than put herself through the pain of saying goodbye and making arrangements for the school, could she have hitched a ride out of town early with some of the Wagon Towners? That almost kicked off a whole new series of thoughts that he had neither the time nor the energy for. By this point, he was starting to feel tired again, though thankfully not as exhausted as he had last night. Checking his pocket watch, he saw that there was still another hour left in the morning. He hadn't eaten. He readily recalled the kerchief full of Miz Raskin's biscuits being kicked aside in all of the commotion. Quickly he heeled on Teddy before any other investigative urges claimed his attention. He'd have to come back to Wagon Town later after he had better organized his questions.

Upon reaching the barnyard, he noticed more than a few chickens were running loose and felt a new dread. He unsaddled Teddy, turned him into the corral with Remington, and started for the back of the house where the chicken coop was positioned adjacent in the back yard, convenient for retrieving eggs for the kitchen.

"Oh no," he murmured as he found Lucinda sitting on the back stoop. Her face was buried in her hands, her sunny hair making a halo of sweat-tamped frizz around her head. "Happened again, didn't it?" he asked as he headed toward her and took a seat next to her, his lower back not liking the maneuver one bit.

She turned and hugged him immediately, reminding him of last night's ordeal and again feeling like he wasn't holding a teenager but his little girl.

"Damn coyote got a bunch of pullets, Papa," she said through a series of sniffles.

He couldn't begrudge her a swear or two now and then, though her mother might have. Looking up, he saw that the wire fence, so meticulously built, had a surprisingly large hole dug underneath it. The boxy coop within, also well-constructed, was intact, but its ramp was knocked askew. Feathers of every variety littered the ground, a few trailing away from the mounds of a few dead young chickens that appeared to have been killed for sport.

"I'm sorry, sweetheart." He knew how much that coop meant to her. Hell, it meant a lot to *him*, and part of him was angry for her sake, but another could not hate a wild animal for acting on its nature. *This* sonofabitch, however, had been nothing but persistent, and he was ready to shoot it for his daughter's sake. "Soon as I can, I'll help you dig a deeper trench to bury the wire."

He felt her nod against him then he lifted her chin. She looked up at him with those big brown eyes that kept breaking his heart, and he nudged away one of her tears with the back of a knuckle. *So... so... like her mother.*

"Fill in that hole good for now, and get Ellie to help you round up the loose hens, all right?" He waved a hand toward the furthest edges of the property. "Take those dead ones out there, spread them a little. Maybe they'll keep that critter occupied a while."

She nodded and got to her feet, dusting off the seat of her skirt and straightening a yellowed white apron with tiny, faded pink flowers on it. Hiram remembered that apron too well. Rachel used to wear it when she did chores, dusted herself off just like that. Straightened her hair, just like that. Quickly he looked elsewhere before he was reminded of her too much. "Where's Caleb?"

"Inside. He's been awfully quiet. Ellie, too, for once."

He gave a small smile to that. Ellie was never very quiet about anything for very long.

"Did something else happen at the jail?"

Hiram paused midway as he started to rise, the sudden stop in momentum sending a charge up his entire back and into his hips. He suppressed a grimace of pain and forced himself into a full stand. "I guess they weren't ready to see the Evans brothers again."

That seemed as good an answer as any to her. She pushed another loose lock back from her face and turned to re-evaluate the chicken coop. "Well," she sniffled, "I'd better start filling in that hole. Send Ellie out, please."

He nodded and stepped up, pulled the door open, and entered through the kitchen. He shrugged off his coat and took off his hat to deposit them over a chair—he'd worry about putting them away properly later— and then lifted a tin dome from a serving plate in the center of the small dining table to find some of Lucinda's dried fruit pie left. He broke off a piece, nibbled it to steady himself, then he went over to the sink, pumped water and splashed his face, gulped large handfuls of it, realizing how thirsty he was after not eating or drinking much of anything other than coffee and last night's sour mash for the last few days. Refreshed a little, he braced himself and headed through the little corridor, past the master bedroom, to the front parlor where he found his son sitting in a chair by the main window. Facing north, the parlor was the coolest room in the house. Its potbelly stove had been left untended overnight, and neither Caleb nor Lucinda had bothered to fire it up this morning.

Caleb sat in a chair staring out the window, past the yard and toward the road and its lining of oaks and cottonwoods. A few of the story pamphlets rested in his slack hands, but a few were scattered on the floor at his feet. Hiram was almost relieved, hoping it meant his son had recovered from the sobering perspective he'd expressed earlier and now begun to read them once more. If anything, he needed the escape. Or maybe, Hiram considered, they seemed particularly tasteless now that Caleb had gotten too good of a look at what a mangled corpse really looked like.

Hiram walked to the narrow stairwell and called, "Ellie girl, you up there?"

There was a distant shuffling noise, the sound of a chair moving. "Yeah, Papa?"

"Come down here and go help out your sister, please."

The whirlwind that comprised his youngest daughter appeared as a silhouette on the top landing and stomped down the steps into full view. She had her doll tucked firmly in the crook of her arm as usual, and Hiram felt far too much relief to see that she did not seem affected at all. His attempt to cover her eyes must have worked because they were sharp and curious, not bleary with tears or trauma. Even last night's ordeal seemed forgotten.

"Lucinda needs your help with the coop," he instructed her and gave her a steer toward the kitchen.

"Wook!" she chirped, then opened her mouth wide and reached in to wiggle one of her front lower baby teeth. "Anothew is comin' out."

"Well, looka there." Hiram cupped a hand under her chin for a better look, inwardly smiled at the gap she already had, soon to be widened. He'd been through this twice already with Lucinda and Caleb, and to see the process for the third time was a tiny agony, especially now.

"Can we see Mama, wike you said? I wanna show hehw."

The reminder caught him for a moment, and then he nodded. The agony was not so tiny after all. "Yes, of course. It will have to be much later, though, okay?" She bobbed her head to that, satisfied, and scrambled off. He waited until her stomps made it through the kitchen, and he heard the rear door slam. After a deep breath, he turned to his next urgent task. "Caleb?" he began. "You all right, son?"

Haunted eyes turned and looked at him, blinked with a mechanical slowness as if Caleb had been so lost in thought that it took a few seconds for him to fit back into his own body, let alone his own head, and register the question. The crust of something white clung to the corner of his mouth and chin. A sour smell wafted in the air around him.

"You throw up?" Hiram asked.

The boy nodded vacantly.

That was not surprising at all. Hiram figured it must have happened on the way home. "Look, if you want to talk about what you saw, you can now, with me."

Caleb's eyes shifted down to the papers in his hands. "Oh," he murmured vacantly and bent over to pick up the ones that had dropped.

Hiram eased into the chair across from him, waited for his son to retrieve them. Caleb tamped them into a neat stack and laid them on the narrow round-top table next to the most decorative lamp in the house. Rachel had prized it for its reverse-painted globe of flowers and vines and its inviting, perfect glow.

"I'm sorry," Caleb said, his voice gravelly from stomach acid burn, "I was just looking through them again. I didn't mean to... I mean I... Those men," he started over, "their heads were... torn off..."

Not *cut* off. *Torn* off. That alone told Hiram how much he had seen. He nodded. "Yeah," he said weakly. It still made his own stomach turn.

"And they had holes in them." On one hand, he pinched all of his fingers together and pressed them against his shirt, around the area of his upper stomach, at the junction of the rib cage, and then his hand angled slightly. Hiram swallowed hard to see that it was the same angle that Becker's pencil had gone into Frank Evans' chest cavity. "Their hearts were taken out."

"I'm sorry you saw so much," Hiram whispered.

Caleb stared into space for a moment longer, and then when he finally shifted his gaze to his father, he looked almost scared to speak. "They looked like they were killed... the way you kill vampires."

Hiram blinked, and his mind went perfectly blank for all of five seconds. Then, what exactly his son had just said, hit him like a phantom punch. *"What?"*

The boy took a breath but remained serious. "You drive a stake through the heart and cut off the head. Sometimes the heart is removed, too."

Before he could stop himself, Hiram rose and paced, ran a hand through his hair, gritted his teeth before he said something too harsh. He wished his brother was right here in front of him, handy for a good decking because this was the last straw on how much those stupid tales had colored his kid's thinking. For a moment, it had seemed Caleb found them too irrelevant, and now he had switched back just like that. "I can't believe I'm hearing this. You've been reading too much of that crap. That's it. I'm writing your uncle and telling him to stop sending them."

"No, Papa." Caleb remained in the chair. "That's how it *looked*. That's all I'm sayin'."

Hiram's nerves hummed louder than a telegraph wire, and pressure built between his temples. "Those men *died*, boy. It's no joke. Do you know what it could mean for me if this gets out?" His boots fell heavier on the floor as his pacing developed longer strides and faster spins from one direction back to the other. "I could lose my job. Someone broke into the jail, killed the Evanses in a very bad… you *saw* how they were killed… and slipped out again. Nathan and I can't even explain how. Know who saw them last alive? Me and Nathan. That's it. We're *both* up the creek. I don't want to hear about any damn vampires from that pulp." He bit back the harsher language he might more readily use around Silas or other adult men.

Caleb cringed, his pale brows rising in a look that hovered somewhere between complete confusion and fear. "I'm s-s-sorry."

As if the boy's eyes were not enough to halt his tirade, that slight stutter hit home. Hiram looked away frantically, ashamed of himself. His gaze landed on the pamphlets, and his son's actual words caught up with him.

That's how it looked. That's all I'm sayin'.

Caleb had not been serious, just making an observation, one that his young mind could understand. The murders were incomprehensible in both how and why. Hiram had seen violence, maybe not on any battlefield, but he and Silas had ventured into enough of the *wrong* establishments when they were young, randy, and stupid. They'd witnessed men stabbed or shot, seen noses crushed and skulls broken in brawls. But brawl injuries made sense. He'd met men who fought on both sides of the war, saw that they were missing limbs or an eye, all of it grounded in the explainable.

"No, I'm sorry," he said. Pinching the bridge of his nose, he dropped back into the chair, leaned his elbows on his knees and *breathed* for a moment. "I am, Caleb. I deeply apologize. This…" Sometimes, there was nothing more relieving than stating the obvious. "This is a huge mess I have to deal with, and it's got me scrambled in the head." He considered confessing that he'd had a blackout last night but couldn't imagine a twelve-year-old completely grasping the aftermath of that or the anxiety. "Let's just…" Another breath. "Let's just keep this quiet for now, okay?" He looked up, hopeful that he'd undone a little of the damage from his outburst.

"Yeah, Papa, of course." Caleb blinked, shrugged sheepishly. "I only meant that…"

"I know what you meant," he said. "I know now. Sorry, your papa is a mite wound up."

"Well, *yeah*." The sarcasm dripped, and the old Caleb began to shine through again. "Don't worry. I won't say anything."

"Good man. Now, if you go into town, I want you to keep your eyes peeled and stay away from the jail for now. You go straight where you're going, whether it's to see Fraleigh about the mail or anything else, you go there and straight back, you stick to the main thoroughfare, no alleys or back ways, and I don't want *any* of you out after dark. Hear me? And make sure Ellie stays quiet about it, too." He would have to repeat the same rules to the girls before he headed back out again.

"She didn't see anything," Caleb assured him.

"Good, but make sure she doesn't flap about Papa not letting her see whatever she didn't see."

The boy finally cracked a smile, and Hiram's heart dropped a little of the aching weight that had piled on. Maybe, if he could just keep it together and stop flying off the handle, he'd get through this.

CHAPTER THIRTEEN

Small though the church was, it loomed in all its weathered-white boxiness, and Hiram approached with an untempered sneer on his face as he had for the last seven months, but he was relieved to see the tail end of Nathan's buckboard peering out from the rear of the building. Choosing to go through the front was a diversion technique because he was suddenly concerned that someone might see and ask why he'd gone in via the clinic. Of everyone in the town, only Becker and Silas truly knew about the crisis of faith that had consumed him. The effort employed keeping his head down as he passed between the narrow pews of the sanctuary, using the lowered brim of his hat as a blind to the altar and cross.

Once to the right side of the altar, he lifted his head and went through the rear door into the clinic-cum-rectory. The herbal smells accosted him, far more welcome than the stench in the jail. Nathan and Becker were in the process of heaving one of the bodies onto the examination table. It was bundled in a length of old burlap that was giving them no end of trouble. Becker's face was an uncomfortable shade of red, so Hiram stepped in to help, impatient to see the examination get started.

He took hold of the corners on what appeared to be the head and shoulders end, while Nathan had the feet. Grunting, they hoisted the mass onto the table then cringed when the coarse wrapping came undone, and the dark red of shredded flesh and loosened vertebrae peered through the gap. Hiram already recognized that this one was the corpse of Frank Evans, so it was his brother who still lay in his makeshift shroud on the floor next to the extra cot.

"How'd it go?" he asked and took off his hat to wipe his brow. "Anyone see you?"

"Don't think so," Nathan said. "We took 'em out the back like you said. I had to bolt the door and go out the front to make sure the whole office was locked up. How's Caleb?"

"He's got a strange way of coping."

A hollow *thunk* sounded on the end of the table as Becker sat down a separate clutch of burlap: the dead man's head. When marshal and deputy both eyed him irritably, he muttered, *"Verzeihung."* Then he unwrapped the body, left the burlap under it to tumble over the edges like a tablecloth.

While Becker positioned the head and began removing Evans' upper clothing, Hiram stepped aside with Nathan to give his debriefing. "Appears the telegraph lines are down, so I can't say if Sheriff Slaughter got my message this morning. Given the possibility that our killer is still in town somewhere, I'm reconsidering keeping this too secret. Slaughter will have to know, and we may need his backup."

Nathan nodded. "What do you need me to do?"

"Take the buckboard and whatever you need for the night, get to Tombstone and tell Slaughter. Tell him everything that happened at the opera house and of the arrest but hold off on explaining *this*." He gestured at the table and its occupant. "I think I better do that myself when he gets here. I'll check out the jail again, keep working the town with patrols, questions, whatever it takes."

Nathan nodded along with that. "If I leave now, I can probably reach Tombstone by late tomorrow morning. Don't know how long it'll take Sheriff Slaughter to prepare to come back here."

"Check by Fraleigh's one last time before you go, see if he ever got a confirmation on the lines. If he didn't, then head on out. Best case, the first message did make it through, or the lines are already being fixed, and you end up running into the sheriff while he's on his way here."

"All right, and what about Watkins?"

"I can keep him in the dark a little longer."

"Don't know how you diverted him the first time, but he sure don't wanna come near us now."

Hiram cracked a grin at that. "I have my ways."

After it became clear that no telegraph response would be forthcoming and Nathan had hit the road to deliver the original message in person, Hiram spent more time at the jail than he had intended and far less time checking in on the rest of the town.

At first, he moved from cell to cell and tested the locks by repeatedly turning the keys in them, but there was nothing wrong with them other than that the one on the right tended to stick.

Finally, he opened the blinds as far as he dared to let in light and placed the oil lamps around the pools of dried blood and piss in Frank Evans' cell, and then his focus deepened like a splinter that could not be extracted by any means.

He tied a neckerchief over his nose and mouth to dull the smell and dropped into a squat to discreetly get closer. There were three blood pools lined up. As already noted by Becker, they were far smaller than a human body should spill with injuries like that. The first was where Evans' head had come to rest, more of a smear than a pool. The second aligned where the stump of his neck had left a trail of shredded muscle and a string of dislocated vertebrae. It was also more of a smear, though there was some pooling near its base where the larger hunk of open flesh had rested. Then there was the actual pool that had accumulated directly under his torso. It had dried into a red-brown stain that had cracked into dozens of puzzle pieces, like a dried pond, with a perimeter of yellow residue around its edges. Just under the bunk was the smear where his crushed heart had lain. Only a thorough scrubbing with lye *might* lift it all from the floorboards. The same went for the stains in the younger Evans brother's cell.

Hiram looked up at the ceiling multiple times as he changed his position, searching for patterns. It was the task of insanity, insistently searching for something that simply was not there, as if he would *finally* spot that *one* blood spatter that had eluded him. Even then, he didn't expect it to tell him much.

Until it suddenly occurred to him what *else* was missing.

Flies, he thought. No matter how much the jail had been shut up for the day, there should still be flies. The coppery but foul scent of the blood and the stink of shit remained, but no flies had slipped into the building to gather in the cells and complicate his examination.

Closing his eyes, he recalled the scene as it had been discovered, from the positions of the bodies and the heads. Their faces held entirely different expressions. Harlan had looked oblivious, eyes open but hooded, mouth slack. His big brother had been wide-eyed, mouth agape as if he'd started to scream.

He saw, Hiram thought. *He saw the killer.* Harlan didn't know what hit him, but Frank had seen it coming, maybe even witnessed his brother's murder first.

But there remained the question of how said killer had gone from one cell to the other without unlocking them, or even how no one had reported hearing at least one scream come from within the jail in the wee hours of darkness.

Finally convinced the stains and the faces in his head would tell him nothing more, Hiram put the lamps back where they belonged, closed the blinds, stepped out of the building, and locked up. He kept the neckerchief on purely for the sake of appearances should Watkins spot him. He'd have to keep pretending there was a cholera threat, but at this rate, cholera seemed like it would be easier to deal with than *this*.

The rectory door had an *Out* sign hanging on its front, but fortunately, no one had needed medical aid. The smell inside, by that time, had risen to new repugnance and penetrated cloth and cupped hand. Hiram noticed that flies still did not seem very interested, but Becker was undoubtedly absorbed. The long strip of rag tied over his nose and mouth did not look nearly enough as he dared to get his face disturbingly close to the edges of torn skin and muscle for Hiram's comfort. The marshal watched as he poked and prodded with tweezers, made incisions in arteries only to shake his head as little to nothing came out. He'd filled the bottom of a glass vial with a blackish gooey substance, which he said was blood, and placed that on the counter for a closer look later. Next to it, Frank Evans' already autopsied heart sat stored in a jar.

Once Becker felt he'd done all he could with Frank's corpse, Hiram helped him switch it out on the table for Harlan's and left him to it. He shared his observations about the flies and the different facial expressions, which Becker didn't seem to take much stock in.

By late afternoon, Hiram had had enough of corpses and getting nowhere. He returned to the house and retrieved Ellie for the promised visit to Rachel's grave while Lucinda prepared supper with, for once, Caleb's help.

With Ellie in the saddle in front of him, he rode back up the street for the final time that day, noticing that the quietude had reached a new low but relieved to see a familiar cart, hitched up to Arsenic, parked outside the Palace. Silas had made it back from his run to Benson.

The sun barely peered over the western horizon when father and daughter reached the other end of town. Hiram stood just inside the fence around the cemetery and stared west, toward a soothing, rosy sunset, as he listened to Ellie's little voice chatter over her mother's resting place. She had come with a handful of paper flowers that Lucinda helped her make. They were half crumpled from being held too tightly, but Rachel wouldn't have minded the least.

"This one's fwom Wucinda, and this one's for Caweb."

A fall breeze muted her voice slightly, so Hiram kept an ear cocked to listen in. He didn't need to look at the grave to see it, for it remained behind his eyes at all times with its carefully painted letters on a simple wood plaque.

RACHEL WELLS
BELOVED WIFE AND MOTHER
1852 - 1888

"These are aw fwom meeee. Okay, one is fwom Papa."

"She died just this year?" a man's calm voice startled him.

"And wook, Mama, Imma woose anothehw toof!"

He turned to find Cage Edwards, who was standing outside the fence as well dressed as he had been at the after-party. *Too perfect*, Hiram thought and did not delve deeper into how that was possible in an environment like this with its dust and wind. He'd heard no coach wheels or horse approaching, so he assumed the man had walked into town.

"Last March," he specified quietly.

"How?"

"Typhoid." He left out the finer details that would drag the memories out of their dark gully and all but paralyze him from interacting at all.

"My sympathies for your loss." Something in his gray eyes looked almost like a smile, even while the lines of his mouth tightened soberly.

Hiram decided he imagined the conflicting expressions. In the reddened light of dusk, he noticed Ellie had gone quiet and turned to check on her, saw that she bowed in prayer, little hands folded together, the flowers scattered at her knees.

"Please excuse me if I startled you. Just out for an evening stroll, and I happened to see your horse at the front of the church. I wanted to thank you again for your actions last night."

Hiram tried not to roll his eyes. One more pat on the back, real or verbal, and he'd be seated at the Palace in no time draining that sour mash, especially since it was on this man's tab. "It's part of my job, Mr. Edwards."

"It's *Cage*, remember? I'd much rather you call me that."

"Cage," he corrected himself. He'd barely thought of the actor all day after the matter of the Evanses. That their bodies were just inside the back of the church several yards to his left did nothing to help him relax at all.

"Well, there are lawmen, and then there are the real protectors," Cage said. He reached into his coat, drew out what appeared to be a thin stack of cards, and held them out just at the edge of the fence. "Please, take these tickets for the show next Friday. It's the least I can do. I understand your daughter has quite the ear for Shakespeare." When Hiram did not immediately move to take them, he inched forward only slightly. "Please…"

Hiram stared at the offering, swearing he saw Cage's hand begin to shake as it hovered just over the juts of the picket, but he appeared rooted to the spot, unable to step closer. His eyes narrowed impatiently, the muscles in his face tensing.

"She does," Hiram said finally. *Thank you for making my life a little more hell for the next week.* He stepped to the fence line and reached out to take the stack.

Cage let it go readily and pulled his hand back while Hiram looked down to thumb through them, one for each Wells family member.

"Hamlet, huh?"

Cage's face relaxed, and he nodded. "It's August's favorite to perform."

There was a suggestion in that, given that *everyone* had likely noticed how much Lucinda had taken to the young and mysterious August Chandler last night, and he had seemed as taken with her. Hiram figured it best not to put too much stock in that, though. One more week and the troupe would be gone, and then supper table conversations could return to normal.

"And who will *you* be performing?" He meant for it to sound derisive, mocking his older daughter's overblown admiration for theater.

"Queen Gertrude," Cage said bluntly.

Before he could catch it, Hiram let out a snort of a laugh.

A slow smile spread on Cage's face. "Ah, you *do* have a sense of humor."

He had to admit, he liked the man, respected him, too, after how he'd coolly offered his watch to Frank Evans in exchange for letting Lucinda go. He wasn't sure he would outright call Cage a new friend, but he *did* feel some trust in him.

"What's Heaven wike, Mama?" Ellie's conversation with the grave continued.

Cage's pale gaze shifted over Hiram's shoulder. "Your little one seems to be adapting well."

"Yeah, she's like a green twig. Always snaps back." With a glance at his youngest, Hiram determined that she was well enough out of earshot to make any sense of what he said next, but he still lowered his voice. "Tell me something."

"Yes?"

"Last night, during the party, did you notice anyone else acting peculiar?"

"Well, that would be a matter for your eyes, Marshal. You're the one who remembers every face you see."

"All right, let me rephrase that." In his mind, he saw flashes of Cage's back disappearing out the batwing doors of the saloon. "You walked back to the Simpson house after midnight. Did you, by chance, see anyone lingering around the jail? Hell, anyone else out that late at all or crossing the thoroughfare?"

"No, why do you ask?"

By now, Hiram had prepared himself for such a question. "It's just, uh… Frank Evans reportedly ran with the Jack Taylor gang. If there are more of them out there than we knew of before, I figure the brothers may have been working with a third party, someone even more dangerous, lurking around in my town."

"I see, and you won't stand for that."

"I won't stand for criminal asswipes who threaten these people or my children."

Cage tilted his head as if examining that statement. The breeze stirred his hair which took on a slight glow across the top of his head as the moon rose in the southern sky. The western horizon looked muddy now, and Hiram realized he'd better be gathering up Ellie and heading home for supper.

"You think this individual is still in town?"

"Likely cut and run by now, but I can't be too careful." Then he decided it prudent to mention the telegraph lines. Anyone who had been into the mercantile today knew about it, and Mr. Fraleigh liked to assure them that "our Marshal Wells" was working around the problem. As outsiders, Cage and his troupe did not hear every piece of news or gossip, especially since they were staying at the Simpson house away from town. "By the way, the telegraph lines are down. I hope that doesn't affect any communication you need to make for your next engagement elsewhere, but I had to send my deputy to Tombstone to report the arrests. I expect Sheriff Slaughter to be arriving soon."

Soon was too ambiguous for Hiram's comfort, but it sounded better than *tomorrow, or maybe the next day.* The truth was, it could be more than two days hence, and that made him think about the horrible smell of dismembered corpses swelling beyond his ability to cope.

"I see." Pale brows drew in as Cage looked down, some thought racing through his head. "Makes sense. And what does that entail?"

"I honestly do not know. I hope the sheriff takes the Evanses off my hands. He played a big part in taking down the Jack Taylor gang. He'll be mighty interested in these two."

"Really?" The corner of Cage's lips turned up slightly.

Before Hiram could continue, Ellie slammed into his side with a knee-binding hug that nearly sent him tumbling. He stepped out of it to get his balance, found Cage smirking in amusement.

Ellie remained half wrapped around one leg while she peeped up at the actor and scrutinized him before asking, "Awe you *reawy* the king of the faiwies?"

Cage played along without a hitch, narrowed his eyes cautiously. "Can you keep a secret?"

That was enough for Ellie Wells to jump to her own conclusion. "I *knew* it!"

Hiram tweaked her nose, inducing a giggle, and began to guide her to the cemetery gate, with Cage following along outside the fence. "Well, I'd appreciate it if you report anyone or anything strange that you see." He swung the gate open and herded his youngest on.

The actor nodded and walked with them toward the front of the church before turning for the north side of the thoroughfare.

"Hey, Cage," Hiram added, "be careful. The troupe, too. I don't want to go through last night *again*." He left the actor to assume he specifically meant the holdup.

Cage only gave a pleasant, unconcerned look to that. "Of course, and it's my honor to be your second set of eyes, Marshal. Good evening to you." He nodded courteously. "And you, too, Miss Ellie."

Ellie bobbed excitedly on her feet to have been acknowledged by the great Oberon himself, and Hiram lifted her into Teddy's saddle. "All right, Sweet Pea," he said as he mounted up behind her. "Let's go home."

CHAPTER FOURTEEN

Becker had barely noticed how dimly the sun fell through the windows before he began to light more lamps. At the distant sound of voices, he'd looked out the back window at the graveyard beyond and seen, in the golden twilight, that Hiram Wells and his youngest child were out there. The little girl knelt piously before her mother's grave, hair in messy golden braids, while her father stood near the fence speaking with a visitor.

Becker squinted to make out the figure of Micajah Edwards, head of the Chamberlain Players, standing near the fence, speaking casually with the marshal. Even from here, it was clear how the man's height loomed, made all the more evident by the heavy black coat that seemed to draw the shadows in around him. Something about him disturbed Becker, but he couldn't put his finger on why. He'd witnessed how Edwards had tried to help diffuse last night's situation, putting his charisma forward for more than the entertainment of strangers. No doubt the actor and the lawman were speaking about the whole matter quietly while little Ellie held her short vigil.

Rarely, in the past months, had Becker seen Hiram Wells visit his wife's grave unless he had one or more of his children with him. He might have bottled up his own emotions, but at least he did not deny them the chances to grieve as needed.

Becker went back to his examination, positioned every candle and lamp he had around Harlan Evans, particularly his head, and proceeded to lean in for a closer look. He guessed Harlan for somewhere between seventeen and twenty, his young face frozen in cold, dull skin, milky eyes, and lids half-open. That brought him to think about the marshal's suggestion that Frank had seen his killer coming and Harlan had not. Typically, facial muscles relaxed at the time of death, so Becker would have readily dismissed such a notion, but after staring at Frank's shocked face versus his brother's almost serene mask, he began to wonder. The boy had the same blackened blood, too. Dead blood could appear black, but it was still just a dark *red*. This, however, *was* black. Iron black and relatively runny, but it was *scarce*. He'd drained as much as he could find out of the settled areas of Frank's body, and it only amounted to a few spoonfuls. Now he found Harlan's body to be in the same bloodless state. He did not bother to cut open the second heart. By now, he knew it would only reveal the same, an empty vessel like the rest of the body, so he'd placed it in a jar next to the other.

"What happened to you?" he said as he looked at the clouded eyes. Harlan's eyes had been blue like his brother's. The pupils were blown open, an element found not only in death but also pleasure as with the eyes of those who chased the dragon. But there was no way, Becker deduced, that pleasure had anything to do with *this*. He considered how Harlan had merely hustled around the opera house with a sack, collecting jewelry and money during the holdup, while it was his brother who dared to hold a town marshal hostage and strike a priest. The kid, it seemed, had just fallen in with a bad family element.

"You poor… poor… boy," he whispered. "What took your blood and tore off your head? What—?"

A cold strum traveled through his middle, and Becker looked away for a moment. He had just asked *What?* not *Who?*

"What?" he repeated and let his thoughts run out loud. "*What* could do that? A persistent animal still couldn't get into the jail and exit so neatly. A person couldn't tear off a human head. What else? Something else, something not hu…

…man."

No, he stopped himself. That was ridiculous. He took a breath, ignoring the putrid waft of the dead, and glanced toward one of his packed bookshelves. The answers were not going to be there, he thought. Despite the wide verse of his little library, the answer couldn't possibly lie in there. Could it?

Well, there was only one way to find out. He gripped Harlan's head and turned it to the side, exposed the side of what remained of his neck.

The flesh had long stiffened, the shreds of the sternocleidomastoid muscles jutting more like splinters now than meat. Hanging from beneath them were the limp tails of torn carotids. That was when Becker realized he'd been focusing all his attention on the neck stump itself, too fascinated by the tears and rips and how someone could possibly do that.

But above the jagged border where mutilation began, where the skin was still whole, he homed in on a small hole caked in the same blackened blood he'd collected from the brother.

A puncture?

He found nothing similar on the stump attached to the shoulders, so if there were others like it, they had been destroyed by the tearing and ripping when the head came off. He would have to explore Frank's head and neck again, too, see if he could locate a similar mark, but first, he'd finish with Harlan.

He reached for a scalpel and cut into the edges of the hole, brought the seam out to the edge of the torn skin, and carefully peeled it back with forceps. He sliced a little deeper, worked in until he found where the hole ended with the severed part of the upper carotid. On this, he tried to keep a stampede of thoughts and theories corralled before they grew too outlandish. Something had punctured the boy's neck to the carotid. Like an awl through leather, it had gone in with force and left some bruising in the flesh around it.

Mein Gott. Something sharp went in here, but that didn't explain the lack of blood. A transfusion apparatus would have been awkward at best to spirit into a locked cell, but it would not draw out an entire body's worth of blood like this, let alone two bodies.

Becker's thoughts were drifting hazardously back toward *what*, rather than *who*, did this when a creak sounded from the sanctuary. He straightened, his scalp and the backs of his arms tingling as nerves set off. "Hello?" he called and relaxed the forceps he was using to hold out a strip of skin. He cocked his head to listen, paid attention to his feet and where they were planted.

For a long moment of silence, he waited. There came another creak of one of the floorboards, and he knew exactly which one because it was attached to the same series of joists that ran under the wall between the sanctuary and rectory, directly under where he stood. That board had been a problem for a while now, bowed with age and in need of replacement, and someone had just stepped on it. The vibration tended to carry, always giving away visitors.

Becker's mood darkened, and he picked up one of the lamps, carried it to the door, and opened it with sudden force. The lamp light surrounded him and the door frame in an orange glow, but beyond it, the sanctuary was a pit of darkness but for the upper silhouettes of pews. Blue shafts of low moonlight were beginning to pour through the windows on the east-facing wall.

"Jimmy Callow, if you're messing about in the sanctuary again, I'm having a word with your father," he announced sternly. Then… "Damnit," he uttered and winced. In his fixation on the autopsy, he'd forgotten to light the sanctuary for the evening. "Sorry." He looked heavenward and waited a few seconds to see if lightning would strike.

It took a moment for his eyes to adjust to the stark contrast in light, and then something bled into view as he stepped forward a few paces. At the far end, the entry doors swung wide open and loose on their hinges, letting in more hazy light and a gust of cold air.

Becker held the lamp more aloft, turned it about until the glow cast on the rest of the room, and found nothing out of order other than the open doors, all of it reeking of the mischief he'd dealt with so much lately now that the town's remaining kids were growing bored. Some of them had no respect for the institution of the church at all. It concerned him more that they should get up to such mischief after dark while he was studying a dead body that should not, reasonably speaking, be dead at all but slumped in a jail cell pondering fate.

He'd not heard any small feet scrambling for those open doors, but he held up the light and swept it around to find the room appeared empty now. Only the long, heavy altar table disrupted his view, and he moved around it to cast light into that corner, finding no one hiding there. With a sigh, he stalked irritably down the center to the doors and shut them, lamenting that he'd never had to bar them before. Now he wondered if it wasn't a good idea. He carried the lamp back and sat it down on the altar, removed the hurricane globe carefully so as not to burn his hand. He picked up the large candlestick on the right and tilted it to the lamp's wick, transferring the flame and bringing more illumination to the standing cross in the middle of the altar.

He was absently reaching for the second candlestick on the left, but his hand passed through empty air before he realized there was nothing there. Upon looking this time to correct his error, he saw that the thick tall candle itself lay discarded on the altar top, a few wax chips scattered around its wick, but the decorative brass stick was gone.

Becker barely had time to acknowledge this before he heard another board creak behind him. He started to turn, and then he found the other candlestick when it came swinging out of the dark behind him and connected with the base of his skull. He heard himself grunt as he dropped, almost hitting his chin on the edge of the altar, and then the darkness of the sanctuary welcomed him into its depths.

She had spent much of her day in a fog, half of her mind focused on fixing the damage to the chicken coop without constantly wanting to cry, the other half trying to forget everything that happened last night without still wanting to cry.

It had all left her tired, so much that she nearly burned the chicken she was roasting, and then she'd discovered that the milk acquired from the neighboring Rand farm had soured already, so she couldn't make gravy. Lucinda hated it when supper was not perfect. Perfect, hearty meals made her feel like she *still* made her Mama proud.

That concern was forgotten, however, when her father and sister returned. They were about to sit down to plates of very dried-out chicken and little else when Papa produced a fold of tickets and handed it to her. "Here, you can be the keeper," he commented.

She took one look at the top ticket, read the title, and screamed, *"Oh my God!"*

It provoked winces—none more pain-stricken than that of her father—and she dove into his arms to hug him, kiss his cheek, which had now grown rough again with stubble. "Thank you, Papa!"

"Don't thank me, thank Cage… er, Mr. Edwards." He pried her loose, and she relished how his eyes softened at her just as they had this morning when she was distraught over the coop.

"Oh, *hell*," Caleb muttered. "Not *another* play?"

It was telling that Papa didn't bother to chastise him, but Lucinda didn't care. She forgot about the overcooked bird and watched her family chew especially hard. At least her latest dried fruit pie was ideal.

"Ellie, stop messing with that tooth," Papa said.

In her room later, she opened the hope chest her mother had started for her. In the space next to a stack of linens, she'd stashed a few books for safekeeping, among them the volumes of Shakespeare that Miz Oliver had given her. She pulled out a single worn copy of Hamlet that had a simple binding of rusted staples, its cover a faded woodblock illustration. She turned up the lamp on her desk and sat down to read, hoping to reclaim the details of the play that she may have forgotten since first reading. It wasn't long, however, before her lids drooped, and her head felt heavy. Determined to keep reading, she propped on her elbow.

Alas, poor Yorick. I knew him, Horatio, a fellow of infinite jest...

Her head started to drop out of her hand when something *clicked*.

Alas, poor Yorick. I knew him, Horatio, a fellow of infinite jest...

She propped up, blinked to realize she'd been reading the same line over and over, dozing off just at the end of it. The little carriage clock on her desk read after nine, so she needed to go downstairs to say good night.

Clack...

It sounded like something dropping against something hard.

Click...

Ah, now she knew where the sound came from. She stood, pushed hair back from her face, and went to the room's single window and pushed up the bottom frame from the sill to get a better look down into the moonlit yard. Cold air caressed her face and cast off the last of the drowsiness.

"Jesse?" she whispered as loudly as a whisper could carry on such open air. "That you?"

"No, it's *me*, August."

Lucinda's heart jumped into her throat. "*August?* What are you doing here?"

"I wondered how you were doing," he called up. A figure moved below, stepped out from the side of the house a little more until she could see him better, his beautiful ivory face fully illuminated. "I didn't see you at the opera house today."

The flattery of that statement made her too giddy for a moment. He had *wanted* to see her there today? She'd been so tired from last night's ordeal and then in such a tizzy over the chicken coop that she'd not remotely considered going into town. Now she could slap herself for that.

"Can I come up?" he asked.

"No! I am not Rapunzel," she laughed. Not that there were any means for him to actually climb up. The outer wall had no trellis or other such access. That didn't matter because for all that her father had let her spend time with Jesse, she didn't know how he'd feel about a new boy throwing pebbles at her window *at night*. "Papa may skin us both if he catches you here. He's already caught Jesse—" Not the name she meant to repeat right then.

There was a moment of quiet from below, and she hoped she hadn't incidentally shooed him off.

"Are you with him, Lucinda?" he asked.

The directness startled her. She hadn't had an answer ready for that. She'd spent a lot of time with the ranch hand, felt attracted to him and sometimes hoped to understand whether their goals and dreams aligned. She'd fished for the evidence to no real avail. It seemed, mostly, that he just wanted to get under her skirts.

"I, uh, can't say I'm *with* him." She decided she could be direct, too. "He's a suitor," she said, hoping it sounded practical. "Nothing more yet."

Silence from below. More awkward humming in her chest.

"I understand you're performing Hamlet next Friday," she said. "Mr. Edwards gave us tickets. I'm so excited."

"Oh, yes." His figure appeared to look around, studying the dusty side yard that faced west, away from town. Lucinda's room was more directly over the kitchen, while Caleb and Ellie shared the room that was over the parlor and her parents' bedroom. Then he looked back up again. "Please, let me in. I just want to see you."

"You can see me fine from down there." The creak of steps rising within the house caused her to almost bump her head on the bottom of the window frame. "I think Papa's coming," she hissed. Of course, he was. It was about time he tucked in Caleb and Ellie across the hall as he always did.

"Come to the opera house tomorrow," he insisted.

"I'll see."

"I'm not leaving until you say yes!"

She tried not to giggle too loudly. "Yes! Yes, now go!" She pulled her head inside and slammed down the window only seconds before her father tapped on the door.

"Lucinda, you talking to someone?" He was polite enough not to intrude on her room.

She tried to force a serious look onto her face and hurried over to open the door. "What, Papa?"

"Who were you talking to?"

"Myself. I was reading."

"Yeah, right." He pushed past her and went to the window. "Jesse out here throwing rocks again? Last time he put a crack in that pane that I had to replace." He slid up the window with agitated force and thrust out his head, looking into the night.

A gust of frigid air pushed into the room, and Lucinda shivered. She swallowed and tried to keep calm. The incident in question had been almost a year ago and left, then, both parents irate with her and her gentleman caller.

He pulled his head back inside and slid the window down, turned the latch. "Listen, I know he cares about you, Lucinda. He also brought my gun to me last night, and I won't discount that, but you tell him to come to the front door and knock like a *normal* person."

Then a loud knock sounded on the front door down in the parlor, and Lucinda almost burst out in nervous laughter. She caught herself just in time as a voice cried out with it, muffled but clear and distressed.

"Marshal Wells!"

It was Pastor Becker, and what began as a loud knock became frantic pounding.

CHAPTER FIFTEEN

"Marshal!" Becker's voice continued to wail from the other side of the door as Hiram hurried toward it, growing more concerned about making it stop before the pounding transferred into a headache.

The marshal flung the door open to find the man outside leaning heavily against the outer frame, a hand holding a rag to the back of his neck. His breath heaved and sweat streamed from his brow.

"What's going on?"

"They were... taken..." Becker huffed before he tipped forward. Hiram moved to catch him, kept him upright. "Someone was in the sanctuary."

"Come on, in here." He steered the shaken man inside, kicked the door shut, and helped Becker onto the sofa.

"The bodies are gone." All of this time, he kept the rag clamped to the back of his neck. It gleamed wetly, and Hiram caught a drip of water that looked like it had thin threads of blood swirled in with it running down under the side of Becker's collar.

"Shhh," Hiram tried to get him comfortable, to look at the injury he was compressing.

"Papa, what's wrong?" Lucinda's voice asked.

He glanced up and found her and Caleb standing at the bottom corner of the stairwell, staring with wide-eyed concern.

"Get back upstairs," he said.

"Is he okay?" Lucinda asked. "What bodies?"

Already in the know, Caleb gaped.

"I said get back upstairs!" Hiram winced at the anger in his tone. They both turned and scurried from sight, but their steps clattered and clomped through the ceiling. *Shit!* He wasn't angry at them. They had every right to wonder why the pastor had turned up on their doorstep mumbling of missing bodies so late at night. He owed them a big apology later. Turning attention back to Becker. "Can you walk?"

"I made it all the way here, didn't I?" Becker griped.

Hiram almost wanted to deck him.

They removed to the kitchen, where he turned up the lamps and got a better look at the injury while Becker leaned over the supper table, his frazzled gray hair spilling around his hidden face.

"Yeah, they got you good," Hiram said. There was a bruise already forming at the nape of his neck, peering out from under his hairline, and a puckered cut that still oozed blood. "You seeing double?"

"I'm seeing just fine."

"Yeah, well, you're only looking at a tabletop right now." He took the rag over to the sink, pumped more cold water into it, wrung out the excess, and brought it back. He laid it gently over the cut and bruise and eased himself into the chair adjacent while his unexpected guest continued to recover. "What happened?"

Becker carefully erected himself onto an elbow and held the cloth in place. "I got so involved with the autopsy that I didn't go light the sanctuary. Someone was out there making noise, and I went to check. Whomever it was hit me with one of the candlesticks."

Hiram cringed at the sound of that.

"I woke up, and the Evanses were… *are*… gone."

Despite Becker having said this from the moment he entered, only now did Hiram grasp it. He took a breath, stood, and retrieved a bottle of whiskey from one of the shelves, poured the last dram into a mug, and set it before Becker.

"I shouldn't," the pastor objected, "booze after a head injury is not a good idea."

"Drink it," Hiram said as he sat the empty bottle down hard on the table. "Settle your nerves." There was no argument. He watched the pastor sip and began to pace, fitting this new development in with the puzzle pieces he already had. "So now we have an upset accomplice covering his tracks *after* he left the bodies for us to find. What the hell kind of sense does that make?"

"Us? Don't you mean *you?* You found them, and it looks more like they were left for you specifically."

"Possibly." He wondered if the person could have been in the audience at the play, but he was confident that he'd seen and known every face. Only the acting troupe had been strangers to him, but they were accounted for easily enough, and now their faces would never be forgotten. "But why?" He slapped his hands down on his sides. "I cannot, for the *life* of me, think of a single motive."

"The life of you," Becker said quietly.

"What?" Hiram wondered if he'd heard correctly.

Becker cleared his throat. "No one has it out for you from some time long ago?" He gradually sat up straighter. "According to Mr. LeBlanc, you two went through a rather sordid spell together before settling down here and amending your ways. Opium dens, brothels, brawls and 'borrowed' horses, breaking the rules of Hoyle."

Hiram shot him a warning look that he'd better bury *that* shit immediately then pinched the bridge of his nose, a habit that he'd resorted to a lot lately. "I need to have a word with Silas," he muttered.

"Was there someone you angered that might not let it go?"

Hiram pondered that but could only shake his head vacantly. "Not permanently. Not after nearly twenty years. I was *eighteen.* Nineteen? Maybe."

"That is old enough," Becker said and checked the blood on the damp cloth before discarding it on the table and adjusting the subject. "I may have found the means for the exsanguination." He looked suggestively at the now empty mug.

"That's all I've got, so you might as well spit out what you're going to say."

The pastor lowered his voice even more. New sweat beaded on his brow, slick in the lamplight. "I found what looked like a puncture on Harlan's neck, where some sharp object had penetrated to his carotid. The tissue was damaged all the way through. That could have been from a spike on a transfusion device. At least I can excuse myself since I have no such apparatus. I've never had to perform a transfusion, and God willing, I never will." He immediately looked like he regretted that statement.

"God willing? Seems to me it would have been a good device to have the night my *wife* died," Hiram spat.

Becker closed his eyes, exhaled a long breath. "Marshal," he said with measured calmness, "do we really have time to debate this again? How about once we figure out how you ended up with two mutilated dead men in your jail, we'll then sit down, and I will explain the *complications* of blood transfusions to you? Ja?"

It was no use, the headache was back, and he couldn't slow down every rotating thought and emotion that fueled it. His jaw clenched as he attempted to rein in the argument that wanted to surface. He turned away from the man sitting at his kitchen table and pressed the heels of his hands into his eye sockets, massaged until some of the pressure ebbed.

Focus, H, that little Silas voice said in his head.

"Alright," he finally started over as he lowered his hands. "About what time would you say you got hit? How long were you down?"

"Just around sunset, I saw you speaking with that lead actor out at the cemetery, but I went back to work. The next thing I knew, it was completely dark outside, and I heard noises in the sanctuary."

"So maybe twenty minutes after dusk then? After Cage Edwards and I parted ways?"

Becker nodded.

Hiram pulled out his pocket watch and consulted it. "It's almost ten now. How long'd it take you to get over here on foot? Thirty minutes?"

"With my head splitting, too," Becker nodded.

"You were probably out an hour and a half, plenty of time for a body heist. The question now is, was it one person or more? Two heavy, stiff bodies? That's a double haul, maybe triple to get the heads. That about how long it took you and Nathan to get them into the clinic?"

Becker nodded. "Exactly three trips."

"The burlap disappear with them, too?"

"Ja," Becker said. "It did."

Hiram sat down in the adjacent chair again and stared at the empty whiskey bottle with a little longing of his own and a whole lot of frustration. "Anything else?"

"The blood samples and the hearts," Becker said. "Those were gone. I had collected a second sample from Harlan."

"They were all on the counter?"

"Ja."

"Huh." Hiram leaned forward on his elbows and stared ahead, let the kitchen around him blur for a long moment, replaced by visualizations of the heist in as much capacity as he could.

He knew the clinic-rectory as well as he knew other locations and faces. In his mind, he merged an image of it bathed in warm lamplight after dark with what he'd seen that afternoon as Becker worked first on Frank, then on Harlan. He imagined a creak in the floor that sent a vibration from one end to the other. Then he followed Becker into the sanctuary through the interior door between the rectory and an utterly dark sanctuary. He allowed that visual to trail off into the blackness that had taken down Becker momentarily.

Then back to Harlan's body on the table, unknown hands wrapping up the head again, bundling up the body. A flash of the same hands gathering up Frank's body from the floor in its burlap cocoon. And last, the vision shot back and forth across the room, scanning for other details, homing in, until he pictured one last pair of hands grabbing the vials of blood and the jars of hearts from the counter. Each jar, being larger than the vials, required careful cradling inside an elbow.

"Taking blood samples and hearts was thorough," he said as he blinked, and the kitchen came back into being around him. "That suggests something else entirely."

"But what?" Becker picked the cloth up, leaving a damp spot on the wood, and examined the blood on it.

Hiram automatically took the cloth from him, stood and went back to the sink to pump more cold water, wrung it out, and brought it back to the pastor. All the while, he considered how to put a new theory into words. "They weren't just taking back the bodies; they were stopping you from discovering something else, maybe something about that blood. It turned black, and you said that's not normal. You think maybe we're dealing with a disease after all?"

Becker opened his mouth, shut it again.

"Not Watkins' cholera," Hiram clarified. "Something far different. It's like someone out there knows about it, knew the Evans boys had it. I know, none of that makes *any* sense, but just think about it a while, okay?"

The pastor nodded. "This point, anything seems possible. The veins in their arms were also discolored. They had collapsed from the blood loss, of course, but they were black, too."

Hiram stood and resumed pacing, daring to ponder last night in greater depth, from how he'd gone back to the jail for Caleb's pamphlets and found himself suddenly out on the street, on Teddy, on his way home. He wanted to ask if he'd walked in on something already going on, but that made no kind of sense. The Evanses had been sleeping quietly in their cells, on their bunks. He remembered seeing their shadowed forms *on* their bunks, heard a breath or a snort, or some grumble.

You boys alright?

The headache became a railroad spike driving down through the center of his brain. "I can't," he whispered.

"Can't what, Marshal?"

"I…" he couldn't bring himself to confide in Becker over the blackout. By now, he felt that plenty of evidence dismissed him as a suspect. There had been no further gaps in his mind, and he had other witnesses to his whereabouts for this evening. How the idea of a disease might fit into it all seemed far too random, but that was Becker's specialty, and given the look on the man's face, Hiram had gotten him thinking.

One thing, at least, was clear. Someone *was* out there, and that someone might be playing a bizarre and twisted game.

"Stay the night, Becker," he said as the hackles on his neck tingled, and all he wanted was a drink, but he'd given away the last of the stock he kept at home. "Don't go back up the street tonight."

He watched the distant fire from a large parlor window at the back of the boarding house. At nearly a half-mile out amid the chaparral and down in a deep gully, it burned so brightly to his sharp vision that it appeared to float in a void, glaring away the landscape around it. Finally, the flames began to die down, and the landscape bled back into perspective, wide open with the backdrop of the mountains that reminded him of an ancient fortress. He'd seen many of those in his wanderings. After the flames ebbed completely, the figures of two horsemen appeared, riding back through the scrub at a trot, their clothing, faces, and other details clear to him. It all marked the end of the first stage of the game. Soon he would cast the dice again and see what happened next, but always within reason, always within the realm of his control.

Cage turned away from the window and faced into the large parlor that had been meticulously decorated with heavy brocade drapes framing the windows, an Empire sofa, and matching chairs with embroidered seats and backs. Lamps burned on the mantle over a small blazing fire, the whole of it warm and welcoming. Genevieve and Nora were on the sofa kissing each other so aggressively as to tear each other's lips, releasing little streams of blood that they licked off and started all over again. One straddled the other in a mound of skirt ruffles, corsets exposed and half untied, their hair disheveled and free. Ever since their blooding, they had been this enraptured with each other, all inhibitions eradicated and passions set free, and after half a century, it still greatly appealed to the voyeur in him. With telescoped vision, he observed Nora's slender hand explore a length of Genevieve's naked leg then work its way under the ruffles seeking more receptive territory. At the same time, Genevieve leaned steeply down to lick the rise of her lover's bosom.

A soft gasp sounded from the doorway, and Cage turned a forced but pleasant smile upon Miz Grace Simpson, who was encountering the blatant love affair for the third time this week.

"What is going on here?" Eyes wide with shock, mouth bobbing open then closed like a landed fish, she tried to comprehend such a level of sexual expression, especially one right here in the rear sitting room of her boarding house.

The two on the sofa completely ignored her.

"Ah, Miz Simpson, that was a delicious supper you served us tonight," Cage said and approached her, stepped into her line of vision. Of course, only Jasper and Morgan ate, but she believed everyone had dug in with gusto, carved their pork and potatoes like perfect ladies and gentlemen. "What are you doing up so late?"

A weak, trembling voice answered. "I thought you might like some tea while you rehearse."

"Curiouser and curiouser, isn't it, Miz Simpson?" he said. "You've seen a cat with a grin, have you not? But have you ever seen a grin without a cat?"

Her eyes dragged hesitantly from the scene on the sofa to Cage.

"A-a g-grin?" she stammered.

He snagged her will readily, calmed her in the space of a breath, and stepped closer. He thought she was still an attractive woman, dark-eyed and mahogany-haired with light streaks of gray. A few soft lines feathered out from beneath her eyes, and the subtle olive tone of her skin suggested she hid some Latin heritage. He quite liked the structure of her jawline and cheekbones. She was well poised—something Cage always appreciated—and wore only the most elegant dresses even when she cooked the food that she served to her guests. If she were more interesting, he might entertain the idea of blooding her, giving her a new life uninhibited by the cling of propriety, and simply watch what happened next. Still, no one else in Mica Bend had proved more interesting than the town marshal, and Cage was far too selective when it came to growing his kith.

"I know," he said gently, "this is such a shock for a woman of your refinement. Doesn't it make you curious, though?"

She took a breath and nodded vacantly as he leaned his face closer, smelled the crook of her neck where the high lace of her collar, pinned at the front with an elegant cameo, guarded a racing pulse. A faint perfume lingered there, not too oppressive.

He reached up and unbound her hair from the proper bun atop her head, lowered the locks to her shoulders, fingered their ends into soft curls. "Do you not long to feel such passion coursing through you? Right here?" He thrust a hand between her legs, crumpling the satin of her skirt until he found the inner junction of her thighs and gripped until he felt the warmth down there grow against the coolness of his fingers. With another gasp, she bowed toward him a little, her eyes wide as they remained fastened upon his.

Something about the response filled him with sadness for her, a lament for her hum-drum life. Just as quickly, he changed direction, in no mood to play with her too much.

"Thank you for the suggestion of tea, Miz Simpson. Why don't you go on up to bed now? Go up to your room and lie down, enjoy yourself, and forget you saw any of this. It isn't proper at all, is it? The rest of us will be quite fine to lock up and turn in when we are ready." Then he pulled his hand free and turned her toward the corridor from which she'd come. "Go on now, Grace," he whispered in her ear. "Jasper and Morgan will see you in the morning for breakfast. The rest of us will see you at supper."

Like a windup doll, she walked, headed straight to the front of the house, and passed August as he came down off the last step. She didn't notice him at all as she turned at the banister and paused. "Goodnight, Mr. Edwards," she said with a soft quiver before she went upstairs.

"Good night, Miz Simpson," he called after her. This was the third time he'd sent her to bed with her memory altered, but the first time he'd burrowed in the suggestion that she drift off practicing a little carnal pleasure. He turned attention back to the sofa and its two randy occupants. "Girls, that's enough," he said. "Genevieve, it's time."

She lifted her head, throwing back her long red tresses, and caught a breath while Nora continued to kiss her chin. "*Now?* You want me to go *now?*"

"I will not say it twice. Just be thorough. You have six hours before you should seek haven."

"Very well." She crawled off of her lover even while they kept pawing at each other playfully. "My love," she giggled and shook out the ruffles on her skirt, pulled taut the front laces on her corset before turning to pad away barefooted. "Duty calls."

"Have fun," Nora said and leaned back again, blissful in her drunken arousal, her small bosom heaving.

The curls on Genevieve's fiery hair bobbed with her stride, and then she was gone down the corridor toward the front of the house, past the figure who lurked there.

Cage had been expecting to hear from him all evening. "*What, August?*"

He stepped closer, bringing with him the scents of the night air, fresh blood, and smoke. He'd fed and cleaned up after himself, but he looked so dissatisfied, his jade eyes bleary as they stared submissively at the floor. "Cage, I… I think we should add a fifth." He stumbled over himself.

"The Wells girl," Cage stated for him. He'd seen them stare with moon eyes at each other so much last night while the poor, young bastard whom she was with had stood by like a cuckold.

"Yes."

"*No.*"

"Why not? She would be a perfect fit."

Nora laughed almost musically. When the troupe chose to perform variety shows, it was her voice that enchanted the audience, left ranch hands and saloon girls alike wetting themselves to meet her. "She's a child, August," she all but sang softly.

"She's sixteen. *I* was sixteen."

Cage closed his eyes and pinched the bridge of his nose. Though August was by no means the youngest of the kith, he certainly appeared so, and the whining of late did nothing to help that.

"And her father is Cage's new toy." Nora giggled at her cleverness and rolled her eyes toward their leader as if to say *oops!*

"Do you enjoy crucifixion, Nora?" Cage said lowly and opened his eyes.

"When I'm watching." She blew him a kiss.

The front door down the hall opened, and Jasper and Morgan entered the foyer, returning from their errand of the night. They discarded the hats and gloves of their uniforms, peeled off their coats and hung them, bulky piles as they were, on the hall tree in the foyer.

Jasper pushed his long hair back from his face as he led the way through the hall and into the parlor, and August stepped quickly out of the way, went to stare out the same window where Cage had been watching the fire.

The red-headed thrall gave a clipped, respectful nod. His face gleamed with the crystallization of sweat marred by streaks of soot. "It's done, just as you said."

"That preacher never saw anything," Morgan said as he stepped in behind his companion.

Jasper smiled. "But feathers were ruffled, I'm sure."

Cage nodded along, curious about the ripples of the deed. "Are either of you needing?"

"Maybe a little," Jasper said.

"Nora, give Jasper his fix. Morgan?"

The quieter of the two shook his head. "No, sir, I'm sated."

On the sofa, Nora assumed a more languid pose, arms draped along the sofa's length. "What if I refuse to move?"

"Now," he said firmly, jaw clenched as he flashed the subtlest glimpse of his eye teeth budding.

She pouted, as Nora was wont to do, and peeled herself up gracefully. "Come along then, Jasper," she purred and took his hand, led him away. "Let's go out back."

"Anything else, Cage?" Morgan asked.

"Not tonight, thank you." As the last thrall went about his own business, Cage turned and walked to the sofa, sat down, and leaned back right where the girls had been frolicking. Their scents lingered, fragrant as fresh roses. "Why the obsession with Lucinda Wells?" he asked pointedly.

August turned from the window. His eyes bore a stung look from Cage's initial denial. "She's smart, curious, sweet."

"Attractive." Cage gave him that. "You will leave her alone, August. Flirt, tease, pull her heartstrings all you want, but you *will not* touch her or blood her or do anything else permanent without my say." He sighed and leaned his head back against the carved wooden frame in the sofa where the flourish made a perfect indention. "None of that family is to be touched." He stared at the ceiling with its frame of crown molding and unlit chandelier, listened to the fire snap.

"Why is that?"

"Because I said so." Normally that was enough. "You want a mate, too, August, I understand, but not her. Not yet."

"Then when?" The boy's voice trod the line of pleading, still deep and composed but bearing the slightest tremor. When no answer came, he asked hopelessly, "Why do you play such games?"

Cage plumbed for patience. Most of the kith minded their own damn business when it came to what appeared to be his whims, but his reasons ran far more profound than personal entertainment, and he was under no obligation to explain anything. A warning growl crept up in his throat, and when he lifted his head and looked at his subordinate, his eyes narrowed with deadly seriousness. "No one in the Wells family is to be touched until I'm done with them." In a fluid, blurred motion, he rose. "Now, excuse me, I'm going to haven elsewhere. I no longer wish to stay in this house come dawn."

August glared at him with ongoing resentment, but he turned away from it. Some night, possibly soon, the boy would learn that there was no game, but a strategy was in place for something else. Something far more significant and horrifying than going through eternity without a mate.

On his way out the door, Cage lifted his coat from its hook on the hall tree and shrugged it on, the length billowing as a gust of moist wind met him at the door. Outside in the front drive where the coach sat parked, the horses all boarded in the barn around the side of the house, he looked up at a sky that rapidly clouded over. A thunderstorm swelled on the northwestern horizon with flashes of blue light, and the air produced a pungent, sweet zing in his nostrils.

He smiled at the sudden change in the weather, held out his arms wide, and let the swelling gales pull him up into the night.

CHAPTER SIXTEEN

After he'd seen that Becker's cut was no longer bleeding and the pastor seemed hearty enough, Hiram had left him on the sofa and gone upstairs to apologize to his children. He found Caleb quiet and ponderous and Lucinda rightfully snappish with him. Ellie, blessedly ignorant on the matter, slept through it when he summoned his son and eldest into the corridor and told them both the truth. He caught Caleb up on the details of the body heist while telling Lucinda the whole story about the Evans brothers' deaths. Just as she was beginning to come around and forgive him for shouting, a storm moved in with heavy winds and a short-lived but pounding curtain of rain that brushed across the landscape. He thought of Nathan, having to camp out on the road to Tombstone, and hoped his deputy had been prepared enough to deal with such elements.

By morning the rain had dried up but left mud puddles that soon turned to crackled pockmarks in the road. Hiram walked rather than rode into town, quietly escorting Becker as far as the mercantile before they parted ways. Becker needed to deliver his Sunday sermon, and Hiram was happy to stay at the far end of town from that. They agreed to meet up later, and then he stepped inside to speak with Fraleigh. His hopes were immediately dashed.

Still nothing had come in on the telegraph lines. That meant Nathan had not lucked out by having Sheriff Slaughter meet him halfway on his journey, and it would probably be another two days' wait. At this rate, he owed his deputy more than a few beers. With the new developments, he fought down a growing sense of despair and, while he rarely worried about his reputation, that also felt at stake. How incompetent would he look to the county sheriff who had been the most instrumental in taking out a ruthless gang? He admired Slaughter just as he had—despite the way Silas liked to tell the tale of the encounter—Wyatt and Warren Earp when they'd vowed revenge for their brother's death. Then there was the most unnerving issue: Mayor Watkins was going to have a field day when he found out what had been going on right under his nose.

He had just stepped out of the mercantile when Jesse Warren rode up, looking equally as rattled.

"Marshal Wells," he called and all but flung himself out of the saddle before fully reining Peso to a stop. The horse grumbled at the conflicting maneuver and stomped as the kid calmed it down.

"Good morning, Jesse." He turned and started walking. "Shouldn't you be working?"

Jesse fell in beside him, leading the irritated gelding. "I am. Tucker sent me. We're missin' some hands. You know Amon Yount and Charlie Preston?"

"Yeah, they got lucky with those actresses." He gave greeting nods to Terry Wilkes, who was opening the barbershop, and a few other known faces that bustled by, including Watkins. The mayor kept a wide berth, much to Hiram's smug delight.

"That's a load of shit. Er, pardon me, sir. Amon is an ass. No actress would want him."

"Well, that's right judgmental, Jesse. Amon seems like an upstanding individual." His sarcasm was lost on the kid as usual.

"But they never came back after the play Friday night. Their lockers are still full, so they ain't bailed. Ain't just them, though. About three others ain't back."

"Really?" Hiram paused and raised a brow to that. "Come to the saloon with me."

They reached the Palace, where Jesse stopped to water and hitch his horse while Hiram went straight inside. Sunlight, freshened by last night's rain, dashed the floors and every tabletop within the vicinity of the windows and batwing doors. Silas was alone, arranging stock on the mirrored shelves behind the bar with a disgruntled look on his face. He sported not his finest red silk vest but a rather plain gray tweed one. His frilled shirt was yellowed in the armpits, which could not be of greater distaste to him.

"Silas… you're looking the worse for wear."

"Good morning, H. Here." He clomped a mug of hot coffee down on the bar with practiced irritation. "No chicory, just your plain ole Arbuckles'."

"Much obliged." He savored the smell of the fresh brew. "Who put a bee in your bonnet?"

"The Chinese laundry," Silas sighed and finished lining up a series of bottles filled with inviting amber liquid. "I took my load over there this morning. John John, Miz Cheng… they're all gone. Up and left on us."

"Huh, that happened faster than I expected. Well, they *were* down to only *one* customer." Hiram looked pointedly at his friend. Upon thinking about it further, he realized he had not noticed a single Chinaman, or woman, for some days, and none had attended the play. Not that there were many left. Since the boom had ended, the more significant handful of them had set out for San Francisco, but Silas had depended on the few remaining to continue doing what he was too lazy to do. "Well, you can always get Izabel to do it." Again, his sarcasm went unnoticed.

"Izabel would sooner eat my boots than wash a shirt. *My* shirt, at least." He poured a cup for himself and settled into place for their usual morning exchange.

"Any news from Benson?"

"No, but did you know the telegraph lines are down?"

Hiram spit a tiny bit of coffee back into his mug. "You don't say?"

"Yeah, apparently the Signal Corps can't keep them up between here and there. Someone keeps clipping them, and I'm sure the storm last night didn't help."

"Between here and Benson, you mean? What about to Tombstone?"

"I guess. Heard it discussed at the freight drop. Why?"

"Tell you shortly." He took a more robust swig of his coffee as Jesse finally arrived at the bar.

"So…" Jesse began again. "Y'ain't seen Amon or any of the others still about town the last couple days?"

Hiram gestured for Silas to pour the kid a cup as well.

"Excuse me," Silas said. "You mean Amon Yount? I thought he and Charlie Preston got lucky."

Hiram leaned over his mug and slapped a hand to his forehead before Jesse opened his mouth again to argue. After some length, he managed to untangle three different conversation threads and keep the focus on just one.

"Well, there was that one group in here guffawing after the play Friday night," Silas said. "Who were they again?"

Hiram saw them clearly in his mind, gathered around a table over near the poker nooks. "Angus McMadden, Reece Johnson, and Jack Briggs."

"Ain't seen them either," Jesse said.

"Well, I sent them to their room and shut down right after you left." Silas looked pointedly at Hiram, silently indicating that there would be another, separate discussion coming. "I left in the morning and didn't open again until I got back from Benson."

"Iz didn't tend while you were out?"

"No, I wasn't going to subject her to that after the night before. I kicked those hands out of here and went on my supply run."

"Well, she was in choice form yesterday morning," Hiram griped over his confrontation with her. "Where is she, anyway?"

"Went to pick up a few things for the kitchen, if she can. Did you know we also seem to be in a milk shortage?"

Again, Hiram laid his head in his palm, and then he rubbed the insides of his eye sockets with forefinger and thumb. "Yeah, I did. If it's not one problem, it's another. You can't get your shirt cleaned, and Miz Raskin can't make biscuits."

"Exactly. We're in Hell."

"Well, I'm just a messenger." Jesse drained the rest of his mug. "I need to go ask around some more, then get on back to Tucker's and fill in for those deadbeats. If they turn up…"

"I'll send them back to work," Hiram said. "Oh, one more thing, Jesse."

"Yeah, Marshal?"

"You crack another pane in Lucinda's window, and I'll appeal to Tucker to put you on the most ass-chapping cattle drive you've ever worked."

"Sir?" The kid looked thoroughly confused, maybe a little scared, then shook his head as he turned away. "Dang, that was *months* ago," he muttered.

"Good luck," Silas called after him.

Hiram watched him leave, wondering if maybe he'd made the wrong call on Lucinda's nighttime visitor. Only then did it occur to him who else had been eyeballing his daughter of late and might dare flip a few pebbles at her window. He sighed as he turned back to the bar and found his best friend staring a figurative hole through him.

"Now, do you want to tell me what's *really* happening?" Silas said. "No bosh this time, H."

Hiram looked toward the batwing doors, still flapping from Jesse's departure and the pleasant shafts of sunlight falling through.

"Stop looking for an escape route," Silas objected.

At least they were alone for the time being, the only interruptions being the distant clop of hooves or a voice from across the thoroughfare, too faint to be understood. Hiram nodded slowly and surrendered. He pushed his mug back across the bar for a refill, and then he began to tell Silas *everything.*

"Alas, poor Yorick. I knew him, Horatio. A fellow of infinite jest, of most excellent fancy." August addressed a skull that he held aloft in his hand.

As promised last night, Lucinda had come to the opera house. After a morning of pacing, waiting for the sun to reach high enough, for enough businesses to be open that she didn't seem too anxious, she'd set out not long after her father and Pastor Becker had left.

Now she watched August stand before a section of the stage on which a small swath of actual dirt had been carefully arranged on a tarp in shallow mounds. There were a few blocks of wood painted to look like ancient tombstones. Only lanterns lit the room along with some ambient daylight through the open front doors. Jasper and Morgan were working on other props. The fairy forest of A Midsummer Night's Dream had been dismantled. Now large panels painted to look like the interior of a castle were going up slowly, the backdrop changed from deeper woods to rolling green countryside. The two prop masters had ceased hammering on a section and now quietly debated how it would fit a specific area of the stage.

"Then, when we're done with the scene, this will be dragged off stage," August explained and indicated the tarp and its load of dirt.

"Brilliant," she said of the instant graveyard while her eyes remained on the skull cradled in his hand. "Is that thing real?"

"Only the most real props for this troupe," he said and sat down next to her on the edge of the stage. He presented the skull for her better viewing.

"Really?" She cringed as the barren, ivory face stared back at her, every detail perfect. Then, like her father might have observed, she noticed the fingerprints of some otherwise talented sculptor embedded here and there in the surface of the cranium. Not to mention, it was too clean for the skull of a long-dead jester recently exhumed. "No," she laughed. "That's made of ceramic."

August feigned a look of puzzlement as he shifted it in his hand. "It is? Huh. Well, *shhhhh*, don't tell the audience." He presented it to her, but she still did not wish to handle it. "What's wrong?"

"Nothing," she stared at it with a sickening knot rising into her throat from her belly. "Please put it away."

"Oh, all right then." He leaned steeply back onto the stage, placed the prop on the edge of the dirt tarp, and sat back up. "It's only natural, Lucinda. It's how we look under the skin, nothing more." He pushed a lock of light brown hair back so that his eyes caught the light, and she felt like she could stare into them forever.

His words were no comfort to hear, but she found his outlook fascinating. "You don't fear death at all?"

He shrugged. "Not really. It's nothing but a doorway."

"A doorway?"

"From one life to another," he said. "It's all one great cycle. Think about it. A bird dies, its body rots and is eaten by worms that thrive only to be eaten by the next bird, which carries on only to repeat the cycle. Death-life-death-life. It goes on, never-ending, each one feeding the other."

The thought of worms eating a dead thing tightened the feeling in her stomach a little more. "I don't *want* to think about it." She stared at the floor and its polished boards and listened to Jasper and Morgan murmur something about maybe adjusting the board's angle to fit the stage better.

Then to her surprise, a delicate but masculine hand slipped over and took hers, drew her attention back. "I'm sorry, is something wrong?" August asked, and she looked up at him, found herself admiring his beautiful porcelain skin yet again.

Her gaze slid down the angles of his cheeks, drifted along the line of his lips, and just like the first day she'd met him, she felt stirrings deep inside that she was not used to, and that certainly did not occur so much the presence of Jesse Warren. Her eyes rose back to his, focused on the creamy jade of his irises. The spokes appeared to move, shifting with the flicker of light, and she felt like she could tell him anything.

"My mother died," she confessed. "Last spring."

"Oh." His brows furrowed so softly there was no question that he must understand what she was going through, even now, months later. "How? That is, if you don't mind."

She shook her head absently, looked down at his hand resting on top of hers. "She got typhoid, but the doctor... he's actually..." she thought to add, "... he's also our pastor, at the church at the end of town."

"Right?"

"He said it wasn't that. She was carrying my new baby brother or sister." She couldn't go further than that. It was enough admission that her mother's death had not been single but shared with a tiny life that Lucinda had never had a chance to know. Her vision blurred away the lovely green eyes that coaxed her to speak, and she drew in a breath. "I'm sorry. I can't."

"Quite all right," he said. "I'm so sorry. I didn't know."

"Of course."

"I didn't mean for what I said about death to sound flippant."

She sniffled out a chuckle, appreciated his concern. "No, August, it's fine." She wiped at her eyes, gave her vision a moment to clear. "So, you see, when you asked me if I would be interested in acting, I was flattered. Really, I was. Very much so. I think I would love nothing more. But right now, my family needs me. And my father... he especially does. I want to leave this place so much, to just run away from it and not have to be reminded of it all or how it happened."

She closed her eyes for a moment, pushed down the memory of her mother screaming that night, Papa crying for help or pacing frantically as Pastor Becker worked. In the end, she had taken Caleb and Ellie and gone into town to stay at the Palace where Izabel had set them up in a room, and it was Uncle Silas who had gone back to the house to face the keening, wailing, and tears that she could not deal with.

The shame she felt over that. *God... the shame.*

And now her father had confessed to her the mystery of the Evans brothers, how they had been murdered only for their bodies to disappear, plunging him into an unimaginable dilemma.

"I was exploring teaching school," she said. "At least, I was until last March. Miz Oliver—that is our teacher who is missing—she was helping me prepare. Of course, that would mean eventually going somewhere else for a job. But I can't leave here," she concluded. "Not now." She sucked in one big sniffle to clear her head, swallowed, and felt it push down the knot in the back of her throat. "No matter how much I'd rather be out on some grand adventure that would bury this hurt, I can't leave him with the pain he's in, and I can't leave my brother and sister."

"I understand."

"And after what happened last night," she whispered, thinking of that hallway discussion, her brother's eyes haunted as Papa apologized for shouting at them and then explained carefully why. She knew she didn't have the entire story but just a piece of it. Just enough.

"You mean the night before last?" he asked, looking a mite confused.

"Oh, right." He was thinking of the holdup on Friday, but by now, the shock of first her father, then herself, being held hostage had worn off in light of the more current news. She had promised her father she wouldn't speak about it. She wanted so badly to tell August that she was afraid.

She was so *very* afraid.

As she started to wipe her eyes, August suddenly did it for her, his fingertip brushing just along the bottom edge of her lashes, and she couldn't help but give him a weak and trembling smile. He leaned closer until his lips hovered over hers, and she was surprised by the same soothing coolness that radiated from them as from his fingers. But she knew she wasn't ready. Despite having kissed Jesse plenty of times on the mouth, she acknowledged that August Chandler felt *different* in some way she could not explain. She was intimidated, for one thing, by his beauty, his elegance, and felt her awkwardness suddenly bloom to embarrassing measure as she leaned back from his approach.

"Um, would you like to go for a walk?" She attempted to compose herself and sat up, dared to cast a look at the ceramic skull lying beside the little fake graveyard. "It's awfully dark in here. I think I need some light."

"Oh, um." He looked toward the far, open doors and back to her. His calm demeanor shifted with what, oddly, seemed like nervousness. "I'm afraid I can't. I was up late rehearsing at the Simpson house, and I'm kind of tired now."

"Come on. Fresh air will do you good." She insisted. Truthfully, she felt that if she could get him out into the sun, she would see him better, see the flaws that were hidden in this dim and golden glow, and maybe he would not seem quite so perfect. Beyond him, out on the floor near the other end of the stage, she noticed a strange silence suddenly bud. Jasper and Morgan had gone very still, stopped discussing their props. Their faces were grim masks in the lantern light, staring hard at her.

"No, I really can't," he replied calmly. "Let me rest, alright?" He lifted her chin, looked her in the eyes again. Though she still admired the rare jade hue therein, she realized that he did indeed look rather tired.

"Alright," she agreed.

"But maybe later?" he said.

She nodded. "Later."

"Have a good day, Lucinda Wells," he said softly.

"The same to you, August Chandler." She smiled back, and he helped her ease off of the stage, walked her halfway to the doors. She stole little glances back at him, then realized she would be remiss if she didn't also say, "Good day, Jasper… Morgan."

"Good day, Miss Wells," Jasper called after her while Morgan, still a man of so few words after over a week in the Bend, only nodded.

Out on the street, the church bell rang at the southeastern end and a moment later was answered by the louder gong of the Catholic chapel behind the school. Lucinda giggled a little over that, then did as her father had told her and kept only to the main thoroughfare as she started for home.

"Lucinda!"

It was Jesse's voice, and a surge of near panic went up her middle as she wondered if he'd seen her come out of the opera house. She hoped not as she turned toward the source of the call and found him riding toward her from the other end of town.

"Hello, Jesse."

"Hoped I'd see you," he said as he reined the horse closer and fell in beside her.

"Did you now?" she asked. "What are you doing in town instead of working?"

"Does everyone have to think I'm slackin'?" he grumbled. "We're short some hands, Tucker sent me after 'em, but I don't think they're around here no more." He sounded gruff, like he'd explained that plenty already and was done with it. "I think your daddy is on edge about something," he said then and slid out of the saddle to lead his horse.

By that, she could assume her father had told him nothing yet, so she left it alone. "That's his job, Jesse. If he weren't on edge all the time, he wouldn't be town marshal."

"True. Bet he'd a'gotten the bulge on Geronimo if it had gone down that way."

Lucinda rolled her eyes. "Perhaps."

"Well, can I at least walk you home? I need to head that way and be gettin' back to the ranch."

"Of course," she said and took a moment to look at him, here, in the brilliance of broad daylight with his tanned face, young but already lined around the eyes, and that tiny quiver he had at the corner of his full but chapped lips. She noticed a few little things she hadn't before, like how his eyes were not simply hazel but had a blue-green ring around their amber centers and a luster that shown bright even while he squinted in the sun. Jesse was handsome, of that she'd never had any doubt in the time she'd known him, but at least he felt genuine. Compared to that ethereal creature that lurked around in the dark of the opera house, on the edge of her heart and with no fear of death, Jesse was very real indeed.

On that note, she held out a hand, and Jesse, pleasantly surprised, smiled and cocked out his elbow for her to take it.

CHAPTER SEVENTEEN

It had been a long time since Hiram took his patrol north of the railroad tracks. The landscape there, while still covered in chaparral and interrupted by scattered fingers of saguaro cacti and large clutches of prickly pear, seemed not as interesting. Unlike the risky gulch that separated the town from the mountains, the washes out here were shallow, their sands softer and less packed. The whole of it spread wider, flatter, and the view of the Arduous Mountains grew hazier, veiled by dust and heat ripples. Without the town and the northernmost block of the defunct train station and water tower for a compass, a man could easily get turned around and go the wrong way.

The northern sky was bluest, peering between clouds that took many forms, from sweeping and feathery to puffed and fat. Hiram paused Teddy many times to admire that sky and question why it filled him with such strange longing. A flock of vultures circled in the distance, further than he intended to ride as he figured that would bear no more fruit than his chase a week ago looking for Maria Oliver. But, for a moment, he envied their flight, wondered what the world looked like from up there, and as his back twinged and he grew tired of the saddle, that envy grew just a little more until he stashed it away as fancy nonsense and returned attention to the land.

Upon turning south again, he realized how far out he'd gone. The train station had shrunk to a tiny box, and the jut of the water tower was like looking at the sight on the end of his gun.

The distance reminded him of how his parents had taken him and his brother to Atlantic City when they were Caleb's age. While James preferred to stay on land building lumpy sandcastles, Hiram had swum out only a little way from the beach. At least that was what he thought until he became enraptured by the wide-open sky over the Atlantic and merrily floated aimlessly on his back, waves crashing in his ears, staring upward entranced. Then upon erecting himself and turning, he found the beach and hotel a frightening stretch away. The figural spec of his father waded out, shouting and gesturing frantically for him to come back, but his voice paled on the wind and cries of gulls. Hiram immediately swam back to shore, the effort leaving him sore for days but satisfied by the whole experience, even if it had ended with his father verbally thrashing him.

Hiram blinked the memory back into its nook in his head and refocused. Next, he realized how westward the sun had traveled. Far though it was from dusk, he wasn't about to break his own rule and be out *here* after dark. Not now. Not until all of his questions had satisfying answers.

He had just started to heel Teddy back into a gallop when a series of snarls and yips rose to his right, and he looked to see movement amid a small section of scrub. A couple of furry tails flicked into view. Another yip sounded, then a deranged giggling noise that was nothing short of hideous. Some three or more coyotes were fighting over something, and given he left no stone unturned, he steered his horse toward them.

"Yah, get!" he shouted and drew his Peacemaker, prepared to shoot should the animals decide to charge at him. He thought of Lucinda's beloved chicken coop and wondered if one of these was the offender that kept destroying the fence.

They didn't charge, but he glimpsed one taking off with something in its mouth, while the others—he could specifically see two now—mulled around scratching, digging, yipping with a sort of desperation. He raised the gun to the air and fired off a shot that caused Teddy to grumble. The coyotes stopped what they were doing and scrambled off, paused several yards out, scrambled again until they were a comfortable distance away. Weaving around barrel cacti and cholla, he found the clearing of wash in which they'd been digging and felt Teddy start to buck as he let out tiny squeals.

"Whoa!" He balanced himself in the saddle as the gelding stomped forward and backed up, refusing to halt. "Teddy, whoa!" A firm pull on the reins ended the revolt, and Teddy finally stood still in the soft sand, hooves half-buried, and Hiram looked down only to feel his stomach turn.

Just out from Teddy's front hooves, the stump of a right forearm lay half uncovered, the hand spread wide as if trying to claw its way out of the earth. Along its grayish skin, black veins coursed.

"Well, damn," he said.

Thirty minutes later, after dusting off his discovery and figuring out a way to wrap it and get it safely back into town, he arrived at the clinic-rectory. The "Out" sign was still up, but Hiram pounded the door as if it were some towering fortress gate. He heard shuffling inside, boards creaking, until Becker emerged looking none too pleased.

"Did you find something?" the pastor asked. He looked pale, tired, no doubt still recovering from his head injury.

"You have no idea." Hiram entered to the scent of herbs, relieved that the place did not reek as much of decay. "Got a present for you." He went straight to the table and unrolled his duster, let the arm flop onto the surface, and joined in Silas' lament over the Chinese laundry being closed. The stump end had left a black stain on the linen that he was sure would never come out, and even if it did, he didn't think he wanted to wear the garment ever again.

Becker grabbed the oil lamp from the counter and placed it over the arm like a prize specimen. "Where did you get this?"

"Some coyotes dug it up outside town. Does it belong to one of the Evanses?"

Becker grabbed a rag, used it to wrap his hand before turning the arm over to examine it. "No, it's a right arm. Frank had a ring practically welded to his finger, which would have left a mark if removed, and Harlan had a cracked thumbnail."

"You made a note of all of that, did you?"

"I may not have *your* memory, Marshal, but I can tell one man's hand from another." He turned the palm to face up. "Look how calloused it is. I'd say this is someone from Wagon Town or maybe a ranch worker."

"Shit." Hiram felt his mood sinking further into a black abyss and the sense of despair rising in its place. He paced to calm the storm, adjusted his hat, rubbed at his stubble. "Jesse was in town earlier today telling me some of Tucker's hands didn't come back in after the weekend."

"Well, whether this is one of them or not, there's still this." Becker hovered his little fingertip over the inside of the arm, indicating the black veins under the skin. "Same discoloration. I'm willing to bet there wasn't any blood on the scene where you found it."

"Not at all. It was in a soft wash. I need to go pick up a spade, go back out there and dig in the morn—"

Both men startled, stepped back at least a foot each when the hand end twitched. The fingers curled, the wrist slightly bent, just a second of tension before it slowly uncurled again. For a long moment, they stood quiet, staring while nerves and hackles slowly settled down. Finally, they looked at each other.

Hiram's mouth went dry as ash, making words a struggle. "So, have you seen anything like *that* before?"

*
**

Papa's presence had never felt so dim and brooding at the end of the supper table. Caleb dabbed at his bowl of beans in quiet understanding as everything he'd seen, everything he knew now, fed one thought after another that he dared not share. To do so would upset his father more, so he let it all coalesce in the heavy pit of his stomach.

Across to him, Lucinda shared wary glances with her brother. They made faces at each other, shrugged, gestured discreetly, but neither could figure out how to broach the silence or dispel the tension.

Ellie nibbled her beans, making a big deal over her loose tooth.

And Papa sat with his elbows on the table, hands steepled over his bowl, spoon dangling from between two fingers while he stared into space.

"No appetite, Papa?" Lucinda finally asked.

He blinked, raised his eyes, and dug at his beans with disinterest. "No, sweetheart, I'm sorry. You know how busy I've been."

Caleb knew it was secret talk to keep from upsetting Ellie.

"I thought that maybe you could actually watch the play Friday night," she suggested. "Maybe Mayor Watkins will allow you a night off?"

"After last time?" he said wryly, propped his spoon in the bowl, and leaned back. "No, I'll be watching the audience again."

"If anyone shows up," Caleb added, putting a momentary damper on that talk. He fiddled with the end of his spoon, scooped up beans, turned the spoon and watched them tumble back into the bowl. He had never thought that he would want things to be the way they were before the holdup, before he'd seen what dead bodies *could* look like. The last one he'd seen was his mother, still as a statue and cold but whole and perfectly situated in her casket. She had looked like she was sleeping, nothing more, and sometimes he still felt the urge he'd felt then, to shake her, to demand that she wake up. Then the lid had been put in place, and the finality of it all struck him.

"Well, it's said lightning doesn't strike the same place twice, right?" Lucinda tried to sound hopeful. "Maybe they will come out."

Oblivious to the mood in the entire room, Ellie piped up. "Wha's the pway?"

Lucinda, of course, had to say something. Caleb rolled his eyes as she went to town on the plot. "It's called Hamlet. It's about a Danish prince."

"Hamwet?"

"*Hamlet.*"

"Wha's Day-nish?" Ellie said.

"From Denmark. That's a country far across the ocean." Lucinda began to gather their bowls up, pausing to check that Papa was, indeed, finished. "He discovers that his father, the king, was murdered, and the king's ghost asks his son to avenge him."

"Ooooh, I wanna see it!" Ellie squealed and bounced in her chair.

Lucinda's mouth drew up into a smug smile as she looked at her brother. "Even Caleb would like it, with all of that creepy stuff you read."

Despite the need for the diversion she was providing, this brought him to only scowl at his big sister.

That it was a diversion, however, was lost on Papa. He rubbed at the stubble on his chin, rubbed his eyes, and took a long, deep breath. "Lucinda, could you please stop trying to civilize the family for one moment?" he said with so much fatigue in his voice it made Caleb want to go to bed right then.

"Oh, um, yes, Papa," she said, but Caleb could tell her feelings were hurt.

Later, as he sat up against his headboard and stared at the penny dreadfuls on the table between his bed and Ellie's and waited for Papa to come up, Caleb wondered how they had suddenly seemed to feel so real. Uncle James had only been printing pulp for fun. It was thrilling, a whole lot less boring than life in the Bend, and until three days ago, it had felt like the perfect escape. Except now it did not. Not even a little.

Ellie, dressed in her long nightgown, climbed into the next bed, snuggled herself down under the covers, and turned to face him. "Okay, wead to me," she commanded.

The unreasonable fear seized him that if he opened the pamphlets again, something else would happen. Someone else would die horribly, with their head and heart removed, and his father would have to deal with it, as he was dealing with this *thing* now. "No, not tonight, Ellie."

"Awww, pwease?"

"No. Say your prayers and go to sleep."

She pouted because Ellie was good at that, and he wished she could understand.

Beyond the crack in the door, a shadow moved, and Caleb realized Papa had already come up and stood outside, watching them. A tired eye was peering through that crack, and then he pushed the door open and stepped inside.

"Did I hear a request for a bedtime story?"

Ellie all but cheered, and Caleb braced himself, worried that maybe Papa would pick up the pamphlets and, for once, read them himself.

That was not the case. Tonight, the story his father told was about Buffalo Bill Cody. It was aimless, no plot, just a lot of talk about shooting targets from the back of a horse, but it was precisely what Caleb needed as he finally drifted off to sleep.

CHAPTER EIGHTEEN

Monday morning, Hiram pulled an old duster from the wardrobe. The linen was discolored from age, frayed along its hems, and far less crisp than the one he'd ruined for the sake of investigation, but it had no black stain on it, and that was something. He got a spade from the barn, packed it onto Teddy's saddle along with a rolled piece of burlap in case he did find something else, then gave his two youngest children a similar warning as yesterday: go straight to school, stick to the main thoroughfare, come straight back home in the afternoon, be inside by dark.

Squinting in the bright light, he rode Teddy north of the tracks again and wound through the scrub. He looked back, visually marking how far out he was then going a little further, again recalling that day at the beach when he was twelve, until he came upon the same wash.

He was still westward from where he'd noticed the coyotes acting up and so turned east and followed the smooth and flowing sands shaped by runoff. At last, he spotted a scattering of coyote tracks and digging points that were much clearer than yesterday afternoon. Not far from them, he found Teddy's hoof prints from yesterday and used those as a compass to locate the very spot where he'd found the forearm. After tethering his horse, he took the spade and stepped into the soft wash, felt his boot sink in almost to the ankle, and began to dig, particularly where the coyotes had started holes. He remembered that he'd seen one running off with something, most likely more evidence, but there was no way he could hope to track and chase down such a varmint.

After around two feet down, with a width of three feet, he gave up on the first spot, wiped the sweat from his brow, and stepped back, his gaze following the wash further east. It wound into sparser chaparral, the sands still fluid, except for a few tracks that veered onto them further up. Adjusting his hat against the glare, he took the spade and followed the wash to the tracks. His leg muscles were already sore from the pull of sand on his boot heels and the balancing act he had to employ walking in it. Thorny brush grabbed at the duster, but the old cloth pulled free as he kept going. Another set of tracks veered in and wove with the first, then another, and the sands ahead darkened.

Hiram stopped, stared at sweeps of black mingled in with the tan and white, like soot, and then he smelled the pungency of something charred, and it *wasn't* wood. The winds had swirled soot along the wash in a marbled effect. After a few steps more, he saw the source, a hole half-filled in but at its center a core of ashes and something jutting up from it. Still maintaining balance, he worked his way toward it, already considering where he would first plant the spade, but then the whole area came into perspective, and he realized that what protruded from the blackened sand was not the remains of any burnt timber. Not from a tree. Not from a wagon.

The most pronounced protrusion was a femur with its ball joint exposed, still holding together despite someone's attempts to burn it. Laying down in the sand, half-covered, was another ridge of bone, perhaps another femur, but he wouldn't know until it was excavated.

His throat tightened at the discovery, and his gut swam anxiously when his gaze drifted to what was clearly the joined arches of a rib cage, and next to it was the most haunting piece of all.

Like its neighboring parts, the skull was half-buried, turned in profile so that the left jawline and teeth were clear, rising to the hill of a cheekbone, higher to an empty eye socket with a dribble of sand and black goo trailing out of its inner corner. Then there was the crusty surface of the head dome not completely burned clean. If that had been the case, there wouldn't be quite as much bone left, but there were also patches of crispy, desiccated skin clinging to the cheek near the withered shell of an ear. At this close, the smell of more than scorched bone grew overpowering, not merely an undertone of rot but something for which there were no words.

So, this was what he'd been scenting on the horizon during some of his prior patrols for the last week. But the smell could not have come from this single, isolated area. He'd mainly patrolled southward, and he'd caught the faint whiff of it out at the Hanson farm well over a week ago now. His stomach lurched, but he managed to keep from dry heaving. If he'd had breakfast, he would have readily emptied it on the sand.

"Sonofabitch," he whispered and raised his neckerchief to cover his nose and mouth. The entire area of his lower back tensed into a solid block of pain rooted at his spine, and Hiram began to dig.

Lucinda couldn't stop thinking about her last discussion with August, especially after what she knew now and how she'd behaved yesterday. Had she seemed short with him when she'd left the opera house yesterday? She hoped not. Oh, God, had she appeared too snippy just because he didn't want to go for a walk? These thoughts nagged her up the thoroughfare as she took her brother and sister to school on Remy with the shotgun her father had custom installed on her sidesaddle. She usually didn't worry about carrying the gun in town as it was there for more extended rides and encounters with rattlers, but things were different now, and she'd promised her father some precaution.

The town was eerily too quiet for a Monday. Granted, all mornings had been quieter for some time, but today there seemed no life whatsoever, just a strange miasma of emptiness hanging in the air. When she thought of the telegraph lines being down, she had a quirky visual that Mica Bend was trapped in a giant bottle with a cork firmly in place. With the air inside growing stagnant, its few remaining citizens were unaware of the glass barrier surrounding them or that they were slowly suffocating.

There were, of course, some of the usual greeting exchanges. Mr. Raskin called out as he swept the hotel's porch, Mr. Wilkes opened the barbershop with his friendly wave, and Izabel smiled back as she had a cigarette on the boardwalk for the Palace. No sign of Uncle Silas yet. All the while, Caleb was quiet behind her, his usual brotherly jabs on hold, and Ellie hummed sweetly to herself.

Once they reached the school, she went through the usual dismounting order with her siblings until they were all safely on the ground. The school's front doors were wide open to let in the morning air, and she could already hear Miz Raskin in there calling roll. Lucinda didn't need to hear Caleb's complaints to realize the woman had no sense of how to wrangle students, let alone teach. Unlike Miz Oliver, she knew very little about the world and could probably barely make it through the sixth grade McGuffey's.

To the side of the building, she noticed that there were no other horses at the hitch, so either someone was forced to walk or had skipped altogether. She couldn't blame anyone who skipped now, given the situation.

"You gonna go work on the coop?" Caleb asked.

Right. That had *been* the plan. Take her siblings to school, go straight home and make some improvements to the chicken coop. But for the first in a long time, she didn't feel like putting that first on a chores day. She gave a little, smug smile. "I'm going to go study Shakespeare."

"Papa's gonna get his back up at you," her brother warned. "You're supposed to go straight home."

"You let me handle Papa. We're in broad daylight, Caleb. Nothing's gonna happen. Now, you better get in there before that harpy calls your name."

He still frowned with disapproval, but slowly he surrendered and went up the steps.

As soon as his figure disappeared inside the doors, she hoisted herself back up into the saddle and threw her knee over the support, arranged her skirts, and rode back up the street to the opera house. She had not noticed on the way to the school that the doors were not open as they often were with Jasper and Morgan working on the stage. Perhaps it was too early for them, or August, to be there, but to be sure, she got down and went to try the handles. Neither door budged.

"Damn," she said under her breath. August must still be at the Simpson house. Perhaps she could surprise him there, escort him into town, then she would have her walk with him, and it would not interfere with his rehearsals. Pleased with this plan, she considered the route there. It was two miles outside of the last bend at the end of the thoroughfare but still close to the main road. There should not be any risk in sticking to the road, plus she had the shotgun.

She mounted up, adjusted her skirts, proceeded back toward the school and onward. To the south on her right, the flat scrubbed land stretched for several miles before the Arduous range rose above it. The range still looked hazy with the sun beaming from its southern angle, giving the high, pillared portions of the mountains an air of mystique. She thought of the ancient temples in Greece that she'd read about in the classics studies Miz Oliver had given her when she considered teaching as a future profession.

The remaining two miles to the Simpson house felt long to anyone who did not typically ride out there, and Lucinda had not been in at least nine months. Miz Simpson had often invited her mother and her out for tea when the house was quiet, but it had become too quiet in the last year as most of the boarders moved on in search of work.

Lucinda felt horrid that she'd ignored the two invitations that Miz Simpson had sent her after her mother's death. All told, she simply had not felt like sitting in the beautiful parlor eating dainty cakes and sipping tea while one chair remained empty. Visiting Miz Simpson had been a special treat back then, a ladies' social day that was now absent the town's best lady. It must, she thought, be wonderful for Miz Simpson to have the troupe there now, even if it was only for two weeks, bringing new and creative life to the house. After they moved on, perhaps she could make an effort to accept those invitations again.

At last, she arrived at the signpost and turned right into the drive that circled up to the front porch where the troupe's coach was parked. There was a barn around to the side where Miz Simpson provided a private livery for guests. It had once been maintained by a hand, but since business diminished, she'd been forced to let him go. Now guests were responsible for their horses, and she only provided the feed.

The house was flanked by oaks that gave it some shade on the east and west, but the south faced directly into the plain and the tapering end of the Arduous. The structure, which rivaled Watkins' house in size and was painted a dusty blue—granted the paint had seen better days—with black trim, was surrounded by a northern porch. The shade there had always been inviting for a sit-down in the summer. The windows usually shared light from the other windows within each room, but currently, they were blacked out by the curtains pulled shut. That was odd, Lucinda thought. Miz Simpson liked to have daylight flooding in, especially when it began to dwindle this time of year. There was a smell of something burning on the air, like a distant campfire, something faintly unpleasant mingled in, but in a moment, it was gone.

She stopped Remington at the hitch and dismounted. He grumbled as she tethered him. "Shhhhh," she murmured. "Hush," and rubbed the velvety end of his nose before she went up to the door and used the ornate brass knocker. After a long minute of waiting, she tried again, but there was no answer, not even the muted creak of feet moving within or approaching the door.

"Hello? Anyone home?" She had not seen Miz Simpson or her small carriage in town earlier and surely had not somehow missed her while heading in this direction. "Huh," she muttered and then cringed that she almost sounded like her father.

After a third try, she huffed irritably and went to the edge of the porch facing east. A gust of smoke blew by, carried off and away from her. So, that was why she had not smelled it again, but the fire must be closer than it seemed at first. She stepped down and went around the side of the house, where the barn and its corral were set back by a good thirty to fifty yards. Beyond it, a half-mile out near the upper end of the gulch that ran past the lower side of the Bend, she saw the smoke rising and even a few licks of flame.

Lucinda gasped. That looked serious, a problem that could spread fast if no one knew about it. Instantly she turned and went to untether her horse and climb into the saddle, rode Remington around the house and set out for the gulch. As she drew closer, the smell grew worse, not merely the smoke of burning wood or brush but a pungency that made her think of roasting meat and decay.

"Uhg." She cupped a hand over her mouth and halted Remington before she got too close. The ruts out here could be hazardous to a horse's leg, so she dismounted and tossed the reins over a bush where they snagged just enough to keep him in one place. Then she drew the shotgun from its holster and carried it with her.

Walking toward the pillar of smoke, she was stunned to find two shovels nearby, each chucked into the soil and left upright with their handles almost like a gate through which she walked just to within view of the gulch, and there she froze.

Her throat tightened as she beheld no mere brush fire, but a cascade of blackened bones dumped into the gap, some with crisp flesh still clinging to them, piles of offal settled at the bottom, gleaming even as they blistered and burned. There was a faint waft of kerosene burning off, likely used to start the blaze. She had never seen a human skeleton or entrails in anything other than neatly ink-drawn medical illustrations in an academic book Pastor Becker once loaned her. At first, she wanted to think the rib cages and the longer bones all belonged to some animal or other, but the skulls, removed and laying randomly about, did not belong to any wild animal. Maybe six in all? She wasn't sure. Her mind wanted to shut down, stop counting, stop looking, stop everything.

God, the eye sockets were *staring* at her even without their eyes. The teeth, stripped of lips, were locked in a permanent grin.

"Oh," she gasped as the shock, and the sting of the smoke, pushed tears up into her eyes. She stumbled back to catch her breath.

"I'm sorry, Miss Wells, you're one of the last people we'd a wanted to see that," a voice with a subtle brogue said from some twelve feet behind her.

She knew that voice, spun to find Jasper O'Brian, in his broad-brimmed black hat with his long ginger hair spilling over his shoulders, stepping out from behind a large patch of mesquite and prickly pear.

"Jasper, what…" she coughed as she accidentally sucked in a lungful of the potent smoke. "What's going on here?" Some part of her connected everything her father had told her about Miz Oliver's disappearance, about the bodies of the Evans brothers being taken. Slowly she raised the shotgun and levered a round into place.

"Now, Miss, you don't want to do that," Jasper said and held up his hands.

"Get back!" she spat. "You stay right there, Jasper." Her arms shook, her palms went slick, and it was all she could do *not* to pull the trigger out of sheer terror.

He only sniffed indifferently, and then his eyes shifted from her just to the side, and Lucinda heard a footfall behind her. She gasped but never made it to a scream when a lightning-fast hand came down in front of her, grabbed the gun barrel, and angled it away from Jasper and, in the same motion, snatched it from her grasp. She spun around to find herself face to face with Morgan Reed.

He stared down at her with those dark, brooding eyes for a mere second, and before she knew it, he had her by the arm, had spun her around facing toward the burning pit again.

"Oh, love," he whispered sharply in her ear. "Oh dear, love, you may have just gotten all three of us killed." It was the most she'd ever heard him say as his elbow locked around her throat. "We'll have to sort this later, though."

"No…" she whimpered, tears now burning streams down her cheeks, her nose running profusely. On instinct, she reached up, her slender hands trying to pull at the man's much stronger arm. If she could turn her neck, she might bite him, but the brute hold forced her to only look up at the sky and the billows of acrid smoke that veiled the morning blue.

"Shhhhh," Morgan continued to whisper. "I'm not gonna hurt you, sweetheart, but you're just going to get a little light-headed now and take a nap."

And she was. Gray patches danced before her vision, and she tried to focus, but soon the patches closed in and turned from gray to black. She felt her hands slipping, unable to grip the arm that was squeezing the consciousness out of her.

"Get her horse," was the last thing she heard Morgan say. "Get it into the stable out of sight."

CHAPTER NINETEEN

He leaned against the counter, arms crossed, breathing through the lingering pain as he watched Becker examine his sandy, charnel discovery, bloomed open from its burlap square. The pastor began to separate and piece together parts of at least two separate skeletons, occasionally raising a magnifier to examine one. Hiram had uncovered an additional forearm—possibly the left mate to the right one that he'd brought in yesterday—which was burned down to the bone like the others in the pit but still had enough connective tissue to keep most of the hand together.

Amidst it all, he'd found pieces of cloth, mostly denim shreds singed on the edges and part of a leather belt still clinging to its brass buckle. To whom it all belonged was to be determined. Could it be some of Tucker's missing ranch hands? Could it be prospectors from Wagon Town? Did one of those rib cages—the more petite-looking one—belong to Maria Oliver? Hell, could either of the skeletons even be one of Silas' missing Chinamen? Did the Raines brothers make it safely out of town, given how the younger had seemed so disturbed?

With his guts tensing into a sickening ball of lead in his belly, he acknowledged the worst part. He'd smelled—but without any means to identify it or where it came from—the same burnt reek on the wind when he visited the Hanson farm. It had been too faint to make much of it, but now it had a potential context that meant Zach and Cassandra Hanson, perhaps even some of their livestock, might also be out there somewhere in a gulch, incinerated down to bones. In the days after that, he'd placed interest in Maria Oliver's disappearance because it had looked far more suspicious. Now he wanted to kick himself over not being more thorough with the Hansons, too.

But the furniture in the house had been covered, the barn was empty, and the buckboard was gone, he reminded himself. Could he be forgiven for accepting all of that as practical evidence? And if it was still practical after all, what about that char smell? Around and around his thoughts whirled until he almost made himself dizzy.

"I'm going to have to tell the town something," he said quietly. "Shit, I'm going to have to speak with Watkins. I just wish Nathan would get back here with the sheriff." How he wished that so terribly much. He needed support and the wisdom of a far more seasoned lawman like Slaughter. They would need to form new search parties and scour the landscape for more burnt remains and then, most challenging of all, figure out who did it and why.

Then, he considered that not all of the remains were successfully burned, and, speaking of which, he looked up in a near panic. "Where's the other arm?"

"I put it in the cellar to keep it cool," Becker replied while his eyes remained on the bones. "Miz McCall died last night. The family came in this morning to arrange her service, and I had to hide it somewhere."

Hiram took a breath, ready to unload more questions.

"Relax, Marshal," Becker said. "The Lord took her honestly via natural causes."

He sighed more relief than felt natural over hearing of someone's death, no matter who they were. He would pass on his condolences to the McCalls when and if he got a chance. "Did it move again?"

Becker looked up at him. "No."

"What do you think caused that?"

"The movement?" Becker put down the magnifier and pondered the bones for a moment. "If we were in the middle of a lightning storm, I might say it was galvanized movement triggered by static." To Hiram's blank stare, he added. "Almost a hundred years ago, in France, Luigi Galvani proved that electrical current can make a dead frog jump, or at least twitch."

"Why would someone want to make a dead frog twitch?"

"That's beside the point." Becker sighed patiently. "I guess that's my roundabout way of saying I have no idea what made that arm move. There *are* perfectly reasonable ways it could happen, but there was no lightning or static or means of stimulation."

"A rattlesnake can still bite with its head cut off," Hiram offered and felt like a complete idiot.

"Within the same day that it was chopped, ja," Becker replied, "but that arm was severed days ago. Plus, a human arm is not a snake, Marshal. It doesn't writhe for hours after its head has been removed."

The pastor looked smug now, which niggled at Hiram's nerves, and his muscles gripped tight. He winced, air hissing through his teeth, as he braced a hand against the small of his back. Digging earlier had put more strain on him than he usually tolerated.

"Did it ever occur to you that the Lord is telling you to take it a bit easier on yourself?" Becker asked, eyes lowering to Hiram's middle in indication.

"Hard to say since He and I aren't talking," Hiram snapped and pushed away from the counter, prepared to leave since he didn't want to get into *that* talk. He'd go elsewhere to keep thinking if that was what it took.

"All right, I don't generally prescribe it, but maybe some laudanum to help you sleep, and—"

"*No!*" he barked, worse than his objection to divine guidance. Hiram cringed, realizing for anyone else it probably seemed like an overreaction. "I'd rather eat a skunk's ass," he concluded.

"Well, that would *not* be interesting to watch." Becker held up his hands to call a truce and got back on the subject. "Look, I think at this point, we can accept that this is not a typical series of murders. These people weren't killed in some saloon brawl or farm accident, and this disposal was systematic."

Hiram paused in his flight and adjusted his hat as he looked back at Becker. "*Systematic,*" he echoed. "Right." It was the perfect word for it all.

"Ja, so I think you can back off yourself. No one, not even the great Sheriff Slaughter, could imagine something like this happening. Not in their jurisdiction. Not at all."

Hiram let those words sink in, though it would take a while before he could apply them to himself. Lightening up was not in his nature, not over something like this, but for once, he appreciated the pastor's sentiment. "Thanks, Norman," he said and started to go.

"One more thing," Becker said, "about that arm."

"Yeah?"

"Other than the discoloration being completely wrong for average decomposition, something else was missing. You were right about the flies. I didn't think much of it when the specimens came from indoors, but the arm was outside long enough that it should have been full of maggots. Maybe those coyotes thought it was a treat, but the flies didn't touch it, and that's not for lack of opportunity."

Hiram nodded along with that and felt the weakest of smiles lift toward the pastor for the first time in months. It was a relief that he was not the only one to have noticed that detail.

By late afternoon, his morning dig had caught up with him in soreness, and Hiram felt every muscle pull as he patrolled, starting from the scorched area of the wash where he'd found the bones and circling the town altogether, but he never came upon another similar site. Now he couldn't tell if the smell of something burnt on the wind was real or in his mind because he expected it to be there.

Upon hearing the train pass through, he reined his way back into town and headed to Fraleigh's Mercantile. As most afternoons went these days, there was little noise in the Bend once that train roar and whistle died in the distance. A rooster crowed somewhere on the south side of town, two of Tucker's hands rode by at a leisure pace heading back to the ranch, and Terry Wilkes was closing up the barbershop earlier than usual. But other than that, nothing. The heat of early fall was cut by a cool, dry breeze that whispered of more trouble to come.

He hitched Teddy outside the mercantile and started to walk in, his mind primarily on his mission to check word on the telegraph lines. Only, the knob didn't turn, so the door did not give, and he nearly kept walking with the expectation that it would. The toe of his boot kicked the bottom of the door loudly, and only then did he register that the closed sign was up. He absently rattled the knob, squinted through the glass.

Afternoon light defined the main counter with its displays of candy jars on one side, and the opposite wall hung with tools and shelves of everything from chamber pots and boots to dry goods, soaps, and tobacco tins. The postal counter with its mail nooks sat shadowed at the very back, with no sign of Mr. Fraleigh.

Hiram stepped back, frowning at this inconvenience. He was sure he'd given the man time enough to get back from the maildrop by the old depot. Next to his reflection in the window, the figure of Terry Wilkes appeared walking up behind him.

"Hey, Terry," he said as he turned. "Any idea where Fraleigh's got to? He should have been back with the mail by now."

"No, Marshal, I was about to tell ya I ain't seen him today at all."

"Huh."

"I mean, he may have been, but I just didn't see him. Could be on a supply run. I personally hardly had any business at all. I'd be willin' to open back up if you'd like to come in for a shave." His eyes darted suggestively along the lower region of the marshal's face and the amount of bristle that had already come in since Friday.

"Oh, no thanks, Terry. Maybe tomorrow."

"About time you had a haircut there, too."

"Um…" Hiram hustled off the boardwalk from the store and untethered Teddy. "I'll think about that another day. Have a good evening."

Wilkes' shoulders wilted a little, but he nodded along. "You, too." Thankfully, he headed back across the street to presumably go home.

In his place, Jesse came riding into town. The kid knew he'd been spotted immediately and didn't wait for Hiram to wave him down.

"Marshal Wells," he greeted, steering closer and pulling down his neckerchief to reveal the cleaner lower half of his face compared to the upper half that bore a layer of daily dust. "Been sent again to ask if you ever turned up McMadden, Johnson, or Briggs."

Ironic words, Hiram thought, considering what he *had* turned up. If those hands had still not shown up at Tucker's ranch, then the likelihood they were amid a pile of burnt bones somewhere on the horizon went up. "No, Jesse," was all he could say, voice dull and gravelly.

"Well, now Rick Henry's missing and maybe Marcus Hall. Headin' to the saloon to check for 'em."

Hiram lowered his head and closed his eyes, hiding beneath his hat brim for a moment. "Shit," he said under his breath. It was time, he figured, to tell the kid what he could. "I'll go with you," he said as he looked back up. "I want to speak to you about something."

CHAPTER TWENTY

The Palace was empty of any other customers, bringing Jesse's search for his colleagues to an end. Hiram treated him to a beer and briefed him, speaking for the third time of the Evans brothers' bizarre murders, the assault on Becker with a candlestick, and the bodies stolen.

Having no one else to serve, Silas hung around behind the bar and listened again, but now Izabel was with him, so it was news for her. Hiram detailed the discovery of charred bones this morning north of town and that there were likely more out there.

"So *that* was the smell?" Silas said. "I remember it on that ride out looking for the Widow Oliver last week."

"You knew about this and didn't tell me?" Izabel snapped and swatted him on the back of his head. For someone so tiny compared to the southern rake, she packed a wallop that made Hiram cringe on his friend's behalf.

Silas recoiled. "I didn't want to upset you, love," he argued. "Besides, I didn't know he found *more* bodies… or bones? Bodies? Help me out here, H."

Hiram sipped his coffee. "Mostly bones, some full parts, like that arm. Becker's been examining it. Miz McCall died," he added. "That has him a little busy, too."

"Letty McCall?" Silas refreshed the coffee cup. By now, the brew had simmered in the pot until it smelled as burned as those bones in the desert, but Hiram kept drinking it anyway. "Laws, that woman was old as the hills."

"Now Nathan isn't back, which is worrying, to say the least. Fraleigh's out, so I can't learn anything new about the telegraph lines."

Silas poured a shot and slid it across the bar to him. "Here, on me."

Hiram passed it to Jesse. "Kid? How're you doing with all this?"

Jesse stared saucer-eyed at him. "You think the same thing happened to Tucker's hands? You think they're a bunch of burnt bones now?"

Hiram gripped the kid's shoulder, tried to convey a little comfort amid so much upsetting information. But how could he do that when he himself felt nothing but tension? "I can't say, Jesse."

"Why would someone do that?" Jesse raised the shot toward his mouth. The amber liquid sloshed hazardously close to spilling in his shaking hand. In a swift motion, he tossed it back and gulped loudly.

"Why do any of it?" Silas said lowly. He turned and looked at Izabel, who simmered but seemed to be handling it much better than the kid was.

"I thought at first the Evans brothers were the only target. The big mystery wasn't even why but *how*." Having already explained in thorough detail the matter of the locked cells, the lack of blood despite messy decapitations and heart removals, he didn't need to rehash the *how* question. "Now, it's all gone to hell in a handbasket. I can't find a rational explanation for any of it."

Jesse sniffled hollowly. "Ain't nothin' rational about it, Marshal. It's just deranged, 'at's all. I never heard the like."

"Who has?" Silas agreed.

"Can I help somehow?" the kid asked.

Hiram took a moment to think. "Yeah, you can. I want you to stay at the house. Keep an eye on Caleb and the girls while I handle town tonight. Don't head back to Tucker's this evening, Jesse. I don't want you riding the trail back alone."

"But Tucker..."

"I'll write him a letter if that'll help. Don't worry about your job."

Jesse nodded and looked longingly at the empty shot glass.

"Sorry, kid," Silas said. "Can't have you drunk on guard duty around my niece."

Hiram smiled to himself at that and gave Jesse another firm pat. "Thanks. Tell Lucinda it's her papa's orders."

"You think Lucinda'll listen to me?" he said and stiffly unhitched himself from the stool.

"No promises to that." He watched the kid wander slowly toward the exit, still digesting everything he'd been told. Hiram had worked on ranches and cattle drives when he was close to Jesse's age, seen the damage coyotes and wolves could do to calves or sheep. He knew Jesse had seen the same, but to imagine what that damage must look like done to a person had to be shocking for the boy.

Beyond the batwing doors, daylight softened into golden hues. He heard Silas' pocket watch click open and automatically asked, "What time is it?"

"Four o'clock."

Hiram looked up at his friend and Izabel, still standing close by, quieter now than usual. Her lovely dark skin seemed paler now, her throat tight with carefully tethered concern.

"You two," he said, eyes darting from one to the other. "Don't go out anywhere tonight. Keep the lights up in the saloon after you lock up. Hang extra lanterns on the boardwalk."

"Yessir, Marshal," Silas said, clearly attempting to sound light as he draped an arm around Izabel and drew her closer. "We can do that."

"I better run the last patrol." He gulped down the rest of the ashen coffee and eased off his stool, muscles still reminding him of everything else he'd done today and what more was to come. But what troubled him most was that if someone could get into a locked jail cell and murder two prisoners, what was to stop them from getting into a locked saloon?

She felt time slipping by even while full consciousness evaded her. She floated, soothed by a feathery cloud that buffered the connection between her mind and body. Occasionally the sensation of *something* came to her. Fingers. Toes. Forehead and eyelids. Then it would slip away along with any ability to form a cohesive thought. Just when she found sensation in her eyes and began to blink, to glimpse and comprehend a bedpost, a curtain, the glow of a lamp, bitter and spicy liquid filled her mouth. Fingers touched her throat, massaging, and a swallow reflex did the rest before her belly warmed slightly, and the clouds returned.

As these administrations ended, she slowly fitted back inside her skin and extremities completely, and when her mind aligned with the inside of her skull, a dull throb began. Someone was dabbing her forehead with a cool, damp cloth. A taste of cloves and sourness lingered on her tongue.

How she'd gotten here remained vague for a moment, and then her eyes flew open, stung by the brilliant glow of an oil lamp on a bedside table, and she smelled the remnants of smoke on her dress. She gasped, coughed and gurgled as her stomach flipped and threatened to send up whatever was in there.

"Shhh, it's alright, Lucinda, you're safe." The cloth returned, patted around her brow softly.

"A-August?" her voice cracked, and she had to roll onto her side because being on her back grew more nauseating by the second. She curled up, and then, "Oh God…" before she gagged and convulsed. A hand supported her head as empty, burning bile shot from her mouth to be caught in a bowl that was quickly whisked away.

"Here, try to drink this." The cool rim of a glass touched her lips, and she sipped, recognized the taste of sodium bicarbonate in water. She lay still, letting it settle, and after a few minutes, burped softly. It didn't wholly settle her stomach, but it helped. She let herself relax into the depths of quilts over a feather mattress as she recognized that she was in one of Miz Simpson's more vast upstairs bedrooms that faced west and was furnished with a four-poster bed, side table, vanity, and a prominent Persian rug.

"I'm so sorry this happened," August said. "I'm afraid Jasper and Morgan overdid it with Miz Simpson's laudanum."

Upon the mention of their names, it all came back: blackened bones in a pit, skulls staring with empty sockets, the wretched smell of burning entrails and why her dress reeked now. Lucinda's eyes flew open, and she found the strength, if on wobbly arms, to push herself up and against the headboard. The room around her was dark but for that bedside lamp, and August's face glowed on one side, angelic and calm.

"It's all right. You're with me. You're safe," he insisted.

"Jasper and Morgan were burning… bodies… bones…" She struggled not to be sick again after sitting up too quickly. A new wave of pain washed through her head, and she fought to keep it upright on a weak neck.

What occurred to her next, as she allowed her weight to settle into the pillows behind her, was that August was not exactly objecting to this announcement.

He was hardly reacting at all.

"Yes," he finally said. "They *were* burning bodies."

CHAPTER TWENTY-ONE

He didn't sweep the town perimeter as broadly as usual but kept closer in, wove through the neighborhood on the south side below the businesses that ran from the empty Grand Saloon to the barbershop and boutique. He'd only encountered a barking dog and council members Wayne Granning and Joseph Briggs, who did not seem vaguely interested in speaking with him as they proceeded through one of the broader alleys toward the main thoroughfare. He rode on past Mayor Watkins' residence, the largest on the end of the block and adjacent to the back of the opera house. North of the main thoroughfare, he drifted past the empty mini village and camp that had been the Chinese laundry, around which still hung a dirty canvas sheet wall, and the rows of tiny one-room cribs. Miners and prostitutes both had rented them over the years, though now they were mostly empty. Nathan had the one on the end closest to the jail and work.

Thoughts for his deputy had long gone from confidence in Nathan's ability to simply deliver a message and retrieve Sheriff Slaughter to unsettling concern. If he retraced the time since Nathan had left late Saturday morning, placing him in Tombstone on Sunday, then, optimistically speaking, they should be arriving late tomorrow morning at the earliest. That also depended on how quickly Slaughter would have been able to wrap up any business he was in the middle of and head out. At this point, Hiram would give anything to see the two coming into town. Because the sheriff thought he'd be coming for the Evans brothers, a few extra of his men should be in the entourage, delivering the kind of backup Hiram needed badly. But with his grim discoveries bundled up in the rectory cellar under Pastor Becker's watch, his hopes were not high.

His patrol ended with a stop by the jail. Perhaps now, he hoped, something new would appear, something he'd overlooked for trying too hard the first time. He braced for the smell to hit him as he walked in. Though it had ebbed, the strange blend of copperiness and rot lingered. He cracked the blinds to let in the last of the daylight, then he simply leaned against the end of his desk, crossed his arms, and faced the cells and their shadowed corners. The stains on the floor were obviously still there, and again he thought of procuring some lye to remove them, but then his thoughts settled back into *that* night.

As with his recollection practice, he inhaled a long, deep breath and slowly released it, letting his thoughts and visualization travel back to the moment he stepped inside, in the dark, looking only for Caleb's penny dreadfuls on the desk along with his badge. Those had gone into his coat pocket before he found himself in front of the saloon. He walked back the memory from that daunting moment to right before, when he had looked into the shadows of the cells. With the late-night given to the kind of quiet that played up every creak and groan from the floorboards, every whistle of air through the door frame, he had lit the oil lamp and seen, beyond the sphere of its light, that the Evans brothers were sleeping. He could hear their breath but found it odd that neither commented on his return, especially Frank. Insults should have been exchanged again, at least.

A subtle throb started in his head. Come to think of it, he got a headache every time he tried to recall that missing piece between the brothers in their cells and snapping to in front of the Palace. He fought past it to continue staring into the shadows past the cell bars, visualizing the shapes of the Evans brothers in there on their bunks. He felt like there had been something else there, but clearly, there had not, just two jackasses sleeping.

Before he knew it, the light through the windows had dimmed to a redder gold. Feeling like the jail would tell him nothing, he gave up and left, got back onto Teddy, and patrolled as far as the church, where he noticed, in the cemetery, that the McCall family was finishing up service for their matron and dispersing. It was only a gathering of six people, including the woman's son William, his wife, two sons, and two others whom Hiram couldn't make out. Becker shook some hands and chatted, but the exchanges were a murmur on the breeze from this distance. Hiram didn't wish to hear it anyway. He didn't feel like giving his condolences, didn't feel like waiting until Becker was freed up to see if he'd discovered anything new about the bones. He turned and rode back to the Palace.

"Did I do the right thing?" he asked quietly as he and Silas stood on the boardwalk and watched the southwestern sky spread out with rose and peach hues on feathery rolls of clouds. Izabel was inside watching the bar in case any customers did come in. "Was I right not to report it to Watkins and the town?"

Silas raised a brow and went about lighting the lanterns on the underhang. "Would you prefer to have had Joseph Briggs nagging you for news on the case every minute? Or Miz Elliot demanding you camp out at her place and protect her specifically? And then there's Mayor Watkins." When he finished with the last lantern, he pulled a silver case out of his jacket and withdrew a cheroot, placed it in his mouth, and used the remaining match to light it. "He'd expect you to solve it in two seconds," he spoke around the slender cigar, "like you did with the late Richard Oliver."

"That took me a week."

Silas puffed a few times to get the smoke started. "Was that all?"

"Alright, those are some of the reasons, and pride, too, I guess."

"Pride?" Silas exhaled a sweet-smelling cloud. "No, I haven't seen any of that here."

Hiram leaned back against one of the supports, looked up the thoroughfare, and felt as if night was falling quicker than it should. Next door, John Raskin came out on the hotel porch to light the lanterns there. When his gaze returned to his immediate area, the warmth he found in Silas' eyes coerced him to open up more than he had in a long time.

"I'm terrified, Silas," he rasped. "Hell, I think I'm more terrified than I was the night Rachel got… sick."

Silas lowered the cheroot and sighed out another cloud. "Damn, knew it was too soon for this." He lifted his boot to tamp out the end on the heel gently, then tucked the cigar back into its case and stepped closer, keeping his voice low as he said, "Hiram."

He wasn't used to being addressed as anything other than *H* from this man who had been his constant companion for more than twenty years.

His attention hooked, he frowned deeply, not sure what to expect.

"I don't need to remind you that it's been a hard year for you," Silas said. "First Rachel and now… I've seen you walk through darkness before, but not quite like this. I didn't realize how bad it had you gripped until Friday night when Frank Evans had a gun under your chin."

"Pardon?" He had a feeling Silas was about to say something troubling.

"Look, it's like this," Silas said, "Ever since I've known you, you've always seen the light at the end, somehow."

"The hell're you talking about?"

"Let me finish, please. Between you and that light, there's this great dark tunnel so black you can't see what's on the path ahead of you. Could be rocks, broken glass. Could be hard ground or a full cliff drop into nothing. Rachel dying… that just made it harder for you to navigate, and that light… it would show you the way if it didn't create such a blind spot that you can't make sure where you're stepping to get to it."

Hiram fought a wave of uncomfortable impatience. Leave it to Silas to get allegorical on him when all he wanted were solid answers. "And your point?"

"My point," Silas said, "is that of all people, you're the one man I know who can walk through that kind of darkness with the absolute knowledge that he *will not* fall in, and you *will* get to that light. I know you're terrified. Hell, I'm terrified, too, especially now that you've told me to lock up tight and keep the lights on." He raised a finger and shook it slowly, not to scold but to drive home an assertion. "But I also know that won't stop you. Nothing will stop you. Nothing ever has."

Hiram stared, speechless, while Silas's eyes grew intense, daring him to disagree. He wanted to argue that he *was* falling, *had been* falling, was going to *keep* falling. It was that fall that had led him to challenge Frank Evans to pull that trigger, even if it meant orphaning his children. But here he stood, maybe not on solid ground, but on a boardwalk, and he was upright, sore back and all, and he was too tired to dispute his best friend after such a presentation whether he agreed with it or not.

"Marshal Wells!" Titus Watkins' voice rose behind him from the street.

Silas's lips drew back, baring teeth as he hissed, *"Shit,"* at the same instant Hiram whispered, *"Fuck."* They both turned to see the mayor walking toward them, cane stabbing the ground rhythmically.

"You've been avoiding me, Marshal Wells," Watkins said. "And lying. The Evans brothers don't have cholera, do they, or anything else? You just wanted to keep me out of the jail. But they aren't in the jail, are they? You tell me what's happening with those two, and you tell me *now*."

The poor timing of it finally plucked Hiram's last good nerve. He took a long, deep breath and exhaled it with return fire. "No, Titus. No, they are not. The truth is they're deader 'n hell. Some other party broke into the jail and killed them before we got to have us a proper hanging for your entertainment. So, you know what, Mr. Mayor? Do you know what? I haven't had time to babysit your swell sensibilities or answer stupid questions or clean up trash. The telegraph lines have been down for days, so I'm waiting for Nathan to hand-deliver Sheriff Slaughter back here so I can have the kind of backup you've denied me over the years."

The evenly delivered tirade halted Watkins in his steps. By the look in his eyes, he was stunned but churning for an immediate response.

Hiram didn't allow him to get there. "To make it worse, whoever killed them is still out there, and may be disappearing some of our own fine folk, including some of Bryce Tucker's hands, maybe even Marie Oliver, and burning their bodies."

"Burning?" Watkins pulled a face.

"Yes, *burning* human remains. If you got on your horse and roamed your dandy ass outside the thoroughfare now and then, you might've got a whiff on the horizon. But despite having smelled it out there all week, I've only managed to find one spot and two—" he thrust out a hand with two fingers up for emphasis. "Two charred-up skeletons that belong to God knows who."

Silence dropped, interrupted only by Teddy suddenly grumbling from his usual place tethered at the end of the boardwalk next to the alley on the right.

The next thing Hiram was aware of, as he stared Watkins down and braced himself to answer all of the new questions he'd just freed upon the world, was that Silas had stepped into his periphery and was grinning from ear to ear.

Watkins gaped a moment longer, but just as he started to speak, he was interrupted by someone loudly clearing their throat. Startled, he turned, as did Hiram and Silas, to look to the right.

Standing out in the street, in his long, black coat, pale hair capturing the last of the dying daylight, was Cage Edwards, who appeared to have witnessed the entire exchange. No one had heard or glimpsed him coming, but there he was, looking rather smug and calm.

"Oh, hell," Hiram muttered.

To no one's surprise, Watkin's attention immediately shifted to buttering the lead actor's ass. "Mr. Edwards! Good golly, I am so sorry you witnessed that." He started toward Cage, quickly spun back around to point the end of the cane at Hiram. "I'll deal with you in a minute, Marshal." Then back to Cage as he stabbed the cane into the ground for emphasis. "I'm afraid our Marshal Wells is making some rather strange deductions here. Out loud. In public. When it should be in a private meeting."

"Nonsense," Cage said and walked past him without another glance. "I've smelled something burning since we arrived. Thought it was peculiar." He walked up the saloon steps and joined Hiram and Silas with Watkins scurrying behind him. "Hmmm, guess this town is proving far more interesting than I expected."

Hiram gripped one of the supports, suppressed a wave of dizziness as he came down from the rush of finally giving Watkins a piece of his mind. "I'm sorry I didn't tell you more at the cemetery yesterday," he said lowly, giving the actor a side glance. "It's been a lot to deal with."

Cage paused beside him, lowered his voice to a rather soothing and understanding tone. "Of course, it has."

"You say you've smelled the same thing?"

"Indeed, I have. Somewhere out there past the boarding house. I can't tell you how near or far. It's just there on the wind sometimes."

"Exactly," Hiram said. "I wouldn't hold it against you if you decided to haul your troupe out of here early for safety's sake."

Cage narrowed his eyes thoughtfully at that, turned to Silas. "Mr. LeBlanc, why don't we move this affair inside? Is there any of that Kentucky mash left?"

"Sure thing, Mr. Edwards, step right in. Izabel will help you get that started." As his one and only customer headed through the batwings, Silas planted a firm hand on Hiram's shoulder and tried to steer him inside as well.

Watkins, clearly stunned all over again that he'd lost any leverage he might have had, lingered by the bottom step of the boardwalk.

"Come on, Mayor Watkins, you too," Silas said, gesturing him on. "You want a private meeting; there's no better place right now."

Hiram would be remiss if he didn't glare at least a little at his friend for that, but he also recognized Silas seizing the opportunity to sell more booze. The saloon keeper had almost gotten his entire catch reeled in through the doors when another voice interrupted.

"Papa!"

"Caleb?" Hiram stepped backward and turned to look up the street. The horse and its clump of riders appeared as a silhouette against the last weak vestiges of light. The lantern glow soon defined the details of Jesse in the saddle with Ellie wedged at his front and Caleb holding on behind.

The horse had barely come to a halt before Caleb swung a leg over and jumped down to run to his father. In his path, Jesse reined up to the hitch and jumped down to reach back up for Ellie. "What's going on? What are you all doing here?"

"It's Lucinda," Caleb started.

"It couldn't wait anymore," Jesse said, catching his breath as if he'd done the running and not his horse. "Caleb says she went riding this morning, but she ain't come home yet."

"What?" Hiram felt a cold prickle run up his arms and the back of his neck. "Did she say where she was going to ride?"

"Said she was gonna study Shakespeare," Caleb reported.

Hiram groaned, knowing *precisely* what that meant.

Ellie came running around them and up the steps into her father's arms. Hiram winced as he lifted and positioned her straddling his hip.

"Whewe's Wucinda, Papa?" the six-year-old murmured, wide eyes blinking in a way that made him ache as if the question wasn't bad enough.

The commotion had now drawn Silas back outside with Izabel right behind him. Watkins and Cage trailed along as everyone's curiosity piqued and focused on the street again.

"She must'a gone to see that actor… *Chandler*," Jesse spat. "That rat bastard." His teeth gritted resentfully, and then he froze as his eyes drifted from Hiram to just over his shoulder, where Cage Edwards stood in the doorway.

Hiram didn't have time to soothe the kid's bruised feelings over Lucinda's other suitor. He turned to the actor. "Cage? You see my daughter today? Did she go to the opera house or even the boarding house?"

"We rehearse at both locations, but I can tell you that I have not seen her today at either place."

"She didn't come looking for August at Miz Simpson's place?" By now, his heartbeat slammed painfully against the inside of his rib cage, and only Ellie's warm head against his chest kept him composed.

"Not that I'm aware of, and I don't think Miz Simpson would turn her away."

"I saw her this morning," Izabel said and squeezed past Silas to the edge of the boardwalk, where she gestured across the thoroughfare toward the corner of the opera house. "She dropped off Caleb and Ellie, then she came to the opera house, but no one was there yet. Then she got on her horse and rode back down the street."

Hiram dropped a kiss on the top of Ellie's head. "Sorry, Sweet Pea," he said as he slid her back down to the ground, "you and your brother stay here with Uncle Silas and Iz."

Izabel was quick to take her hand and coax her into the saloon while Hiram turned to step down and look across the street at the opera house sitting fully dark, its doors shut and probably locked. With his mind on scorched bones and a killer lurking around somewhere in his jurisdiction, he had not bothered to check the place earlier. "No one in your troupe is there?" he asked Cage.

Cage shrugged. "Not that I'm aware of. It's a night off. Everyone else is at Miz Simpson's place."

"Watkins, you have the keys to the opera house?" The way he all but barked out the question made the mayor startle.

"Uh, yes, I should right…" he patted down the pocket of his coat and stopped, stared up the northwestern street with a deepening frown. "…here."

Through the roar of his own pulse building in his ears, Hiram heard the rumble of wagon wheels and multiple horse hooves pounding, growing closer, then a horse squeal.

"Who is that?" Jesse's voice asked next to him.

Hiram dragged his attention away from the opera house to look up the thoroughfare. The horses and wagon came from the same direction that Jesse and the children had come, the same route that led to his house. Beyond there, it kept following the tracks until one could either keep going to Benson, veer toward the Hanson farm, Bryce Tucker's ranch, or turn south completely and head to Tombstone.

The horses were not coming in at a full run but a sluggish gallop, the buckboard creaking on its axles like it would fall apart. Their harshly ghosting breath caught the lantern light, and it became clear that no one was in the wagon's seat, but Hiram recognized both horses and their burden. He'd sent their owner out two days ago now, had hoped to see his return already, but tomorrow had been the more practical expectation.

"Whoa!" he shouted as the team grew closer. They slowed down just enough at the command that Hiram could step forward in time to grab a rein on the gelding closest to him and not get trampled. "Whoa, boy…" he said with a firm but soothing voice. The horse squealed again, snorted with agitation, and pulled forward a few more tromps, forcing Hiram to dig in his heels, dragging out ruts in the sandy road until at last horses and wagon stopped with a loud groan from the axles.

Next door, John Raskin and his wife had emerged from the hotel, drawn by the noise. Hiram turned and gave a gesture that Jesse and Caleb stay put. Upon the boardwalk, Izabel stood in the doorway holding Ellie's hand while Cage had stepped to the end away from the others, his face obscured by the shadows there. Watkins stood against the railing, one side of his face illuminated, eyes squinting nervously.

Only Silas came down off the boardwalk and stepped forward. "Is that Nathan's buckboard?"

With new weight settling upon him, Hiram swallowed down a thick lump, tried to grasp what exactly was happening here. "Yeah," he said as he attempted to soothe the horses and examine them. Both bits had been pulled so hard that there were sores in the corners of their foaming mouths, and more sores peeked out from the edges of their breast collars and other hauling tack. The animals were not only winded but steaming with sweat.

"Never seen horses so lathered up," Silas said as he came closer.

"Yeah." Hiram swallowed again, losing words. His little girl was missing, and now so was his deputy. His body suddenly felt mechanical, as if his joints had rusted in place, along with his back, at this new development. Certain the geldings would not lurch away on him immediately, he let go of the rein and stepped to the front of the buckboard and the seat where he reached in and gripped the brake handle, shifted it into a locked position. It wouldn't stop the animals from dragging the wagon off again, but it would at least slow them down. He wandered further back, looking into the wagon, which was empty but for a rumpled blanket and a coil of rope.

Silas stepped closer to the tailgate, stared into the corners along the low sides. "Looks like everything got jostled out on the run back."

Hiram stared as his inner vision worked out the possibilities. "He had started to make camp," he said, voice droning, "hadn't yet unhitched the team."

"Do you think maybe they just got away from him?" Silas tried to weigh in some cautious optimism. "Could mean he's still out there and perfectly fine if he at least has his water."

"Nathan knows how to handle them. He came here all by himself from California with this wagon. He knows how to handle it and his team."

"But what if something spooked them after he got out of the seat?"

As if the suggestion alone were not enough, the horses suddenly did spook. Both let out squeals which Teddy and Peso echoed at their hitches. The geldings stamped to work themselves back into a run. The buckboard groaned in its frame, and the wheels turned partially. Then all of the horses acted up at one time. Teddy bucked against his tether at the corner of the saloon, Jesse's horse reared slightly and stamped back, while Nathan's geldings reared in as much as the wagon hitch would allow them and pulled. The buckboard jolted forward, and, in its wake, a vicious snarl erupted as something came out of the dark from the alley closest to the clothing boutique and launched into Silas at almost his head height.

He shouted as he went over on his back, and the world spun out of control.

It took a matter of seconds for Hiram to comprehend that what was hunched over Silas and tearing at him was the largest coyote he'd ever seen. Its fur was a matted mess with a bristly ridge standing high from its nape down to its ratty tail. Its shoulders appeared thicker than those of the normal rangy varmint and powerful enough to pin a man down.

"Get it off!" Silas' cried.

Black jowls curled back from needle-like, unnaturally long teeth that gleamed as they gnashed at his throat. He wedged a forearm against its neck, and then his shouts became hysterical screams as the teeth lunged in and grazed their target. A gleam of red sprayed upon the ground beside his head. Another gnash and graze, another helpless scream as he kicked and tried to roll to get the damned thing off.

Across the street, Jesse fought to get his horse under control while Izabel shouted, and Ellie wailed at the top of her lungs.

Hiram reached across his belt, drew his Peacemaker, and did the unthinkable by fanning the hammer back with his free hand repeatedly, filling the air with the ear-splitting crack of rapid gunfire. Smoke filled the air with the sulfurous stench of spent powder. He didn't stop until the fifth round went off and the cylinder was empty.

The animal yelped as black blood spewed from its neck, head, and the side of its body, and it collapsed on top of its victim. Hiram didn't bother to holster the pistol as he dove forward, pushed the beast off his friend, and tried to shove it as far away as possible. On his knees, he frantically examined Silas, who was gripping his bleeding throat, the pool next to his head growing larger by the second.

"No... no... no..." His own voice sounded so distant to him. His ears rang after the gunfire as he tried to focus on how to staunch the bleeding. A flap of bloody skin slipped between his fingers, and he tried to pin it back in place.

"Ya... got it... H..." Silas gurgled. "G-good..."

"Yeah, got 'im good," he said, attempting to keep the both of them calm, an impossible task as he reached up and pulled on the sleeve of his old duster. It ripped readily enough, so he tore it free, wadded it up, and compressed it over the side of Silas' throat. "Jesse! Go get the doc!" he commanded without looking up. Within his periphery, he saw the kid manage to get his horse to plant all four hooves long enough to fling himself up into the saddle, and from there, Hiram heard only hooves kicking into a run going southeast toward the church. He looked down, locked eyes with Silas, and held it as he pressed harder on the wound. "Hold on... hold on..." Hot tears welled up along the edge of his lashes as it became clear Silas was losing consciousness.

Then movement again, footsteps hurrying closer.

"Papa!"

It was Caleb with Izabel right behind him. To his side, the buckboard shifted, creaked and rattled unnervingly as the horses spooked again and dragged it several feet.

Without thinking about it, Hiram raised his right hand in a halt gesture. "Caleb, get back! Both of you, back!" The last thing he needed was his kid or Iz in the way or getting trampled.

There was a blur of movement. Caleb shouted and stumbled back, fell over onto his elbows. Izabel screamed next to him, and then came a louder, angrier snarl as Hiram found the wretched creature back on its feet, its mouth clamped over his forearm. Sharp fangs pierced fabric and skin down to the bone, sending a lightning bolt of pain up his arm. Hiram screamed, impulsively pulled his arm back, but the thing wouldn't let go. Instinct overpowered his desire to save Silas as his left hand released the pressure on the wound, and he fumbled to grab his empty Colt from the ground. He gripped the barrel, hammered the beast on the side of the skull with the hilt, heard bone crack. It yelped and let go, leaped back and recoiled, its teeth bared and slathering with red swirls of Hiram's blood.

In the next split-second, he saw his own death in the thing's glossy black eyes. Not the amber-yellow eyes of a regular coyote. *Black.* Oily black, glaring orbs. It gnashed its teeth again, making a hideous cackling noise that was not uncommon for a coyote, but coming from this *thing* made his belly fill with ice and his throat tighten. Hiram braced, knowing it would leap at him, go for his throat as it had Silas'. He remembered the Derringer in Silas' boot and made a slow move to lean back, to try to fumble Silas' pant leg up and get into the pocket between boot and calve, but before he could finish, the coyote lunged. He knew he would not have the small gun extracted, aimed, or the hammer cocked in time.

A hollow, sickening *THUNK* sounded as a tall black boot appeared swiftly, stomp kicked the beast in the side, and sent it rolling with a yelp, and then the figure to whom the boot belonged came into complete focus with a sweeping black coat and a streak of pale hair. Cage Edwards seemed to have moved unnaturally fast, or maybe it was that he simply took the thing by surprise while it was focused on Hiram. He carried with him a lantern from the boardwalk, the wick within the globe turned up to create a brilliant, dancing flame.

In a handful of seconds, the coyote recoiled again, recovering from the kick, and Cage swung the lantern in a high arc by the handle, brought it down so fast it caught the beast directly on the top of the skull. The glass globe shattered as kerosene traveled up through the burner, past the wick, and dashed across the beast's head, down its back, catching in the bristled fur in the space of a blink before the path of the spill erupted in flames. There was a loud pop as the fuel reservoir split with a brighter burst, and the metal bloomed open somewhere around the coyote's chest.

Blinded, it backed up awkwardly, swung its front half back and forth in a blazing frenzy. Its mouth opened wide to let out a blood-curdling screech. A slathering tongue frilled between its abnormally long teeth, and its black eyes exploded from their sockets, spraying ropey ooze upon the sand.

Hiram winced as the fire grew, the heat too close, pungent smoke billowing at him. In a moment of added desperation, he grabbed Silas by the shoulders of his jacket and dragged him a few feet. New agony shot through his arm at the effort. He collapsed and tried to resume pressure with both hands, even as his right hand failed him, shaking under the pain that seized his arm. All the while, his gaze was drawn back to watching the beast burn.

It screeched and writhed as the flames engulfed its fur and the skin beneath split, exposing slick muscle that quickly blistered away down to the bone. The smell of burnt hair and flesh billowed up on dark smoke, and then the coyote collapsed with one last screech that reduced to a horrid mewling noise, then a drawn-out gargle, and finally nothing.

For an instant, Hiram glimpsed his unlikely savior still standing on the other side of the burning carcass. The smoke drift parted briefly to reveal Cage staring down at his handy work, his brow furrowed deeply into a glare that looked more like anger than fear. His eyes, too, illuminated by the flames, seemed less silvery gray and almost white, pupils closed to fierce pinpoints. Then another drift of the noxious smoke passed over him, and he stepped back, seemed to fade against the darker street behind him. Hiram's eyes stung, and his vision blurred.

Horse hooves pounded closer again. Jesse's voice shouted, "What the hell!"

Becker's voice rose then. "Mein… Gott…"

But Hiram couldn't see him. Couldn't see anyone who had been standing outside the Palace or the hotel. Not the Raskins, not Watkins, not Caleb or Ellie, though he could hear Ellie still wailing her lungs out somewhere on the other side of the crackling dead thing.

Shit, he *hoped* it was finally dead.

Then Izabel was suddenly there with him, on her knees at Silas' head, but she was as blurry and obscured to him as everyone else. "Silas!" He could hear the tears in her voice. "Mi querido, please." She sniffled, and Hiram felt his friend's body jitter as she shook Silas frantically. *"Silaaaaaas!"* Her voice reached hysterics.

To Hiram's relief, Silas groaned, and he blindly continued compression even as his right hand lost strength. It wasn't enough. It couldn't be given the way he felt so much warm blood escaping through his fingers. "Somebody, help me." His voice cracked through gritted teeth. He drew in a breath, almost choked on the disgusting smoke, and forced it out of his lungs with a cry of his own that echoed up the thoroughfare, bounded off the false fronts and the shuttered windows of the Bend.

"Somebody help me!"

It was some time before Lucinda could sit up without getting dizzy or wanting to vomit again. She continued to sip the soda water a little at a time until her stomach stopped churning, and then she finally dropped her legs over the side of the bed and braced herself upright. August's hand was on her back, rubbing gently while she fathomed all that he had told her, what he had *shown* her.

Before her eyes, he had lifted a hand into the light and from there pulled back the curtain on her reality just so. The change was subtle at first. His neatly groomed fingernails began to grow rapidly, ivory white tips forming and rising to sharp peaks—*claws*—while at the same time his finger bones crackled and lengthened. His lips parted, and she glimpsed long canines descend from his gums, forming needle-sharp points. His tongue absently flicked at one, drawing the tiniest bead of red, before he closed his mouth and hid them away. As quickly as his hand had transformed, it reverted into a normal-looking, graceful hand with the nails rounded down near the quick.

"History has given us many names," he said. "In Macedonia and Greece, we are the *vrykolakas*. In Europe and Russia, the *strigoi* and *upyr*, the *strix* in Rome. More ancient still, the *uttukku*. Ever since Lord Byron and his inner circle told ghost stories to each other, we are called something else."

"Vampires," Lucinda whispered.

He smiled lightly at that. "Yes."

Her emotions tread a narrow path between fear, awe and, strangely enough, pity. One moment tipped into terror only to be up righted and sway toward amazement, and when she looked at him, with his pale green eyes, the cut of his cheekbones, she wondered how something so beautiful could harbor such a creature inside. He had stepped from the pages of her brother's ridiculous horrid tales, a thing that could not walk in the daylight without bursting into flames, could not survive on anything but blood. *Human* blood.

"How can you do what you do?" she asked.

August stood and went over to pull open the drapes on the window across the room. A wash of dark blue and lingering streaks of peach graced the sky beyond. The sun had set, and Lucinda felt new dread tighten in her chest.

"There is an instinct," he explained. "It's a thirst that cannot be denied, but it comes with a cost." He turned from the window, half a silhouette, half a ghost with his pale skin and white shirt as the lamplight barely reached him over there. "Essentially, we carry a pestilence. One bite drives it into the veins of our vic—" He swallowed the word, clearly didn't want to use it in front of her.

"*Marks,*" he amended. "What it does from there is terrifying, even for us. The infection takes on a life of its own and transmutes the body into a thing that is both living and dead, a phantom of its former self driven only by the instinct to feed, and it cannot be controlled, so before we are done, we have to dispose properly of the remains.

"That is what you saw today when you came upon Jasper and Morgan. They serve as our daylight ambassadors, seen when we cannot be seen, and utmost they help clean up our messes," he added almost miserably. "The heads and hearts must be removed to keep the body from rising again. But to keep the disease from accidentally spreading, it must also be burned."

He stepped closer, bleeding back into the light and coming to sit on the edge of the bed again. "Ah me," he murmured. "I *hate* telling you this." He reached up to caress her face, and Lucinda unwittingly flinched. She had noticed how cool his fingers were when he'd wiped at her tears yesterday, but now they burned colder. Maybe it was all in her head, perceived now that she knew what he was.

"You kill every night?" she whispered.

"Yes."

"You've been feeding on the people in this town?"

"Lucinda, please…"

"*Don't,*" she spat. "How could you?" She felt new tears, new sickness, and utmost a new sadness so vast it was incomprehensible. "How *could* you?"

"For one, I do not know these people as you do. They are nameless faces. That does not mean that I *like* that I do it, but the reward of immortality is worth it," he said.

At that she stood, wavered and swallowed down another threat of bile. "Immortality? I don't understand."

"Remember how I told you that death is a doorway?" He stood, looking down at her. "Life-death-life, remember?"

"Yes." She had to look away from his intense, mesmerizing eyes. "Yes, I remember." The speech had disturbed her because it incidentally brought her mother to mind.

"My kind are part of that cycle like anything else." He sounded argumentative now. "Death is required for anything to live. It may be ugly, but it's the truth. You eat animals for sustenance, and we consume blood. One nation wars with another over resources. Men rape and poison the land for gold so they can make their fortunes to survive. Do you think that isn't killing *something*? Do you think that isn't a disease of its own? At least we are honest in that we cannot help our nature."

His voice, his intensity, sliced through her, made her shudder as she tried to back away but collided with the bedside table and halted when the oil lamp nearly tilted on its heavy base. The flame flickered erratically for a moment.

"I don't *want* to think about those things." She moved away, started backing toward the door, trying not to trip on the Persian carpet.

"But you must, Lucinda. Otherwise, how will you live your life? Shying from the truth, or facing it and grasping the world before you and *owning* it, living to the fullest? I am *sorry* your mother died, but you cannot let it destroy your chance to live. To have a daughter like you, she must have been a lovely and extraordinary woman. She would not want you languishing here in this fading town, would she?"

"Don't you talk about my mother." She spun and grabbed the doorknob, but in an instant, his hand gripped her wrist. He'd moved in such a blur, faster than she could blink. She started to scream, but his other hand clamped over her mouth, the cold making her shiver. He turned her to face him, pulled her back near the light.

"Look at me… look at *me*…" he insisted and uncovered her mouth. "Lucinda, you have nothing to fear from me."

"Then let me go. Please, August. I won't tell anyone about this, not even my papa." She looked up at him then, hoping that he would at least find some empathy, understand why she was so scared, but when her eyes met his, her fear ebbed into a warm feeling. She swore tiny creamy flecks danced amid the green, soothing and arousing.

"The most objectionable thing about immortality," he said softly, "is that it can get quite lonely."

"Lonely?" she uttered. "I can only imagine what it must be like never to see the sun again." She blinked, felt like she was still shaking the effects of the laudanum. "But you were at the opera house during the day. When I first met you, and then yesterday."

"I didn't go outside, remember? The idea is to be *seen* during the day, but whether it is inside or outside doesn't matter." His lips curled up wryly at the corner. "People fill in the rest of the illusion for themselves. Besides, there is a safe margin at dawn and dusk when the light is low enough for us to be out. The first time I was there to oversee props, and yes, there *were* rehearsals going on in the basement, I assure you, but then I heard a new voice, and I came upstairs, and there you were, a vision unlike any other. I felt like… I felt like I woke up suddenly, Lucinda. Like I didn't even know I was asleep, just going through the motions of existence, and then there you were, and a hundred years of weight fell away from my shoulders, from my heart.

"As I said, immortality can be lonely, even in a kith as we are. Genevieve and Nora have each other. Cage shares nothing of himself or his past." He sounded particularly frustrated with this as he held up his hands in a shrug. "Jasper and Morgan, well, they work separately."

"Genevieve and Nora?" she asked and couldn't stop the little chuckle that rose, and her cheeks grew warm. "They're together? As in… lovers?"

"Perfect companionship is all that matters. As for missing the sun, there are options. To my vision, the moon is almost as bright. There are colors in the night sky that human eyes cannot see and so many other things that you are *all* blind to. I only want to share my world with you if you'll let me. Would you consider it?"

How lovely he made it all sound. If she ignored that blood was his sustenance, it sounded alluring indeed, a strange world free of human sadness and regret. She opened her mouth to speak but only sighed when she found his lips hovering over hers. She wanted to kiss him, frightened though she was. He moved, instead, to drop a gentle peck on her cheek, then the shell of her ear. It tickled sweetly and sent shivers down her middle into the junction of her thighs, the same sinful and delicious sensations she'd felt the day she met him.

"You smell so good." His breath ghosted against the side of her neck.

"What part of *don't touch* did you not understand, August?" Cage Edward's voice, lowered to a menacing growl, said from somewhere in the room, and then August was gone, literally ripped away from her by a force so strong it lifted him from the floor. He went flying back, hit the door and crashed through it, out into the hallway. Large splinters of wood spilled around him while a quarter of the door still hung on its hinges, and the panel with the doorknob on it landed with a loud *thunk.*

Lucinda screamed and stumbled back, fell against the bed and gripped the covers for the need of something to keep her from collapsing entirely.

In the hallway, August slid to the floor against the far wall. His lips curled back in a pained grimace, teeth bared so that she saw the fangs extended, so long and narrow that they dug into his lower gums.

To her immediate left, Cage towered. He watched the younger man struggle to get up from amid the shards of wood. Knowing now what he was, Lucinda understood why he had so much presence both on the stage, pretending to be something else, and here now. Predatory power emanated from him, channeled by the straightness of his tall figure, the set of his broad shoulders, the ferocity in his eyes.

A second later, Jasper and Morgan appeared in the hallway. Each stepped to one side of August, took him by the elbows and hauled him to his feet. They started to shove him back into the bedroom, but he shrugged out of their grasps aggressively and dusted himself off, glared at Cage with eyes changed from soft green to black onyx.

As she watched them with shuddering breath, Lucinda began to realize that neither she nor August had seen Cage enter. He had not come through the door. He was simply *there* as if he'd materialized from nowhere.

"I can't have a moment to myself anymore but what some *shit* happens," the troupe's leader snarled.

"Cage, she came here, she saw Jasper and Morgan disposing of—" August started to argue.

"They have already informed me, and that is now the least of our concerns," he replied.

While Jasper and Morgan lingered out in the hallway, Nora and Genevieve appeared and slunk through the door. Lucinda had already perceived their beauty as ethereal, the kind that projected well from a stage, that seduced audiences and especially men, but she had a new perspective on them now, and she cringed when Nora looked back at her and ever so subtly licked her lips.

"Yes, August," Nora jeered, "Cage told you no touchy." Her full, red lips opened into a wide smile. She did not display any fangs, but Lucinda felt like she was being devoured with those dark eyes alone. "Don't worry, girl. We'll take good care of you." In the same kind of blurry movement that August was capable of, she was on the bed pushing Lucinda over. Her hands, no bigger than Lucinda's own, grabbed her wrists and pinned them at the sides of her head. "Mmmm, pretty."

Lucinda's heartbeat kicked into a panic. With the only light on the bedside table, Nora's head was silhouetted, her face shadowed, but her eyes still peered from it like black pits, and her teeth shone white and feral. Lucinda closed her eyes and tried to push herself as deeply into the feather mattress and quilt as possible.

"Get off her!" August shouted. The bed jolted violently, and Nora's weight lifted, followed by a row of ferocious growls, ripping noises, like two angry animals tearing at each other.

"Enough!" Cage's voice boomed.

Lucinda's eyes snapped open in time to see Cage briefly gripping August's throat in one hand, Nora's in the other. Both bore deep, bleeding scratches on their faces, and their hands had sprouted into the spindly claws that August had revealed earlier. But then, to her astonishment, the scratches healed instantly, the claws reverted, and Cage dropped both of them to their knees.

Lucinda boosted up into a sit and crawled backward, disheveling the mattress and covers as she tried not to snag her skirts until her back pressed against the headboard. She drew her knees to her chest, tried to make herself as small and unnoticeable as possible.

"Someday, August," Cage said, "you will learn why you don't go for the first human to lift your prick in a century." He stepped further into the room then turned, positioning himself before them all. "Do I have everyone's attention?"

No one answered, but it was clear he did. Genevieve knelt next to her lover and laid a hand on Nora's shoulder while August stood up, his face a tight mask of lingering anger.

Once everyone else seemed calm, Jasper and Morgan stepped fully into the room but maintained their distance. August had called them daytime ambassadors, but Lucinda began to realize that *servant* was probably a more apt definition of their station. Their matching clothing had, from the start, seemed more like uniforms, and their stance was submissive to Cage's domineering presence. She tried to calm her breath and do as she guessed her father would, observe, learn more. God, what would he think of this? she wondered.

Cage closed his eyes and took a breath as if figuring out where to begin. "Some critical errors have been made here." His eyes snapped open, focused upon one individual. "Jasper."

"Why? What're you lookin' at me for?" already his voice trembled from being singled out.

"You were in charge of outlying disposals," Cage said. "An infected animal just appeared in town, the result of poor clean up. Another fucking *coyote*, Jasper. And where there is one of those, there are more to follow." In a blur, he shot forward, grabbed the accused man by the throat and lifted him easily off his feet until only the toes of his boots touched the floor. "You made the same mistake two towns ago in Contention City, remember?"

"I swear, Cage…" Jasper wheezed as he pried pitifully at the grip. "I was… thorough."

"Wells and his friend, that saloon keeper, were attacked and bitten in front of witnesses," Cage snarled.

Lucinda gasped sharply, covering her mouth. Reactionary tears flooded her eyes, and she couldn't help but shake her head. No, *not* Papa, not after what August had told her about the disease. As she stifled little, sharp breaths, she found August watching her. The glossy black in his eyes slipped back like oil trailing away into his sockets, revealing the soft jade again. He gazed at her as if to apologize for what she heard now and what it meant for her father.

Cage continued. "They were both taken to that clinic in the church, where I cannot set foot. Given the degree of his injury, LeBlanc will be a revenant by morning."

"*Uncle Silas?*" she gasped again. "No…"

"I'll take care of 'em both," Jasper rasped.

Cage's hand let go and dropped the man, who fell to a knee gulping in air and massaging his throat. "No. Leave Wells. He has a little more time. but ensure that the other one finds peace. Do *not* be seen." Cage's mouth remained pressed into a thin, angry line. "No more mistakes, Jasper." He didn't wait long before an angry, preternatural roar came out of him that rattled the panes in the window. "*Goooo!*"

Lucinda cringed and tucked her streaming, warm face against her knees to mute her sobs. Jasper half crawled toward the door before pushing himself up to hurry from the room.

In the awkward silence that fell, Cage's eyes darted to the two women, still kneeling on the floor, and he gave a clipped toss of his head for them to leave. Morgan, with his always reserved look, gave his boss a nod and proceeded out. Genevieve and Nora started to follow.

"Genevieve," Cage suddenly spoke up.

She froze in the doorway, her hand in Nora's, and turned to look at him. "Yes, Cage?"

"When I sent you after that deputy, what happened?"

Nathan? Lucinda's sobs shuddered a little harder. She felt her tears spread over the fabric of her skirt against her knee.

Genevieve's mouth formed a soft "Oh" and she looked down. "I found him, already almost halfway to Tombstone. He'd just stopped to make camp when I took him out. He never saw me coming."

"And you let his horses and wagon go to find their way back here? Worse, they picked up the interest of that pestilent beast that tailed them into town."

"Cage… I…"

"This is a critical time we are in."

"Yes, Cage."

"I don't care if you love horses, Genevieve." His voice hardened again. "You do what you're told, or I'll hold you as accountable as Jasper."

Her shoulders lifted with a quiet breath. She looked none too happy at the reprimand, but she nodded. Before anything else was said, Nora herded her from the room, and Lucinda suddenly wished they were all still here. The women with their catty smiles, Jasper and Morgan, too.

She was alone with Cage and August now, and she shivered as Cage's attention finally turned to her again.

"Now, as for you, sweet Lucinda," he purred her name and stepped to the bedside, sat down and leaned over to look her in the eyes. "Under normal circumstances, I'd clear your head and send you back up the street to your father, but it's too late for that. There are things out there in the dark right now, so I have a mission of my own."

"What's going to happen to my Papa?" Her voice came out like a soft mewl through her sobs.

"Ah, well." Cage reached up with surprising gentleness and swept a few strands of hair back from her face. She felt his cool fingertip graze her earlobe. "He was a potentially dangerous man before, but now he surely will be soon. We shall see where this goes."

"You had Genevieve kill Nathan, too?" she stuttered.

Cage sighed patiently. "I do not take pleasure in having to make such decisions, girl."

A new thought occurred to her, terribly delayed, but considering how her entire day had been spent in an opium stupor, she couldn't penalize herself. "W-what about Miz Simpson? What have you done with her?"

"Miz Simpson? Well, she is quite fine, for the time being. She's down in the kitchen happily making supper for Jasper and Morgan. Would you like some?"

His gaze leveled more intensely with hers, pewter eyes with bright-cut silver flecks that seemed to pour into his pupils continuously. She couldn't help but follow their paths like streams that pulled her along placidly with them. It barely occurred to her that her tears began to dry, that she'd stopped shuddering and felt the tension in her body ease. Her stomach growled a little, and she nodded vacantly. Yes, food would be good. It might help her recover from the laudanum.

"Very good," Cage said. "I'll have a tray sent up, and then after you eat, then piss, or shit, or whatever your human body needs to do, you're going to lay back down and sleep long and deep until your papa wakes you."

She nodded again and slowly relaxed, turned on her side to rest her head on the pillows, and remained curled up. Having something to eat sounded very good indeed.

"I have to say that you do have good taste, August," Cage said. "She really does look like a china doll."

"You bastard," August growled, but Lucinda barely heard it.

"Wonderful," Cage said pleasantly. "Now, I've got work to do."

CHAPTER TWENTY-TWO

The chaos of the coyote attack had begotten more chaos until the marshal and company had finally settled into the rectory-cum-clinic. With no disrespect meant to Nathan, since his buckboard was already there and the horses hitched, Hiram and Becker had loaded Silas into the bed. Becker had taken over compressing the wound while Hiram raced the wagon up the street with Izabel clinging to the seat beside him. Having no time to douse lamps or lock the security doors, they'd left the Palace fully lit and opened to anyone.

For the duration of the journey, he replayed the scene in his head, every detail up until the moment the smoke had briefly blinded him, and he had lost track of Cage. He had called out for the actor a few times, but the man had departed without notice. After that, Watkins had loitered around the commotion, looking rather green until he was advised to join the Raskins for the night and not risk running into another such predator on his way home. Jesse had followed the wagon with Caleb and Ellie in the saddle with him while leading Teddy. The horses had been turned loose inside the cemetery as a temporary corral in hopes that the fence would deter other predators. Given how high the first beast had sprung, Hiram didn't bank on that, but a little sacrilege was better than having them hitched and less mobile.

In the wagon's wake, the beast burned down to nothing but bones and a scorch mark in the street, and Hiram did not think too hard about how he would deal with that mess.

Now he sat on one cot and leaned back against the wall, boots planted on the floor. His duster and gun belt—with the Peacemaker restored to its holster—had been removed, his throbbing right arm exposed and elevated with a towel underneath. The bite consisted of two sharper piercings from the coyote's front canines followed by two rows of molar prints that had been just as sharp, leaving long razor cuts. If he held still, the bleeding ebbed, but the moment he flexed a single muscle, it welled up and threaded over his arm onto the towel.

On the other side of the room, Silas shivered violently on his cot, breath coming in short little hisses through his teeth, while his eyes rolled up in his skull, and Hiram couldn't tear his eyes away.

"It's shock," Becker had explained when the quivering began. He was busy holding the compression on his patient's neck and giving instructions to Caleb and Jesse with calm calculation.

Izabel was on her knees at the head of the cot, crying softly, pleading in Spanish with her lover to hold on.

Hiram swallowed, blinked away a flash of that night in March, himself in a similar place to Izabel as he hunched over the master bed and held Rachel's hand, not sure where his tears ended and hers began.

Smell of blood…

"Caleb, get that knife into the fire. Jesse, check that water kettle, and then over there in the counter cabinet, you'll find a bottle of carbolic acid. Has a red label. Ja… ja, it's marked poison. No one's going to eat it, Jesse. Pour a little in those pans there and add the water. Make sure it isn't too hot." He indicated a couple of speckled enamel wash pans in a stack on the end of the counter.

Becker was good at this, Hiram realized. His instructions focused the boys on a job that kept their panic down and resourcefulness up. While Jesse found said bottle and added some of the contents to the pans, Caleb propped the blade of a Bowie knife on the edge of the open potbelly stove with the blade resting amid the brightly glowing coals. Jesse then hefted the substantial iron kettle off the stove to pour as instructed.

Ellie, meanwhile, was curled up on the cot next to Hiram. Her frightened wails had, thankfully, reduced to little keening sobs, but she was far from settling down. The thing had scared her and good, and Hiram reconsidered his philosophy of not hating an animal based on its nature. No, he told himself, something was *wrong* with that thing, something that went beyond its nature and beyond rabid. A rabid animal would not have had such strength. Viciousness, yes, but it would be dehydrated and thin, weaker, and it would *not* have gotten back up after taking five slugs to the neck and side.

Then there were those eyes.

Hiram inwardly shuddered and tried to banish that visual, but as with everything he saw, it remained engraved deep and wouldn't fade. Worse was the image of it pouncing upon his best friend, tearing at Silas' throat. Far worse was the happiest, most enthusiastic man he'd ever known stretched on a cot, seizing and pale, face slick with cold sweat. Diminished from composed and gracious to *this* in a mere blink.

"Okay, wash your hands, boys," Becker said. "And bring it to me, too. Jesse, one more thing, see that piece of leather on the counter? Hand that to me, please." He alternated dipping his own hands in one pan and went back to examining his patient. He gently tugged a lower eyelid down one at a time for a better glimpse of Silas' whites, looked at the edges of the compression and uttered a none too pleased, "Hmmmm."

Hiram didn't like the sound of that.

"Alright, take that other pan and go start cleaning the marshal's arm, Jesse."

"Just pour some whiskey on it," Hiram said through his teeth and impatiently started to sit up. A dizzy wave sent him back again, and his shoulders sagged. *Useless.* He felt so goddamned useless here, and while his arm was waiting to be cleaned and wrapped, his eldest was out there somewhere in the dark of night, and where there was one monster—a bona fide *monster*—there might be more.

"Whiskey is for drinking," Becker said, maintaining his focus. "You've lost a lot of blood yourself, Marshal. You stay put. Jesse, start cleaning his wound. Caleb, bring me the knife. Careful, don't burn yourself."

The boy used a cloth wrap around the knife handle and lifted the glowing blade from the embers, carried it carefully before him. A stream of smoke briefly trailed from the tip.

Hiram braced himself, though he was not the one about to be cauterized. All he smelled now was blood. Silas' and his own. As he watched Silas shiver and seize, he felt a coldness spread through his chest as shock tried to claim him as well. *Dammit, no.* He needed to stay alert because he had a mission.

Jesse brought the second pan of water over to Hiram's cot and doused a rag in it, sloshed it around for good measure. A sulfurous odor swirled up on the steam.

Across the room, Becker locked eyes with Izabel, asked her calmly to help him roll Silas onto his side so that his head tilted for better admittance. The saloon keeper's shirt, one of his favorites with its high collar, was saturated in red and torn back from his shoulder and chest. There were claw marks below his collar bone, but they were shallow and only oozed.

He'll be really upset about that shirt, Hiram thought. He *had* to think that way because the alternative was unbearable. "Caleb," he rasped after he watched his son hand Becker the knife. "Take your sister into the sanctuary a while. Bar the doors."

Becker noted this, paused a little longer in silent agreement.

"Yeah, Papa." The boy gently pried Ellie up from the cot, got her on her feet.

After the door shut behind them, Becker handed Izabel the piece of leather. "Keep this wedged between his teeth," he said. That done, he aligned the flat side of the Bowie and addressed Silas directly. "I'm sorry I don't have a proper cauterizing tool, Mr. LeBlanc," he said, "but this knife'll do the trick." He removed the compression bandage, briefly freeing a fount of fresh blood, and immediately lowered the blade.

With the hiss of searing skin and Silas' strangled cry, a violent stinging sensation shot up Hiram's arm, and he cried out, looked down to see that Jesse had wrung the hot, treated water over the bite. Blood marbleized into the streams and bloomed out over the towel.

Across the room, Silas bowed violently, and Becker shouted, "Hold him still!"

Izabel reached to grab at his flailing arms but, so much smaller than he, she struggled, while Becker attempted to pin him, to hold the knife in place just a little longer.

Done with sitting still and helpless, Hiram pushed himself up past Jesse, grabbed the towel and clamped it over his arm, pinned it with his elbow against his chest. Then he stumbled across the room, dropped down beside Becker, and grabbed one of Silas' flailing hands in his.

"Silas, brother, come on," he grated out. "Just hold on a little longer."

As the crackling tapered off, the injured man finally passed out. His mouth slackened, and the leather strip dropped free. Becker carefully lifted the blade, making sure it didn't stick to the skin, and revealed a nasty red seal that appeared to have successfully cemented the loose flap of skin back into place.

Hiram took a breath. "That it?"

"Hopefully he'll stabilize, but if that coyote was rabid—"

"No," Izabel interrupted desperately with a sniffle. "It can't be *that.* Fue el diablo!" She crossed herself then.

"It wasn't rabid," Hiram agreed flatly. "But it was definitely *something.*"

"It wasn't the devil, Izabel," Becker argued.

"Oh, it was pretty close," Hiram replied.

"With an attack like that?" Becker looked from one to the other, likely assuming they were both in denial. "It's clear it had been pacing with those horses for some time, followed them into town, went after the first thing it saw as a threat."

"You didn't *see* the attack." Hiram tried not to be snappish. "You didn't see me empty my gun into it and the damned thing get back up." He slowly let go of Silas' hand, laid it at his side as Izabel and Becker gingerly rolled the patient onto his back again.

By now, Jesse had stood up from the other cot and hovered nearby as if shy to contribute to the debate, but he finally found his tongue. "He's right, Pastor Becker. That wasn't no ordinary coyote."

Becker sighed patiently, got up and retrieved a tin and a roll of gauze from the counter, brought it back to start applying some smelly herbal balm to the side of Silas' neck. Izabel, murmuring what sounded like a prayer in Spanish, helped him lift Silas' head so he could wrap his neck with the gauze.

Hiram turned to sit on the floor, leaned against the corner of the cot with the towel still clamped between his forearm and chest. He almost couldn't feel his fingers, and then a second cold wave braced the inside of his chest. He gasped and found Becker staring dubiously at him. "I'm *fine.*"

The pastor chose patience again as he reached for Hiram's arm. "Let me see it."

Hiram surrendered to unfold his arm and reveal the bite that still oozed but no longer bled excessively. Becker frowned as he got his first good look at the lacerations.

"See, that ain't a normal bite either," Jesse observed from where he stood. "Those teeth were too big. That whole critter was *too* big."

"That critter was *definitely* too big," Hiram echoed him.

Becker examined it a moment longer and then got up to prepare a gauze pad with yet another ointment. He came back to kneel by Silas' cot, laid the pad over the bite, and began to wrap Hiram's forearm.

Hiram gritted his teeth as the gauze grew a little tighter with each pass. "Alright, that's enough." He gave Becker just enough time to tie off the end. "Jesse, you ready?"

"I am if you are, Marshal."

He held out his good hand, and Jesse responded by reaching down to help him haul up to his feet, steadied him before he fell over from getting vertical too quickly.

"What do you think you're doing?" Becker stood up behind him.

"You didn't hear yet," Hiram explained, "but Lucinda didn't come home this afternoon."

"Oh…" Becker gasped. "Oh, God."

"Jesse and I were about to go look for her before this happened."

"Then I'm not going to stop you," Becker said. His eyes shifted to the young ranch hand and narrowed grimly. "Look after him, Jesse. He's about to fall on his face as it is."

"I'm standing right here," Hiram muttered and tried not to hobble as he went to go put on what was left of his duster.

"I'll take care of 'im," Jesse affirmed.

"And I'll finish treating these other wounds on Silas." Becker knelt, reached for the pan of water. "Go on then. I'll pray that you find her safe and sound."

"You do that," Hiram said bitterly and shrugged on the linen coat that was lacking a sleeve. Then he stared down at his friend for a moment longer. Silas was beginning to shiver again, but at least it was a sign of life.

With that, he pulled on his gun belt and struggled stubbornly with the buckle because shit if he would let Becker know how wretched his hand and arm felt. Dignity spared, he finally settled the holster in place on his left hip, then he drew the Peacemaker and opened the loading gate on the cylinder. He ejected the spent cartridges one after another and replaced them with new ones from the belt's loops, filling all six chambers. He closed the loading gate and eased the hammer back down steadily.

The danger of six loads seemed nothing after what he'd witnessed, but to have just one more round in the last chamber was a cold but worthwhile comfort.

*
**

Some nights he let the winds simply carry him where they would. Other times he followed a trail below or weak house lights on the horizon, depending on his needs. Tonight, he pursued a scent that resembled old leaves, decaying blood, and wet dog.

A waning half-moon shone above, though its dark half was still clearly defined like an empty section of pie plate. The illuminated half looked like a piece of fine crystal as it cast veins of silver through the clouds. A faint green aurora slithered along the *Winter Road*—as he had once called it so many ages ago—the pulsing river of stars and dust that arced across a sky that was as blue to his vision as it was in daylight to a human, but for him it was richer, fused with shades of violet. Below, the landscape showed bright, yellow sand and red clay peering up through patches of scrub and cacti. To his left were the mountain columns of sandstone that he had come to adore. They were full of caverns and crevices that were perfect havens, especially since they faced north, away from the deadliest of the sun's rays. Upon the kith's arrival, he had fed in the most outlying miners' camp there at the foot of the columns, where the missing went hardly noticed at all. Disposal was distant from any habitation and neat, easier.

But when it came to tightening the circle, closing in on any town, cleaning up became more hazardous, the risk of discovery greater, the more need of help to get it done. That was why Jasper should have been more cautious, more studious to see that no burn pit was left half-finished before it was filled in. Nothing should remain, and that was why Cage now swept down toward the scent he was seeking and found his quarry.

Four of them sped toward the sleeping town, barely a mile out.

He dove and materialized into full form before landing in a three-point kneel some fifty yards before them and stood up. The wind that followed his descent billowed through his hair, his coat, and the loosely buttoned old shirt he'd worn. He removed the coat and laid it neatly over a sizeable gray spindle of driftwood before he stepped directly into their path. He opened his hands, felt a long-familiar soreness as bone and nail extended into sharp talons, then he raised one hand and sliced a deep cut down through his palm.

The scent of fresh blood permeated the air around him, and his quarry came to him, all of them, all at once.

The two just ahead of the others dove at him together, snarling, baring teeth that gleamed like shards of glass. He pivoted on one hip and side kicked one away from him while reaching out and grabbing the other as it came in. He gripped the grimy fur of its scruff and the ruff under its jaws in both hands and slammed it face-first into the ground where he heard and felt vertebrae crush against each other. He got a tighter grip while he planted a foot on its shoulders, braced, and twisted its head completely off, trailing strings of torn flesh, scattering broken bone. The tense body went limp, twitching. He dropped the head and spun to ready for the next attack.

The one he'd kicked vacillated between growls, yelps, and hideous hyena-like giggles. Its crushed ribs crackled against each other, trying to heal, but these creatures had not fed enough yet. Perhaps the first one that appeared in town had initiated the whole cycle by attacking one of its pack, which in turn attacked another, and around and around they went until this moment. For a fraction of a second, Cage watched it stagger sideways, unable to get its bearing like a half-crushed bug, and then he focused on the other two that had been bringing up the rear.

He backward sidestepped as the next dove at him and let it pass by in a flash to land somewhere behind him. He pivoted back around to punch the second between the eyes, putting the whole side of his body into the swing. The snout bone and frontal skull caved in, resulting in a strained screech as the creature smacked the ground and scrambled back in a recoil. Its teeth gnashed aimlessly at the air. A black, oozing eyeball dangled from the crushed socket, while the beast let out a grating gibber that made even Cage want to cover his ears.

He spun into the one that had glanced past, found it rebounding and coming back. It opened its jaws wide as it leaped to head height. His left hand shot out, caught it around the throat, and squeezed, forcing its maw skyward where its wails and howls carried the loudest. His claws gripped deep into the mess of matted fur, black flesh, and esophagus so that its roar died into a gurgle that collapsed into a mewling sound. While the body twitched and its clawed feet flailed, he thrust his free hand forward, up under its ribs into the chest cavity, where he found the heart, clutched and ripped it free before dropping the body with a meaty *thunk*.

Black ichor arced into the air with every attack and kill, gleaming in the moonlight as it splashed upon the ground. With every scrape of claw or tooth to his skin, his rage grew and burned behind his eyes. The heart fell away from his hand as he reengaged.

Down to two, he rushed upon the one with its side crushed, kicked it again in such a way as to send it over and pin it by the neck, then with a simple side twist of his heel, severed the spine to immobilize it.

The remaining one, gibbering and screeching while one eyeball swung against the side of its maw and the other glared out from a hole brimming with putrid discharge, made its last advance only to miscalculate and come at him sideways. He snatched its upper jaw and pulled the beast against him, shoved fingers into its mouth and gripped the lower half of its maw. The needle-sharp teeth dug into his fingers, but he channeled back the pain as he pried the hinge of its jaws apart with a wet crunch. It keened and tossed its head violently to get free before he shoved his right hand down its throat. Past esophagus and windpipe to effectively cut off the infuriating sounds, and when his hand emerged, the skin of his forearm tore in long gashes against the angle of its fangs. His hand slipped free, gripping another pulped and crushed heart, and the creature collapsed.

Cage held the heart before him for a moment. It was unrecognizable in his grip, with his claws curled into its collapsed chambers. His teeth gritted, angry breath huffed as he stared at the lacerations to his arm, oozing red against thick smears of black. A moment later, they closed, his skin seaming back together, leaving no scars until there was nothing but the gleam of the ichor under the moonlight. This immediate healing had long ago ceased to fascinate him. That he should have to go through it at all made him nothing but angrier.

The night grew as quiet as it would ever be for ears such as his that heard every insect crawling nearby, every drop of night dew settling.

Cage composed himself, let the anger burn itself off in his head, let all transformations he'd assumed fade, and began to gather the pieces of his carnage into one pile. In the end, the heap looked like little more than large chunks of torn fur, a paw here, a severed jaw and teeth there, and then he took off his shirt, used it to wipe down his upper body, until the fabric was little more than a black stain, and threw that into the heap. He retrieved his coat and reached into one of the pockets to withdraw a match safe.

He struck a match and threw it onto the pile, which instantly flared up with the most revolting reek. At their core, the flames burned green, putrid as the abominations they consumed. Revenant flesh was highly combustible to fire, to sunlight, but there was nothing wrong with giving it additional help. Cage held out a hand and concentrated, called in gusts of air to feed the flames, building them higher and hotter and ensuring that they stayed corralled within this isolated spot and did not spread through the chaparral.

Then he waited.

…and waited…

…and waited…

He stood still and tolerated the brilliance and the pungency for perhaps an hour, maybe more. When the cleansing finished, and there were only fragments of bones that no carrion creature would touch now, he put on his coat and moved on.

The coat, trousers, and everything else that may have gotten the ichor on it would also be burned, and his body would have to undergo a cleansing ritual, too, and to think about it made every part of him quiver with new fury, but he choked it down. If there were more revenant creatures out there, he needed to find them.

So, he stepped away from the smoldering ring of bones and, sniffing the air for a trail, took a running start and launched himself into the night again.

CHAPTER TWENTY-THREE

Before they went anywhere, Hiram stopped by the jail. He went inside, moving as quickly as the darkness and his sore arm would let him as he lit the lamp on his desk, and opened the desk drawer, withdrew an extra badge, and palmed it. Then he carried the lamp over to sit on top of the safe. His hand shook as he dialed the lock open, but he managed to get it right the first time. Inside, the light flickered over Frank Evans' Peacemaker and belt. He took out the gun and topped off the cylinder but left the sixth chamber empty in case Jesse was not used to handling a pistol the way he was the shotguns and rifles typically wielded in his line of work.

Then he closed the safe and started to turn the wick on the lamp back down only to pause, once more looking into the shadows of the empty cells, still braced by the sense that there was an answer floating in there somewhere that had simply escaped him since Friday night. With that thought came the familiar headache. It occurred to him how little he'd been sleeping now, how little he'd eaten the past three days. Chastising himself for that, he turned down the wick and hastily headed for the door.

Outside, in the chill of the moonlight, Jesse was waiting on his horse next to Teddy. The kid was staring with frightened saucer eyes up the thoroughfare and toward the expanse to the southwest between the town and the Arduous range.

"You hear that, Marshal?" he asked.

Hiram listened and felt an icy bloom in his middle that shot up his back to his nape and then branched down his arms.

Though the din was distant, it filled the night air with wails, vicious snarls, unearthly cackling. A normal pack of coyotes attacking one of their own out there sounded horrible enough, but this went beyond the mundane and left nightmares in its wake. The hellacious chorus tapered off with one greater note, a prolonged howl that strained against the night and died into a strange gargle and then nothing at all.

The noise weighed on Hiram as much as it terrified him. His daughter, and now his deputy, were missing. There was no way Nathan could have made it to Tombstone without his horses and wagon, and that meant another search tomorrow, after he found Lucinda, after the night gave way to brilliant day and he could see clearly what was coming at him.

"Focus, Jesse," he said, and his voice sounded like an intrusion on the moment. Jesse blinked and looked down as Hiram handed him the gun and belt, then the badge. "Can you handle that?"

"You wanna deputize me?"

"Position's likely open," Hiram said grimly. "Hell, I should have just done it before anyway and let Watkins and the council gripe. I always needed more help. Besides, it makes you carrying that thing in town more legal."

"Sure, I'll do it." His hands shook a little as he pinned the badge on his jacket lapel.

Hiram didn't have a Bible, so it was the shortest swearing-in he'd ever performed with the kid still on his horse, a hand raised as he took the oath.

"Now, what about the gun?" Hiram asked as he went back to the boardwalk and began to light two lanterns. "You good with it?"

In the silver glow, the kid's eyes were in shadow though it was clear he was staring at the Colt in his hands. He nodded vacantly. "But Marshal," he said with helplessness in his voice, "You put five bullets in that'n in the street, an' it still got back up." He slid the weapon into its holster and pulled the belt on, secured it to his hip, and resituated in his saddle.

"A bullet may be a small deterrent, but it's something." He brought the lanterns over to the horses and handed them both up to Jesse. "That's what these are for. I wish we could carry more." With his right arm giving him no end of grief, he braced, climbed into the saddle, and took back one of the lanterns. "You saw what Cage did. We encounter another monster like that, you throw that lantern at it hard. Don't worry if you set the whole damn desert on fire. You just turn and bolt. I'm sorry we don't have time to put some better plan together."

Jesse nodded, his face now half-lit by a warm glow, the other dark and cast in blue. His eyes remained down a moment longer.

"What?"

"I love your daughter. You know that, don't you, Marshal? Even after how she's been all week since those actors came to town."

Hiram's chest, already gripped in a vise, tightened a little more. "I know, kid."

"Somehow, I feel like she's all right. She's probably with August Chandler." There was a sad resignation in his voice.

"You questioning my daughter's honor?" Hiram asked gruffly, though he couldn't begrudge Jesse for any confused or unmannerly thoughts on the whole matter. Hell, he didn't care himself how he found his daughter. If she was naked in August Chandler's arms, at least she was *alive,* and that was all he cared about.

"No, just saying I know she doesn't love me the way I love her." Then he said the thing that won Hiram over forever. "But I'd still do anything for her."

The marshal nodded. "You're a better man than August Chandler, Jesse. Trust me." He held his lantern aloft with a shaky right arm, realizing he'd have to alternate his hands on the reins, which would slow them down somewhat. "We better get going."

"So, how are we doing this?"

"First, we visit Miz Simpson and the troupe, and if Lucinda isn't there like Cage said, we go door-to-door in the south neighborhood."

Coming out of his mouth, it sounded practical, easy enough, until he discovered that a two-mile ride out of town, in the middle of a night lined with streaks of icy light and long shadows, felt like forever. As with chasing vultures on the horizon, the Simpson house felt like it slipped a little further away with each stride and the fear that there was something else out there. They heard no more distant howls and screeches, but that didn't make Hiram feel better.

At long last, the shape of the Simpson house loomed with the star-dusted sky and the branches of larger trees as its backdrop. For the most part, the place was dark, but there were flickering creases of light in the windows, leaking between curtains not completely drawn. The shadow of the troupe's coach sat in the front drive, spider-like the way its slender, elegant wheel spokes made strange patterns against the moonlit backdrop behind it. Around the side and further back, the barn and corral stood draped in the eerie lace of shadows cast by an oak tree that had lost most of its leaves already.

Hiram raised his nose and sniffed the air, frowned at the smell of burnt *things* drifting in from the scrubby plain. Just as Cage had said, the scent wafted in and out on the breezes.

"You trust the troupe?" Jesse asked. "You trust Cage Edwards?"

"I don't have any reason not to," Hiram said as he dismounted and headed for the porch and front door. "He did finish off that thing in town. I just hope he made it back here safely." Considering the man seemed to walk everywhere he went, Hiram had to admit he felt as much concern for the lead actor's wellbeing as his daughter and deputy. The odd thing was that Cage had not hung around to explain the inclination to set the beast on fire, but it had worked, and Hiram was grateful.

With the lantern aloft in his left, he raised his right hand to grip the knocker, winced at a strange tingling through his arm. Then an odder sensation washed through him. For a moment, the night around him flared brightly, and his hearing dulled as if plunged underwater, only the sound of his breath and heartbeat reaching through, while a hollowness dug into his middle, gnawing with the worst of hunger pangs. He clutched a hand to his stomach and blinked rapidly, shaking his head.

"You all right, Marshal?" Jesse asked. There was impatience in his voice. *Knock on the door already.*

His vision cleared to normal, his ears unstopped, but the gnawing only reduced. Hiram remained aware of it still there niggling at his belly, in his chest. His left arm had lowered, and he quickly erected it. He took a long, deep breath but felt like it wasn't quite enough. Gripping the knocker, he pounded it three hard times and waited, thought he heard the creaking of steps from within the house. "Miz Simpson?" he called and knocked again. "It's Marshal Wells. Can I speak to you a moment?"

He heard no more floorboards groaning or creaking as steps approached the immediate area of the door, so he naturally startled when it opened abruptly, and there before him stood Genevieve Blakely. She wore a silk dressing gown for bed, and her fiery hair was backlit from lamps burning down the hall in the rear parlor where, he recalled, Rachel and Lucinda used to have tea with Miz Simpson.

"Hello, Marshal Wells," she said in a near purr and leaned against the frame, allowing a shoulder of the gown to slide ever so slightly free, revealing the curve of creamy skin.

It distracted Hiram far more than expected, given how often Izabel unabashedly presented her own assets—meeting no objections from Silas—in front of him. This young woman, however, could give Izabel a run for her money.

"Miss Blakely," he almost croaked, then cleared his throat.

"What do we owe the pleasure at this hour, Marshal?"

"I was wondering if… I mean… I…" He clamped his mouth shut, pulled himself together. "Miss Blakely, have you by chance seen my daughter today? Lucinda went for a ride and hasn't come home."

"Oh… oh no," she gasped, sounding sincere. "I haven't, but maybe Miz Simpson has." She turned to look down the hall as footsteps approached, and Hiram looked past her to see the silhouette of a woman in a more conservative dress approaching, tiny waist cinched, hair down in neat ringlets around her neck and high collar.

"Miz Simpson," he greeted her as she came nearer, and behind her trailed none other than August Chandler. Her face formed in the light of his lantern and gave him a sweet smile.

"Why, Marshal Wells, how unexpected."

Something about the entire scene before him did not fit. He would never have expected to see Grace Simpson standing next to a sultry actress with the tall, attractive figure of August Chandler right behind her. August leaned a hand against the door frame from the inside, all but creating a shield around Miz Simpson's petite figure.

"Actually," Hiram cleared his throat again and looked at August. "You're the person I want to see, Mr. Chandler."

"Me?" August blinked, looked slightly astonished.

"Have you seen my daughter today?"

The question, so point-blank, seemed to take the young man by surprise. "Why? Is something wrong?" His eyes roamed past Hiram, clearly focusing out into the drive where Jesse waited with the horses. A fierceness beamed in them, easily interpreted as suitor jealousy.

"Have you *seen* my daughter today? I won't repeat that."

August opened his mouth, but Miz Simpson answered for him.

"Lucinda did come by, Marshal Wells, but only briefly this morning." She sounded strangely relaxed as she said it, perhaps trying to keep him calm.

Hiram's gaze unlocked from the young actor's, and he looked at the lady of the house. Cage had claimed not to have seen Lucinda at either of the troupe's regular locations, but that did not necessarily mean anything if the man had been out on one of his walks. "She did not come home this afternoon," he informed them.

"What?" August started to nudge past Miz Simpson. "Where could she be?"

"Funnily enough, I was hoping she'd be here with *you*. Even if it ended with me shooting you in the ass, Mr. Chandler."

The casual threat gave Chandler pause for a moment but then seemed to fall on deaf ears. "Can I help?" the young actor asked anxiously. "I can get one of our horses, help you search."

"No," Hiram said. "There are dangers out tonight. I'd advise you all to stay inside. Is Cage here?"

"No," Genevieve answered a little quickly, but she appeared to have walked back her smiles and sultry charms as she tugged the shoulder of her gown back into place. "He hasn't come back."

New nervy tightness strummed through Hiram, and he pinched the bridge of his nose. *Not another one.*

"He went into town for a drink hours ago," August said. "Should we be concerned?"

"Yes," Hiram said. "Yes, you should." He returned his gaze to Miz Simpson, who blinked sleepily back at him. "I need to get back to it then. Keep your doors locked. Only let Cage back in if he comes back." Where the lead actor was concerned, Hiram hoped he'd been shrewd enough to take advantage of the Palace remaining unlocked and stay in there. He added checking the bar to his list when he and Jesse got back into town.

"Oh dear, of course," Grace Simpson replied, still sounding distant.

Hiram frowned at that, gave them all a nod goodbye before he turned away. He heard the door shut behind him as he stepped down off the porch. Ahead of him, he could see that Jesse was still staring most intensely at the door. "Jesse, grown-ass men don't have staring contests," he commented as he handed the kid his lantern so he could climb back into the saddle. A dizzy wave caught him as he righted himself and adjusted the reins.

Jesse blinked. "You had a staring contest with Frank Evans."

"That was a diversion."

"Something was off about that." Jesse nodded toward the door and the house.

"I know," Hiram said as he took back the lantern, but in his worries over his daughter, he didn't have time to nail down what it was. "I trust Miz Simpson, but the others…" He shrugged. "Let's go."

The ride back into town was as strenuous as the ride out. Two miles felt like it turned into twenty as the ache in his arm branched into other parts of his body and wrung out little shivers that he suppressed. He put it down to riding around in a duster that was missing a sleeve. The night had turned so cold, and it tingled in his fingers and toes. At least they could be grateful that no more haunting screeches, howls or warped chortling noises sounded in the distance, and no stalking growls arose from the scrub and shadows on the sides of the road.

They veered off from the southwestern bend when they reached the main thoroughfare and headed toward the old Spanish mission and chapel that stood back behind the block for the school, Bixby Brothers' Carpentry, and the bank.

Father Ramirez came to the door of the little adobe parsonage behind the chapel in his long johns. Rubbing sleepy eyes, he answered Hiram's questions with deepening concern, but all it came down to was *no*, he had not seen Lucinda all day.

They moved west and past Watkins' big gabled house with its long porches. They didn't bother there since the mayor was accounted for over at the hotel for the night. In the neighborhood, Hiram pounded on door after door until he couldn't anymore and began to send Jesse. Terry Wilkes came to his stoop, looking a little green and tired, and a few houses up, town councilman Wayne Granning appeared to see what the commotion was about. Finding their marshal and a ranch hand on their doorsteps so far past midnight initially provoked irritation until they learned the reason for the visit. Grumbles turned into apologies that they had no information, and the search continued.

Upon reaching the end of the neighborhood, Hiram noted the lower angle of the moon and how soon a majority of their light would be briefly gone before the sun came up. "Where the hell is everyone?" he whispered and saw his breath ghost away. Not even the Kranes had answered their door.

"You don't look so good, Marshal," Jesse said, holding his lantern up closer to Hiram's face.

The flame inside the globe flared to a stinging brilliance that forced Hiram to squint. Then there it was again, that same peculiar flash he'd had while standing on Miz Simpson's porch. A fresh chill moved through him, and the gnawing kicked up in his gut while the landscape around him flashed brightly. It was only an instant, the effect like watching a slow bolt of lightning bring out the paths of white sand, the scrub and cholla, rocks and other details that were more apparent during the day. Once more, his hearing took a plunge into an imaginary lake, ears flooding with water that wasn't there.

He felt like he could… *sink*… away… just fall to the bottom of a vast inner sea.

"Marshal?" Jesse's voice reached him, muffled over the thunder of his own heartbeat, the echo of his breath growing shallow as he exhaled.

… then inhaled sharply as he snapped to again.

Hiram shuddered and looked up to find Jesse staring with worry at him. "I'm sorry, what?"

"What now?" Jesse asked.

He looked down the line of houses platted unevenly during the Bend's early days. "We could try again," he suggested. "Maybe the first pass at least roused some folks."

"A'right."

They started to move back westward again when Jesse randomly nailed the problem with the Simpson house visit. "Ya know, I saw that lady's shoulder. Funny how Miz Simpson didn't get 'er back up about it."

The little scattered puzzle pieces of that whole scene fit into place as they hadn't when Hiram was standing right there in front of it. Grace Simpson was too conservative to have an actress parading around her house showing off skin, even just a little bit of shoulder, in a dressing gown that was barely there. And then there had been August Chandler hovering over her, not protectively, but more like…

Controlling?

"You're right," he said, his head clearing as he shook off the last of this second weird episode. "Miz Simpson seemed like…"

"Like she drank all the laudanum," Jesse finished.

Hiram suppressed a snort. Yes, that described it well. There was an opium-induced vacancy in the way the woman stared, the relaxed way she reacted to the news of Lucinda being missing. She *knew* Lucinda. Had known her since she was a child. Cared enough about her not to be quite so passive to such news. He knew too well what opium did to one's wits.

"Drugged?" he whispered more to himself than to Jesse. The thought stirred an old discomfort in him that had long been suppressed. "She was definitely way too passive about it all," he said. She had not, he realized, even reacted when he commented on the possibility of shooting August Chandler in his gamy, young rear.

"Yeah, like way… way…" Jesse perked up. "You're not sayin'…"

Something else occurred to him, and Hiram chided himself for not thinking of it before. In the end, they were all, save Miz Simpson, *actors*. Genevieve and August… they sounded sincere, but were they just as good at playing off stage as on?

"We're going back to the Simpson house," he declared.

"Oh, okay. We're not very far from sunup, you know?" He gestured toward the eastern sky. "And no offense, but can you stay in that saddle, Marshal?"

"Mind your damn business, boy."

That was when they heard the crack of a gunshot. It was muffled, likely fired indoors, and came from somewhere on the other side of the schoolhouse at the end of town. Hiram straightened to full seated height in the saddle, cast aside all dizziness and aches that tried to grip him. A few seconds later, a louder shot sounded, this one clearly outside. There was only one other gun that he was aware of in that vicinity of the town.

"That was Silas' Derringer," he said and heeled Teddy into a full run.

After Marshal Wells and Jesse left on their mission, after Becker cleaned the claw gashes on Silas' chest and applied more salve, bandaged those, and dared to *hope* that his patient was stabilized, he took care of the elementary things. He and Izabel got Silas out of his bloody vest and shirt, pulled off his boots to hear the heavy thump of his mother-of-pearl-handled Derringer falling out of its ankle holster. Becker placed the gun and Silas' pocket watch on the center exam table then covered the shivering patient with every quilt he had. He stoked the fire in the stove, kept it roaring and the room warm. The bloody clothes went into a heap at the foot of the cot next to the boots, and Izabel sat on the floor at the other end where she tucked her knees under her and folded her arms to rest her head next to Silas'.

Now it was just a matter of waiting and allowing him to rest.

The frenzy of saving a man's life ebbed, replaced with the soft crackles from inside the stove and Silas' short, sharp breaths. Caleb and Ellie had remained, blissfully, out in the sanctuary—Becker had last seen Caleb distracting his sister by getting her to pray in one of the pews—which was perfectly fine.

He made a cup of willow bark tea for himself to combat any forthcoming headache and sipped it at his desk as he flipped through *Van Schaack, Stevenson & Reid's* apothecary catalog. Although there were supplies that he would need to replace after tonight, browsing was more of a distraction from the growing dread inside him. The man on the cot was Hiram Wells' best friend, clearly more of a brother than Wells' actual sibling back east. He'd been an adventure companion, a partner in crime long ago. Silas LeBlanc's death would be an added blow, and Becker worried further about the marshal's recovery.

Worse, Silas' life had been left in Becker's hands, and the slightest thought of failure stirred cold nerves in his stomach. Worse still, while urgent treatment was going on in the rectory, right below them all in the cellar, a metal-lined and locked chest contained the remains of several unidentified people, haunting Becker even while he was holding Silas down and cauterizing his neck.

Becker felt dirty, tired, haggard.

His head dropped heavily over the catalog as he nearly fell asleep with his cheek propped in his hand. No, he *had* fallen asleep. He sat up, rubbing crusty eyes, and had the sense that quite a length of time had slipped away. He pushed sweeps of wiry gray hair back from his face and stood to check on his patient.

The room had grown quieter, cooler, the fire in the stove down to embers that snapped occasionally, but Silas' shuddering breaths had subsided. The latter caused Becker to brace himself as he knelt beside the cot.

The face turned upward was still, peaceful but pasty compared to its usual olive complexion. There were blackish hollows under the eyes, and dark veins showed through the translucent skin at his temples. The veins branched along the sides of his face, over the sharp hills of his cheekbones, and trailed down under his jaw.

Becker reached over to tug the quilts down from Silas' chin, caught a breath to see the black traces continue down the sides of his neck. When he dared to angle Silas' head to get a better look, he found the greatest concentration of black came from beneath the bandage from the main bite area. Hearing no breath, unable to note any rise in Silas' chest, he felt for a pulse.

There was none.

Becker shuddered, and the last vestige of hope in him withered. What remained was holy terror at the now all too familiar black veins, and given where they originated, it was safe to conclude that the bite had caused it. Hiram Wells was right, it was *not* from rabies, but they *were* dealing with a disease.

Becker wobbled Silas' head right to left to note that there was still plenty of flexibility. Rigor mortis was a while from setting in, so Silas had not been dead very long. The movement on the pillow startled Izabel awake next to him, and slowly she raised her head, lifted her face from behind the veil of her wavy black hair.

"Though I walk through the valley," Becker rasped. Swallowed to find his voice to keep going. "...of the shadow of death..."

"*No*," Izabel gasped. "Silas? Mi querido?" She shook him a little, waited for a response, but when there wasn't even a flutter of an eyelid, she burst into tears.

Becker took her hand, knowing it was cold comfort, and suppressed his own urge to mourn immediately. He needed to stay focused, work fast if he was to find out more about what had killed this man, what *had been* killing days ago. Whatever it was, it had infiltrated the landscape, the wildlife, the people, and someone out there had known about it, known enough to try to stop it, albeit in the most brutal fashion without any warning to the town.

While Izabel cried, Becker stood and went to grab vials, a syringe, and a pair of scissors, to extract as many blood samples as he could. Kneeling beside the cot again, he cut away the primary bandage around Silas' neck, peeled back the pad on which he'd applied salve as much for the cauterization as the abrasions, and gaped. The entire site was a large, glistening black spot, the skin warped by the blade-shaped burn mark, the chaotic corona of veins reminding him of some kind of blight growing on a white petal. He had barely pushed the syringe into the site when something more occurred to him, quickened his breath and worried him.

Hiram Wells had been bitten, too, and the man was out in the night doing no less than riding around on a horse when he should be back here now, getting treated in as much as Becker could hope to treat him.

"*Scheisse*," he muttered and then glanced upward. "*Entschuldigung*," he added and crossed himself. He drew out the syringe full of black fluid and transferred it to a vial. Capped it. Drew another.

"What are you doing?" Izabel demanded.

"Iz, I know this is a hard time for you right now, but I need to try to find out what that coyote was carrying."

"El diablo!" she spat.

"Oh, I'm past arguing with you about that, *leibling*," he said as he transferred the second sample into another vial. He had just capped a third when she grabbed his wrist and squeezed.

"What was that?" she whispered.

Becker straightened and cocked an ear. The door into the sanctuary was open, all the better to keep an eye on the children, who had remained quiet, presumably asleep. The candlelight from the altar flickered sparsely through that opening, but more distantly came the rattle of a door in its frame. Faint at first, then harder. It came from the far end of the sanctuary at the main doors, which Caleb had secured on his father's orders. There was no other sound from out there.

Holding a finger to his lips for Izabel to keep quiet, Becker rose, placed the vials on the examination table near Silas' gun and pocket watch. Having learned his lesson two nights ago, he picked up an iron poker from beside the stove and took it with him, then he stepped into the doorway and looked into the sanctuary. The altar candles blazed brilliantly enough, but he couldn't see the Wells children anywhere.

The circle of light reached far enough to see that the main doors remained closed, the inside bar set firmly in its brackets. He came out to the front of the altar and incidentally interrupted the silence as he stepped onto the same board that had alerted him to intrusion the other night when he'd been fixated on studying Harlan Evans' corpse. If someone did rattle the doors, they had stopped now. Becker wandered farther out to the front of the altar, looked behind the first two pews for any sign of the kids.

Soft scuffing drew his attention to the other side of the altar to what was probably the deepest corner of the entire church and rectory. An angle of weak yellow candlelight reached so far down, and just within its lowest line, he found a blond crop of hair over a pair of wide blue eyes staring back at him, the rest of the face obscured. His gaze adjusted, and he put the whole picture together. Caleb was tucked back into the corner on the floor, sitting up. Below the angle of light, he had his little sister curled against him, asleep in the darker recess. By the look in the boy's eyes, he'd heard the doors rattling, too. Perhaps he'd been sleeping and was awakened by the disturbance.

"You heard that, too?" Becker whispered.

Caleb nodded slowly, remained still with his arm protectively pulling Ellie close. The boy had good instincts, Becker thought. It was the most shadowed corner, the one where they would be best hidden, and he couldn't blame Caleb, after everything he'd witnessed, for choosing it.

"Stay there," he whispered.

Caleb started to nod again when Izabel let out a blood-curdling and long scream on the other side of the wall in the rectory. Becker and Caleb both tensed up, eyes wide, and Ellie startled awake.

"Wha's at?" she murmured before Caleb clamped a hand over her mouth and tucked himself tighter into the corner, pulling her with him.

Izabel's scream was followed by a crashing sound, scraping on the floor, glass breaking, a soft pounding of footfalls. By the time Becker got to the rectory doorway, a *bang* sounded as the rear door was thrown open and a gust of cold air sucked into the back room and through the sanctuary. The gale whistled as it blew Becker's wiry hair back from his face. His heart now thoroughly rammed up into his throat, he looked around the room frantically to assess what had just happened.

Izabel lay sprawled at the foot of the examination table, which had been shoved aside by several feet. The Derringer and two of the vials of blood had fallen next to her while the third remained on the table. The gun was in one piece, but its pearl handle was stained with splashes of the blackened blood samples Becker had just drawn from Silas

Who was no longer on the cot.

Becker's throat tightened all the more to see the covers thrown aside, the door wide open and swinging on its hinges as night air continued to chill the rectory, rustled the clutches of herbs hanging from the ceiling.

Izabel stirred, attempted to sit up, clamped a hand to the back of her head. "Silas?"

Becker rushed to kneel and help her, set aside the poker so he could check her eyes as she blinked them open. "What happened?"

"Silas… he woke up," she said. "He's… alive." She groaned and massaged her head.

No way possible, Becker thought. Even if he'd misread the man as dead, how could he have the strength to push Izabel aside and bolt out the door? Even if he was delirious, *why* would he even do either of those things?

"But h-his…" she stuttered. "His… e-eyes…" There was no question that she had been momentarily frightened, but then her mouth quivered into a smile. "Alive…" she whispered with relief. "I think he's just confused."

Boot steps pounded up the steps outside the door, and Becker was suddenly aware of a figure standing there. From the corner of his vision, he could surmise that it was not Silas returning, calmer after the shock of rising from the dead. Nor was it Hiram Wells in his torn-up yellowed duster.

The coloring was wrong: all black clothing, a shot of long ginger hair.

Becker looked up to find Jasper O'Brian standing in the doorway, staring toward the empty cot with a sour face and wide, desperate eyes, but what stood out most was not that the Irishman, of all people, was here at this moment, but that he held in his right hand a *sword*. More striking, it was a straight broadsword with a crossguard that looked like it came from the Old Country and another century completely, not something more expected like a cavalry saber. The blade gleamed with a deadly sharpness in the dancing light.

"Where is he?" O'Brian asked, eyes darting toward the cot. At first, the question came out weak, and then he swallowed, took a step deeper into the room, and raised the blade out before him. "*Where* is he?" he repeated with added rage through gritted teeth.

"Where is *who?*" Becker asked. Why one of the Chamberlain Players' stagehands should suddenly arrive like this made no sense. O'Brian had no connection to Silas or anyone else in the town whatsoever, so who could he be looking for in such a frenzy and with an ancient weapon in his hand?

"I don't have time for games, preacher! The man you had in here tonight, one nearly had his throat torn out… where is he!" The tip of the sword, reflecting a point of light like a tiny golden star, wavered before Becker and Izabel by only a few feet. "It's almost dawn!"

Their eyes remained on the intruder, both of them far too confused by his appearance, let alone why he had come brandishing such a weapon looking for Silas LeBlanc. In the next few seconds, Becker became aware of Izabel's hand groping over the floor, grabbing something.

There was the click of a hammer drawing back as she thrust out her arm toward the deranged man, wielding the Derringer.

"Bastardo," she spat and fired without hesitation.

Jasper O'Brian half spun as the bullet grazed his upper sword arm and struck the wall to the side of the door frame over the desk.

His ears ringing from the shot, Becker watched as Jasper raised a hand and clamped it over the wound while staggering back, the sword lowering. The blade's weight was apparent as it wavered over the floor.

A second more, and Izabel had already cocked the hammer again. She had one shot left, and O'Brian was not willing to tempt fate again. He backed toward the door while Izabel pushed herself up to her feet and stepped daringly closer.

"Iz, *wait!*" Becker shouted as he stumbled to his feet. The rest happened faster than he could completely register it.

O'Brian disappeared out the door, his boots thumping down the steps like his feet were more tangled than tumbleweeds, and Izabel ran to the opening, gun still raised at the fleeing man. She stepped outside and fired again. Becker grabbed the end of the offset table to steady himself, took a step and heard glass crunch, looked down to see that he'd stepped on the broken vials of Silas' blood.

Scheisse.

"Silas!" Izabel's voice shouted desperately in the dark outside the rectory.

"Izabel!" Becker shouted. "Izabel, wait!" He hurried to the doorway and looked out, squinted to see two figures running toward town, one accompanied by the thin sliver of steel, the other petite in swishing skirts. Izabel was too wound up to care that she was out of rounds or that her target had a long sharp object in his hand.

"Silas!" Izabel's voice called further out. They were now near the block of the mayor's office and the jail. "Silas, come back!"

Becker looked back into the room, found Caleb standing in the sanctuary door on the far side. Ellie was with him, rubbing her eyes and blinking blearily. "Stay here," he said. "Shut that door and keep your sister in there."

"Yessir," Caleb said as he put an arm around Ellie to keep her back and pulled the door shut.

Becker looked around the room, grabbed his coat from the peg by the door, and went back to retrieve the iron poker. Just as importantly, he grabbed his Gladstone, which he had a feeling he was going to need more than ever. He shoved it under one arm before he stepped outside and shut the rectory door behind him.

Ahead, the sky above had dulled from its greater nighttime splendor with the moon so low, the stars fading back into their consuming void, and the ground before him became a great chasm of dark gray. At least he knew that it was even ground between here and there, and the buildings were clear enough in shape and space. He'd tread there so many times that he shouldn't worry about crossing in pursuit of a sick man, but why, he wondered, did the night always seem so much darker before the dawn?

CHAPTER TWENTY-FOUR

Somewhere behind him, after they passed the scrub and reached open road, Hiram was forced to drop the lantern into the dust as he galloped toward the source of the shots. His arm could not take it anymore, and he needed both hands on the reins.

Behind him, he heard Jesse keeping up.

Ahead, he saw only movement against the dark of the northern landscape beyond the church, but he heard Izabel's voice shout, *"Silaaaas!"*

"Izabel!" Becker's voice shouted from near the back of the church. Racing closer, Hiram could see the pastor's figure outside the rectory, the light from the window on his back as he started to cross the darkened ground, running—or rather staggering—as fast as he could. Then he noticed the rumbling of hooves and stopped where he was near the mayor's office as Hiram and Jesse arrived.

"What's going on?" Hiram asked as Teddy stamped with agitation beneath him. The gelding grumbled against his bit for a moment until Hiram calmed him with a soft, *"Whoa, shhhh."*

Becker huffed to catch his breath. "I think we've got a madman on the loose, but Silas is out there somewhere, and I don't know how."

"Wait... Silas is okay?" Hiram asked as Jesse caught up. He looked down to see that Becker had an iron rod in one hand and his bag in the other.

"I didn't say that, but he may be wandering, I don't... I don't know what happened, Marshal." His voice trembled in a way that Hiram had never heard before. Something had completely spooked him.

"Who fired those shots?"

"Izabel. She was shooting at…" The shape of his head shook in the dim light. "You won't believe this, but one of those stagehands, the Irish one."

"Jasper O'Brian?"

"He just barged in, demanding to know where Silas was. I have no idea why." He heaved a deep breath. "He's got a *sword*. I think he wants to kill him."

Hiram swung a leg over the saddle, dropped to the ground, and steadied himself before he tethered Teddy to the awning support on the corner of Watkin's office. "Did you say, sword?"

"Ja, a big damn sword," Becker snapped in lingering disbelief. He sounded tired, with his accent creeping out heavier than usual. *"Mein Gott,"* he murmured, and Hiram saw his head shaking again.

Having climbed down from his own saddle, Jesse joined them to ask, "Why would a stagehand come after Silas?"

Becker groaned.

Hiram rubbed his chin. "But Silas is up and moving around?"

"Ja."

"Where would he go? Why?"

"I don't know!" Becker suddenly grabbed his right arm too close to the bite for comfort. "What about you, Marshal? How are you feeling?"

Air hissed through Hiram's teeth, and he pried his arm free. "Damn, Becker. I'll hold up."

"I have something to tell you about that coyote bite." The desperation in his voice, the mention of the bite alone after all that had happened, did nothing to calm Hiram's nerves.

"Sounds like it's got to wait. I'm going to get Silas. Where are Caleb and Ellie?"

"Safe," Becker said. "They're still in the church."

"Alright, keep 'em there. Jesse, you stay with the pastor. Keep your eyes peeled and listen."

"Yessir."

Hiram pondered what he'd seen and heard so far. From a distance, he'd witnessed two figures moving toward the shadows of town, but now he knew that there was a *third* out there, too. *Silas? But how?* He didn't know what to make of that claim, given the last time he'd seen his friend and Silas' condition. It made more sense that he might be wandering in a fevered haze, though Hiram couldn't fathom how that was possible after so much blood loss. With all this to consider, he set off and passed the mayor's office to reach the corner of the jail.

"Be careful," Becker gave a breathy call behind him. "That sword..."

"Well, then it's a good thing I have a gun, isn't it?" He looked up the thoroughfare but saw no one, no shadow disappearing in the distance, heard no scuffling of feet. It was clear the parties he was after had veered down an alley somewhere along the way.

"Silas!" Izabel's voice called, thinned out by distance, coming from somewhere on the other side of the northern block. That would put her, and possibly Silas, near the Chinese laundry, of all places. How damned ideal that a delirious Silas would wander in that direction even while pursued by a man with—if he understood Becker correctly—a sword.

But why did a stagehand and actor want to kill a saloon keeper he did not even know, whom he had no connection with? And with a *sword?*

"The hell?" Hiram whispered at that thought. Steeling himself and surrendering to the lack of answers, he simply followed his nose. Literally. Faint scents in the air rose into swirling trails. A whiff of perfume— Izabel's? A stronger scent of blood—Silas had it all over him earlier. And *smoke* so malodorous as to be offensive. He *knew* that particular smell now. He'd inhaled it far too much while digging a hole out in the desert yesterday morning.

"Sonofabitch."

If it was a new puzzle piece, it was a damned scary one. He turned the far corner of the jail and set off north, creeping along the western wall of the bathhouse until he reached the corner and peered around at the long row of cribs, including Nathan's that had not been used for days now. Hiram ached that he had no time to think about his deputy, who was as lost out there somewhere as his daughter was.

Shit, what was *happening* to his town?

He moved on, listening, smelling. There was something feral about the urge to use his senses, something inside him operating on pure instinct that felt strange and natural at the same time. As he stood gazing, listening, smelling, he became acutely aware of the blocky structures around him and the ground, going from shadowed and less defined to more varying shades of gray. Details crept out from the boards on the crib walls to the roof on the long shed that used to cover half of the Chinese laundry. The abandoned sheet wall shone brilliantly white to Hiram's vision, though he knew it to be nothing but yellowed canvas used as a divider between imaginary districts. He blinked, but the white brilliance remained, cranked up like everything else crowding his head. Silas had said the Chinese all picked up and left, but why they left up their boundary didn't make sense. Didn't matter now. He only wanted to find Silas, to put at least a single thing right in his spiraling world. Then he could look for Lucinda again.

He tried to focus again and grew far too aware of his heartbeat thrumming with surprising steadiness in his chest. Then another overlapped it, distant, slower but just as steady, while on top of that another beat, faster, anxious.

"Silas?"

It was Izabel's voice floating over the beats that echoed each other. She sounded pleased, gasping relief.

She's found him, he thought with relief of his own. But there was still a madman—with a sword no less—somewhere in the mix, and Hiram couldn't hear the fourth heartbeat wherever its point of origin lay. He drew his Colt, cocked the hammer and held the gun pointed up but still ready, his finger resting across the trigger guard, and eased around the corner. From there, he followed the back of the block, around the bathhouse to the now-closed gunsmith's shop and the haberdashery. To his right, the canvas wall had a gap torn in it, framing the view beyond. The laundry yard was a ghost town in and of itself with some wash tubs and equipment abandoned, poles and drying lines still standing. A chill breeze that bore early morning dampness stirred the wall, made it flap loudly in his ears, forced him to focus past it. Beyond that was the back of the blacksmith and the corral for the livery, but the sounds Hiram was following kept him along the rear of the block.

"Silas, mi corazón."

Their hearts were beating close together now, one anxious, the other weirdly calm. Hiram cocked an ear forward to follow them, heard something that sounded like a soft pop and a feminine gasp, and then it all *stopped.*

He blinked, shook his head as all noise around him dampened back down to an average volume. As if a flaming wick in a lamp had been turned down in his head, his senses calibrated back to normal again. The scents around him, played up to an almost sickening degree a moment ago, ebbed. The unnatural brilliance of his surroundings faded into gray shades again, though now tones of blue joined them. The sky had lightened above. That reminded him that the sun was not far from rising, that he had not slept all night and, despite that, still felt far more awake than he should.

He still, at least, had a sense of direction to follow and proceeded to the corner of the bakery. The space between that wall and the Palace's east-facing was too narrow for a horse, but it was a favorite passage for a shortcut, and the town's kids had enjoyed it as a play tunnel over the years. He kept along the rear wall of the Palace, finally reached the far corner, and there turned to look down the wider alley toward the street.

The gap was entirely shadowed but for the long column at the end where pre-dawn light showed between the walls of the saloon and the hotel next door. He thought of that dark tunnel in Silas' flowery speech, with its light at the end. This light was bluish and weak, and before it, leaning against a wall, two figures clung together in silhouette. The larger one pressed against the smaller, head lowered and angled deep into the junction of shoulder and neck. He could see part of Izabel's profile raised upward, her mouth open, ready to breathe another soft gasp, and though the heightened sense of hearing had vanished, he detected little ongoing sucking noises.

Oh, fuck's sake.

Hiram stood for a moment staring, allowing his vision to adjust. The sucking noises persisted, grew more passionate, and he shook his head. Leave it to Silas and Iz to reunite with kisses when everyone else was worrying about them, but he couldn't be the least humored by it. There was also still a danger out there, so this needed to stop right now, and Silas needed to get his injured self back to Becker's clinic. Still, he opted to keep his gun out, the hammer cocked. The barrel remained aloft, the whole of the weapon cradled in his hand to balance just right to reduce the soreness and shaking in his arm.

"Dammit, you two," he finally said. "Silas… Iz…"

A wet ripping sound answered him as Silas raised his head and pulled away from Izabel, who did not remain standing. She slid down the wall. A damp gleam trailed behind her until she fell over on her side with a soft hush of skirts.

Hiram frowned, wondering why Silas did not try to catch her at all, but as his eyes rose from the form on the ground, he stared into the figure before him. Definitely Silas' silhouette with its close-cropped hair and the sculpted shoulders he'd earned boxing for so many years.

With the slowly inching light, more features presented themselves. He only wore his trousers and belt, his feet bare and dirty. One shoulder was crossed by the gauze wrap that helped keep a bandage in place over his chest. A large dark stain soaked the dressing, originating at his mouth. The entirety of Silas' lower face was one great smear of blood that had dripped down over his chin to his neck, pooled slightly in the dips of his clavicles, and where his eyes should be, Hiram made out only black chasms.

"Silas?"

A chesty, inhuman growl rumbled up that made Hiram's entire body hum with tension. He didn't think of any land animal like the coyotes he'd encountered lately, either the normal ones that had dug up the arm or the monstrous one that had attacked Silas. He thought of the gators he'd heard years ago chuffing and bellowing out in the Louisiana swamps at night. They'd made his skin crawl and his attention turn to noting every possible escape route, whether it was a forest path or a dock.

He stood now within an alleyway, with the passage ahead blocked off and only one way out. The last thing he wanted to do was level his gun at Silas, but every muscle coiled as he backed up slowly.

Then the figure before him shuddered, breath picking up for an instant, and a raspy voice whispered, "H…"

Something about it was all wrong, detached, lost. It wasn't filled with the comity that commonly graced Silas' voice, whether in his jabs or chatter. That hollowness sent little icy bugs running down Hiram's back. There was not even any recognition behind that single letter, spoken so often before.

"Silas," he finally spoke up, cleared his throat, hoping he could get through whatever cloud had consumed Silas' mind in his sickly state. "Silas, what are you doing out here?" He glanced past the figure to that of Izabel laying so still on the ground. The light had risen, bringing out the streak she had left on the wall.

It was *red*. So very red.

The rumble of that unearthly growl grew again, and in a blink, Silas dove at him far too fast for a man who had lost so much blood. Hiram tumbled out the back of the alleyway and landed flat on his back. His hat flew free as he managed not to bang the back of his head on the ground, and while he didn't pull the trigger on the gun, the impact of his hand on the ground set off the hammer. The shot rang in his ear and echoed down the rear block. The Colt slipped from his grip before he brought his arms up to push against Silas' chest, felt his hands slip against the blood-drenched bandages.

"Silas, *why* are you doing this?" he gritted out through his struggle and then, pinned down, gaped up into a pair of eyes that froze him to the spot.

Oil-black orbs glared down at him, resembling others he'd seen recently, those on the coyote that had attacked Silas last night. Branches of delicate black veins framed Silas' chalk-white face, fanned out from the prominent rims of his eye sockets.

Silas paused, his lips curled back in a vicious grimace, and Hiram shuddered to see that his friend's mouth was crowded with a set of long, pointed canine teeth. They were thin, needle-sharp on the tips, almost translucent with swirls of blood clinging to them or dripping from his lower lip.

If Hiram could have opened the earth beneath himself and retreated into it, he would have, but he remained straddled, pinned down. The rumbling growl persisted but did not pick up into a more threatening timbre. Silas's nostrils flared as he sniffed, leaned down, smelled the crook of Hiram's neck. Cold breath gusted on the skin there, and Hiram imagined those fangs suddenly opening wide and closing back in on the flesh like a bear trap, points spearing into muscle and vessel, pulling, tearing, thrashing back and forth to maximize damage and blood flow.

He acknowledged now that Silas had ripped Izabel's throat out. That was why she lay in a heap in an alleyway, a crimson streak on the side of the wall. Any second now, it would be *his* throat, too. He imagined the mess, a pool of red, tendrils of torn tissue twisted across the sand.

"Silas…" His eyes teared as part of him tried to make sense of it all, how he'd been plunged into such a nightmare. He waited for the inevitable, to either wake up or die, but it did not happen. Silas only hovered there, keeping him pinned, and continued sniffing almost dubiously as if he couldn't make up his mind to kill again or not.

That was when the shift happened again, all of Hiram's senses flooding with incomprehensible stimulation. The sound of his own heartbeat rose once more in his ears, pounding in terror, and above him, Silas' beat… steady… slow…

The coppery smell of blood invaded his nose, the ground beneath him became harder, grittier, and the blue of the morning sky above brightened, the last stars seeping away. He became aware of another heartbeat approaching, this one beating as quickly as his. There was a nearby scuff of feet, a soft ring of steel.

Silas suddenly rose onto his knees, teeth still bared, and issued a long, seething hiss as a figure loomed just within Hiram's periphery. Then Silas sprang back as a flash of silver arced sideways through the air, directly over Hiram, and barely missed Silas' neck. The weight lifted from Hiram's body followed by a soft scrambling of feet, so fast it didn't sound humanly possible before it faded down the alleyway going toward the main thoroughfare.

Hiram boosted up, scrambled for his gun, grabbed it and rolled up into a kneel as he aimed at Jasper O'Brian. "Hold it right there, fucker!" he hissed, cocking the hammer.

The stagehand had already drawn back into a stance with the sword raised to strike again. Becker had only said *big damn sword*. He had not said how damn big, as in that it was an enormous damn broadsword the likes of which Hiram had only seen in the illustrated books on King Arthur that he'd read as a kid. Little Hiram had *dreamed* of having a sword like that, an Excalibur of his own.

O'Brian froze in that stance. His head cocked eerily as he appeared to scrutinize Hiram, and his heartbeat gradually lowered from frantic to steady. He took a breath, slowly began to lower the blade. "Please, don't shoot," he said, tone entirely reasonable. "I know this all looks fucked to hell." The tip of the blade dipped to the ground.

"That's one way of putting it," he said through gritted teeth.

Then Jasper O'Brian said what Hiram knew but still did not have the stomach to admit for himself.

"He isn't your friend anymore, Marshal."

The distant gunshot made Becker straighten up, grip the iron poker in his hand tighter. Anxiously he looked back toward the church, relieved to see Jesse emerge from the rectory door and hurry across the distance to the corner of the mayor's office. The kid had gone to check on Caleb and Ellie just as the sky was lightening quickly, the eastern horizon a muddy wash of pink and orange.

"I hear what I think I heard?" the young ranch hand asked as he reached Becker's side again.

"Ja, gunshot, as far up as the Palace." Becker braced himself. Both the doctor and the man of God in him could not wait any longer. "I'm going up there."

"I'm going with you." Jesse's hand hovered over the handle of the gun on his belt.

"That new?"

"It was Frank Evans', the one used in the holdup. Marshal gave it to me." He lifted the collar on his jacket. "Deputized me, too."

Becker gave a clipped nod. At least the Colt gave them a little more support than his measly iron poker. He hoped—no, *prayed*—that Jesse wouldn't have to use it. "All right." He took a deep breath. "Let's go."

Jesse started to jog ahead only to stop and look back, patient, waiting.

"I'm not a runner, Jesse," Becker grumbled.

"Oh, sorry." He backed up, kept pace.

They stayed on the thoroughfare and at least twelve feet out from the boardwalks and alley openings because both agreed it prudent to be able to see Jasper O'Brian emerge with that sword if he did.

They had just reached the front of the haberdashery and, in the lifting darkness, saw a figure dart onto the street up ahead. It veered with such speed as Becker had never seen, but he glimpsed a pale face and upper body with corded arms before it vanished into the shadows of the boardwalk at the Orleans Palace.

"Was that Silas?" Jesse asked.

Becker gulped hard as he asked himself how a man in that condition could still be on his feet and move so fast, but he already had an idea. He didn't like it, didn't want to believe it, and the only way to find out if he was right or not was to go forward.

Despite Jasper O'Brian wielding a sword and Hiram equipped with a gun that could split the man's head before either of them blinked, somehow Hiram felt that he was *not* the one with the upper hand. As he listened to their hearts beat, his own hammering, Jasper's still fast but gradually easing up, he knew that the other man understood what exactly was going on, and that made all the difference.

"He didn't kill me," he said, trying to raise some defense for Silas.

"That's 'cause you don't smell very delicious, not like his pretty señorita, and now I'm goin' to have to take care of her, too." The stagehand—no, he was far more than that to be here now, equipped with a weapon no man carried anymore—sounded gruff, tired. "You feel it don't you? The change coming?" The corners of his mouth curled, but it was less a sardonic look and more one of *knowing*. "He didn't kill you 'cause your blood is spoiled already. He knows his own kind."

"What?" Hiram slowly got to his feet, maintaining his grip and aim, though his hand shook endlessly. "What're you talking about?"

"Oh, I think you *know*, but we'll have to address that later." O'Brian straightened up completely. "And I don't have time for this." He turned and started to walk, ignoring that there was a gun on him.

"Stop," Hiram growled. "You stay right where you are."

O'Brian turned the sword into a reversed grip, so the blade was half-hidden up the back of his arm, but the crossguard still peered out from the side of his hand. He all but ignored Hiram as he stepped around at a wide berth and started for the alley. "At least he's going for familiar territory, even if he doesn't understand the how or why anymore."

"I said *stop*." Hiram tried to sound firm, to banish the plea in his voice. He pivoted with O'Brian's movement, gun still trained, but they both knew that he would not shoot, not yet, not with all the questions in his head that only O'Brian could answer.

O'Brian got to the corner of the alley, gave him one last look, and then darted in.

"Shit." Hiram listened to the pound of footsteps through the passage and turned the corner in time to see O'Brian's silhouette disappear out the far end, and then he ran after, pausing as he came closer to Izabel's body. The coppery reek of blood accosted him as he skirted around her, staring with a new ache in his chest.

She had collapsed on her side, knees bent together under the ruffly pile of her skirts, head turned sharply to the side. Her eyes stared, empty of life, through locks of curly hair. Blood dripped from the corner of her mouth and a small amount pooled under the area of her chin. The side of her neck that Silas had bitten into was mostly hidden, and Hiram felt shamefully thankful not to see it. He continued edging around her, then hurried out into the thoroughfare past the support post and trough where he usually hitched his horse.

Across the street, something else briefly caught his attention, made him freeze again. The large uneven scorch mark remained in the dust along with the pile of coyote bones. The creature still reeked of burnt hair and decay, and even from some twelve yards away, he could make out the skull with its incredibly long canines, the caves of its eye sockets still projecting the illusion of an enraged beast. The busted reservoir and wire handle from the lantern Cage had used to kill it were tangled with the rib cage.

To the east, the faintest golden rim of sun peered over a cloud bank and crept up into an explosion of light. The brilliance stung, forced him to lower his eyes. Just below the glare, he found Becker and Jesse standing near the eastern corner of the Palace.

He heard his own voice, distant, echoing inside the space between his ears, tell them to remain outside. "Izabel's in the alley. Silas killed her." It didn't sound, didn't *feel* like his voice. He could see the wash of disbelief descend on them, heard their hearts racing, adding to the echoes, detected a gulp in Jesse that indicated the kid wanted to throw up.

Then the loud flapping of the batwing doors into the saloon drew his attention next. Normally they fanned back and forth with a softer *whap-whap-whap* before settling into place, but now their hinges groaned, the panels beat the air. From inside came the sound of glass breaking, a crack of wood, Jasper O'Brian's boots hollow on the floorboards.

"Stay out here." Hiram pulled himself together and ran up onto the boardwalk, crossed and went in.

The place was dim but for one oil lamp in its mirrored sconce, still burning weakly, but that little flame beamed back with so much intensity. Hiram looked away from it, shook his head and blinked, listened for the heartbeats that had guided him before.

Silas' was *here*... somewhere. He heard the unwavering beat within the vast front room but couldn't pinpoint it, not with O'Brian there, too.

The stagehand was in the middle of the room amid the tables, looking up toward the balcony. He'd assumed a guard position with the sword, ready to swing. "How 'bout you come on down from there, eh?" he coaxed, his brogue coming out a little stronger.

Hiram's gaze rose to see what had O'Brian's attention. His keen vision adjusted to the shadows of the upper floor and balcony, where he made out the shape hunkered there.

The creature that had been Silas clung, facing out, to the highest corner, clawed hands and feet dug into two adjacent walls and the ceiling. It glared down with those slick onyx eyes, lips drawn back into a full grimace, fangs bared.

"Holy shit," Hiram uttered.

And Silas sprung.

With impossible speed, he leaped to the banister, gripped it for less than a second before vaulting over and going straight at O'Brian only to bound back as the sword swung and missed him. He let out a reptilian roar and swiped with clawed hands as the blade followed through. O'Brian's feet shuffled backward, assumed a new stance, legs slightly bent before he lunged forward and repeatedly swung, advancing in a relentless attack.

It was like watching a mesmerizing dance while recalling the days of Silas' boxing matches. He had been *good*, and whatever he was now, that experience was fused into his muscles, his bones. He ducked the swings, took jabbing swipes as he went. Razor-sharp claws opened up O'Brian's sleeve, the front of his coat. O'Brian, on the other hand, seemed to know what he was doing, each lunge and swing controlled, one attack following through into another, advancing one second, retreating the next to avoid another swipe with those claws.

"Don't just stand there, Marshal!" the stagehand shouted. "Shoot 'im! Slow 'im down!"

Hiram snapped out of his daze and aimed, his hand shaking, and fired, but it was too much for him to hit anywhere vital. He still could not bear to do that. Silas let out an ear-rending shriek as the bullet grazed his side, and his next movement blurred when he bounded up onto the bar and crouched with predatory grace.

O'Brian tried to turn with the movement but wasn't fast enough as Silas streaked down from his perch, dug both sets of claws into O' Brian's collar, and heaved him up with ungodly strength. The sword dropped and clattered across the floor while its wielder was flung across the room, over the bar, and collided with the mirror and shelves.

The mirror shattered. The shelves collapsed, and bottles smashed upon the floor behind the bar. O'Brian's body descended with it, a pained *"Ooopb!"* sounding from behind the barrier while individual shards of glass continued to drop and ring.

Hiram gaped, his hand automatically cocked the hammer on the Colt again, but before he could refocus and aim, Silas lunged at him. The saloon keeper didn't strike with claws but delivered a blunt hand shove so powerful Hiram felt his feet lift from the floor.

Hiram's finger pulled the trigger impulsively and fired into the air. Then he crashed down into one of the tables. The legs shattered underneath while the top split in two, sending out a fan of splinters. He let go of the gun but managed to keep the back of his head from bouncing on the floor. His back, ever a growing nuisance in the pain department, experienced a new wrath of agony while his breath shut off. His mouth bobbed open and closed as he fought to draw in just one gulp of air. His body convulsed, and for a moment, there was nothing but his own heartbeat again, and the agony, and the world around him rippled as he tried to focus.

Silas seemed to hover nearby and looked toward the doors as if considering an escape, but brilliant sunlight spilled onto the boardwalk now, reflecting upward. He backed away from it, rumbling with that irritable gator growl that still terrified Hiram.

Something popped in Hiram's chest, and he gasped in a sharp breath, recapturing Silas' attention. The pale head snapped sideways to glare at him. The blood-stained muscles on his chest, the cords in his arms all tensed, prepared for a new attack.

If this thing, up until now, had retained any fragment of Silas still within its being, Hiram could finally see that it was gone. It did not recognize him, did not care for him, was not the brother he had known. He desperately fought past the near paralyzing pain, pushed up on his hands and feet, crab crawled backward until one of the balcony supports stopped him. His hand reached out, tried to find something to use. Anxious fingers felt over pieces of the broken table, hoping to find his gun, but came across the handle on the sword instead.

As his hand curled around it, he noted the strangeness of the weapon again, groaned as he lifted it with his right arm, and as not-Silas lunged at him, he swung it around to present the tip of the blade forward in defense. He caught a glimpse of some other movement behind the incoming thing, but it was more than he could calculate now.

His eyes snapped tightly shut, and he drew back his lips in a grimace, braced for the worst.

There was a jolt, the heavy blade jarring in his grip as its broadside smacked against the naked side of his assailant, and then its weight pushed back, the blade suddenly freezing in place before him and holding there. A sickening crack sounded, and something stung sharply on the surface of his chest.

Then… nothing.

In the shock of silence that descended, Hiram took a long moment to catch up that he was *not* further injured, that Silas' teeth were not lodged in his neck and tearing him apart, but there was a significant amount of weight against him, pinning his sprawled legs down, and then a burbling, cold breath sounded next to his ear.

He opened his eyes and took in that Silas was slumped, oily eyes staring down at the sharp protrusion of a broken table leg thrust through his back and coming out his chest. The splintered point had lined up with Hiram's own heart and ground, stinging like a sonofabitch, through his skin and into his sternum. The sword, still weakly gripped in Hiram's hand, rested against Silas' side. Hiram had not managed to swing it in time to stop Silas' attack, but it had stopped something else.

Jasper O'Brian, hands still on the other end of the broken table leg, was kneeling behind Silas, but the stagehand had come in off-center enough to impale himself through the lower belly incidentally.

For only seconds they remained like that, but it felt like forever as Hiram got his bearing, put his hands on Silas' chest and pushed back to keep the sharp tip of the bloody table leg from penetrating any further. With a heave and a groan, he shoved, and the weight on the sword blade shifted as O'Brian backed up and extracted himself from it with a wet sucking sound and a cry of agony. The weight of the blade returned, too heavy for Hiram to hold it up anymore, and his arm collapsed to let the steel fall flat with a *clank* on the floor.

O'Brian stumbled back and up to his feet with a hand clamped over his pierced middle. Gleaming red saturated the front of his coat and dripped, bright at his feet, and then he looked toward the beams peeking under the bottom of the batwing doors.

"I'm sorry, Marshal," he said with a quiver. His eyes looked frightened now, glistening. "Guess I've fucked up for good now." He coughed, caught his breath. "But I'll be seeing you." His next motion could not have been more shocking as he reached out, planted a hand on each of Silas' shoulders, and dragged him backward with him. The point of the table leg came free from Hiram's chest, but the whole thing remained lodged through Silas's body. Hiram immediately slapped his good hand over the shallow gouge, felt an ooze of blood blooming through his shirt.

Silas did not seem able to fight anymore as he went almost limp, but he still let out a low keening noise that provoked new chills.

"I'll see you soon," O'Brian repeated. Then he pulled his gruesome load with him, flung himself and Silas out the batwing doors, feet stumbling awkwardly, and both fell into the sunlight, the doors flapping wildly behind them.

Hiram pushed himself away from the support, got onto all fours, and crawled his way to his feet. Then he leaned himself into a rush for the doors, pushed through in time to see O'Brian fling Silas the rest of the way out into the thoroughfare. Then O'Brian let go and dove away from Silas, arced into a skilled roll, and came up in a kneel. He pivoted around to look back at the results.

An unearthly screech rose as Silas' body ignited in flames before it even hit the ground. They spewed out in long seams, like fissures opening in his back, down his arms, splitting his skin and exposing muscle. His mouth hung open, teeth exposed, but only that ghastly keening came out as if the table leg—also now on fire—had blocked off his windpipe, killed the monstrous growls and replaced them with pain.

"What the hell!" Jesse's voice cried from somewhere to the right, where he and Becker were at the other corner of the saloon.

Another outcry rose from the porch of the hotel next door as Watkins and the Raskins emerged, drawn by such commotion and gunshots at the break of dawn.

Hiram cringed at the brilliance of the sunlight, at the flames consuming the man who had been his true brother for almost half of his life, seen him through more than one tribulation, and the unanswered questions swarmed in his head, sickened, angered, confused and paralyzed him.

O'Brian, arm clutched over his belly, got to his feet, backed away, his figure lost for a moment to the spears of sun flares behind him, then he turned and bolted, hunched over but surprisingly fast. Blood saturated a spot on the back of his coat where the blade had exited.

"Hey!" Hiram shouted and stumbled down the steps, made to give chase, the whole town around him rippling, tilting, the morning sun blinding and stabbing. He could not keep his legs under him as O'Brian's figure vanished into the light. It was all he could do not to fall over like a board and smash his face into the ground, but he almost did exactly that. His knees buckled and hit hard before he collapsed onto his side.

"Marshal!" Becker's voice reached him muffled by the throb of his heart. Then there was nothing but the beat, hollow, detached, and the last ambient sound Hiram truly recognized, as his cheek ground into the road and his eyes closed, was Silas still keening and gurgling horrifically as he burned.

CHAPTER TWENTY-FIVE

There was no way to understand what had happened and think within the realm of the normal. He could not walk back time and observe with an omniscient eye where and why it all began or how it had led to Silas LeBlanc's corpse burning in the middle of town only feet away from the remains of the creature that had attacked him not twelve hours before. Becker left the all-knowing aspect up to God, but he did at least have puzzle pieces that were fitting together into a grim picture the likes of which he would never have believed.

Tears streamed from his eyes as he knelt over Hiram Wells' unconscious body and watched the flames rapidly sizzle away the last of Silas' flesh and muscle until the belly cavity was exposed. The blistering pile of blackened entrails that remained continued to cook, the smoke carrying a horrific smell.

"That sonofabitch," Jesse growled and started to bolt past, heading after the fleeing figure of Jasper O'Brian.

"Jesse, wait!" Becker called after him. "Leave him! We know where he's going!"

Jesse spun back around on his heel, breath heaving, his dusty face pulled into a grimace while streaked with tears. "He killed Silas!"

"That may be, but there's more going on here," Becker replied. "We saw only part of it, but we'll have to determine what bigger role Jasper O'Brian played in this later." He looked at Wells lying on his side, limp as a sack of grain, waves of dirty hair covering his face. He reached down and swept it back, then gulped down the heavy rock that formed in his throat. Creeping in along the man's temple, just along the hairline, were a series of tiny, blackened veins. "I need you to help me get him back to the clinic," he said. Then he looked up at the audience that had come out onto the porch of the Raskin.

John Raskin was in his long johns with trousers pulled on over them and held up by suspenders, his wife bundled up in a frilly dressing gown with her hair still tucked inside the bulbous shape of her night cap. Their son, Toby, was not in sight, a slight relief given the traumatic nature of the entire early morning event. Mayor Watkins, already fully dressed as likely he'd been ready to go back to his own house the moment light rose, came down from the porch but only walked as far forward as he dared. He seemed to be figuring out the best way to go around the flames as they bloomed in one direction then the other. Occasionally a small pop and squeal of burning organ tissue arose.

"What just happened here?" Watkins asked with a tremor.

Becker could see in his eyes that he was winding up inside, preparing to figure it out for himself and start throwing blame because that was how the man worked. "You want the complicated version that ends with how a stagehand killed Silas LeBlanc?"

Watkins' head snapped up. "That's Silas?" The cane paused in mid-raise. "How?"

"Did you miss what I said?" Becker griped. "One of that troupe—the troupe *you* arranged for—did this."

"Don't," Jesse said, sniffling. "Let's not do this now."

Words of wisdom from the youngest person on the scene, Becker thought. He was relieved when John Raskin, not quite as timid as Watkins, approached, moved around the blaze and came to stand over him.

"What did I just see, Norman?" he asked incredulously.

"I don't know what to tell you, but I need to get the marshal down to the clinic, and as for that…" He gestured at the burning body, what was left of it. The smoke, greenish in the morning beams, had begun to taper down. "Normally, I'd say dowse it, but leave it alone. Don't touch it. Don't let *anyone* touch it even after it's gone out." He had a sick man to focus on, and maybe he couldn't save Silas, but he'd sure as hell try to save Hiram Wells. He gestured to the alleyway. "Izabel's in there, dead. Her throat's been torn out."

"My God."

"Ja."

"What do you mean her throat's been torn out?" Watkins finally got up the nerve to step around the burn zone. He shifted back and forth on his feet. "Did another of those animals come into town?" The cane raised and angled toward the charred pile of coyote bones.

"I promise I will tell you everything later, Titus," Becker argued and then looked back to Raskin. He swallowed again, braced to keep his voice firm, but the slightest tremor still crept in. "Would you cover her, please, John? Stay with her? As soon as Jesse helps me get Mr. Wells into the clinic, I'll send him to fetch Father Ramirez. Izabel was a member of his flock. He'll need to bless her body."

Raskin nodded with a stunned vacancy in his eyes. On the hotel porch, Miz Raskin had her hands clamped over her mouth, tears of shock on her cheeks. "Soon as I give my wife a drink or somethin'."

"Where's your son?" Becker asked.

"Toby's sleeping in," Raskin replied. "Thank God."

As Becker and Jesse struggled to get a handle on Hiram Wells' limp body, Watkins suddenly walked in the other direction, not toward his house but past the hotel.

"Where are *you* going?" Becker called after him.

Watkins turned, raised that ridiculous cane like he was about to demonstrate, then shook his head and proceeded. At the far corner of the hotel, he turned right and disappeared, sending him in the direction of the livery. He kept a horse there, but he was hardly ever seen on it or going anywhere that required it.

Becker didn't have time to wonder what the mayor had in mind. "Let's go," he said to Jesse.

It was no easy feat even though the marshal was not the heaviest man, being of average size and height. Some fifteen minutes later, they passed the mayor's office. Still tethered at the corner, the horses watched them stumble by with ears pricked forward and curious. About that time, Watkins rode by in a fast gallop on his roan, only reining in for a pause.

"You said *that stagehand*. Which one?" he demanded as the horse stamped around beneath him.

"The red-headed one," Jesse said irritably.

"I'm sure there's a perfectly logical explanation. Once I speak to Mr. Edwards, I'll get to the bottom of this."

"You do that," Becker replied.

Without further word, Watkins rode on.

"Idjit's going to the Simpson house," Jesse said. "Should we stop him?"

"You can't change a fool's mind, Jesse," Becker said. He did, however, feel a slight twinge of guilt and spoke under his breath, "Bless me, Father, for I've no damns left to give." But he could waste time verbally brawling with the mayor, or he could get Hiram Wells into care, and he was pretty sure the Lord understood his dilemma.

What felt an age later, they managed to deposit the marshal on the cot he'd used last night. Every crease under his clothes drenched with sweat, Becker pulled Wells' boots off and put his feet up while Jesse handled the upper half and removed the duster.

Their clumsy movements, clunks and thumps in the rectory alerted Caleb and Ellie to their arrival. Becker heard the door into the sanctuary creak open. "Stay in there, Caleb!" he called over his shoulder.

"Is that Papa?"

"Stay there. I'll call you in a minute."

Caleb had seen almost as much as his father in the last few days, and he seemed glad not to see too much more as he remained peering through the crack, keeping Ellie pushed away even as Becker could hear her complaining.

"The marshal gonna be okay?" Jesse asked as he unbuckled Wells' gun belt and awkwardly worked it out from under the patient. He held it up, noting to Becker that the holster was empty.

Becker moved to gently pry open each of the marshal's eyes and peer in, finding the pupils responsive to the light that fell through the window over the cot. "Man hasn't eaten or slept well in days. And then there's this." He laid Wells' injured arm out straight. On the edges of the bandage, the veins near the surface of his skin were the same color Silas' had been in his last hours, the same coal-black as those on the Evans brothers' bodies, or on the severed forearm that Wells had brought to him two days ago.

Jesse gasped. "What kinda coyote bite causes that?"

Becker understood the reaction but needed to work without too much side commentary, even if it was only meant in concern. "Jesse, I want you to go get Father Ramirez now and take him to Izabel. Tell him what we know so far and help him secure a casket for her."

"Yessir."

"But also, when Silas' remains have stopped burning, I want you to gather them."

"Me?"

"Do not touch them. Use a shovel or pitchfork. Maybe Randy Miller will let you borrow some tongs from his forge. Get them onto a canvas or some such. I trust you to take the utmost care."

The kid looked like he would be sick, but he nodded. "Yessir." He backed away from the cot side and headed straight to the door. Rattled though he was by it all, the focus of clear orders seemed to do him good. Becker considered how Jesse had been up roaming about all night with the marshal, and he still took orders without complaint when he had to be thoroughly exhausted.

"Can we come in now?" Caleb asked.

"No, just a moment more, please." Becker almost envied his patient's unconsciousness. He himself felt exhausted, and he was the one who had managed a few winks last night while Silas LeBlanc had been dying of stranger causes than blood loss alone. Then again, he was no longer in his prime, and everything of late had torn him away from his usual pace, his meditations and prayer. He'd had no time to harvest the last of the fall herbs to replenish the clinic for the winter months, a practice that fed his inner peace as well. Granted, helping a lawman with his investigation had been a sort of meditation in itself that stirred his curiosity and wonder, but the onslaught of dead involved had not left him feeling connected with the Divine, the thing which fueled him most.

He retrieved a pair of scissors and prepared himself as he cut off the gauze wrap and peeled back the pad underneath. The slick remains of the salve he'd applied helped it peel off, and he was relieved—surprised, really—to find that there was no puss or inflamed edges that expressed when he gently prodded them.

"Huh," he murmured. The area was a mix of fresher red blood and scab surrounded by the splay of black veins, which was now the more troubling matter. No disease he knew of caused this.

His mind backtracked to the bizarre thoughts he'd had outside the saloon when he had watched Jasper O'Brian emerge and fling Silas' body out into the sun. He'd seen, fleetingly, that there was a long spear of wood protruding from Silas' back, but then the man's body had combusted on immediate contact with the sunlight, consumed down to muscle then bone and organs in seconds.

Or so it *seemed* the sunlight caused it.

Becker turned and looked over at his askew examination table, knocked off-center by Silas shoving Izabel away before he'd fled. On the floor, at its feet, lay Silas' pocket watch and the two shattered vials of blood that Becker had drawn. He had no idea what had become of the Derringer after Izabel had run off with it, but at least one vial had survived and still lay on the table, precariously close to the edge.

Becker rose and retrieved the remaining vial to remove it to the counter, a safer spot. Then he looked around anxiously for a means to gather the glass shards. He had crushed some of them under heel as he'd stumbled toward the door to stop Izabel. He settled on the ash pan beside the pot belly stove and grabbed it along with the whisk broom, and then he swept all of the shards and stoppers into the pan. Most of the blood had dried on the shards though there were some stains on the floor.

The rectory steps were still in an angle of cool shade, and he stepped away from it and out where the light of morning was most brilliant. Sun glinted on the shards, and thin wisps of smoke rose as the spots of blood ignited, made tiny sparks in the pan. A whiff of copper, decay, and char, and the glass gleamed bright and clean.

Becker tried not to drop the pan altogether. He took a deep, calming breath then made his way back into the rectory. He had another experiment to do and books to consult before he confirmed the outrageous theory that suddenly consumed his thoughts.

And if he was correct, then Hiram Wells did not have much time left.

"I swear, Cage, it couldn't be helped," Jasper insisted as he barely held himself up on his knees and haunches in the parlor, a hand clamped over his belly. His uniform coat had been stripped off to reveal the white shirt underneath drenched in two great blooms of blood front and back.

The rich smell of it cloyed the air in the space dimmed by the drawn curtains. For it to be spilled so readily with the expectation that Cage could simply replace it was an insult he could not let stand. "So, you waste the blood we sacrifice to give you life? Then you come back here expecting to be replenished as if it were that simple?"

"No… no, you know it isn't like that. I couldn't get to that saloon keeper with Wells and that kid riding up and down the road and all over town. You wanted me to stay away from the marshal, I did, and then I finally got desperate, and then LeBlanc… he *changed* before I got there."

"Let me make sure I understand this correctly," Cage said, kneeling to take Jasper's face in one hand, lifting his chin. He looked the servant in the eyes, found the corneas clouded though not so much as to blind him completely. The man's face, frozen for centuries at twenty-eight, now developed lines that fanned under his eyes and etched grooves along the sides of his nose and mouth. "It was, somehow, the very person you were supposed to stay away from who impaled you with your own sword. You were trained better than that, Jasper. Worse, you left that sword behind." Cage stroked a long lock of ginger hair that now had streaks of white in it before he stood back up. "Unless you're trying to tell me something else. Is that it?"

"W-what do you mean?" he coughed, hoarse and dry as an autumn leaf as his body tissues slowly withered.

"It happens, and I understand. Thralls grow tired of service and get sloppy. I've seen it before. Is that what is going on here?"

"What? *No.*" His body quivered from the loss of blood. "I've served you well. You know I have. Please… Cage…" His voice broke down into a whisper as he wavered forward and back on his knees, eyes rolling to stay conscious.

"You have, that is true." Cage sighed, looked around the room at his companions. August had lodged himself in the doorway, head down as if he couldn't bear what was coming, and Nora and Genevieve were near the sofa, each flanking Miz Simpson, who stood trapped in a soft mental cloud and staring vacantly.

Morgan—quiet, loyal—lingered at Cage's side as readily as a lieutenant holding an empty burlap sack in one hand.

"The point is, you *were seen*," Cage said. "It's not enough that I just cleaned up a near epidemic, but you were seen in such a way that we are all now connected to the loss of a well-known citizen of the town. Now I have to purify again, and we may need to move on sooner than planned."

Jasper's heartbeat droned, and Cage detected a light rise in the man's temperature as desperation flared and years of loyalty vanished for the sake of a few last, spiteful words. His brogue, which had gradually refined over decades, devolved toward its original Cavan thickness. "Yer a right sorry cunt, Cage. Purification? Bah! Ya didn't mind it when ya slaughtered those two wasters right under the marshal's nose."

Cage's jaw tightened briefly. Such backtalk would normally drive him to act impetuously and slit the man's throat or worse, but maybe that was what Jasper wanted to speed his demise. Otherwise, the thrall's decline was a long, torturous process. "That was a *choice*, Jasper," he replied. "There is a difference." With that, he began to strip off the rest of his dirtied clothes. He slipped off his boots, unbuckled his belt and slid off his trousers. They were black and thus did not show the dried black ichor, but he could feel it, stiff on the fabric, and smell it penetrating the heavier aroma of Jasper's fresher blood. Irritably he stuffed the items into the burlap sack that Morgan held out.

Looking down at his body, he noted the remnants of ichor on his alabaster-white skin. Patches and streaks interrupted the uniform smoothness of his sculpted chest, arms, and drum-tight stomach muscles, a physique earned in the former life he could barely be bothered to recall. His corded right forearm was particularly stained, given he'd shoved it down that beast's throat going after its heart. The ichor had settled into the lines around his knuckles, in the junctions of his fingers. To merely wash it off was forbidden, an ancient law handed down for millennia, and he dared not defy it the way he dared not leave any hunting ground befouled by revenants, human or beast alike.

He gave a clipped side nod to Morgan, who put down the bag and picked up a large quilt dampened with cool water.

August and the girls retreated down the corridor to the foyer at the foot of the steps, safely shadowed from the sunbeams that would soon burst through the picture window that faced south in the parlor. Miz Simpson remained, lost in her trance, and Jasper on his knees near the hearth, too weak to go anywhere on his own.

Cage stepped up to the heavy curtain and gripped its edges, braced himself, closed his eyes, and flung it open. Light flooded through his lids and stung tears to the surface while searing heat consumed the front of his body as he spread his arms wide. His teeth gritted, fangs budding to full, narrow length behind his crusting lips, as he suppressed a scream for the matter of seconds that he allowed his own flesh to burn, just on the surface of his face and for the length down to his loins and feet. Not one inch was spared the deadly light. He spun around, back to the window, and felt the flesh there crisp and smoke, agony digging into the back of his skull, causing hair to singe and wisp away in huge patches.

The deed done, the light quenched as Morgan swept the blinds shut on the rod and then threw the damp quilt over Cage's back and shoulders. The pain remained, but Cage could open his eyes again and stare into the room while his fangs retracted back down to the appearance of ordinary canine teeth. An acrid layer of smoke drifted across the ceiling, swirled around the chandelier.

Slowly the rest of the kith crept back in from the foyer, and Jasper, hunched in the same place, sneered up at him, perhaps drawing some final satisfaction in witnessing the pain of Cage's self-immolation. His body healed sluggishly. The brittle layer of split and flaked skin formed into a layer of scar tissue.

That was the awkward moment there came a loud knock on the door. Cage's head snapped up, and he turned an ear to listen to a human heartbeat outside, slamming furiously. He sniffed the air to catch a scent of piss, nerves, and a faded cologne cutting through the linger of roasted preternatural flesh.

"It's the mayor," August said, having caught the same distinct odors and sounds.

Cage chuckled. "Let him in."

August went back into the foyer and opened the door. The dim light on the northern side of the house beamed in, but its blue cast was far more tolerable as it highlighted the polished wood side panels in the hall, caught on the angle of stairway banister visible from the parlor.

In the doorway, Mayor Titus Watkins stood a purely dark silhouette until Cage focused out the glare around him and defined the man standing with his cane. Watkins' eyes, often affecting stoic control—Cage had seen through that from the moment the man shook his hand—peered inside, blinking to adjust to the low lighting in the house. Only the lamps on the mantle burned along with a candelabra on the sideboard in the hallway. Watkins looked confused to discover the house shrouded in such darkness. It submerged him in a palpable unease that Cage found satisfying.

August exchanged a casual greeting with the dandy, who sniffed the air and wrinkled his nose before following him into the parlor. "What's that smell?" he asked.

At the last moment, August turned sideways and let Watkins pass him by, then he stepped into the passageway, affecting a barrier that kept the mayor unwittingly trapped.

"Mr. Edwards—" Watkins started to speak up then froze as he gazed around the room, eyes pausing on each figure with growing disturbance. "Miz Simpson?" He absently lifted a hand to wave at her. "Hello?"

When Grace Simpson did not acknowledge him, his attention drifted to Nora and Genevieve. The longer pause he made on Jasper was marked by his heartbeat jerking up a pace, a side trip to note Morgan, and then finally he reached the coup de grâce, Cage himself.

Cage let the quilt fall away from his shoulders, strolled forward in full, naked display allowing Watkins to see better the silken pink scares from his face and half-bald head down to his manhood, legs and feet. His flaxen pubic and leg hair had also singed away but would soon return. "Hello, Titus," he said casually while the unexpected visitor took it all in. "To what do we owe this unexpected pleasure?"

"There w-w-was an occurrence in town very early this morning," he replied. He reached up and took off his derby, held it strategically to hide the fact that he had just pissed himself slightly. The acrid odor mingled with the other smells in the room, from Jasper's blood to the smoke borne of their leader's temporarily marred skin. "Silas LeBlanc and Izabel Martinez were killed in a most strange fashion.

"Your man here—eh, Mr. O'Brian, I mean—appeared to be involved." At that moment, Watkins looked down at Jasper, fully saw that the face peering from behind graying red hair was considerably aged. "Oh…" he cringed as if his eyes were fingers that had touched something slimy. He tore his gaze away and back to Cage. "I thought I would… inquire for myself as to what happened. I thought surely one of your troupe could not have killed them. I thought perhaps it just *seemed* that way."

The man was trying so hard to act unperturbed—and failing—that it was pathetic.

"Oh, just be afraid already, Titus," Cage told him casually. "Unfortunately, it is true. Jasper did kill Mr. LeBlanc. It was a necessary evil. As for Miz Martinez, this is the first I've heard of that." His eyes narrowed and cut toward Jasper, then up again. "Tell me about this occurrence."

"N-necessary evil? Now hold on." He took a breath, attempted to falsely steel himself and shake off the shock and sheer confusion of what he'd walked in on. "You tell *me* what is going on here? I came to give you and your troupe the benefit of the doubt, to hear your side of the story. Frankly, I was afraid the coyote attack last night might have impacted your choice to stay for your final show, but then this…"

Cage tilted his head, his crispy brow furrowing. "A man was attacked and severely injured, and you were more concerned about whether we would stay and entertain you?"

The question—more of a statement—did not seem to reach the man. The cane rose, gestured up and down at Cage's body. "What happened to you?"

"Nothing that a drink won't fix," Cage said dryly. In a blur, he was right before the shorter man, towering over him. "You are quite a worm, aren't you, Mr. Mayor? No wonder the marshal thinks so little of you."

Watkins stumbled back, gasped. Oddly, it was not Cage's speed but rather the comment that caught his attention more. "You wait just a damned minute," he spat. "That man withheld information from me. He knew something was happening in this town, and he told me nothing."

"I can't imagine why."

"What *really* happened this morning, Mr. Edwards? Why did Mr. O'Brian kill Mr. LeBlanc?"

"Just wrapping up a small problem that could have been a much bigger one for all of us. Now, I've already had enough of you, little man."

Every vessel in Watkins' face presented a warm, red glow to Cage's hungering vision. "You can't speak to me that way."

"I can speak to you any way I like. I can *do* anything I like. You invited us in, Mr. Mayor. *You* opened the town up to us." Then he stared into Watkins' eyes with bitter intensity. Watkin's weak mind put up no resistance as he gazed back, eyes going blank as he wavered on his feet. "Tell me what happened after the saloon keeper's death. Where is the marshal now?"

"He collapsed… unconscious," Watkins said in a flat voice. "He's at the pastor's clinic, in the rectory."

Cage sighed. *Always with that damned clinic*, he thought. *Why does it have to be on holy ground?* "And what happened to Silas LeBlanc's remains?"

"Still in the street, along with that coyote. Pastor Becker said not to touch them."

Smart, for a holy man.

"What about his woman?"

"Father Ramirez is taking care of her body."

Cage raised a gradually re-growing eyebrow to that. Well, that would not do either. He considered how to handle that matter among many others. "All right, Titus," he said, digging little hooked tendrils into the man's vapid mind, "you are going to go back into town now. Go back to your house and stay there until you hear from me again. Do you understand? Sit *still* and wait."

Watkins nodded vacantly.

"Good boy, run along now." Cage watched him turn stiffly as a Swiss automaton while putting his hat back on. The scent of his piss curled through the air in his wake.

August stepped out of the way to let him through and saw him to the door down the hall. There was one more flood of blue-gray light, and then the door shut, and August returned.

Cage immediately went back to the matter at hand. Jasper had not made a peep during the entire encounter with the mayor, but his breath wheezed in the quiet parlor. Cage felt the wounded thrall's clouded eyes still upon him as he turned to Morgan, gestured him closer and gave a clipped, dismissive nod at his counterpart.

"Leave him," he said. The man would be dust soon, his body depleted of its resources to the point it would not even hold together like a normal corpse. It did not take sunlight to purify that.

"Cage… please…" Jasper coughed again. "Not like this."

"We'll need a replacement," August said, ignoring the pleas. "Someone will have to drive the freighter when we leave."

Cage pondered that. He had ideas of his own but decided it was time to let the *youngster* have some fun. "Why don't you sort that out, August? Be creative."

"And Lucinda?" the pleading almost returned.

"Patience. I need her human just a little while longer."

He approached Miz Simpson, whose hooded eyes stared straight forward, and he reached up to touch her cheek, willed her attention just to the surface enough as he whispered gently in her ear. "Thank you, Grace, for the use of your house. I'm afraid we'll be moving on soon."

"Oh," she murmured. "I do hope you enjoyed your stay."

"Yes, dear, we certainly did." He kissed her cheek, gently nudged her head sideways, exposing her high lace collar. One hand reached around her side and crept up her back to find the series of tight, round buttons that ran up her spine to the nape of her neck. He extracted one claw, severed their threads, and heard them pop off and spill softly upon the sofa cushions where some bounced off and clicked on the floor. The collar came loose, and he peeled it down to reveal the warm skin beneath her ear and the pulse there, inviting him to replenish and rejuvenate.

She sighed sweetly as he bit deep and clean, not spilling a drop as the warm coppery taste of her blood filled his mouth, and he gulped repeatedly, hastily. It pooled heavily in his stomach briefly before it drained off into his veins, flowed out to the rest of his body, plumped up every nerve and fiber affected by the sun's wrath. His skin tingled and shifted as scars smoothed back into subtle skin, and in moments his hair, too, had regrown. Her body sagged, but he caught her in both arms, held her firmly up until her heartbeat slowed to a stop. He drew out the last and smallest sip, detached and licked the bite marks, then hefted her up to cradle in his arms for a moment before handing her gently over to Morgan.

"Do what needs to be done," he said to the thrall. "We need to prepare to leave now." He looked around at the others. "Gather your things. We're getting in the coach. Morgan will take us south of town for the day."

"What about the girl?" Genevieve asked.

"Leave her here," he said. "Her father will be coming for her."

"Are you sure?" August asked. "He's as good as dead already."

"I'm positive." The corner of Cage's mouth curled slightly. "Death may be coursing his veins, but he's not one to give up easily."

"Won't be a very long reunion," Nora added. "You'll have to do something about him."

"Oh, I will. Trust me."

For a long moment, as he surfaced, his mind remained numb, mute, memories floating out of reach. It was pleasant, a place in which he wished terribly to stay. A long time ago, he'd have fought to remain there, but in the now, his eyes opened on their own, and that was the end of it. He stared up at rafters crowded with clutches of colors: dull green, yellowed white, brown. The herbs came into better focus, and when he took a deep breath, their warm, earthy scent filled his nose. He felt padding and blanket under his fingers, woven threads worn smooth, and utmost heard voices that he put names to gradually.

"Ja, well, Calmet thought there was evidence that they all potentially exist in our world together." Becker, obviously.

"Angels *and* vampires?" And this was Caleb, sounding dubious.

"Well, it's complicated but an interesting treatise."

"I bewieve in angews. Mama went to be wiv them."

His heart jumped a little. Or maybe that was his stomach, and he drew another breath to make words, "Caleb? Ellie?"

"Papa!" Ellie's sweet, excited voice pierced his ears right before she barreled into his resting place.

Hiram *Ooofed!* as his whole body was jarred on the cot and tried to raise his head. "Hey, Sweet Pea," he grated out. Seconds later, Caleb hovered over him, concern on his young brow.

Then Becker's grim countenance horned into view. "Excuse me," he said, herding both children out of the way and kneeling by the cot. He reached up toward Hiram's face, the slow movement a warning that he was coming in for an examination. "How do you feel?" he asked as he laid a hand to Hiram's forehead. Then he gently tugged down a lower eyelid and peered in. Moved on to the other.

Hiram would much rather see one of his kids hovering so close instead of Becker's big white mustache. For once, he let his language slip around his children. "Like hammered shit."

"That's no surprise. What about your arm?"

"Not as bad, actually." Hiram raised his head for a look. The bite, cleaned and wrapped again, did not hurt so much now, but the veins reaching out from beneath the dressing, like the dark branches of winter trees, were another matter. He gaped, tried to find his words again. "It's like... Sil—" Another breath to find the strength to say it. "Same thing Silas had." A statement, not a question, because there was no denying it. He'd seen veins like that around oil-black eyes and framing his friend's face and neck. The next thing to strike him was just as hard. "And Lucinda's still..."

"Still missing," Becker said. "What else do you remember?" His face withdrew from the proximity of his patient's, and he disappeared from view.

Hiram stared at the herbs above again, feeling displaced in time from having dropped so hard. A dull headache pulsed behind his eyes as the light from the windows still seemed too bright, but at least it was not the blinding sun that he last recalled. Then the series of mental photographs lodged firmly in his consciousness crept back into place where they haunted him with every detail.

"Silas," he whispered and couldn't stop the silent tears that flooded up, spilled over, blurred the room around him. They streamed over the sides of his cheeks into his ears, tickling and itching, and his nose began to run as well.

Becker returned, out of focus, knelt to hold a teacup over Hiram, helped him raise his head to sip the bitter brew. "Just some willow bark tea, as I'm assuming you've got a right good throb between your ears."

"It true about Uncle Silas?" Caleb's voice asked softly.

"What have they heard?" Hiram asked, raised the back of his left hand and wiped at his eyes, gave a slobbery sniffle.

"What they needed to hear," Becker replied. "No use keeping the truth from them, but I didn't let them go up the street. I sent Jesse to get Father Ramirez for Izabel and to collect Silas' remains. I didn't want to leave them here alone anymore or you without care. Mayor Watkins went tearing out to the Simpson house as we were getting you in here. Saw him come back about an hour ago and head home looking a bit glassy-eyed, I must say."

Hiram only grunted at the last part. Watkins was the last person he felt like thinking about.

Along with the headache, his gut twisted into a lead ball. The images flipped before his inner eye, starting with a burning corpse in the street and moving back in time to Silas straddling him, gone limp with a splintered table leg protruding through his chest far enough to dig into Hiram's own.

Hiram laid a hand on his sternum where his shirt had been unbuttoned, felt a scab there, oily with one of Becker's salves smeared on it.

Next, he envisioned Silas on his feet, a growling, screaming wild thing that had somehow lost all of its humanity overnight, become more like the creature that had attacked him just a matter of hours before. He'd seen Silas with his mouth clamped over Izabel's throat, seen him draw back, tearing skin and muscle, and let her fall to the ground as if she meant nothing to him.

He blinked it away, refocused on his children and Becker huddled at the cot side like they were waiting for something. Even Ellie was patient. "I can't explain anything that happened," he admitted. "Just that... that guy from the acting troupe... Jasper O'Brian... he killed Silas. But then before that… Silas killed Izabel. I think."

"We both saw what happened in those last minutes," Becker said, maintaining an eerie calm as he put the teacup aside and walked over to the counter to his microscope, opened a vial of some dark liquid and siphoned a drop out onto a glass slide. "Silas was beyond help. I know that now." He turned and pointed at some stains on the floor at the base of his examination table. "I took blood samples from Silas in vials that were dropped and broken when he fled. All but this one. I swept the glass up and took it outside as an experiment, exposed the stains to the sun. Just like Silas, they burned away. So, *think* about the order of events. All of it. Can you stand?"

Hiram carefully pushed himself up into a sit, then got to his feet with Caleb's help. The room spun for a moment before he reached out to grip the corner of the central table and used it to further guide him to the back of the room.

"Come look at this," Becker said and helped him get the rest of the way to the counter. The pastor lit two short finger lamps, each with a miniature hurricane globe, and moved them both closer to the microscope, one on each side to illuminate the underside of the stage. "You have to see this for yourself," Becker said and showed him how to look down through the brass cylinder and adjust the focus via a little, spoked wheel on the side.

Hiram propped himself on the edge of the counter for support. He had looked through a spyglass before but never a microscope, which was fascinating as hell as he squinted his left eye shut and peered with his right. A spread of dark circles came into view, their edges raggedy and barbed so that they tended to cling to each other in clumps. Eerily enough, they appeared to pulse hungrily as if trying to grow. "What am I looking at?"

"Those are Silas' blood cells," Becker explained. "What became of them, anyway, and no, they should not be moving like that. Now, here—" he gingerly traded out the slide for another. "Here are normal healthy human blood cells. These are mine."

Hiram looked down through the cylinder again and gave a "Huh," to that. Strange to see that blood, what he typically encountered as a runny liquid that separated, congealed, and dried quickly depending on the environment, should be made up of countless tiny red circles with a translucent red middle. "They look like Miz Raskin's donuts."

"Hardly." Becker chuckled at the comment. "Now, watch this." Again, with the utmost care, he switched out the slides, replacing the view of red, healthy cells with Silas' sample.

Then the tip of a hypodermic needle, magnified to a startling degree, appeared and pushed out a minimal drop of normal red cells onto the slide. The black, raggedy cells spread toward them in seconds, shadows crawling across the glass to reach the new cells where the barbs immediately attached and dug in. The red cells began to blacken, some faster than others, while some quivered in fits of minuscule dissent. But, like a blight destroying a young tree, the sick cells prevailed until the slide was covered in more of them, and none of the red remained.

Hiram pulled back from the cylinder abruptly as if worried the black barbs would reach up through the lens and snag him in the eye.

"You were correct when you suggested a disease might be part of the equation," Becker said. "The samples I took from the Evans brothers were stolen before I could run an experiment like this, but now I think we can deduce why someone has been burning corpses."

"I need to sit back down," Hiram said and worked his way carefully back to the cot.

"Consider this," Becker said, moving to help him resettle and picking up the teacup again. "First that arm, then the coyote, and now Silas. *Think* about what you saw, Marshal, and think about that blood sitting on that glass over there."

Hiram accepted the teacup and drained it quickly, all the better to diffuse the TNT now going off in his head. He coughed, almost sent tea up into his nasal cavity and out his nose. Sniffled it back down and handed the cup back. "More... please..." Better yet, he needed some of that Kentucky mash. A *lot* of it.

Cough.

As Becker got up to prepare another infusion, Hiram looked at his son, the primary expert here on the subject, and said something he would never have expected to say.

"Caleb—" *Cough* "—tell me about vampires."

CHAPTER TWENTY-SIX

Jesse had employed Nathan's buckboard and horses to retrieve Father Ramirez and then gone to the blacksmith's adjacent to the livery not far back behind the Palace, but Mr. Miller was not there. It looked like he had not been there at all given the cold hearth, the eerie quiet in the shed, so in desperation, Jesse borrowed a pair of tongs and a coal spade without asking but planned to bring them back immediately after his task.

Having taken the alleyway between the hotel and the Palace, he had passed the canvas tarp that covered Izabel. By the time he came back through, Father Ramirez had peeled back the upper part of the canvas and revealed her face. Her eyes were closed now, and the light caught a gleam of oil smudged on her forehead in a little cross. Ramirez looked a shade paler than he'd been while riding up the street next to Jesse in the buckboard, but he conducted his blessing quietly in Spanish.

Jesse picked up a few of the words, but his Spanish was not particularly good.

… may God open the gates of Paradise…

He wasn't Catholic, so he didn't linger, afraid it would appear disrespectful when all he felt compelled to do was stare at the blackening mess that had been Izabel's throat. He went on about his own business and stepped back out onto the thoroughfare with the tongs and shovel.

Mr. Raskin stood over the bones, which had finally stopped smoldering. He'd already laid out another tarp for Jesse to use to round them up. "You're a good man, Jesse, to do this. I wouldn't want to touch them even with those." He indicated the tongs and spade.

Jesse had no words, just a tight, dust-crusted throat. Thank God, he thought, that Silas' guts and other organs had completely burned up. He didn't think he could deal with scooping up human entrails.

It's just bones, he tried to tell himself. The organs had reduced to a scattering of flaky, fragile ashes that made him think of a chicken's downy feathers after it had been ravaged by a predator.

He thought, out of nowhere, about Lucinda's struggle with the coyote that had plagued the coop she and her mother had so lovingly built together. Suddenly he wished he'd been more understanding of that struggle, that he'd volunteered to help her fix the damages rather than try to get up her skirts.

"I'm gonna get inside now," Raskin said. "The missus is a mite torn up over all of this, as you can imagine."

Jesse nodded absently and crouched down, immediately focusing on the skull that sat up almost perfectly on its lower jaw, complete and still together, except that the canine teeth were so long that they propped the mouth open slightly. That couldn't be Silas, he thought. Not with *those* teeth that had ripped into little bitty Izabel and opened up her throat so brutally.

His lips thinned out in a grimace as he carefully used the tongs to pick up bone after bone. Small clouds of the finer ash gusted away uncontrollably on a breeze, and Jesse endeavored to stay out of its path. Finally, he used the spade to slide under the skull and maneuver it onto the canvas. Once he'd removed all the black that he could without picking up too much of the road dirt underneath, he stood and propped his hands on the shovel's handle.

He looked up to check the angle of the sun, realizing how time had already crept to late morning, and the silence in the Bend still lingered. By now, he should have gathered an audience. Should have had to explain, somehow, what happened at the break of dawn, but there was no one. No questions. No swears of exclamations. He should have had to fend off the nosy ones like Terry Wilkes and Miz Elliot, but they were nowhere around.

Wilkes should be opening the barbershop right now. Although the town had been quiet of late anyway, there should at least be one or two horsemen coming in for some reason or another, not to mention the other shop owners.

The nothing happening in the thoroughfare was as unnerving as scraping a dead saloon keeper's bones off the street. Despite the sweat collecting within his hatband, Jesse felt like a cold fire erupted across his shoulders and down his arms. It shot through his core into his groin and filled him with the need to go around the other corner of the Palace before he pissed his trousers.

He hurried into the narrow alley, relieved himself against the side of the bakery, and took a deep breath to calm his nerves. For all of his prior talk about liking how quiet it was out here in the wide-open spaces, now he'd give anything to hear kids screaming, horses clomping by, business owners arguing. Fuck, he'd love to see a parade right now, anything to relieve *this* silent hell.

He buttoned up and stepped back into the thoroughfare just as Father Ramirez emerged from the opposite side.

"Jesse," the priest called quietly to him. "I'm ready to take her back to the chapel."

He nodded and headed to the other alleyway. Neither man said anything as they turned the canvas Mr. Raskin had supplied over and maneuvered Iz's body onto it before folding it over her, wrapping and tucking it as tightly as possible. She was so light that Jesse carried her on his own to the back of the buckboard, and then Father Ramirez stood by, waiting.

Jesse bundled up the collection of bones and tied off the corners of the canvas, looking across the street at the remains of the coyote. He refused to touch that *thing* at all. If the pastor wanted to study that, then he'd have to take up the tongs and shovel himself.

Jesse put off returning the borrowed tools and tossed them into the back of the wagon. He was too damned tired now, needed water, food, and to see how the marshal was doing or if new explanations had come to light. "Just a moment, Padre," he said, his voice like dead leaves. "I wanna look at one more thing."

Ramirez nodded and waited with the wagon and body while Jesse went up the Palace steps and through the batwing doors. It was his first glimpse of the inside since he and Pastor Becker had stood outside listening to the short battle. Daylight through the front windows showed him enough. The mirror, shelves, and bottles behind the bar comprised a busted mess on the floor. The tart, oaken smell of whiskey hung in the air, and a table had been smashed in half, its legs splayed out from under it, all but one remaining. Jesse put together the noises he and Becker had heard from outside with the visual he had now. He knew the missing table leg had been the one stuck through Silas' middle when Jasper O'Brian booted him out into the sunlight.

There had also been a gunshot, and he recalled that he'd taken the marshal's gun belt off to find it empty. *There...* he saw it. Near the busted table, the Peacemaker laid against a long shard of wood and a glinting piece of bottle glass. Jesse walked over, picked it up, and wedged it into the back of his belt. He turned for another last glance around the saloon, his heart heavy to think that he would probably never hang out here again, not with Marshal Wells, not with any of his former co-workers.

Then a silvery glint caught his attention, and he looked to see the sword lying on the floor by the nearest balcony support. He knew he didn't have the keenest of eyes, couldn't analyze much more of the scene before him and cleverly form a puzzle piece to save for later the way the marshal could.

But he did know it would be stupid to leave a weapon like that lying about.

Something told him it would be useful, so he reached down, gripped the handle, and lifted it. The blade rang gently against the floorboards. He'd never held so much steel in one hand before, was pleasantly surprised. It was heavy, but the weight balanced well between handle and blade, and then he noticed patches of dried blood along the blade. Jasper O'Brian, he recalled, had fled with an injury through his side. That meant the marshal had managed to turn the blade on its owner. It was the only logical conclusion he could figure, and Jesse smiled to himself, feeling not so stupid after all.

But *who* would need such a weapon to begin with? he wondered, and that mystery kept stirring his thoughts as he carried it outside and headed for the buckboard.

Halted.

As sunlight touched the blade, the blood lifted, turned to wisps of fine, smoky dust and drifted away.

But to see this did not stun him, not after watching an entire man burn.

Father Ramirez stared at the blade with a frown, but he said nothing of it as Jesse slid the sword into the rear of the buckboard alongside Izabel's shrouded body.

Then he climbed into the seat, quickly joined by the priest, and together they fled the Bend's silence.

"…and if a vampire bites a human, that person will die and become a vampire," Caleb went on with growing, if cautious, enthusiasm. "Usually, you have to hammer a wooden stake through their hearts. Best if it's hawthorn."

"And cut off the head," Ellie chimed in from the crook of her father's good arm. "It's gotta be thowough."

Hiram reclined on the cot, still regaining his strength while he sipped more of Becker's headache tea. He looked blandly at the pastor as he listened to all the valuable lessons that could be learned from reading a penny dreadful. "And all this time, I thought my children were reading crap."

Ellie giggled.

Becker's mustache lifted on one side, suggesting there was a smirk hiding under there somewhere. "Well, crap in the pulp sense, but all legends come from somewhere, Marshal."

When Hiram had first awakened, hearing Becker's and his kids' voices debating something to do with angels and vampires, he had not noticed that Becker had already withdrawn several old volumes from his books and had them spread out on the examination table.

The pastor went back to one of the open books now and gestured over the pages. "This is a translation from French to German of a work by Augustin Calmet, a Benedictine monk who wrote not only clerical papers but this volume on angels and demons, vampires and spirits. It collects stories from all over Europe, especially from Poland and the Austro-Hungarian Empire."

Caleb stared over the books with awe, even though he didn't know a word of German. "See, Papa, maybe my penny dreadfuls aren't so—"

"Dreadful?" Hiram suggested.

"Bad," Caleb finished with an irritated glare.

"I wouldn't say that yet." Hiram inwardly smiled as Caleb *harumphed* over his father's sheer stubbornness. He was secretly glad to see the boy's renewed interest in them. Having watched his son abandon his childish excitement and wonder over the pulp tales had been depressing, and Hiram had felt to blame.

"There is more," Becker said, looking up from under his brows in a way that made Hiram feel like he should be at a school desk. "Almost a hundred and thirty years ago, there was an actual vampire scare in the Empire, an *epidemic*, if you will, in the villages of Serbia. News reached the empress, Maria Theresa, in Vienna. Her subjects were digging up corpses, staking and beheading them, burning some of the bodies out of the fear that they were rising from the dead as vampires and feeding on the blood of their relatives. She sent her court physician, Gerard van Swieten, to investigate. He found instances of corpses not decomposing in a natural fashion and theorized that it was because of environmental circumstances."

"Like what?"

Becker shrugged, making circling hand gestures in the air. "Lack of oxygen in the graves, salt minerals in the soil. All reasonable conclusions for a man of science, so he reported that it was all nonsense, that the villagers were acting on superstition.

"Thing is, he went in biased to begin with. He planned to debunk it all no matter what, to put the peasantry and their superstition in its place." Becker closed the book. "But what if he shouldn't have been so dismissive? What if he had *really* studied those corpses?"

"What an ass," Caleb commented, and Hiram was not inclined to chastise him. Rachel would not be pleased about that.

"What happened then?" Hiram asked.

"The empress laid down a law forbidding the exhumation of corpses, and the epidemic came to an end. At least, that's the claim."

"How do you even know all of this?" Hiram unwound his arm from Ellie to sit forward. His head was feeling better, and he was growing new faith in Becker's teas and other concoctions. Still, he had to prop on his knees, suppressing little waves of dizziness.

"My father was a physician before me, but he also had vague interests in the occult." The last he admitted almost defensively. "He felt that medical science and religion did not have to be incompatible. These books were his. He introduced me to both van Swieten—pure science— and Calmet—pure spirituality. Both men wrote their treatises and reports within the same period of years. Then I further studied van Swieten's works at the University of Vienna in medical school, and then Calmet again when I went into the church. I mainly focused on his theological works then, but now, looking at the whole picture…

"Maybe what seemed like peasant superstition had something more to it. Something scared people enough to perform holy rituals defiling corpses and placing crosses and garlic on their doors. Fear drives desperate measures, but *something* starts it, and maybe it isn't always gossip and fairy tales."

"Crosses and garlic?" Hiram asked, rubbing the bridge of his nose.

"You really should read more, Papa," Caleb chided him.

Again, Becker's mustache lifted, and Hiram almost couldn't stand it anymore. He felt like the butt of some huge joke, but he could not ignore any of it, given everything that had happened. Not anymore.

"I think—" Becker started more soberly as he leaned over the book, arms crossed and swallowed as he stared emptily for a moment. Then he blinked to, shook his head. "There may have been signs."

"Like what?"

"Maddie Krane's baby." Becker's gray eyes took on that distant, watery look that spoke of disturbed thoughts. "Should have been born alive, healthy. I felt that child kick in her belly for months, and then... suddenly... dead." He drew a long breath, pursed his lips as he blew it out slow and steady. "I always felt like there was more to it, something out of reach that I couldn't put my finger on."

Hiram frowned as a new dread rose in him, a hum under his skin just from hearing of the stillbirth. "How would that be connected?"

Both of his children had fallen into uncomfortable silence. Ellie chewed on her bottom lip, but she hadn't burst into frightened tears yet.

"It happened the day *they* arrived," Becker said.

"You mean the troupe?" It seemed so unrelated on the surface, but now it was painfully clear that everything had indeed started the day the Chamberlain Players rolled into town in their customized coach and freighter. Maria Oliver had disappeared, likely that very night, and the smells of charred remains had lifted on the winds out at the Hanson farm. That triggered a new thought. "If they are somehow the cause, they could have been here sooner," he speculated. "Could have been hitting the outlying farms, people who don't come into town much."

"And then there's this situation with milk turning sour on all the farms," Becker added. "Maybe that didn't start right away, but you can't deny that its timing is still strange."

"Yeah," Hiram murmured. "I would dismiss it all as coincidence if not for Jasper O'Brian. He came after Silas specifically. He *knew* things, and he was *hunting* him." Then he thought of how Silas almost attacked him only to back off and O'Brian's words explaining why.

He knows his own kind.

Hiram knew what it meant but wasn't ready to speak of that now, especially not in front of Caleb and Ellie.

"But did the troupe bring it, or do they just know something? They're not like Silas. They seem like regular people." He thought of last night's visit to the Simpson house, how bizarrely passive Miz Simpson had been with August Chandler and Genevieve Blakely draped around her almost as if she were a plaything. "Or maybe they *are* like Silas, but just different somehow. They aren't like wild animals. They have all of their wits and still seem normal enough."

"In the lore that I've read," Becker said, "there are varying cases of alleged vampires apparently passing as human, walking around in the villages where they were born and grew up."

"Then there's the sunlight. Is that in the lore?" Hiram asked. "Silas burned in the sun. That's what killed him, not just that table leg O'Brian put through him."

"It isn't specifically mentioned, just that they are usually active at night."

Hiram nodded along absently with that. "We've seen Jasper O'Brian and Morgan Reed out during the day, but when did we see Cage Edwards and the other three taking a stroll in the sun? Lucinda's been seeing August Chandler at the opera house, but as far as I know, he's stayed pretty holed up there."

"Out of the sun," they both chorused.

He and Becker stared at each other for a long, mute moment. Then that was all it took to compel him to his feet. He needed more answers, needed to find his daughter. "I'm going out to the Simpson house again." This time, he'd knock the door down if necessary to find out what was going on in there.

"You can't go alone in your condition," Becker argued.

Right at that moment, Jesse opened the door and wedged himself inside.

"I'll go with you!" Caleb finally spoke up. "Please, Papa!"

"No, you stay here."

"Go where?" Jesse asked. The new deputy stepped into the room and surveyed the situation. He held Jasper O'Brian's sword in one hand, keeping the blade carefully away from his person. "Marshal, glad to see you're up. Look, I retrieved your gun from the Palace." He reached behind his belt, drew out the familiar Peacemaker and handed it over.

"Thanks, Jesse."

"Did you get everything done?" Becker asked gently.

The kid nodded, his eyes glassy pools amid the dust around them. "Father Ramirez took Izabel's body to the chapel. I helped him get a casket for her and everything at the Bixby Brothers', but no one was there." The glassy pools widened into haunted lakes. "Nobody's anywhere, Marshal."

Hiram nodded grimly to that. "Yeah."

"I took tools from the blacksmith without asking, then Father Ramirez and I just left a note and took a casket for Izabel. I just... What is happening?"

The marshal stared at the floor, at a loss of words for a moment before he said. "We'll tell you everything, Jesse, but just give us a minute."

Jesse nodded, then added gently, "I have Silas in the back of the wagon, and I also grabbed *this*." He lifted the broadsword, keeping the point on the blade aimed at the floor. "There was blood on it," he said, "but then I took it out in the sun."

Hiram and Becker slowly looked at each other.

CHAPTER TWENTY-SEVEN

Hiram determined that Becker would accompany him out of medical precaution, while Jesse would stay at the Wells house with Caleb and Ellie. First, however, preparations were made, and Becker encouraged Hiram to eat something before he fell over again. They used Nathan's buckboard yet again, and everyone went up the quiet thoroughfare together with Teddy and Peso tethered and trotting alongside.

Jesse made sure the horses were fed and refreshed, then he and Hiram sat in the kitchen and nibbled on the remains of Lucinda's fruit pie while Caleb cooked eggs. Jesse listened to Becker explain everything again, and Hiram saw that there was no denial in the kid's eyes. There was no argument that there must be some other logical explanation. He had seen enough evidence that the time for denial was past, and he fixated on Becker's every word about the new suspicions.

The food sat heavily in Hiram's stomach, but he kept it down, thanked Caleb for his efforts on the eggs, then drank coffee and water until he felt a little less lightheaded and could oversee the other precautions as they were put in place.

Hiram sent Jesse out to the storage bin in the barn to try to scrounge up some old paint supplies and see if they were still good. Becker, having read that holy water should work as a deterrent to vampires—there was no garlic available—pumped water in the kitchen into a bowl, sprinkled in salt in the form of a cross, and blessed it.

After a brief final word with Becker in the kitchen on how they would approach the Simpson house, the marshal went into the parlor and smelled distemper pigments and old hide glue mixed with some of Becker's makeshift holy water.

"That gonna work?" he asked, watching Jesse smooth out gobs of clumped distemper. "That pigment's probably two years old."

"It'll work good enough." Jesse painted a decently neat cross on one of the windows considering he was using a brush that looked like rats had gnawed on its bristles. Noticeable streaks of desert grit were mingled in with the ugly ocher shade. "I mean if that stuff about crosses isn't bosh."

"Let's hope it isn't. Did you talk to anyone in town when you were cleaning up?" He couldn't bring himself to say *Silas' remains.*

Jesse paused. "I would've if I'd seen 'em, Marshal. Mr. Raskin didn't say anything about anybody comin' around askin' about that coyote or even…" Another pause, this one palpably uncomfortable. "Silas' bones," he finished.

Hiram swallowed hard, which made his stomach feel heavier, and nodded. Just outside the front door, he heard a new argument on the rise and went to intervene.

"Wemme hep!" Ellie's voice rose as Hiram pulled the door open and winced at the late morning light.

"You're makin' a mess more 'n anything!" Caleb shouted back as he held up a tin can, put to a new purpose, that had a few dollops of the dubious paint mixture in it. He stirred it to get the holy water mixed in better with the distemper powder and glue, but Ellie was tugging on it, a patchy paintbrush in her hand. In the tug-o-war, the brush, loaded up with just enough paint, had left a streak on the outside of the door.

Hiram had nothing left in him to get upset over it. "Hey, walk it back, you two. Caleb, let your sister paint."

"Yes, Papa."

Hiram closed the door, took a deep breath, and looked at Jesse, who grinned as he finished his project.

"Don't worry. I'll look after 'em."

"Thanks, Jesse." He noted that the huge sword leaned in the corner nearest where Jesse worked. "You intend to use that, huh?"

"What?" He finished the cross.

"The sword."

"Oh." Jesse looked at it and shrugged. "Looks reasonable enough to me since we don't know what bullets will do anymore."

"Right," Hiram said and lost himself in thought. "Bullets." He reached down and drew out his Colt, considered some possibilities. "It may be a long shot," he added. "May be more bosh, but I've got an idea."

Soon he had Jesse, with Becker overseeing, situated at the kitchen table with both of their guns and belts, working on another task while he went to get ready.

Though he grew anxious to launch the next search for his daughter, there were some other matters to take care of first. He went into the master bedroom, shut the door, then reached under the bed and drew out Rachel's old lap desk, which he carried to the vanity. He opened the box to fold back the tilted writing platform with its leather surface, and underneath that found the compartment with creamy stationery and a nib pen. Along the upper edge of the leather, other compartments housed stamps, glue, and an ink bottle. His throat and chest tight as if he'd inhaled the sharpest dust, he got out a sheet of paper, dipped the pen nib in the ink, and started writing.

When he finished, he let the ink dry, folded the two separate letters, addressed them, and put them aside. Then he closed the box and looked up. His eyes met the framed tintype of Rachel with her hint of a distant smile that had made it tolerable to look at for all of these months. She didn't seem so distant now, as he stared into the large, dark wells of her eyes, standing out all the more because the rest of her coloring had been soft and pale, the same traits that Lucinda had inherited.

"I wish you could see our daughter," he whispered to the portrait. "She has your grace and eyes, and I know she has your courage. We always joked that she was on the delicate side, but I know that's not true. She's stayed so strong for us all these past months. I just wish she were able to follow her dreams. As for me, just give *me* strength. I can't lose her, too. Help me find her." His eyes roamed from Rachel's to the little silver cross hanging on the edge of the frame, and he caught his breath as his eyes watered.

Rachel's death, he understood now, had far more complexity to it than he'd accepted at the time. He'd blamed himself, blamed Becker, blamed God. How could such a beautiful soul be here then gone so quickly? He picked up the little cross, held it in his palm, and recalled how it once graced Rachel's slender neck. She had always taken a gentle sort of pride in her faith, always strove for generosity, kindness, and patience with everyone she'd known, and, he realized, she would *never* have blamed anyone for what had happened to her or their unborn child.

Her death had made no sense to him, just as it made no sense that the creatures in his son's pulp stories were proving *real*. Maybe nothing made sense more, he thought, than how he dealt with the loss and the unbelievable. If, he thought, such things as vampires existed and were the cause of what was happening in the Bend, then there had to be an opposing force, something good to combat the darkness. Rachel had believed in the mysterious ways of the divine, so surely there was a balance.

Surely...

Then Hiram Wells, stubborn cuss that he knew himself to be, bowed his head and prayed.

Before finally setting out, Hiram adjusted the wrap on his arm and put on a shirt that was not torn up and bloodied, a vest, and pulled his good coat and Stetson out of the wardrobe as he had nothing else left. His usual hat, he remembered, had been left on the ground somewhere behind the Palace, and he had no desire to go back for it. Then he picked up the letters he'd written from the vanity and tucked them into the inside pocket along with Rachel's cross.

He stopped on his way through to accept hugs from his children, heard Caleb sniffle against his shoulder. "It'll be okay, son," he whispered in his boy's ear while one hand stroked the silky top of Ellie's head, and then he had to make himself let go before he broke down. It all reminded him how tired he was, that he had not slept in nearly two days and could not foresee when he would sleep again, not until he had his other child back and knew they would all be safe.

By the time he emerged via the rear kitchen door, Jesse had gotten the horses ready. Becker, who was borrowing Jesse's, was already in the saddle waiting, his Gladstone bag strapped to the back where a bedroll usually fit. The sun hung at a position easily read as noon without consulting a pocket watch.

Jesse handed off Teddy's reins to Hiram along with the marshal's gun belt with its new, modified load. "Guess we'll see if your idea's sound," the kid said.

Hiram buckled on the Peacemaker, tied down the holster around his thigh, then climbed into the saddle. "We'll see," he echoed that. "If we aren't back by dusk, you keep yourself and the kids inside. I don't want you out trying to look for me or even the pastor, understand?"

"Yessir."

They rode straight through town, once more, passing the pile of coyote bones in the street that seemed to have cursed the entire thoroughfare with silence. The only living face they saw was John Raskin peering out at them from a window on the hotel's top floor. Hiram nodded up to him, but he couldn't tell if there was any signal back.

They paused at the opera house to look down the alley where the big black freighter was still parked. If they did not find Lucinda or any clue to her whereabouts at the Simpson house, Hiram planned to return and break down the door to check the vaults below the stage. He'd have checked it last night had the atrocious situation with the coyote not occurred.

By the time they passed the church at the southeastern bend, his head was throbbing again, and he was grateful for the shade the hat cast across his eyes. After the last turn heading into the final two-mile stretch to the boarding house, some relief came from the oaks and cottonwoods lining the sides of the road. A mile in, they veered off and wove through the copse to the southern edge where the open spread of sand and scrub reappeared. The plan was to reach the Simpson house from the rear rather than go right at the front door again. But on this side of the trees, the sky became a great blue canopy with the white sun at its core, and that was when his senses bloomed open again since he'd last collapsed that morning.

"Shit," he hissed to the blinding sting. "Shit… shit… shit…" as his hands let up on the reins, his heels relaxed in the stirrups, and Teddy coasted to a stop.

"What is it?" Becker's concerned voice was an explosion in his ears from only five feet away, and the skittering and buzz of fall locusts surrounded him

Hiram loosened his feet and hoisted a leg over, hit the ground, and stumbled back into the trees, eyes clenched shut against the brilliant light, heartbeat pounding—echoed by Becker's—and felt his way to the north side of a large, crooked oak. There he sank, back against the bark, hat falling off, and took long, deep breaths. A metallic taste developed in his mouth that made him grimace and smack his tongue against his soft palate.

A moment later, Becker knelt next to him, Gladstone bag in hand, and felt his forehead. "Good Lord, you're freezing."

"Why I wore my coat," he said. "I'm okay. Just give me a minute."

"What's happening?" Becker asked in his analytical tone and opened the bag, ready to pull some remedy from its depths. "Head pain again?"

"No, nothing like that." Hiram forced his eyes open. At least he'd picked a decent hollow to tuck into, where the glare was nowhere as bad. "Something's happening that I… I can't explain. Started last night when Jesse and I were out looking. Felt like the ocean in my ears at first and … *sinking*… like something was trying to pull me under. Then when I was looking for Silas, it shifted.

"It was like suddenly I could hear better, see better, smell. I didn't fight it. I used it to track Silas, all instinct. I could hear *my* heartbeat *and* his. I hear yours now, too."

Becker's brow sank into a deep furrow, and he continued to prod his patient, examined Hiram's eyes. Then he carefully took hold of Hiram's coat and shirt collars on the right side and pulled them back as far as possible. Hiram didn't know what the man saw, but it made him gulp, the sound not only very present, but the flex of his throat muscles far too obvious, and his heartbeat picked up the pace. The frazzled gray head bowed, and Becker closed his eyes.

"What do you see?" Hiram asked.

A whisper rose from Becker's lips, but it was as loud to Hiram's ears as direct speech. *"Dear heavenly Father, intend this man's body to be a temple of Thy Holy Spirit. May it be your gracious will that he enjoy Your healing power…"*

"You praying for me, Becker?" Hiram asked, sounding more agitated than intended.

"I'm sorry if that offends your current sensibilities, Marshal," he replied with his head still bowed, "but at this point, I think you need all the help you can get."

"No… no, you're right, I do." Freezing lightning shot through his body, forcing out a violent shiver.

Becker's head lifted, and he opened his eyes in surprise at the comment but also to examine the new symptom.

"Thanks for not saying too much in front of my kids."

Becker seemed as fascinated as he was concerned. "The infection in your arm is spreading."

Hiram tilted his gaze steeply down, made out a thin branch of black crawling over the ball of his shoulder toward his collar bone. "It's already spread everywhere," he said and shrugged his shirt and coat back into place. "You weren't there behind the Palace. Silas started to attack me, but then he stopped. Jasper O'Brian said, *'He knows his own kind,'* as in Silas didn't kill me because I'm becoming like him.

"And I am, you know?

"What's going on under your microscope with those blood cells… that's what's going on inside me. I can feel it, and there's no way out, so when I go the way he did, you know what to do." He reached into the inside pocket of his coat, fumbled until he pulled out the two squares of neatly folded stationery, one addressed to Becker, the other to his brother. "I wrote some instructions for you and an address. I'll need you to contact my brother in Philadelphia. Don't be too surprised if you meet James."

"All in good time." Becker took the letters but only stashed them down into his bag somewhere between bottles and jars. "But right now, you're not giving up this fight, Hiram. You hear me?"

"I don't blame *you*," he said, feeling like he had to keep talking to stay anchored, even with his voice a flood of raw noise in his head. His fingertips, touching the ground or the bark on the tree, were overcome with the rough sensations. The dry, earthen odors of the forest around them and Becker's sweat—and blood—packed tightly in his nose. Soon, he was afraid, all he would be was a creature of pure instinct with no human identity at all. "I don't blame you for Rachel's death. I shouldn't have. I'm sorry for the way I've talked to you, sorry I kept pushing about a transfusion."

"There were other things I could have tried," Becker insisted. "But a transfusion would have been too risky. I know you were desperate and didn't understand *that*. I just wanted you to realize that it could have made her passing so much worse. Sometimes the body rejoices in the gift of another's blood, but more often it rages against it, and we don't know why."

"Would you just shut up and let me apologize? Say my piece?"

Becker halted and blinked at that. "Well, then go right ahead."

Another shiver hit him, and he grimaced, trying not to swear this time. He'd wept once for Silas, quietly, but *this* grief came with shudders and a flood of tears that could not be forced back down. After their long and enterprising friendship, how appropriate that one should follow the other down into death so soon. "Why did I have to kill my best friend?" he rasped.

"The way I saw it, you weren't the one who did it," Becker said.

"No, but I was so close. I had that sword in my hand, tried to use it to stop Silas from coming at me. Got Jasper instead." He remembered the feel of the man's weight as O'Brian had incidentally impaled himself while coming in with the chair leg behind Silas—the stake through the heart as Caleb and Ellie would think of it. Even though he was not directly the one to end Silas' life or suffering, he felt responsible.

"It's strange that I'll never have to deal with him slipping chicory into my coffee again, never hear that embarrassing story about the Earps or how I saved his ass on that plantation.

"But there were other matters that even Silas didn't gab about." He wanted someone to know that there was more to the man's memory than a saloon keeper who once readily beat a trail through every poker den and brothel he came across. "He liked to talk about how I saved his life, but the reality is… he saved *mine*."

Becker's tugged at Hiram's coat, tried to bundle him a little more, but wrapping up tighter did nothing when the cold came from within, and Hiram brushed his hands away.

"You know I have this memory thing," he said. "Everything I see, everything I experience. It never goes away, never fades. I can stash it away, but it's always still there."

"Ja, I've heard of such things. It's a rare gift."

"Gift? Hell. It comes in handy now and then, but other times it's more of a curse." He took a moment to organize the story in his mind, to present it as gracefully as possible, but in the end, he surrendered to the embarrassment. There was no other way to tell it with dignity.

"When we were in San Francisco, we used to visit Hop Alley there, chasing the dragon."

Becker's brows drew in profoundly, eyes narrowed to indicate he saw where this was going.

"We had a favorite den, well hidden under Chinatown. It was just—" he shrugged, shook his head "—recreational for Silas. Me though… For those few hours we'd spend there, my mind was finally quiet. Every image flashing by, *everything* I've ever done since childhood, just *hushed*. It was bliss."

"I see." Becker sat forward a little more, listening patiently.

"Silas saw that I liked it a little too much, especially when I started sneaking off on my own. I was on my way to becoming a dope fiend, but he's the one who kept a clear head. He dragged me out of the city, got us both to Placerville and stashed in a hotel. Then for... I don't know how long... may have been days, maybe weeks. It's one area where I have a hole in this *gift,* as you call it." His teeth ground on the word gift, but he didn't bring up the more recent hole that had occurred or the anxiety it had wrought. "He cleaned me, wiped up my puke, wiped my ass, got me eating again, and he never let us set foot in one of those places again."

"So you weren't just on your way," Becker said pointedly. "You *were* a fiend."

"Won't even let me candy coat it, will you? Yeah, okay, I was," he admitted. "It got *that* bad, and God... Silas paid me back in spades for what happened in New Orleans. It's funny to think that he, of all people, was the first to keep me on the straight and narrow. It was my biggest secret, and he kept it all these years."

"Did you ever tell Rachel?"

He nodded. "Had to. The first time she offered me laudanum for a headache, I just told her. Didn't want to risk going back, and she understood that, never over questioned me about it."

"So that's why you objected so readily when I suggested it for your back pain."

"Yeah."

"Marshal, I never thought of your friend as anything other than a good man. I doubt Silas saw it as paying you back. He was proud of you. That's why he liked to tell people about how you saved his life or that time you mouthed off to the Earps."

Hiram nodded vacantly, sniffled back a nose full of watery snot. There was no relief in the confession, not like he'd hoped. If anything, anger rapidly replaced grief. "First Rachel, now him. I don't know what I'm going to do without them." He squeezed his eyes shut, felt that anger swell in his head and throat, and more so in the thrum of his heart. "And this... all of *this*... Knowing what else is out there now, that there are these *things* in the world, whether they're Caleb's pulp monsters or something more, I'll never be free of that either, and I'm scared. More than ever. Not for me, but for my kids."

"Understood."

"I want to find them all, Becker, these things... *vampires*...whatever the hell they are. I want to *burn* them out of this world, the way they've been burning out our town. But I'm not going to be able to do that. Not now that I'll burn, too, like Silas."

"Listen to me," Becker said, teeth gritted. "Your progression is not like Silas' was. I'd say his degree of injury contributed to that, but you're still here, still holding on. Maybe, like many illnesses, this will run its course if you just *hold on*. Some people survived the plague, you know? So, fuck Jasper O'Brian and what he said. You hear me? *Fuck him*."

Hiram's eyes cracked open, draining out more tears, but he raised a brow. "Pastor, such language."

Becker sniffed. "I mean it. *Er hat nur Luft im Sack*."

Hiram felt the tiniest smile quiver up past the hurt. "Somehow, I think that's worse than something you could say in English."

"It's enough. You need anything? Some water, maybe?"

Hiram shook his head. The pastor's words were nice but not as encouraging as intended. The man could not honestly know what it was like to have this—whatever it was—raging through his veins. He did, however, need to pull himself together and use what time he had left wisely.

Closing his eyes again, he tried to focus on narrowing down the deluge of his senses. They had come and gone on their own before, but maybe, with some focus, he could tamp each down to a bearable level. Instead of smelling everything around him at once, he focused on one scent: earth. Instead of hearing everything, including his and Becker's heartbeats, he focused on the skitter of some insect along the bark of the tree. Instead of feeling the soil and every bit of bramble against his fingers, he focused on the crisp curl of a large, dried autumn leaf. That took care of everything but vision.

After a few minutes, he felt like a strange weight lifted as smell, touch, and hearing settled down to normal again. He still had a metallic taste in his mouth, still had to squint against the glare of daylight, but it was not nearly as disorienting.

Blinking, he stared back at Becker, who waited patiently. "I'm good," he finally said, if still a little weakly, and retrieved his hat from the ground beside him.

"Ja? Well, then let's get going. Your daughter is somewhere waiting for you."

CHAPTER TWENTY-EIGHT

When the western face of the Simpson house came into view through the trees, a muted blue interruption in the landscape, they tethered the horses a safe distance out and crept the rest of the way on foot. Hiram had not had any more incidents with his senses, but cold chills still racked him, particularly in his chest, and neither his coat nor the sun on his back still did any good.

The south side of the house, lacking any foliage and facing the plains, appeared to have no activity with its blackened windows. Hiram led the way as they moved toward the corner and then carefully under the parlor window. A soft breeze rattled the nearest brush, and with it came the acrid smell of smoke from somewhere further south. He turned to Becker, silently raised a finger to his nose.

Becker nodded, indicating that he smelled it, too.

If there were more time, he might have traced it to its source. It was alarming that he knew, without a doubt, that he *could* trace it now with no problem, just focus his nose and follow like a hound, but he was determined to find Lucinda alive before he found her burnt remains in a gulch somewhere out there. To consider that a possibility was too painful.

Also, to think that Cage Edwards had spoken of the smell out around the boarding house as if it were strange to him sparked a new flame of anger in Hiram. He was saving it from turning into a complete, internal bonfire until he knew more, but it was clear now that the actor may have carefully worked to earn his trust. He'd defended Hiram twice to Mayor Watkins, which carried its own weight, but he'd also attempted a peaceful intervention during the holdup last Friday.

Cage. He was the one Hiram wanted most to speak to, to ask questions now. But first to find him, and when he did, would he get those answers?

From the most southeastern corner, they turned, and Hiram continued leading the way. To their right, set well out from the house, was the barn and large corral that surrounded its front section. The doors were open, and three of the six colossal draft horses were out behind the fence, while he could see only the glossy rear end of one of the others standing in the doorway. The three that were out pinned up their ears and watched the visitors. Hiram paused, head tilted, and held up a hand to Becker to wait a moment. Running with his instincts again, he cocked an ear and focused, listening for one thing specifically.

His heartbeat, and then Becker's both drummed to perception again, loudest because they were right beside each other, but in the barnyard, he heard the heavy drum of the draft horses' hearts. Given how they boomed steadily, they must be powerful organs considering the weight the beasts pulled in the troupe's freighter. The beats overlapped, but he carefully weeded through them, counted six that matched in tone and thus likely from the same breed. Then just on the other side of the six thundering powerhouses, he detected a seventh beat, not quite as loud, but still as strong.

Without a word, he turned and walked across the shaded yard and up to the corral gate at the corner of the barn. Becker trailed hesitantly behind him but stayed outside the corral when Hiram opened the gate and eased through. There was a series of grumbles from the draft horses, and big solid hooves shifted back and forth uneasily to have a perfect stranger so near, but then Hiram turned into the darkness of the barn and let his vision adjust naturally. All became as clear as the outside but blessedly without the glare. The rich smell of hay and manure swirled around him, and dust motes danced in the slender rays that slipped between the boards in the rear wall.

The other three drafts, including the one poised in the open doors, were munching happily on the last of some grain out of an elevated feed trough. He'd noted plenty of water in the troughs outside, so they all appeared to be well cared for.

Missing, however, were the six elegant black Saddlebreds that pulled the troupe's coach and were also used for riding. There was certainly plenty of room for them, which made their absence stand out even more, but then, in the very rear stall, he focused on the source of the seventh equine heartbeat. Where a thin needle of light shone through not on a sleek black coat but a deep chestnut, he spotted Remington.

Hiram's breath hitched, and he hurried to the back, stirring grumbles from the drafts, and reached the stall. "Remy," he whispered and next noticed that Lucinda's sidesaddle was draped over the end of the stall door. The customized shotgun holster was empty, but then he spotted the familiar shotgun on the back wall on a rack. He grabbed it, opened it to see that the shells had been removed. Whoever had taken Lucinda had made sure she was defenseless, but had no interest in keeping the gun per se.

So, August and Genevieve had lied to him right to his face, and so had Miz Simpson, though he let that slide as likely from coercion if not something more sinister. That meant that Cage had lied, too, or at least dodged the truth skillfully when he'd appeared in town early last night, right before the coyote attack.

For the time being, he left Remington right where he was, spun and stormed toward the doors, swept past the draft horses, and emerged from the barn.

"Find anything?" Becker asked as Hiram opened the gate and stepped out.

"My daughter's horse is here." He did not bother to creep toward the house now but walked upright, straight toward the eastern corner of the porch, and looked into the shade of the front driveway. "The coach and its horses are gone. The freighter was still at the opera house, but there was no coach."

"So, they knew we were coming? You think they've left?"

"Maybe they've gone out somewhere to lay low away from town, but I have a feeling they haven't *left*." Hiram stepped onto the porch, approached the front door with Becker hot on his heels, and simply *listened*. He attempted the same focusing trick he'd come up with under the tree, wove past his heartbeat and Becker's, pushed away the more distant ones of the horses in the corral. Now he heard a new beat, muted from somewhere inside. He leaned closer to the door, ear almost touching the brass knocker, attempted to put direction to the sound.

Coming from somewhere on the upper floor… to the right…

Soft, steady, alone…

But then another emerged, this one elsewhere, lower in the house, with sluggish, long pauses between each beat. Who could *that* be?

He stepped back from the door and, without thinking it through, raised a leg and stomp-kicked the area right under the knob. He'd expected to have to kick again, but surprisingly, the door crashed open, swung so hard around on its hinges that it banged into the wall, and splinters rained on the floor from the frame and broken bolt.

Surprised he'd summoned such force, Hiram paused briefly then stepped straight in. He sniffed the air, detecting something tart and coppery, like blood but edged with the slightest flowery perfume. Miz Simpson had always worn perfume. It had cloyed the air around her everywhere she went.

"Miz Simpson?" he called, voice hollow against the hard surfaces of polished wood. To his left was the dining room, which he knew to go straight back to the kitchen. Straight in front of him, the corridor ran into the cozy parlor that always seemed to be every guest's favorite place. Just to the right was the stairwell to the second floor, where five bedrooms lined the hall. The place should have been pitch dark with all the heavy drapes pulled as they were, but for him, it was almost perfect.

He could still see details in grayer shades, like the grain in the mahogany sideboard or the pattern on the Persian rug in the parlor ahead.

"Miz Simpson?" he called again, and this time Becker echoed him.

"Miz Simpson?" The pastor moved into the dining room and flung open the drapes to let in more light.

Hiram lifted an ear, found that first heartbeat again. "Up there," he said and ran up the steps.

Becker hesitated then followed, his bag still at the ready in case.

At the landing, they looked down the upper corridor that was lined in polished wood with a Persian runner down the center. The bedroom doors hung open, but the one in the middle looked similar to the damage Hiram had just done downstairs. He hurried to that one, looked into the room, and thought, for a moment, that he felt his heart stop with a painful inner punch.

Lucinda lay in the center of the bed, one hand draped across her middle, the other turned palm up and resting on the pillow beside her gently tilted head. The bodice of her dress, while a bit loose and disheveled, did not look torn or tampered with, and her skirts were neatly spread over her legs.

"Lucinda!" He was on the edge of the bed in an instant, shaking her gently at first, but when she didn't respond right away, he lifted her by the shoulders and cradled her head. "Lucinda, honey, wake up."

To his relief, her eyes fluttered slightly, then as they rolled open, she startled, jumped in his arms, and caught her breath. "Papa?" she whispered.

"Oh, thank God," Becker said softly and hurried to the side of the bed.

"Yeah, it's me, sweetheart," Hiram said, and when her arms wrapped around him in a tight hug, he sighed and closed his eyes in a moment of thanks. "I thought I'd lost you." She sobbed softly into his neck, and then she drew back, brow furrowed.

"Why're you so cold?" she said. When Hiram didn't answer, she looked to Becker as if the pastor might have the answer. "Pastor?"

"How are you, dear?" Becker asked. "Did they do anything to you?" He reached out, pressed his hand to her forehead, took her slender wrist and checked her pulse.

"No," she said, "nothing, but you won't believe what I've learned."

"Oh, I believe plenty now, honey," Hiram interrupted her.

She looked back up at him, perhaps thinking she might have to argue on that, but then the seriousness in his own eyes must have tipped her off. "You know what they are, Papa?"

"Vampires? They're all vampires?"

Her eyes narrowed in disbelief. He half expected her to accuse him of reading Caleb's pulp. She wouldn't be far off, anyway. "All but those two hands, Jasper and Morgan," she said when this new shock wore off. "August told me everything about them. Then Cage Edwards said something about you and Uncle Silas being attacked by a *pestilent* coyote. Is that true?"

"What were you doing out here to begin with?" Hiram said, diverting.

"I just came to see August yesterday morning, thought I'd maybe—" She blinked long and hard, still shaking off whatever stupor had kept her unconscious on the bed. "I thought I'd surprise him, and then we'd ride back to the opera house for his rehearsals together." A new thought occurred to her, and she began to sit up on her own, body going rigid in Hiram's arms. "I promise, Papa, that's all I intended to do."

"I know," he said calmly, hoping not to alarm her anymore.

"I got here and smelled smoke, and I just went around the side of the house. It was coming from way out there, where the gulch starts. Jasper and Morgan were burning bodies, and I *saw* them." Large brown eyes teared up again, and she shook her head. "Papa, I had no idea."

"I know," he repeated and decided not to tell her anything more about Silas yet, all the better to keep her focused on getting out of here. "They didn't try anything with you? No one bit you, touched you?" Just saying the words brought bitterness to his tongue. "Not even August?"

"He wanted to. I think he would have tried, but suddenly Cage was here. He was so angry and… and strong. He threw August out that door."

Hiram looked at the panel in question, broken in two, one half hanging off the hinges, the other lying flat in the hallway. "Cage did that?"

She tucked her bottom lip as she nodded up at him.

Hiram's brows shot up. "Huh." He might no longer trust the man—if he could still be called that—but he appreciated the defense of his daughter.

"Is Cage their leader?" Becker asked.

She nodded. "I know what they've been doing here, Papa. They didn't just come to entertain the town." The tears threatened to come up again, and she shook her head. "How could I be so stupid?"

"Sweetheart," he said, "you're anything but stupid. We all fell for their charms, and now we need to get you out of here."

"Wait, where are they?" she asked, on the verge of new panic.

"They're gone," he said. "The coach is gone, anyway, and the house seems empty, but there's something I need to check before we go." He reached an arm under her knees, braced the other under her shoulder blades, and found it strangely effortless as he lifted her from the bed and stood.

A look of amazement washed over Becker's face. "Marshal, doesn't that hurt your back?"

It took a moment for Hiram to realize what he meant. He should have had a crippling spasm the moment he tried to lift his daughter, but there was hardly a twinge. There was no time to ponder it, though. "It's fine," he said. His arm also, oddly, did not feel as sore.

Becker still didn't appear to approve, but he backed out of the way then said grimly, "I think we can assume Grace Simpson is no longer with us."

Hiram took a breath, nodded. "Another one, just like the rest." Then he carried his daughter from the room and down the steps with Becker hurrying behind.

In the bottom foyer, Lucinda stared at the door he'd shattered as he finally put her down on her own feet.

"Stay here," he told them both and then turned into the corridor, where he went back to listening for that second slow heartbeat that was stifled somewhere lower in the house. It was still there, thumping only every few seconds. He could almost count it the way, as a boy, he'd counted seconds between a lightning flash and the rumble of thunder.

Behind him, Becker gestured Lucinda into the light of the doorway and proceeded to examine her, checking her eyes, feeling her throat. "And you're sure none of them did anything?" he was asking. Their voices became murmurs, filtered out for that specific sound Hiram was hunting for.

One-one-thousand, two-one-thousand, three-one-thousand. He made it to six counts.

Thump.

He took a few steps, counted again.

Thump.

He stepped into the parlor and looked around, but his keener vision was drowned out by a thread of light shining between the drapes over the far window. The bright beam defined lines and shapes like the mantle's edge and the slopes in the carved wooden back of the Empire sofa. It created points of light on the glass in the room: the crystals in the small chandelier, the oil lamps on the mantle. He crossed the room, lowered his eyes to brace for the glare, and flung the curtains open.

A flood of light unleashed, accompanied by a high-pitched but short scream from behind him. He spun back into the room and found Lucinda had followed him as far as the parlor doorway. Her hands clamped over her mouth, she stared toward the floor in front of the hearth.

Just as Hiram followed her gaze, a raspy cackle of a laugh sounded.

"Scared ya again, girl," Jasper O'Brian—or what was left of him— wheezed at her. Only the brogue bore any familiarity.

A second later, Becker joined Lucinda in the doorway and crossed himself.

Hiram almost made the gesture, too, as he took in the withered creature propped against the side of the hearth, limp arms thin as broomsticks at his sides, spindly legs stretched out in trousers that hung limp as did the shirt on his upper body. The ridges of ribs showed through material matted with dried blood. Clouded eyes, set in a face of shriveled skin and deep hollows, shifted and watched the marshal approach. The stagehand's long red hair had mostly turned white and fallen out, some laying like tangled feathers on his shoulders, while a few clumps still clung to his flaking skull.

This was the source of the heartbeat Hiram had heard, barely hanging onto life. As his shock dwindled, he stopped to stand over the dying man who was just out of range of the sun.

"What happened to *you*?" he asked, void of any empathy at all.

Becker eased around Lucinda and came forward to kneel, examining the living skeleton on the floor. "Ja, seriously, what happened?"

The eyes remained on Hiram, the paper-thin lips pulled into a rictus, showing that a few teeth had fallen out. Some had caught in the drapes of his shirt. "Ya feelin' the 'unger yet, Marshal? Yer friend felt it right away."

He barely realized he'd moved, only that he was suddenly on one knee in front of the pathetic thing, gun drawn and pressed under its chin. "I want answers now, you freak."

Another hoarse chuckle. "'Course, ya do." The curled leaves of his nostrils shrunk inward as he drew a breath. "I'll tell ya everythin' ya wanna know… for a favor."

"No favors, you just talk." Hiram drew back the hammer.

"Well, tha's premature, inn'it?" His bony hand lifted, managed a gesture for Hiram to lower the gun. "Jus' end my sufferin'. Ya can do *that*."

Hiram lowered the hammer. "Fair enough."

"Jig's up, 'cept he has somethin' else in mind," O'Brian said and coughed. "He killed yer two thieves, right there'n the jail, jus' wanted to see what ya'd do about it. Then 'ad *me* clean up 'is mess."

"Cage," Hiram said.

O'Brian answered him with a bland, milky stare that simply said, *Who do you think?*

"So, you're the one who hit me from behind," Becker said. One hand rose absently toward the base of his skull, then lowered again.

"Sorry, preacher. They canna walk on holy ground. It's the *enérgeia*, ya see? It messes wiv 'em. As fer me… I 'avn't served yer God in o'er two centuries." He broke off coughing, took a moment to get his bearing. "I've served Cage an' his kin, never 'intent to be one. Their blood is the elixir I've now been denied." Another coughing fit racked him. Every breath the pathetic creature heaved in made Hiram's own throat feel tight just from hearing the dry wheezing. "He's through wi' me. Tossed me like rubbish."

"But they aren't like that thing that Silas changed into," Hiram said. "Why are they different?"

"They're nobles, whole 'n powerful, 'specially Cage by far, 'specially at night. But you 'n me, we're incomplete creatures, trapped on the threshold. Soon ye'll jus' be a mindless husk, like yer friend." He paused, clamped his mouth shut, but his jaw moved like he was chewing on his tongue, trying to work up enough saliva to keep talking. Then he swallowed, the thin skin of his throat flexing with the sound of sand grinding.

"Papa?" Lucinda uttered. "What's he saying?"

He only put his finger to his lips and gave her a gentle *shhhhh* gesture.

"Their blood gave you longevity, but didn't change you?" Becker said. The medical analyst in him was fascinated.

"Long as we get it reg'larly."

"You mean you and Morgan Reed?"

"Clever preacher."

"Is there a way to stop the change? A cure?" Hiram asked.

"Fer you?" The glassy eyes lowered to him again, and the crusty, balding head rocked from side to side in a *no* gesture. "Not fer you, Marshal. Ther's a cure if ya can take it in time. Ya kill a noble if ya can get that far, burn the heart 'n consume the ashes in holy water and vervain. Give't to yer family, anyone exposed, bit'n er not."

"Holy water is a defense then?" Becker asked. "And crosses?"

"Ag'in," O'Brian coughed. "All 'bout the *enérgeia*. Holy ground, holy objects 'n water… they bind it. Neither a revenant nor a noble can stand ta be 'round it fer long. Does'n always matter what faith channeled it." He cackled pathetically at the look on Becker's face. "Divin'ty comes in a lotta forms, preacher."

"But the cure won't work for me," Hiram said hollowly and looked up when Lucinda sniffled. A flow of tears gleamed on her face as she leaned in the doorway, a hand still over her mouth. "One more thing," he said, returning to O'Brian's pathetic mug. "Where can I find them? The opera house?"

"They made lairs right un'er yer nose, but Cage always keeps a secret haven, dos'na always say where he'll be even to the kith." He raised a wavering hand, a crooked finger, gesturing Hiram closer.

"Kith?" Hiram frowned, leaned in but only by a fraction, the Colt still ready, though he doubted the poor husk could try anything.

"He's lookin' fer somethin'… Cage is. Was mighty interested in *you*, Marshal."

"Why?"

"Once I'd've thought he was jus' playin' with ya. Now… dunno. He's too serious. There's somethin' happenin' among the nobles. Not just Cage'n 'is kith. Been goin' on fer some time. Can't say wha', but they're…" His eyelids drooped heavily as if he were about to pass out.

There was that word again, *kith*. "Hey—" Without thinking, Hiram reached up and grabbed one of the stick-thin arms under the cotton sleeve to shake it, winced as he heard a sickening crack, felt the arm give as if he'd snapped a brittle, dry branch. The lower half dropped, caught in the fabric of his sleeve.

O'Brian's head lifted, and he let out a raucous cry. Hiram jerked his hand back, bit down an apology because he didn't feel a bit damned sorry for this flaking, mummified bastard.

"They're *what?*" he insisted.

"Ya swore," Jasper whispered. "Kill me… p-p-please."

"What about the nobles?" he asked more desperately.

"Yer wasssstin' time, Marshal. Ev'ry second ya sssssit there, ya become lesssssssss… huuuuuman…" He strained harder to speak now. "An' you've lef' yer lil ones alone, 'aven't ya? Only way ye could be 'ere." Another long wheeze for breath. "End me… now… p-please…"

The very mention of his younger children, and the thought that Cage and his kind were still somewhere near or in town, was enough to end his questions. Hiram stood, reached over and dragged Becker to his feet as well. Then he raised the Colt again, cocked back the hammer, and shot point-blank into the top of Jasper O'Brian's skull.

O'Brian's body immediately turned into grayish-brown dust that held its shape for the space of a blink before collapsing in on itself. The clothes remained and fell in while the fine dust billowed out of his sleeves and trousers; his hollow boots fell on their sides. Hiram stepped back as the crawling cloud settled, leaving the toes of his own boots coated. Becker pulled a handkerchief from his pocket and covered his mouth while Hiram moved over to Lucinda, embraced her, let her hide her face in his shoulder for a long moment.

"Morgan Reed is just like him," he said to Becker, "so it doesn't matter about the sun. The others may need to hide for a little longer, but Reed can go anywhere, whether it's in the church or even my home. All the crosses in the world won't keep him out."

"Dear merciful Father," Becker gasped.

Hiram saddled up Remington quickly while Lucinda and Becker waited, got the horse out of the barn, and then the three of them headed back around the southern edge of the woods to gather Teddy and Peso. Soon they had woven through the thicket and got on the main road.

Hiram could tell that Becker's thoughts were spinning, his medical mind and his theological mind attempting to balance everything he'd learned from Jasper O'Brian while remaining in motion.

They rode as fast as possible, considering Lucinda was riding sidesaddle, but the closer they got to town, the more he smelled smoke. At first, he attributed it to the char he'd smelled all week, but then he realized this was *cleaner,* purely the scent of wood burning and much stronger than the little acrid whiffs that had teased him off and on. He looked across at Becker, who was keeping pace decently.

"Smell that?"

The pastor nodded, and when they finally reached the lower end of town, they reined to a brief stop with the horses grumbling, stomping, and winded.

A column of smoke undulated into the air ahead by another half-mile, originating from somewhere behind the school and the vicinity of the Spanish mission.

"Father Ramirez," Becker gasped, and before Hiram could stop him, he reined his horse on.

Damn, was all Hiram could think, and the only thing to do was follow.

The adobe walls of the mission chapel held in the flames, but they had eaten through some of the support beams in the roof and caused chunks of the adobe to fall in, creating a chimney effect as the smoke drew up into a perfect column.

Becker had already reined Peso to the other side of the structure where the doors were.

"Shit," Hiram hissed under his breath as he heeled Teddy on and stopped at the old wall ruin from the original mission.

Becker had already dismounted and run across the former courtyard and thrown open the heavy wooden doors only to let out billows of smoke.

"Stay here," Hiram commanded Lucinda, who was not far behind him. He dismounted without tethering Teddy and hurried around the wall to catch up with Becker.

The pastor at least had the wits not to run blindly inside and fanned feverishly at the thick veil, coughed. "Javier!" he shouted into the smoke.

Hiram pulled a handkerchief from his inside pocket. "Becker, stay back." He had to shove the distraught man aside, then he covered his nose and mouth and squinted as he eased into the small foyer, trying to get a glimpse into the chapel. Fortunately, the wind tunnel effect of opening the doors caught, pushing the smoke back into the chapel and sucking it up through the hole in the ceiling. It did not clear the air entirely but made it bearable. He did not go any further than the entry from concern that more of the roof would collapse.

Once within the arch of the second entry, he could see more of how the fire had spread. It roared primarily near the altar ahead, and that was where rubble from the first chunk of the roof lay as well. Still, much had caught upon the pews and was spreading, grabbing onto anything wooden or cloth, while the brightly painted frescoes of angels and saints on the walls watched helplessly.

Hiram's eyes stung and watered, but beyond that haze, he saw the blackened shapes engulfed by the flames. Izabel's body was already mostly gone, little more than a skull and a few bones that lay on the platform where Father Ramirez had placed her casket. The casket's pine sides had already burned down to ridges of flickering coals. The priest's body lay sprawled on the steps below her, only half as burned but beyond saving. He lay face down, one arm reaching toward the altar.

"Javier!" Becker's voice blared in Hiram's right ear as the pastor finally attempted to work his way in.

"It's too late!" Hiram shouted over the roar. A new crash sounded as another section of the roof came down, adobe chunks obliterating the altar while a burning cross beam collapsed upon the steps and rolled. Parts of the adobe chunks ignited as the organic matter within was exposed. "Becker, stop!" He turned and grabbed the man's lapels, pushed him back out through the doors into the fresh air, both of them coughing.

"He's gone already!"

Hiram lamented that there was nothing either of them could do but let it burn. Mica Bend had a fire wagon stashed in a barn on the other side of the neighborhood on the south side, but with no team of horses, no water, no people to operate it, and no time left, the thought was fleeting. Only hopelessness streamed in steadily, as it had for days now.

"Reed! It had to be Morgan Reed!" Soot dusted Becker's face and streaked with rivulets of tears. His large white mustache stood out amid the grime, and his lips curled back in a grimace of anger. "Bastard made sure Isabel didn't rise like Silas did!" He coughed and turned away. "But why Javier, too? Just… why?"

"Because he was a witness," Hiram said and wiped his face down with the handkerchief, clearing the smoke particles from his eyes as he blinked out tears of his own. "If not for Morgan or Jasper, anyone would be safe on holy ground. The padre hardly ever set foot out of here except during the day to have breakfast with you or pick up the mail or food."

Becker's face pinched up, and his throat flexed tightly as he swallowed down his sobs.

"Papa," Lucinda called gently from where she waited upon Remington. "Look."

Hiram noted the alarmed look on her face as she pointed into the distance toward the southern neighborhood, the first large house belonging to the mayor. Watkins' roan horse, still saddled and bridled, was wandering around the porch of the place, nibbling on whatever looked appetizing.

"Didn't you say something about him coming back from the Simpson house and heading straight home?" Hiram said.

"Ja," Becker coughed, wiped his mouth, and refreshed his focus on the horse. "Ja, he sure did."

Without further prompting, Hiram took Teddy's reins and began walking toward the big house, a good thirty yards, and approached the other horse slowly. "Hey, what are you doing out here alone, huh?"

The horse nuzzled his hand, looking for a treat, velvet snuffles tickling his fingertips before he stroked the scant blaze up to the forehead. "Where's your owner?"

Lucinda had stayed on her horse as she rode toward the front steps to the porch. "The door is open," she called.

Hiram led Teddy and the roan to the front and tethered them to the porch railing. "Titus?" he called as he stepped onto the porch. A distant heartbeat met his ears from somewhere inside. It was rapid, that of someone stricken with fear. The hinges on the front door creaked as a breeze stirred through. Hiram stuck his head through the opening and called again, "Mayor Watkins?"

"Do you think he's all right?" Lucinda asked, keeping her distance.

"Watkins!" Hiram called in more sharply.

By now, Becker had stepped up to position himself on the other side of the frame. "We should check on him."

Hiram nodded but reached across his front and held his right hand over the grip of his gun. He gestured for Becker to keep behind him as he moved into the foyer and made sure to keep calling to make it clear that he was no stranger or a threat stepping into the house. "Mayor? It's Marshal Wells?"

The rapid heartbeat continued from somewhere ahead.

Watkins' house had a similar layout to Miz Simpson's, with a front stairwell to the side of the foyer, going to the second floor, and a short corridor straight ahead that led into a rear parlor. Doorways to the sides of the entrance led to a larger sitting room and a dining room.

The parlor was smaller than the Simpson one, but Hiram was as familiar with it. Occasionally, he'd been called there to make reports on various cases or to be reprimanded depending on what burr Watkins had up his ass at the time. He walked on, beginning to relax as he reached the end of the corridor and looked into the comfy room with its hearth and mantle displaying crystal lusters. There had never been a Miz Watkins, but the man knew how to decorate. A round Persian rug of rich, warm colors covered the floor, and a reverse-painted lamp that portrayed an autumn landscape sat on the side table. A short bookshelf displayed a collection of beautiful leather-bound classics that would have made Lucinda swoon, but Hiram was sure they were more for display than actual reading.

The half-closed curtains on the one big window let in ample afternoon light to reveal the figure sitting up in one of the winged-back chairs. Watkins' derby hat was placed on the table beside the lamp while its owner stared straight ahead. But for the accelerated heartbeat, he seemed simply trapped in deep thought.

The reek of dried piss permeated the room, so strong it didn't take enhanced senses to smell it. Both marshal and pastor wrinkled their noses.

"Titus," Hiram said sharply to try to get his attention. "Did you know

the chapel is on fire?"

"It's my fault," Watkins barely whispered.

"Your fault?" Hiram approached the mayor and looked down. "The chapel fire?"

Becker came to his side, then knelt next to an arm of the chair to get a better look at the man's face. "Titus? How are you feeling, Sir?" he asked, voice pitched to break through the apparent catatonia. He felt Watkins' wrist to check his pulse, laid a hand to his forehead. "Feels normal," he said, looking up at the marshal.

"I let them in," Watkins murmured. "I invited them."

"Something done broke his mind," Hiram commented.

"I know he's not your favorite person, Marshal," Becker said as he stood back up, "but a little compassion goes a long way."

"I'm sorry something broke his mind," Hiram said smartly.

Becker sighed patiently. "Who'd you invite in, Titus?" he continued.

"He told me to wait," he replied. "Just to wait... sit still."

"Who told you to wait? Wait for what?" Hiram took three paces then back again, his boots louder on the floor as his agitation and impatience rose. "Oh, fuck'sake." He leaned over and grabbed Watkins under the chin, giving a little rough shake as he tried to lift the man's face. "Look at me, you pompous ass. *Who* told you to wait? Cage Edwards?"

"Sit still and wait..."

Hiram let go, nostrils flaring as he huffed out a breath and inadvertently chewed on his bottom lip for a moment before he reached down again, started to take Watkins by the arm. "Alright, Mr. Mayor, let's take this over to the office."

Watkins jerked his arm away and screamed. His heart pounded harder as he huddled back into the chair tighter. "No," he peeped. "No..."

"Whoa," Hiram commented at the reaction.

Watkins settled back down, glassy eyes still staring toward the hearth.

"It's not like we have a lot of time to interrogate him," Becker said. "Sun will be down soon."

Hiram looked out through the opening in the curtains, noted the angle of the light. "To hell with him," he said then. "Let's go.

CHAPTER TWENTY-NINE

Jesse was on the third chapter of *Tales of the Vampire, Lord Covington: A Romance of Intrigue and Horror*. He was not particularly interested in the story so much as the nuggets of information it imparted since he knew so little about vampires, fact, or fiction.

He'd been sipping coffee all afternoon at the kitchen table as he struggled through the tale. Besides him being a slow reader, the frilly nature of it versus what he'd witnessed—when Silas LeBlanc had come plunging out of the Palace with a makeshift stake through his heart and landed in the sun—were utterly at odds. The prose was too pretty, too silly for him when he'd seen the ugly case firsthand, so he primarily relied on Caleb to break it down for him.

"Well?" Caleb sat back in the opposite chair, eating a piece of rock candy. He didn't look like he was enjoying the candy at all, and more like he was distracting himself while his lucky little sister was upstairs in their room taking a nap.

Jesse wished he could have napped, but too many things haunted him, from that coyote to Silas, and utmost, Lucinda being missing. Her father and Pastor Becker had been gone too long, as far as Jesse was concerned. A glance at the window over the sink revealed a landscape rapidly descending into golden afternoon light.

"Well," he finally said. "This stuff's pretty gospel, huh?"

"Close enough, after what Pastor Becker said about it."

"Giant bats, Caleb? Really?"

"Okay, maybe not like that," he amended. "But the stakes, holy water, crosses.”

“Sunlight,” Jesse added. “Doesn’t say anything about sunlight, but ‘least there’s that, too.” For a moment, the memory of scooping up Silas’ bones with a coal spade flashed behind his eyes, and his hand went slack with the pamphlet in it. “I’m sorry about your uncle. He was a big part of your life and your daddy’s best friend. I know he’s hurtin’ from it.”

“Yeah, we knew Uncle Silas better than our real uncle,” Caleb said sadly, “even though Uncle James does send me those stories. I ain’t seen him since I was little, and Ellie’s never met him.”

Jesse rubbed at his tired eyes, took another sip of the brew that he’d accidentally almost burnt on the stove because he was too used to the coffee Tucker’s cook made. He heard soft footfalls from the other side of the house on the steps that led up from the front parlor. “Well, in a way, your real uncle did you a favor sending this pulp. Taught you some useful things.”

Caleb sucked on the candy and nodded. “Funny.” There was no humor in the comment, though.

Ellie came wandering in, her rag doll gripped tight in her little elbow and rubbing her eyes. “I’m hungwy,” she announced.

Jesse drained the rest of his coffee and nudged the pamphlets aside. “What do you got?”

“Canned stuff in the pantry and some dried meat,” Caleb said with no enthusiasm at all. “Leftover beans, but they make Ellie fart.”

“Hey, you fawt, too, Caweb,” she objected.

“Okay, dried meat it is,” Jesse said and got up. He went to the pantry and had just opened the door when he heard a commotion of squawking and clucking from the chicken coop outside. Then Nathan’s horses grumbled in the corral. A nervy shiver shot through him, like spotting a scorpion climbing on his arm or a Gila monster in his path. He thought of Lucinda’s coyote problem and the attack in town, both so far apart in terms of menace, but still, he would love to put an end to at least one more of those critters, normal or otherwise.

He turned and looked back at the table and the chair next to his where he’d propped the sword, pommel up. Why the old weapon fascinated him so much, he wasn’t sure and didn’t really care, only that it seemed ideal to have not only should bullets run out but because the blade had a reach for almost any kind of necessary close defense. Not that he’d choose it over the gun first, but he grabbed the long handle before he headed for the back door.

"What is it?" Caleb asked.

"Hopefully nothing. Stay here with your sister."

Caleb got off his chair and went over to grab Ellie's hand. Her eyes grew saucer-side, and her arm cinched up to draw the doll in tighter.

The door creaked on its hinges as Jesse tried to open it slowly and not alarm any animal that might be in the yard. There was reasonable doubt that a monster like the one that attacked Silas and the marshal would be in the yard. Just enough sun remained to keep such a thing at bay. He stepped down from the stoop and crossed the dusty little patch of the yard to see, to his dismay, that there was a huge opening in the coop fence. The wire was not cut, but one of the wooden supports had been pulled out of the ground along with its neighbor and swept aside, wire and all. Thus, several of Lucinda's prized chickens were running loose in the yard, and some had already made it over to the corral. A few downy feathers were scattered across the dusty flat, and a few floated in the air, not so much a sign of an attack so much as chickens just being chickens.

Then he saw that the corral gate was open, but the horses had not taken advantage of it. Jesse's back muscles coiled at this. Someone was here, had done this on purpose.

He kept the sword in his left hand as he wanted his right ready to draw the Colt and made his way toward the corral and barn, from which he could get a better view toward the front of the house and the main road going by. He paused at the end of the corral where he'd hung his lariat and bedroll over the corner post when he'd cleared the saddle for Pastor Becker to use it and strap on his Gladstone. Quickly he moved to close the gate and slide the bolt back into place. The two horses only watched him, but their ears pinned back with agitation.

He thought he heard hooves in the distance, and he smelled smoke, squinted as he scanned the horizon from the west, sweeping around to the east, past the distant blocky structures of the town as they began a quarter mile from the house and stretched on.

Then he saw it, on the far side, a distant black billow rising against the dimming eastern sky.

"Shit," he said under his breath. That was not some small fire. From here, he couldn't be sure which structure burned. It could be anywhere on the other side of the neighborhood, behind the opera house and school. His best guess was the old Spanish mission.

And that *was* hooves that he heard coming, just up the road, obscured by the last slight stretch of trees opposite the Wagon Town grove.

Two horses… no… *three*.

He wanted to rush to meet them, but the marshal had said to stay put, and he didn't want to make any assumptions until they were in sight. He waited just a moment more, and then Ellie's high-pitched scream sounded from within the house. Jesse wanted to pin it on shenanigans, but he couldn't take that chance. He turned and hurried back up the stoop and into the kitchen, took three long strides into the room, and found both children standing right where they'd been when he left them.

They were both staring at him, frozen to the spot, still gripping each other's hand.

"What?" he asked.

No… they were staring *past* him.

Jesse followed their gazes, spun just in time to see the fist coming at his head. It cracked directly on the corner of his jaw at the junction of his ear, the effect immediate as blackness consumed his vision, and he barely felt himself collapsing to the floor or heard the clatter of the sword falling from his hand.

The ride up the thoroughfare sped by in silence but for the pound of hooves. They had shut the door to Watkins' house, and then Hiram had confiscated the mayor's horse, wasn't going to leave an innocent animal out and vulnerable. So he clamped two sets of reins in his hands as he led. He left Becker to his thoughts, whatever they were, for the journey. The pastor and Father Ramirez may not have been as tight as Hiram had been with Silas, but it was enough of a friendship for Becker to grieve.

They stopped by the hotel to tell the Raskins about the fire in the mission. He warned them to remain inside with Toby and, ultimately, to tap every ounce of faith they had as they barricaded themselves in a room with every cross they owned hung on its walls. John Raskin had nodded along with that since he'd witnessed enough that morning to listen and take the warning seriously.

There was no time to go door-to-door elsewhere, to try to find anyone else that might be left, and Hiram hated that. Hated everything about the situation. Even if he could find others, who would believe him?

The only thing keeping him in any positive frame of mind was that he had his daughter back, and he didn't know whether to thank Cage Edwards for that or plunge a stake into his heart if he achieved the chance.

Upon reaching the house, he frowned when three fluffy chickens dashed through the yard, and he heard Lucinda utter, "Oh no."

Something felt far more off than a damaged coop. As Hiram had grown accustomed to doing, he raised an ear and made out not three distant heartbeats as there should have been, but *four*. Two of them were rapid, one steady, the fourth one slower. Young shouts followed, suddenly grew louder, going from inside to outside.

"Ow… stop… you'w puwwing my haiw…"

"… be quiet, Ellie!"

"Shut up, both of you!"

The third one, gruff, hateful, did not belong to Jesse, and Hiram heeled his horse ahead of Lucinda and Becker and made the rear corner of the house only to pull on the reins and shout, "Whoa!" so suddenly that Teddy nearly reared.

The kitchen door hung open while Morgan Reed reached the bottom of the back steps with both younger children presented in front of him. He had Ellie's hair gripped in one hand, using her as a means to steer while also forcing her head back and exposing her neck. The sword that Jesse had laid claim to was in his right hand, the blade tilted so that it aligned with both Caleb's throat, and Ellie's.

Hiram dismounted and shoved Teddy's reins away, sending the gelding wandering and drew his Colt. While Ellie's eyes ran with tears, Caleb tried to keep calm with his hands down at his sides, but their heartbeats gave them both away as frightened beyond belief.

"Careful, Marshal," Reed said with his teeth gritted. "One wrong shove and both their little throats touch this blade." His dark eyes beamed in a way Hiram had not seen before. His initial impressions of the man had been of someone quiet, withdrawn, but now he saw the killer in there, the other servant who had helped Jasper O'Brian cover up the long murder spree of their inhuman masters.

"What do you want, Reed?" He kept the gun raised, realized that his right arm was nowhere near as sore now, the shakes minimal. With the evening light falling and his remarkably sharp vision, he felt like he could pull the trigger with certainty and hit the man directly between the eyes. But then Becker and Lucinda caught up, the roar of their horses' hooves coming in behind him, and he thrust out his left hand to halt them.

"It's not what I want," Reed said. "It's what *he* wants."

"Cage," Hiram said, lips drawing in as his jaw tightened on the name.

"He wants a word with you. He'll be waiting for you in the opera house."

"And if I don't go?" The question arose out of sheer stubbornness. He'd been manipulated by Cage enough already, hadn't he? Why did the man—or whatever the hell he was—want to speak with him?

"Then soon you'll be feeding on your own children," Reed replied, and the cold already ramifying through Hiram's body dropped a few more degrees. "I hear young blood is the sweetest. Can't you smell it already, Marshal?"

The question rendered him mute because the crux of the matter was, he *could* smell it. Coppery, salty, sweet. The harder their hearts pumped, the more he smelled it diffusing off of them, an undertone to Caleb's sweat, to Ellie's tears.

"Papa, just shoot the sonofabitch!" Caleb cried.

Morgan laughed dryly. "I do like this one's spirit, but will he be so spirited when his own father goes for his jugular?"

Heartbeats thrummed all around him now: Lucinda's and Becker's behind him, Caleb, Ellie, and their abductor before him, and then another began to stand out, just inside the kitchen door.

Hiram tried not to look, to not give it away when Jesse appeared in the frame. "Is Cage there now?" he asked, sounding resigned.

"Soon. You'll know when. It won't be long now." Reed's lips curled back into a smile that betrayed a strange kind of madness or fascination.

"Oh my… God," Becker was the first to declare as the last of the sun in the west disappeared not slowly below the horizon as it should and leaving behind a warm, rosy sky, but in seconds.

Hiram inadvertently lowered the gun as his gaze angled upward, and he gaped at a rising cloud of thick orange dust that blotted out the blazing disk. It swelled and spread out, a wall of intangible boils and swirls, and in mere seconds it surrounded the northwestern end of town. A gust of wind came in, carrying tendrils of the dust, but the wall itself did not roll in on the Bend like a regular dust storm. It kept growing upward, swirling and gathering.

"Impressive, isn't it?" Reed said. "You see, now, why I serve."

Becker and Lucinda got down from their horses, grappling with the fact that it was not a typical dust storm that would have everyone scrambling to get the horses into the barn and themselves into the house before they breathed in any of the grit and spores that could make a man ill.

Ordinary storms did not *wait* as this one did, Hiram realized with astonishment. It built up, strengthened, and *waited* for further command.

While Morgan gloated, however, enjoying the reactions to the spectacle, Jesse had kept his wits. The kid had eased himself down from the stoop in utter silence and managed a few steps approach before he drew the Colt and cocked back the hammer.

Click.

"That fucking hurt," Jesse growled.

Reed jolted, turned slightly to gaze over his shoulder. The motion caused him to pivot his arm outward, angling the blade away from Caleb and Ellie enough that Caleb could bring his arm forward in a bend and then jam it back hard, elbow connecting with his captor's ribs. Reed cried out and bowed slightly, his other hand letting go of Ellie's hair. That was enough for Caleb to dive into his sister and carry her with him as they toppled off to the side, and Hiram had a clear shot.

He took it.

Reed's body jerked as the first bullet got him below his right clavicle, causing his body to sway in that direction, his arm to go limp and drop the sword with a loud clang on the ground.

Hiram drew back the hammer and fired again, hitting somewhere under the man's ribs on the left side.

Reed shouted and bowed outward at first, then bent forward, hugging his middle before he fell over on his side. His teeth remained gritted for a moment longer before his face went slack, and he passed out. He was not dead yet, as Hiram could tell by the continued beat of his heart, but it did slow down with unconsciousness.

"You two okay?" he asked, holstering the gun and stepping over to where Caleb huddled over Ellie.

"Yeah… yeah… we're fine." Caleb got to his feet and helped Ellie up. She immediately ran to her father, hugging his hips, hiding her face against his belly.

Hiram looked at Jesse. "You?"

"He just rung my bell good," Jesse said as he held a hand to the side of his jaw. He laid the hammer back down on his gun and holstered it.

"Jesse!" Hurried footsteps approached, and Jesse turned directly into Lucinda's incoming embrace.

The kid looked shocked for a moment as she hugged his neck tightly, and then, slowly, a small smile spread on his face. Hiram watched this with an inner smile of his own, hoping Lucinda finally saw Jesse's worth in full.

The reunion didn't last long. Becker joined them as they all looked up at the dust storm. There was still light enough in the sky, but the wall towered higher, expanded, and began to curve around the Wells house and surround the entire town. They turned and watched it flow past on both sides with river-like fluidity. Two parallel walls rolled and tumbled until they met at the far end, an entire mile away but still visible for its sheer size.

"You really think this is Cage?" Becker asked.

"A few days ago, I'd have thought that sounds crazy, but now…" he shook his head. "Jasper O'Brian said the nobles have power. Maybe this is one of them."

"To control the elements? No, that can't be. Only God has that power."

"You willing to bet your life on that, Norman?" The howl and rumble of the winds grew and his new ability to focus on heartbeats, or any other individual sounds, grew harder, and he had to raise his voice. "I have to go see what he wants."

"No, Papa," Lucinda pleaded. "He wants to kill you. He said you were bitten, that you'll become a…" she paused, tried to find the word. "A revenant. That's what August called it."

"Yeah… I know, honey," Hiram said hollowly. "I know what it is."

"So, what I heard about Uncle Silas is true?" There were already fresh tears in her eyes.

"It is," he said remorsefully. On the other side of the barnyard, the horses grumbled and stamped, disturbed, and Hiram let out a short yelp when something grabbed the back of his coat, and Ellie's little arms ripped free of him. He felt the woolen fabric bunch and pull as a force lifted him, flung him backward effortlessly to crash into the side of the chicken coop. In the motion, and for the second time, he lost his hat as it came off and blew away. The wall broke inward but did not collapse entirely at the same instant he heard Jesse shout and Lucinda scream.

He dropped flat onto his ass, legs splayed in front of him, winced at the shock to his tail bone and lower back, and looked up, saw that August Chandler had arrived along with the two women from the troupe, Genevieve Blakely and Nora Long. They stood on the edge of the yard, some thirty yards out from the corral.

The two women had already ensnared Lucinda. She struggled in their grasp, her dirtied dress whipping in the wind, one arm raised, her hand balled into a tight fist as she attempted to deck one of her captors. Despite them both being as petite and slender as she was, they held her easily.

Genevieve grabbed her chin, forced Lucinda to face her, and stared into her eyes with a smile. Lucinda appeared to calm as the tension in her body ebbed, and suddenly Genevieve leaned in and kissed her. It was no mere peck on the cheek but a passionate exploration of her mouth that Lucinda did not resist as her eyes rolled, and she appeared to pass out, falling back into Nora's arms.

"No!" Hiram shouted and boosted to his feet, broke into a run at them, going for his daughter and failing to keep up with August, who became a blur as he shot in, meeting the marshal halfway, and Hiram felt a punch in his gut that lifted him off his feet. He came down on all fours, palms barely keeping his face from tilting over and banging his nose on the ground. The punch had knocked the wind out of him. He coughed and gripped his middle, and right before him, he saw August's boots step up. He started to raise his face and look up, only to have a second punch come down on his right temple.

White light flashed behind his eyes, almost to be followed by blackness as he caught himself again. His ears rang from the blow, but he still heard his younger children screaming for him. His elbows threatened to buckle under him, but he shook it off again, forced himself up to his knees, and rocked back onto his haunches, blinking to clear the patches still undulating across his vision. The sinking feeling he'd experienced while looking for Lucinda last night, revisited in a frightening wave. This time he felt an astonishing flair of blinding rage, but it weirdly bore no focus, just a heated urge to tear at something… anything… *anyone*. He gritted his teeth, choked it back, and gazed up at August Chandler, who stepped closer.

The young man's mouth was set in a bitter grimace as he reached down, gripped the front of Hiram's shirt and vest, and hoisted him up. "It's time for you to let your little girl go," August said through gritted teeth, then his voice deepened into an inhuman growl. "She doesn't want to stay here in this shit hole anymore! Haven't you kept her here long enough!" He drew back another fist and let it fly, cracking across Hiram's left cheek and whipping his head sideways.

The words stung more than the third strike, plunged the marshal into a split infinity of questions, guilt, denial, and anger at this little bastard for even going there. He pried at the hand gripping his front and tried to make the world around him stop spinning long enough to get an upper hand of his own.

Then it was there in the form of a wooden cross, directly in front of him. Instantly August's steel grip released, and Hiram sank back to his knees, found that it was Becker standing just off his left shoulder with the cross thrust forward.

"Get thee behind me, you piece of shit," Becker said, and August moved backward in another blurry flash and stopped.

His body shook slightly, appeared to blink in and out, and Hiram saw that his eyes had changed into glossy onyx orbs that were now all too familiar. Unlike Silas' eyes, however, they were not framed in branches of disease-ridden veins, and they maintained the intelligence behind them while they remained undeniably angry.

"Freak of nature," Becker spat.

"On the contrary, preacher," August said. "We are in perfect harmony with nature." Then he angled his head to make it clear that he was glaring at Hiram. "She's mine now, Marshal, and soon you'll be joining your friend in bones and ash."

"Noooooo!" Jesse's voice shouted from somewhere to Hiram's left behind Becker, and gunfire rang over the howling winds. August turned toward his rival, who was running forward, unloading the Colt as fast as he could without fanning the hammer.

Hiram knew how hard it was to hit anything while moving like that, jerky and so emotionally charged even at such close range. As the last shot pierced the air, Jesse halted, stared hopelessly. He seemed to have gotten a better look at August's eyes, and reason caught up with him.

August Chandler only grinned back at Jesse. "You know where we'll be," he said.

A gust of dusty wind blew past him, and he appeared to meld into it. Beyond him, the girls did, too, and Lucinda was gone with them.

Hiram hunkered over to catch his breath, fought the delayed dizziness and pain in his head and face from taking two good cracks so close together. That was when the punch he'd taken to the gut turned into something else. Sore abdominal muscles gave way to more profound pain, a clench in his stomach that felt like it clawed its way up into his mouth and triggered some animal part of him he'd never encountered before: to bite something, to dig in with his teeth and tear and shake and rip. He groaned and strained to staunch it, to keep *Hiram* in the foreground.

"They got Lucinda again, Papa," Caleb said, now right in front of him, a hand on his shoulder. Ellie approached, too, and Hiram heard their hearts again in a chorus of *thrum-thrum-thrum*, smelled them both not as his children but as something savory and begging to crawl down his throat and into his stomach to soothe the pang that clenched and gnawed and…

"Get away from me!"

He twisted around on his knees and clambered to his feet, stumbled several paces away from them and grabbed onto a section of the corral fence to hold himself up. He could feel their eyes on him, the stunned silence as loud as the storm.

"Caleb, Jesse," Becker said with a sharp edge of caution in his voice, "go collect the horses. Ellie, stay here with me." His footsteps approached but kept within a certain distance. "Marshal?"

Hiram took several long deep breaths, focused on the smell of twisting, surging earth to replace the tang of blood. Strangely, the pain in his face ebbed when he knew his temple, possibly even his eye, should be swollen and tight already. Slowly he turned, let go of the fence, and balanced. His heart lurched a little to see that Becker held up his cross while keeping Ellie tucked behind him.

It was not the symbol itself that hurt, but the fact the pastor found it necessary to use it, but nothing trembled inside Hiram at the sight of it. He reached out toward it, testing the air around it, encountered no force that compelled him to turn and flee as August had.

He lowered his hand. "That doesn't work… yet."

Becker lowered the cross. "Well, that's something."

"I don't have a choice now," he said as Jesse and Caleb approached, leading Teddy and the other two horses. "Cage has answers, and August has Lucinda again. I'm going to the opera house." He took a step away from the fence.

"*We* are going to the opera house," Jesse amended.

"This isn't your battle alone, Marshal," Becker added.

He could see from the stubborn looks on their faces that they weren't going to hear any argument. Then he looked down at Caleb and Ellie who, so help him, were *not* going to the opera house.

"All right, but first, we're stopping by the church."

CHAPTER THIRTY

They turned Remington into the corral with Nathan's horses, and Becker rode Watkins' roan as they raced up the thoroughfare. The dust wall loomed on both sides, spinning like an angry desert demon that kept the remnants of the town's populace trapped. Despite that, they made the trip without any further encounters, and it was a relief that the wall did not reach so high as to blot out the entire sky. Although Hiram's vision was not a problem now, at least the half-moon climbed now, graced the street with some silvery light for the others to see.

They passed the Palace, and Hiram dared not look at its dark open doorway. Just as swiftly, they crossed the front of the opera house, which showed no sign of anyone there with its windows blackened in, and then on, past the jail and the mayor's office. The storm wailed at its loudest here, for just beyond the church and graveyard, the wall looped back around, closing off the southeastern bend going out.

It occurred to him that the night of the coyote attack, he'd had the horses corralled inside the graveyard rather than tethered, blasphemy or not. He had not known then that it was not the fence but likely the holy ground that truly protected them. On that note, he determined that Teddy, Peso, and the roan be left inside the fence. Saddles were left on to save time, but once the horses were safely ensconced, Hiram and company entered the church through the rectory. Becker delegated duties as readily as he had while attempting to save Silas' life.

"Jesse, start breaking legs off the spare chairs in the sanctuary. We'll need stakes. Caleb, Ellie, there are two crosses on the walls out there. Go pull them down."

Hiram watched Jesse purposefully carry the sword with him through the door and soon heard cracking noises. He pulled his Colt out of its holster, opened the loading gate, and started replacing the cartridges he'd spent on O'Brian and Reed. "What's that?" he asked as he noted Becker pulling an entire clutch of small purplish flowers from the dried herbs hanging above.

"Vervain," the pastor said as he shoved the whole batch into his Gladstone. "*Verbena officinalis,* also known as holy herb. Jasper said it's part of the cure, remember? It's hard to grow here, so this is all I have. I use it to treat kidney stones and gout in my patients. Never imagined I'd be using it to treat vampirism. Next, we need one of their hearts. I confess I'm not looking forward to that."

"Guess everything has a purpose." Hiram clicked the loading gate into place and holstered the gun, now watched Becker grab a handful of empty vials from the counter drawers.

"Yes, Marshal, everything does have a purpose. Maybe all this *scheisse* happening now has some kind of purpose. Perhaps, your affliction even has a purpose. I trust the Lord knows what He's doing, mysterious ways and all."

"Yeah, well, I wish He would not be quite so fucking mysterious." He sighed. "You still have my instructions in that bag, right?"

Becker turned to look at him, mute for a moment. "Of course."

"You follow them to the letter, understood?" Now was not the time to get emotional again, but he needed to know that his affairs were in good hands when he left this world tonight.

"I will." Becker only took the uncomfortable silence for so long before he held up the vials. "Sanctuary," he said and grabbed his bag before exiting the rectory at a relentless clip. Hiram followed him through the door and down the aisle between the pews, straight to the holy water font at the entrance.

Caleb and Ellie had collected two crosses from the walls, and Jesse had busted apart three small chairs stored against the back wall as extras from when the church had that much attendance and the Bend had a population worth bragging about.

Becker went to the font and began to fill the vials with holy water. "This glass is thin; it'll shatter easily," he explained as he submerged one vial after another and corked them.

"So, we can use them as holy water bottle bombs?" Hiram said a little too flippantly, earning himself a glare.

"Here you go, Pastor," Caleb said as he and Ellie rejoined. He held up the crosses. "The one on the altar is too big."

"Those are for you," Becker said to them. "Keep them with you. Use them as a shield. Clearly, we've seen that they work."

Jesse joined them with a bundle of chair legs tucked in one elbow while his other hand remained occupied with the sword. "This enough?"

Hiram counted twelve makeshift stakes, and the kid had made damned sure that each had one end splintered into a sharp point. "I'd say we're covered."

The kid handed out the unlikely weapons, though Hiram intercepted him before he almost gave one to Caleb. Each man was left to figure out how to carry them on his own. Hiram hid one in each boot, wedged a third under his coat between his belt and the waist of his dungarees while he noticed Becker sliding one up his coat sleeve and adjusting it. Next, the vials went around, slipped into coat and jacket pockets for quick access. So ragtag they all were, Hiram thought, preparing for the strangest guerrilla warfare he'd ever heard of.

"Staking them should put 'em down," Caleb said, citing his penny dreadfuls again. "But it won't kill them. We'll have to behead them."

"Then good thing I got this." Jesse proudly indicated the sword.

"And burn them," Becker added hesitantly.

"Isn't any *we* where you and Ellie are concerned, Caleb," Hiram interrupted. "You're staying here, on holy ground."

The look on his boy's face broke Hiram's heart. It didn't take Ellie long to catch on, too.

"No, Papa, I wanna fight with you."

"You'w not weaving us, Papa," Ellie objected. "I wanna fight, too."

"Jesse." Becker nodded toward the doors. "That's our cue."

"Right."

Becker unbolted the doors and opened one side to the swell of the storm. Jesse stepped out ahead of him, and Becker followed, pulled the door shut, tamping the din back down.

For what felt a longer moment than it was, Hiram stared down at his children, knowing they could not see him in the dim light as well as he could see them. Caleb's eyes were as blue to him as in any daylight, Ellie's, too. Tears made rivulets down the boy's dusty cheeks, and Ellie's little mouth gaped, showing off the double gap in her lower front teeth.

Hiram's breath hitched as he realized she had finally shed the most recent loose baby tooth, but he had been too caught up in all of *this* to see it happen. First the investigation, then Lucinda's disappearance. It had all caused him to miss another crucial little piece of his life. He swallowed and got down on a knee, putting him eye-to-eye with Ellie and looking up at Caleb. If this turned out to be the last time he saw them, he wanted it to be from this angle, looking at them square in their beautiful young faces.

"You two…" he said and laid one hand against Caleb's cheek, the other against Ellie's. "I love you more than life itself. You know that, don't you?"

"We love you, too, Papa."

"Yeah, wuv you, Papa."

"After your mama's death, if it wasn't for you two and your sister, I don't know what I'd have done. And I know you're both brave enough to take on a thousand vampires, but you're too precious to me to let you go out there and face those things. Please stay here and safe *for me*. Please?"

Caleb sniffled, and his bottom lip trembled. "Papa…"

"You know I'm sick, Caleb. It's not just them you have to stay away from. It's *me*. You need to be safe from *me*."

Tiny keening noises came out of their throats as Caleb suppressed his sobs, and Ellie let hers out. Finally, the boy nodded.

Hiram couldn't help himself. He took a deep breath and held it, pulled them both into a double embrace, kissed their foreheads, wiped their tears, hating that he dared not smell the sweetness of Ellie's hair or the hint of newsprint ink on Caleb's fingers. He withheld his own shudders and sniffles until he let them go and had to push them back, terrified he'd finally, completely awaken the thing in him that had threatened to surface earlier.

"Bolt the doors again," he said as he backed away and stood. "Then you get into the rectory if you want, but lock that door, too. Don't come out on your own until morning, and if you haven't heard from the pastor or Jesse, you go to Mr. and Miz Raskin."

Caleb nodded as he sniffled and wiped his face.

In his mind, as always, the memory of their faces like that embedded itself permanently. Hiram closed his eyes, enjoying it for a moment longer, then he turned away and opened the door to the howling storm.

⁂

The last thing Lucinda had heard was the dust storm raging around her family's home, felt the winds buffeting her. Before that, everything else had been happening so quickly, from her brother and sister as Morgan Reed's hostages to the moment her father shot him after a little distraction from Jesse.

After that situation was handled, they had all dropped their guard for the tiniest moment, and new confusion started, everything happening in obscure flashes. She heard her father shout, then a crash at the same moment arms swept around her. They were thin, willowy, and accompanied by tendrils of wind that embraced her entirely and pulled her away. Jesse, right in front of her one moment, now diminishing with distance as she was pulled struggling across the barnyard and came to an abrupt stop. She flailed and fought and recognized that it was Nora Long and Genevieve Blakely that had her. They were a couple, she remembered. Lovers. And they were working together here, laughing gleefully as they toyed with her.

While she struggled to make a fist, to throw a punch, *anything*, Nora held onto her wrists with uncanny strength, and Genevieve grabbed her by the chin, forcing her to stare into emerald-green eyes with flecks of gold. *Not again*, she thought, remembering how Cage Edwards had done the same, how her brain had instantly become muddled. The bejeweled irises that shifted and broiled and captured her again were far too fascinating to look away.

Then Genevieve's mouth covered hers, and it was not the hypnotic power of the eyes but the kiss that sent Lucinda adrift, loins quivering pleasantly as she dipped backward. Before the darkness closed in, she felt Nora lean in from behind and whisper in her ear with a soft, tickling gust of breath, "Welcome to the kith, little sister."

She startled to, still hearing that whisper, still feeling aroused and yet sickened by it now that she knew what those women were. A dull throb nested in the space between her eyes as she stared up at a warmly lit ceiling of wooden joists and planks and recognized it as part of the underneath side of the stage in the opera house. She'd been here before many times when the school had put on performances in years past or when she had helped her mother organize town meetings that required the stage.

Slowly she raised a hand to press the heel of her palm into the bridge between her brows, massaged gently and tried to force some sense to the surface. It was nothing short of embarrassing to have been snagged again, but then she reminded herself that these were not simple, regular people who had grabbed her in either situation. Having interacted with all of them at some point over the first week they had been here, she'd come to trust the troupe from Jasper and Morgan to all of the players, especially August. All of them had seemed like decent folks, presented themselves with polite comportment. Couldn't she be forgiven for falling under their spell? Now, having been held hostage by Frank Evans, with a gun to her head, felt so *normal* compared to what she'd witnessed in the last two days.

Think, she told herself, asked herself what her papa would do. Turning her head, she looked into the room to observe her surroundings, to try and locate her abductors.

The *vaults*, as they had always been called, were a series of rooms in the brick foundation beneath the opera house. The deepest rooms that ran toward the front of the building were used for storage. Town signage, decorations, and props for festivals and public presentations were stashed in there, along with construction supplies and tools. The two rooms under the stage were for old props, costume racks, and mirrored vanity tables for makeup. She was in the room most directly below the stage where performers prepared themselves. Oil lamps glowed on the vanities, their light reflected by the mirrors, and two heavy folding blinds for changing stood in the corners. She saw, from her vantage lying on the chaise lounge—part of a small sitting area—that the blinds were still draped over with discarded costumes from *A Midsummer Night's Dream*, including Titania's gossamer fairy wings and dress. The antler crown which Cage Edwards had worn as Oberon lay discarded on one of the vanities. A rack near the back of the room, somewhat blocking the dark passage into the storage area, stood loaded with colorful costumes of dresses, men's doublets and tunics, with a sign loosely tied to the end that read *Hamlet*. The entire room system smelled of must, perfume, and the waxiness of stage makeup.

It was when she started to crane her head up for a better view of the steps against the wall on the far side of the room that she felt the slight sting at the junction of her neck and collar bone. "Ow," she uttered and touched at it, found two little round punctures there, perhaps an inch and a half apart, mostly scabbed over already but oozing enough that when she lifted her hand, a smear of blood gleamed on her fingertip.

"Genevieve bit you." It was August's voice, speaking from somewhere near the foot of the lounge. "She did it for me."

It took her a moment to acknowledge what *bit* meant in this case, and then Lucinda closed her eyes and pushed out a stream of tears. They were not tears of fright this time, but betrayal, anger, confusion. "Yesterday, you *asked* me if I would join you," she said. "You gave me a choice. I thought that, despite what you are, that you still had some honor. Now you take that choice away?"

She opened her eyes to peer steeply toward him, then tried to push herself up on wobbly arms and drop her knees over the side of the cushion.

"It will take some hours," he said as if he had not listened to her at all. "The pestilence needs time in your body, and then I can *blood* you. Once you have undergone the transformation, you will understand. You'll see the world in a whole new light."

"You took away my *choice*, August!" Her hands formed fists on her knees as she felt her face heat up. "I want to be with Jesse! Do you understand that?"

His green eyes went cold at that. "Really?" he said with feigned disbelief. "That hick? You told me yourself that you'd like to run away, see the world, go off on a grand adventure. I'm giving you *that*. This is your chance to shine, Lucinda, to see it all, to have it all, and we can do it together."

"And what happens when I start missing the sun?" she said and attempted to stand. "Or my family?"

"You *won't* miss it," he replied confidently and moved to assist her. "You won't miss *them*. Trust me. Once you see how the night comes alive, the sun and this old life will become a distant, dull, boring memory."

She pulled her elbow free of his grasp and glared up at him. "I'm the one who should be the judge of that, not *you!*"

"You *can't* be the judge of that." His eyes suddenly lit up with mildly flirtatious glee. "It has to be experienced, Lucinda."

"But you've made up my mind for me that I'm going to like it! You have no right!" She quickly looked away from his lovely eyes and hated that, but she wouldn't risk losing her will again. She kept her gaze on his chest instead, purposefully examined the mother-of-pearl buttons on the front of his silk vest. Next, she thought of the other consequences he had explained to her. "And then there's *what* you do to survive."

He sighed softly, banished the attempt at humor. "That… I am sorry for that, but you'll adapt. It will come as naturally as breathing." He stepped closer, and a hand lifted toward her, beckoning. "Please, Lucinda, give me a chance."

She wavered dizzily, wondering if the disease he'd allowed to be driven into her veins was already at work. She'd seen enough of what it was doing to her father. How pale he had looked, eyes slightly sunken and tired, and she'd noticed the black veins crawling up the side of his neck. Would that happen to her before August did whatever he needed to do to finish the *transformation*, as he had put it?

Reluctantly she nodded. Surrendering made her feel sick, the pain in her head traveling down to grip her heart in heaviness, despair.

"You'll see it for the gift it is," he insisted and swept a lock of hair back from her forehead, pressed his lips there in a gentle kiss. "I promise you."

Lucinda took a deep breath, and then she turned and bolted for the stairs. "No!" she screamed as there was a blur to her side, and August instantly appeared in front of her. She tried to sidestep around him, but he caught her wrist, so small in his grip, and pulled her toward him. "Let me go!"

"Lucinda, stop! Listen to me; it's not as scary as it sounds! You'll see!"

"Let me *go!*" Her voice reached hysterics. She raised one leg under her skirts and kicked him in the shin. It was as hard as she could muster with all of her pulling, pushing, wrenching and struggling, but it worked. He let go of her with a wince and bent over to rub at the area under his trouser leg, but he was still between her and the steps.

In a heightened frenzy, she spun, looking for the next place to go, and without thinking any further, hurried out of the dressing area and toward the deeper vaults. She ran up against the rack loaded with Hamlet costuming, grabbed the end and pulled with all of her strength to dump it against August as he came after her. The top-heavy frame tipped into his path, but she knew it was only a brief diversion.

"Lucinda!" he shouted after her.

While he swatted a tangle of clothing and hangers aside, she plunged past the props in the next room and further, deep into the smell of mold and dust, and into a darkness that seemed surprisingly grayer to her vision.

CHAPTER THIRTY-ONE

At the end of the thoroughfare, they lined up, facing into the empty town, while the monstrous whirlwind persisted, and Hiram felt like he had fallen into another world. How things had *changed* so much in only a matter of days, starting with two bodies in his jail. He almost expected to wake up in the clinic, having suffered a head injury. Maybe he had gotten himself shot during the holdup at the after-party last Friday and had dreamed all of this because he heard Caleb talk about vampires far too much.

But dreams were not *this* tactile, did not cause his stomach to punch itself with growing inhuman hunger, did not scour his ears with the roar of winds and dust, and now it was time to walk into the eye of the storm.

He accepted that he could not have imagined any of this, never could have expected something so vile to slip into his town, right under his nose, and feed on what was left of its good people, wipe them out in so short a time. The best he could hope for was to stop it from spreading to another similar town and to pull his family from the tempest alive and safe.

On Hiram's right, Jesse had the sword propped on one shoulder, cocksure and stupid as hell. To his other side, Becker was only armed with his Gladstone—as full of holy water and vervain twigs as it was tinctures and balms—faith, and a stake up his arm. They began their walk, straight up the middle, because out in the open, Becker and Jesse could see better in the moonlight, and anyway, stealth did not matter since they were expected. Separate winds scattered the dust of the street across their path, and unlit lanterns creaked as they swung on their hooks over the boardwalks.

"When this is over," he said, having to raise his voice over the gales, "burn the jail and the Palace." He didn't take his eyes off the street. "The Simpson house, too."

"What?" Jesse asked, startled.

"There's still spoiled blood on the floor of the jail, and I'm sure there's some of Silas' left in the saloon somewhere. Fire purifies. If it's good enough for these bastards to dispose of their kills, it's good enough for us."

Becker said nothing to this, but Hiram sensed that silence meant agreement.

Ahead, to their left, a golden, flickering light appeared in the now open doors of the opera house. Hiram picked up his pace until he stood directly before them and looked in, heard the eerily calm heartbeat within, two more muted ones deeper inside. He took a long deep breath through his nose and examined every particle that tickled and teased. "Cage is waiting there," he said, "Lucinda is in the vaults with August."

Neither bothered to ask how he knew this.

The wind whipping his coat about, he stepped ahead into the opening. There was no pretending he was anything but scared, knowing that Cage could read his heartbeat as well as he could read Cage's. Harder still was the fact that Cage was long adapted to his abilities, giving him the advantage. Hiram proceeded forward, under the front balcony and into the great hall beneath the chandelier. All of the candles hanging amidst the crystal lusters glowed, as did the stage lights and the oil lamps set in their wall shelves

The head of the troupe stood on the main floor, straight ahead, leaning casually back against the edge of the stage, which was still partially set up for a performance of Hamlet that the troupe had probably never intended to undertake. Fragments of castle interiors towered against a backdrop of rolling hills, and a tarp of dirt comprised a miniature graveyard with its painted wood tombstones, complete with a skull prop left in the soil.

Cage stood with arms crossed and head tilted as he examined his reluctant guests with narrowed eyes. He was dressed in his usual finery though his coat had been removed and lay on the end of the stage, his tie loosened, shirt unbuttoned halfway down as though he were ready for a scrapping. Then he spread his arms out in a manner of greeting.

"Tomorrow, and tomorrow, and tomorrow," he said in a manner of announcement, "creeps in this petty pace from day to day to the last syllable of recorded time, and all our yesterdays have lighted fools the way to dusty death." He drew out the end of *death* into a long, serious hiss.

Hiram cringed. "God, I hate theater."

Jesse stepped up to his side, the tension in his young body evident in the air around him.

"Welcome, both of you," Cage said. "I see you've come for your lady love, Mr. Warren."

"Where is she?" Jesse said, voice lowered to a tone Hiram had never heard before. For all that the kid could sound so tragically innocent at times, what spoke now was the man who had had enough. "If you people have so much as touched a hair on her head—"

"Downstairs, you're welcome to go collect her."

Jesse looked at Hiram uncertainly.

"Go on, I'll handle him," the marshal said quietly. "Be careful, Jesse."

He got a nod, more uncertainty, a little piquant waft of understandable fear, then Jesse made his way across the open floor toward the door that led to the vaults below the stage. He lowered the sword from his shoulder and disappeared into the shadows there. Hiram counted his footsteps descending until Cage spoke up louder, interrupting him so that he could not decently track the kid's movements. The problem was, if he could hear Jesse's steps, then so could August.

"As for *you*." Pale silvery eyes fell upon Becker. "I'm afraid you were not invited, preacher."

Too late, Hiram heard them coming. Somehow, they'd lain in wait, perhaps keeping enough distance that he hadn't sensed them, heard them, but they moved in from the street, swept on a gust of wind, heartbeats rising and falling with a chorus of laughter that sounded melodic and sweet.

Becker shouted as they grabbed him from behind. Hiram spun to reach for him but was too late as all he glimpsed was Becker reaching out with one arm as he disappeared through the doors and back into the night, still clutching his ever-important Gladstone. The doors slammed shut, pushing a billow of dust across the floor.

Breath quickening, Hiram turned back into the room. He'd seen how these creatures could move with such speed at the house, felt how strong they could be, seen them take his daughter easily enough, but it was still stunning that two petite women should also snatch a man the size of

Becker and sweep him away just like that.

Cage had not so much as budged. "Don't worry, Genevieve and Nora will keep him well entertained once they relieve him of that cross." At that, he unhitched himself from the edge of the stage and stepped forward several feet before standing tall and firm. "You have questions, Marshal Wells."

For all that it was true, Hiram suddenly couldn't think of a good place to start. He gestured around him, at the hall and stage. "Why this?" he began. "Why this ruse?"

"Oh, *this* is because I enjoy art," Cage said tritely. "But if you want a more practical reason, that's simple. No one would suspect a troupe of actors. They are only visitors bringing some much-needed diversion to a town fallen on hard times. How could they have anything to do with the citizens going missing?" He gave a wistful smile as he clicked his tongue behind his teeth. "I know, we're *awful*. Vultures circling the likes of Allen, Contention City, Bradshaw. Other towns have given up the ghost to us, but they were all on the decline already.

"Go ahead, ask me the other obvious ones. What are we? Where do we come from? Why must we burn our victims? Is there a cure?"

Hiram's chin lifted at the last one. "Is there? Your man mentioned a cure."

Cage gave a bitter chuckle. "You mean Jasper still had it in his withered old husk to tell you about the heart of a noble, vervain, and holy water? For you, there is no point. You've borne the pestilence for almost two days now. At most, the holy water would make you vomit your insides out. I'm afraid your time is up on that one."

"Then so is yours," Hiram said and with that drew, tapping a speed he'd never known before as he reached across his body, gripped his Peacemaker, and skinned it from the holster in under a second, aimed at Cage's heart, and fired.

Only Cage's hand moved, blurring as it swept up and over at the same instance as the *bang* sounded.

Hiram felt a disorienting shock to his entire body as the smoke from the spent cartridge cleared, and he found that his opponent still stood, one fist poised in the air in a tight grip. The next thing he noticed was that the muted rumble of the storm beyond the walls rose into a greater quaking of the very ground and floor under his feet. The windows behind the giant drapes and the front doors rattled as some great force struck them outside.

Cage's eyes were tightly shut while he shuddered slightly. His body appeared to ripple in a mirage-like effect, and then he opened his hand, palm up, presented the bullet and looked at it.

"You had them blessed, *and* you tapped a cross into the tip of the lead," he said, examining the slug though he seemed considerably uncomfortable holding it. "You made me lose my concentration, Marshal." He tipped his hand and let the round fall to the floor with a clatter. He rippled and twitched a second more, and then the effect seemed to wear off. "Well, that was just rude."

Around them, the quaking subsided. Clouds of red dust pushed through the cracks at the top and bottom of the doors. Then it all fell into an eerie lull.

Hiram was still shaking it off that his target had caught a bullet in midair—and fired from less than fifteen feet away at that—when Cage dashed forward, pivoted a forearm up and diverted Hiram's hand, knocked the gun away while his other hand came in with an uppercut directly to the chest. Hiram hurled backward, landed flat and slid another ten or more feet before coming to a stop, sprawled and staring at the ceiling. Oddly, he did not feel as much pain as there should have been. Hell, the blow could have potentially killed him, and the fall should have at least knocked him out, just as August's punch to his temple should have made him kiss the dirt and stay down.

Cage snapped back into view, standing over him, cool calmness restored. "I can do this all night, Marshal. You may be a little faster now, a little stronger, but you're still just a man with a raging disease in his veins. Once you reach the point of no return, I'll have no choice but to kill you, to tear you apart and burn you as I've done a million times throughout my existence." He knelt directly over the downed man and put a heavy knee on Hiram's chest to pin him. "But it doesn't have to be that way. You could join us. It is still not too late for me to *blood* you, to bring you into the fold."

Hiram strained under the pressure, raised his hands to push back and try to relieve it. "No," he gritted out, even though he didn't know what exactly any of that meant.

"I've watched empires rise and fall, Marshal. That experience could be yours, free of that crumbling spine you have, free of regret. I've met very few men who are worthy of it. Hell—" he chuckled, "I can't even explain how *August* came to be one of us. The kid was just lucky, I guess.

"But you deserve the reward. You're formidable, a valuable ally. I've told you that before."

"W-what?" Hiram coughed, recalling no such conversation. He groaned as Cage applied a little more pressure. The pain of it was also causing his stomach to squirm, that vile hunger rising in him.

"Oh." Cage's brows rose in surprise. "Oh, that's right. You're still under suggestion. I almost forgot. Let's clear that up." He lowered a hand directly before Hiram's eyes and positioned his thumb against the middle finger.

"Remember," he said and then *snapped*.

Caleb couldn't stop pacing before the altar, the cross held in a tight fist, protruding from one side of his hand while the other side gently tapped his palm. Ellie sat in the front pew, watching him, sober and quiet for a change, though occasionally he heard her sniffle. Neither of them, he knew, could accept that they might not see their father again. To stay safe for him, here, was a painful promise to keep, and Caleb couldn't suppress the hum in his body, the need to run up the street and see for himself what was happening.

But a promise was a promise, he thought. Papa had kept his promises, hadn't he?

Outside, the storm continued to thrash through the nearby trees. Stray winds occasionally swept toward the church, and the eaves creaked against their nails. He wasn't sure how much more he could take hearing it, even if it did seem to keep a certain distance.

"Papa's gonna be okay, isn't he?" Ellie asked softly.

"I don't know," Caleb said, the most truthful thing he *could* say. "Come on, let's go into the back." He hoped it would be a little quieter in the rectory since the front of the church faced the end of the thoroughfare and the storm's edge. He took her hand, and they went through the rear door together, still holding their crosses. He shut the door behind them and, to his relief, found the rectory quieter, at least enough to better address the storm of personal worries whirling around in his head. Part of him kept pondering for a solution, a way to help from here without going against his father's orders, but it was pointless, and he knew it. He and his sister were stuck here and helpless, and he hated it so very much.

He went over to the counter, where one oil lamp burned, and turned up the flame

"Maybe we make up ouw own stowies," Ellie suggested.

That would be something to pass the time, Caleb thought. "Vampires or gunfighters?"

She looked up at him, lips pursed in profound thought. Her mouth opened, but a squeal sounded from one of the horses out in the cemetery. Then another, and a few loud grumbles.

Caleb ran to the window and looked out, cupping his hands to the glass to see out into the dark. It was not, thankfully, absolute darkness as he made out the outlines of the cemetery fence and a streak of moonlight along a horse's back as it stamped in a circle behind the gate, which hung wide open, swinging with a loud creak in the wind.

"Damn," he said under his breath as the shape of another horse slipped through the opening. By the moon on its blaze and the shape of a saddle, he guessed that was Teddy escaping.

"Wha's happening?" Ellie said with a new edge of worry.

"Stay here," he said and ran to the door, unlocked it and stepped out. The gritty wind whipped at his hair as he descended and started for the cemetery only to have Teddy gallop by. "Teddy!" he shouted. "Come back here, you stupid horse!"

The gelding only whinnied and proceeded toward the thoroughfare while Peso started to trot by.

"Oh no, you don't!" Caleb yelled and reached out to catch the reins dangling off one side of the second gelding's neck. Peso veered around, grumbling and squealing and tossing his head. Caleb got a hold near the bit, but the horse wrenched away, the motion dragging the strap sharply through Caleb's palm and burning as if he'd touched hot iron. "Ow!" He let go right as Peso bucked, and Caleb stumbled to get out of the way, tripped over his own feet, and fell backward, catching himself on his elbows.

"Caweb!" Ellie shouted, suddenly at his side, squatting to grab his arm. "Papa said stay in!"

"Your papa is a smart man," a gruff voice said behind them.

Caleb got to his knees and spun to look around, speechless to find Morgan Reed half defined by the moonlight, half silhouette against the church's outside wall. There were dark spots on his clothing at his collar and his lower belly where he'd been shot. No one, Caleb remembered, had checked to see if he was dead, but despite his injuries, he had still managed to come around and get himself up the street, and he looked to be standing as strong as ever.

"Believe me, kiddies, I still have it in me to snap your little necks!" He started for them, the light shifting with his movement, clarifying how he seemed to have aged slightly, but that was not stopping him. The white of his eyes showed bright and wild, and his lips curled back into an angry grimace.

Caleb panicked. If everything he understood now were true, no cross would stop the man. He was not like his masters, could go anywhere he wanted, and sword or no, he looked strong and dangerous regardless of his injuries. He also stood right between them and the rectory door, blocking off their way back to safety and any number of medical tools and devices that Caleb imagined would make good makeshift weapons.

"Come on, Ellie!" He grabbed his sister's arm and dragged her to her feet, started running just in time to feel fingers scratch across the back of his jacket but gain no purchase.

Her legs so much shorter than his own, Ellie stumbled, slowing him. Without looking back, Caleb reached down, hooked his hands under her arms and lifted her to ride on his hip, and then he ran for their lives.

Disorienting how they picked him up off his feet and pulled him from the opera house. One moment standing next to the marshal in a staredown with Cage Edwards, the next watching helplessly as Hiram Wells' figure shrank with the expanding distance, a figure in his coat, spinning and reaching helplessly.

He was aware of arms around him. Thin, beautiful pale arms and cool curls of air buoyed him along, whistling in his ears with the speed and the ethereal laughter of his captors. By some instinct, he hugged his Gladstone close to his chest, felt the awkwardness of the short piece of chair leg he'd strapped to his arm under his coat sleeve, but he did not dare let go of his Gladstone with its important cargo of vervain and additional bottles of holy water.

The doors slammed shut as he cleared them, and he was deposited upon the ground out in the middle of the thoroughfare.

Becker's breath jarred from him, and he coughed at the street dust that swirled around him. He scrambled to his feet and pulled the cross from his pocket, held it ready as he spun from one direction to another, looking for their shapes in the moonlight shining from the top center of the storm surge. A chorus of laughter accompanied the rumble of the monstrous winds. Giggles and breathy gasps echoed around him, bounded off the false fronts of the opposing buildings and the hard brick of the opera house.

"I think he's rather handsome," a soft voice spoke up, so close behind him and startling that Becker nearly crawled out of his own skin to get away from it.

He spun, cross out, and found the moon cast on Genevieve Blakely's mane of flaming red hair. The thread of silver light defined her naked shoulders like those of a classical goddess carved in marble. Any man would wish readily to kiss and caress shoulders like that.

"Too much like a walrus with that mustache," Nora Long replied as she stepped into view, willowy as she tilted her head. "The collar cuts a swell, though. Never tasted a holy man before."

"What do you say, Pastor Becker?" Genevieve said. "Is your blood bitter from all of that abstinence? Or will you surprise us with something sweeter?"

Becker thought about lecturing her on how abstinence was for Catholics. Instead, he reached into his coat pocket and drew out one of the vials he'd filled with holy water. Though his initial plan for the thin glass vessels was to use as bottle bombs, as the marshal had indelicately put it, a new idea struck him. The mere sight of it caused both women to freeze. They did not look so much frightened as annoyed, and he recalled Jasper O'Brian's words regarding the holy in general.

It's the enérgeia, ya see? It messes wiv 'em.

Besides medical science, Becker had also enjoyed following physics and maths, if only in hobby reading, and his home country was replete with brilliant minds in both fields.

Enérgeia, he thought, from the Greek for *being at work*, but time and science had linked it to a deeper meaning, more like *power*: an unseeable power felt in the blaze of a fire, the vibration from loud noise, a shift in the wind. It acted differently depending on the matter it inhabited, but it could not be created or destroyed, only transferred from one form to another.

But for Becker, it also meant the power of the Divine, the *living force* of God, that he'd experienced since he was a young man after medical school failed to satisfy his seeking heart, and he'd answered a second calling. He'd hoped to find the balance between science and faith and, personally speaking, he had. Perhaps other men fell to only one side of the fence and stayed there, but he considered himself fortunate to walk in both worlds.

If the living force, no matter what faith it came from, could condense into specific areas and objects that these creatures could not tolerate, then it stood to reason that a man could be a vessel as well. He snapped off the stopper on the vial and drank down the contents in three big gulps. There was the subtle taste of the salt mixed in, a tinge of rankness because he hadn't changed out the font enough over the last few days due to obvious distractions, but given the way both women stopped approaching him, it worked. He didn't know how long it would last, perhaps only until he took his next piss, but for now, he appreciated the time it bought him.

"Well, shit," Nora said. "That ruins a perfectly good meal."

Becker covered his mouth politely and burped.

Behind him, from within the closed doors of the opera house, a gunshot cracked, and a moment later, the flowing winds around the town ebbed, and the next rumble to sound was that of thousands of pounds of desert dust and sand settling from the tremendous heights to which the winds had borne it. It did not simply drop straight down but flowed, waves and layers shifting over each other in the moonlight, earth transformed into ocean. The sheer amount hitting the ground at once created an avalanche effect. Both women disappeared in pale blurs. Supernatural creatures or not, neither wished to have the red dust surrounding them.

Becker watched the next rising cloud, uncontrolled and billowing, pushing in on the town from all directions. He knelt to give himself some purchase, then grabbed his coat collar, pulled it up as high as he could. He closed his eyes tight, tucked and hid his face deep in the wool to filter the dust as the forces rolled in and buffeted him. Small bits of flying debris stung his exposed hands, one tight on his bag, the other keeping his coat in place. He smelled some of the dust that penetrated through vulnerable seams and openings, but for the most part, the coat did its job of shielding his face and lungs.

When the rumbling subsided and the air stopped pushing him to and fro, he lifted his head and stood. A thin veil of dust still hung in the air, illuminated by the moonlight, giving it the appearance of a putrid, yellowish fog, and like a fog, it muted the world beneath its blanket. There came a distant crashing sound from behind the doors of the opera house, and Becker listened with growing tension for one or both of his assailants to come back from out of nowhere.

Instead, the whinny and snort of a horse answered him, coming from the direction of the church. Faint at first, it was soon followed by a snuffle and hooves approaching before a form appeared out of the haze, first a silhouette, then the full outline of Teddy, still saddled. Becker wondered how the horse had gotten out of the cemetery and if that meant the other two had as well. The gelding slowed to a halt some twenty feet away, snorted with his ears pinned back in agitation as he paced.

From behind the horse, thinned by distance but growing closer, a high-pitched voice yelled, "Caweb, he's stiw thew!"

"Ellie?" Becker said under his breath.

Seconds later, he saw the kids materialize, Caleb carrying his sister on his hip and running for dear life. Red dust clung to their skin, their hair, their clothes, and Caleb coughed hoarsely. Not far behind them, another silhouette appeared, tall, male, and Becker's heart sank. It could only be Morgan Reed, who had been left on the ground at the Wells farm in the frenzy to get to the church and opera house.

How the man, with his injuries, could have gotten up the thoroughfare to flush Caleb and Ellie out of the church *would* have been a mystery, but then Becker reminded himself that Reed had existed on a strange diet of vampire blood for who knew how long. It had not only granted him long life but also made him harder to kill, as it had also done for Jasper O'Brian.

Ellie screamed again as Caleb tripped, obviously out of breath and tiring from carrying her. She tumbled from his arms, but he dragged her back to her feet and got her running again.

"Caleb!" Becker shouted to them, hoping to draw them his way. "Ellie!" He didn't know how he would deal with Reed, but it was time the man started picking on someone his own size. "Over here!" He waved an arm to get their attention.

Something struck him from out of the haze, carried him the rest of the way across the thoroughfare where he landed near the boardwalks for the bakery and haberdashery. His bag slipped from his arm somewhere en route, and he barely kept the back of his head from slamming into the hard-packed ground. He coughed and groaned as he fought for breath, then a weight came down, straddling him.

Becker forced his eyes open wide to see the silhouette of a head and shoulders against the half-moon piercing the veil, a thin, feminine arm raised with the hand opened wide, fingers warped long and spindly, tipped with fine, sharp points.

"I don't care if you did drink holy water," Nora's voice hissed at him. She gave a soft grunt, and her body shivered. "I don't need your blood anyway."

Then her hand, with its deadly claws, swiped down toward his throat.

Before he descended the steps into the vaults, Jesse ran over a few things in his mind about what he was dealing with and how he could handle it. In his job, he wrangled animals that, while not predators, could be highly unpredictable and dangerous. The horns on an angry, out-of-control bull could pivot around, gore and flip a man in a blink. The hooves of a bucking half-grown calf could end future hopes of having kids, and a horse that refused the bridle could bite the shit out of you and never have a single regret about it. With all of this in mind, he considered that his opponent had more incredible speed than any animal, had the strength to pick up a grown man and throw him many yards.

From what Jesse had witnessed back in the Wells' yard, August Chandler was also off his mental reservation. That, combined with his speed, made him far scarier than the refined actor who had been a competitor for Lucinda's affections a week ago.

Jesse considered his options. The sword—he didn't know what kind of skills it took to use it other than swing and put more than arm muscle into it because the thing was heavier than any machete or other type blade he'd used. The stakes in his boots—had to get close enough to use those. The Colt with its bullets that he had carefully etched crosses into while Pastor Becker blessed them—best choice except that Lucinda was down here somewhere, and that meant being sure his target was true before shooting.

"August, please stop!"

A nervy bolt surged through him. Her voice, screaming with something between rage and terror from somewhere deep in the vaults, forced him to a quick decision not to wield a weapon but something else. He shifted the sword to his left hand and pulled a vial of holy water from his jacket pocket, held it ready, and completed his descent, turned into the first room.

He'd never been down here before, so he gave himself a matter of seconds to take in the place: brick foundations, mirrored vanities with lamps glowing upon them, standing blinds for changing, a lounging area with a chaise lounge and two Empire chairs, a costume rack knocked over, colorful fabrics strewn around, and the gaping dark opening into the next room.

"Get away from me!" she screamed again, followed by a crashing noise, and Jesse couldn't help his reaction as he ran to the opening.

"Lucinda!" he shouted into the darkness beyond the reach of the lamps in the dressing room. There was a short pause as if the vaults themselves gasped.

"Jesse! Jesse, he's coming!"

Another crash followed, then silence.

Jesse backed up a step as August appeared to meld out of the darkness, staring at him with glossy black eyes as if the root of all evil dwelt within them.

"You're just the man I was hoping to see tonight," August said.

Jesse raised the vial and threw it on the ground at the actor's feet, ensuring it shattered. Glass shards and water sparkled as they fanned across the floor. August darted back, teeth gritted and issuing a long hiss as if he'd stepped on hot coals. The overall effect was the same as when the pastor wielded a cross against him.

There was a mirage-like rippling effect about August, as if he might dematerialize, his face straining as if he were holding on to his very existence. His eyes clenched shut, and he shook his head as if clearing it.

At that moment, Jesse brought the sword up into both hands, prepared to rush into the second room and swing.

Then August's eyes snapped open, and he took another step back, shoulders hitching slightly, the whole of the gesture making Jesse think of a rattler recoiling to strike. Before Jesse could get in a single step, August shot forward, clearing the puddle and shards, and once in the main room, the flickering, rippling effect ceased.

Jesse responded to the movement by swinging the sword desperately like a club, but August only blurred out of the way. As Jesse tried to track with him the way he might an angry wild bronco, he discovered how easy it was to overswing as August danced back. Jesse cried out angrily as he tried bringing the sword up in an arc, but his target only sidestepped fluidly, and the weight of the blade pulled Jesse forward.

Stupid, he thought. He'd had no idea how to wield such a weapon, and it was proving harder than expected.

The end of the blade came down on an arm of one of the chairs in the lounge area, broke through the finely carved wood and pierced the upholstery where the end of the blade snagged in the thick embroidered material. He started to pull back to slide the blade free when August's fist came down, hammer style, on his right wrist.

Jesse screamed as the bone cracked in two, the lower break tearing through muscle and skin. A warm, red stain soaked his sleeve. His hand, immediately useless, let go of the handle.

"Oops, did I break it?" August sneered.

As tears of agony welled up, Jesse started to pull the handle free with his left hand, gave up at the awkwardness, and bent slightly to try to retrieve the stake in his left boot, got a slight grip, started to extract it.

"I don't think so," August said and back fisted him across the face, shattering his cheekbone.

Jesse spun, one eye seeing stars while the other registered the tilting room. The sword and stake were both forgotten when he landed on all fours, including his right hand. He screamed at the lancing pain and tucked the injured, awkwardly angled wrist against his middle, shielding it as he used his good hand to push onto his knees. Agony-driven tears made a flickering blur of the room while his cheek throbbed, and he incidentally tongued at a loosened molar.

His left hand fumbled to try to draw the Colt, but he'd worn it the way Marshal Wells sported his because he liked the idea of drawing across the body, and he was right-handed, so the best he could do was pitifully hook his left thumb on the inner curve of the grip. He lifted, wrenched his hand around to try to close on the grip but suddenly sensed August standing directly behind him.

A strong hand cupped over his left and clenched until he almost screamed again and let go of the gun, heard it clatter somewhere on the floor. He barely heard a popping sound, a wet tearing, then before he knew it, the same hand that had relieved him of his gun gripped him under the chin, forced him to face up, and August Chandler pushed his freshly opened wrist into Jesse's mouth, forcing his jaw wide open.

Jesse burbled and choked as the blood gushed across his tongue and hit his throat. In trying to reject it, he gagged and sent a flood up into his nasal cavity. He heard his own stifled screams, felt the hand under his chin massage his neck muscles in such a way that triggered a swallow, and once that happened, the gate opened. Eyes squeezed shut, he gulped... and gulped...

"There are different ranks of thralls," August said with vicious zeal. "You'll be on a tight leash, like the dog you are, where you can watch me with her, watch me *have* her. Forever. And you won't be able to do a damned thing about it."

Jesse keened madly against the fleshy gag and tried to thrash. His good hand clawed at that over his throat, then at the wrist that delivered the foreign substance into his body. August's grip only tightened, his wrist pressed deeper, extending Jesse's jaw open until the hinges burned. As more blood flooded in, his mind spun. The events of the past few days spiraled into a soupy nonsense that he could not separate back out, and only one thing made sense now, that he had a new purpose, a new place in the world. A different pain crawled through his broken wrist as the bone shifted and reset itself, and torn skin sealed, briefly itchy as a scab ready to come loose. The ridge of his cheek rose back into place as fragments fit together like puzzle pieces and mended with little healing tingles.

At long last, August declared enough and pulled his wrist free, but the deluge continued to course through Jesse's veins, germinating under his skin, behind his eyes. August shoved him unceremoniously forward on all fours again, where he hung his head, wavered and shivered as the blood renewed him in ways he never dreamed.

"You'll come to me for more when you're ready," August said, calmer but commanding. "Understood? *Only* me."

Jesse worked his mouth, swallowing down the last of the coppery sweet taste, reveling in the high, already craving it again.

He quivered and whispered, "Y-y-yes."

CHAPTER THIRTY-TWO

Cool night air stirred around Hiram, along with the smell of dust and kerosene from the lamp on the overhang. Teddy was grumbling at the hitching post, disgruntled that his owner had turned around and gone the other way when they were supposed to be going home.

He stepped through the door of the jail expecting to be greeted with fresh insults from the Evans brothers since he'd left them sitting in the dark to steep in the consequences of their deeds. He'd suffered many a zinger in every line of work he'd ever taken, but especially in law enforcement, and ignoring them had always proved the best tactic.

Enough moonlight and other ambient illumination fell through the front windows in large shafts that he easily found the oil lamp on his desk and lit it. He positioned it over the desk drawer and located Caleb's pulp chapters and his badge. That was when it came to his attention how quiet the jail was. There was not a single grump over his entrance, and no fresh insult rose from Frank Evans' cell. He did not hear any grunting or snoring at all.

"You boys alright?" he asked and looked up, focused past the glow of the lamp. He could only make out their shapes hunched up on the bunks in the back of each cell. But then he thought he saw a third, not laying down or curled up on a bunk, but standing just inside the bars of Frank's cell on the left. From this side, the bars, dulled with age though they were, still had a subtle gleam, a patina worn into them along the middle from so many hands gripping them over the years.

At first, he thought it must be a trick of the light, his eyes adjusting, but to be sure, he lifted the lamp and stepped closer with it out, only to freeze when he saw that there was indeed a figure, and he knew who it was. An icy block seized his belly and chest, and he took a step back from the sight of the pale gray eyes staring at him while the lower face was shaded by the angle of the uppermost horizontal crossbar.

"Hello, Marshal," Cage Edwards said with disturbing calm for a man who was standing in a locked jail cell. He seemed cloaked in a dark length like an especially bulky cape with a cowl pushed back from his long pale hair. Whatever the case, his entire body from the neck down was an imposing shadow that brought out his height and broad shoulders.

"How did you get in there?" Hiram asked and then took an unwitting step back as Cage stepped forward.

The actor didn't stop at the bars. His face came more into the light as he continued forward and stepped *through* the bars. For seconds he became a watery blur of only the skin tone of his face and the black of his clothing. Hiram blinked, trying to clear the apparent illusion, only to find his unexpected guest suddenly clear again, fully-formed right in front of him. His mind spun to explain it away. Perhaps he'd seen it all wrong, and Cage had not been inside the cell but outside, and there were shadows cast upon him from elsewhere, perhaps by a combination of the windowpanes and blinds, that had given the illusion that he was in the cell. Except now, he was much more clearly in view, and if it had only been an effect from the windows, he'd still have bars of shadows cast over him.

Hiram gaped as the light revealed that the lower half of Cage's face from his lips down over his chin was slick with a sheet of fresh blood. Not the mere trickle of a bloody nose, not like a man who had taken a hit to the jaw and lost a tooth. Worse, Hiram could smell it. The closed air in the jail brought out the reek of copper and an undercurrent of shit. He next acknowledged that the Evans brothers were still slumped in their bunks, and neither had moved an iota or spoke up in fear of the intruder. His next instinct was to reach across his belt for his Colt, and that was when he found himself grappling through more confusion.

"I don't think so," Cage said as, in one fluid motion, a hand appeared out from under the black cloak to grab Hiram's wrist before he remotely found the grip on the gun. In a blink, Cage's other hand swept out and grabbed the pedestal of the lamp, clamped tightly over Hiram's. "Look at me, Marshal," he whispered. "Shhhh… calm down…"

Hiram gritted his teeth, tried to push and pull against his restraints. His assailant was so strong that he couldn't move his arms. In desperation, he attempted to use his body weight to push forward and make Cage back up, but it was to no avail. Hiram's feet back peddled, boots clomping awkwardly, and the smell of blood drew in closer as he found Cage's eyes more directly in front of his own, staring not at but *into* him.

"Interesting," Cage said huskily. "You are a *very* willful man, and you're drunk at that."

The gray spokes around deep black pupils *moved*, glinting as the color—or lack thereof—dropped into the voids at each center, and Hiram gasped as he felt himself falling into them, too. The link between body and mind started to detach with a soothing warmth all too familiar and inviting even though it had been *years* since he'd spiraled down *that* path.

"No," he whispered and attempted to pull back, blink it away, look elsewhere. Shit, he still had a weapon right there in his hand—the oil lamp—even if it meant he set his assailant on fire. All he had to do was tilt it hard, use the glass base as a bludgeon. But the grip over his hand remained firm, impossible to move. He heard himself groaning, straining.

"I don't want to hurt you," Cage said and angled his opium-laced gaze further into the light. "Just *looooook* at me."

His vision could only take in those silver eyes, and he had the fleeting horrifying revelation that they were fucking their way into his mind, worming around, taking over his entire body, freezing him to the spot. "No," he repeated with a grunt. If only he could look away and focus on that bloody mouth, maybe he would snap out of it. Maybe... His eyes rolled slightly but only drifted back into place, staring.

"Shhhhh..." Cage repeated soothingly. "I'm intrigued." The drug of his gaze reached deeper, numbing fingers and toes, and Hiram barely realized his arms and hands were going limp or that Cage had carefully extracted the lamp from his grasp. "That's better."

Hiram put up one last struggle to form a cohesive thought, to ask what was happening, but in a moment, there was only space around him with no sense of depth, his body balanced upright and wrapped in a gauzy peace that felt familiar, welcoming, really... *good*.

Cage's eyes withdrew, but the drugged effect remained. His voice was still clear as he moved around Hiram, examining his transfixed subject like a butterfly under glass. There came the clunk of the lamp sitting down on the desk, the scuff of a heel dragging intentionally, languidly, fingertips tapping idly on the edge of the desk. "Well, this was unexpected," Cage said, smooth as honey. "I thought you'd gone safely home. Come back for something, did you?"

A deep compulsion moved Hiram's lips for him. "My son's stories."

"Ah, I see. Well, let's just work with the situation, shall we? You are an enigma, Marshal Wells. First, that miscreant over there held a gun to your chin, and you did not back down, now this. You were surprised to see me here but still not really frightened. Of course, I understand that this is all quite confusing, but I know *fear* when I smell it. Most men would have shit themselves the moment they saw me standing there. Most would have bent to my will immediately, too. You just cost me a refreshing amount of effort even in your state."

On the edge of his consciousness, Hiram sensed more so than acknowledged, the footsteps circling him, Cage still talking. "So… yes, you have me very intrigued indeed. Most humans do not deserve the life they're given. They don't notice the finer things, the details in the world around them. They don't appreciate what they have, where they are. They're not interesting enough to shine my boots. Take these two, for example. I may be a parasite, but am I really worse than the likes of them?" There was a flash of a gesture, a hand waving flippantly toward the quiet cells. "Yes… I've taken them off your hands for you. That's beside the point."

Hiram could not think, only listen, the words making sense but not really, especially the odd way Cage kept saying *humans* as if he was not, the way he called himself a *parasite…*

"But you… you are interesting. Interesting and sharp, and you pay attention. How old are you, Marshal Wells?"

"Thirty-nine." Hiram barely heard his hollow response.

"Is it true that you remember every face you see? Every name?"

The question buoyed him a little closer to the surface again, pushed away some of the pleasant fog. He distantly felt his jaw clench.

"Stop fighting it, Marshal," Cage's voice whispered in his ear.

The numb comfort closed back in, and the compulsion returned. "I remember everything," he answered.

"Fascinating. Can you recall memories of the womb?"

It was a question that would make Hiram nearly choke in normal circumstances, but with his mind so muddled, floating and compliant, he stared within at a flash of soft orange glow framed in branches of red. Ears packed with fluid through which two tiny heartbeats thrummed steadily, suspended in warmth and peace.

"Yes."

"Hmmm. I have a thousand questions for you now. Ah, but we haven't the time for that now. As it stands, that memory of yours complicates things. It may even mean something far greater if it's the sign I think it is." His voice dropped to a more reflective, concerned tone, "Far greater indeed...

"But all that aside, you're keen enough to discover what we're doing here on your own if I drag it out long enough, then you'll either make a formidable enemy or a great ally. Thus, I'm going to save you for last and then see what I should do with you."

And there were the silver eyes again, in front of Hiram, driving the narcotic effect deeper. He felt a cool hand on his chin, holding him firm to ensure their gazes remained locked.

"So here is what will happen tonight. For once, you're going to *forget*. Everything you've seen here from the moment you saw me, everything we've discussed. Or rather, that *I've* discussed. The memory will still be there but lurking just out of your grasp, a strange itch that you won't be able to scratch for the time being. You're going to blame it on fatigue. You're so tired and tipsy. It has been such a long night, and so much has happened. You'll go home and sleep it off, sleep later into the morning than usual, but you'll awaken with a clear head ready to come back here and see this little mess that I'm leaving for you to clean up. I'm curious to see what you'll do with it. Do not disappoint me."

A hand appeared before Hiram's hazy eyes, thumb and middle finger fixing together before...

Snap.

Becker raised a forearm in time to stop the deadly claws from swiping at his face, heard Nora shriek in a fury, perhaps as surprised as he was at her loss of strength. That must be the way of the *enérgeia*. The forces of faith might not destroy these things, but they were weakened, perhaps disoriented, given the way their bodies behaved in its presence. No wonder they kept servants that were just human enough to withstand it.

Still, it was a struggle holding her back. She raised the other hand to swipe, and he caught that wrist, cringed as the sharp tips grazed one cheek too close to an eye for comfort. Ellie's repeated screams reached him in a Doppler effect, growing louder, compressing, and then thinning again along with her and Caleb's footfalls chucking past, going straight toward the Palace.

"Ellie, not there!" Caleb's voice shouted. "Elllllie!"

Becker tried to turn his head, get a look, but they had already faded into the haze, and right behind them, Morgan Reed's figure was catching up. He wasn't running at full speed, so maybe his injuries lingered, but it was enough given his shorter quarry.

He stared up into his assailant's shadowed face, making out angry black eyes and white teeth as her lips curled back. She didn't seem to want to bite him, not after his holy water stunt, but he still maneuvered to keep her from trying. They were almost in a stalemate. He couldn't let go, she wouldn't stop trying to rip his face off, and all the while, he could feel the stiffness of the stake hidden in his coat sleeve, held carefully in place by the cuff of his shirt.

"Hey, over here! Leave her alone!" Caleb's voice shouted from somewhere further up the thoroughfare.

Ellie screamed out long shrill notes, barely pausing, from somewhere around the front of the Palace, accompanied by an enraged, "Come here!" that was Morgan Reed.

Sometimes risks needed to be taken. Concern for the Wells children gave him enough strength to push Nora off. For seconds she teetered back, and he wiggled his arm to manipulate the end of the stake into his palm. It was not the entire length, but when she came at him a second time, he was already raising the point. He saw her open hand flashing toward his face, closed his eyes, and turned his head while he shoved the point up into her side and rolled to his left to get all the leverage he could behind the thrust.

The claws came down in a full swipe. His right temple and cheek took the blow, three burning lacerations opening up at the same time she let out a scream and tossed back her hair as her body bowed. Becker kept putting pressure on the stake, estimating the point had penetrated up to two inches into her stomach, maybe her upper large intestine if vampire anatomy maintained any resemblance to its prior human structure. As he turned onto his side, he let go of her other wrist and tucked his chin, further getting his eyes out of range before she took one out. Flailing claws slashed into his hairline, and blood trails ran down his forehead, and then he was over, putting his weight on the stake and shoving the point deeper. By his estimation, it was passing her stomach now, angling upward to get under her rib cage. Skin and muscle sealed around the weapon, making impalement all the more challenging. With one loud cry of his own, Becker gripped the stake with both hands and shoved, drove it as deep as it would go, and in the next move freed a hand to fumble the second vial of holy water out of his other coat pocket.

By some miracle, the thin glass had not gotten broken in the struggle. He popped off the stopper with his thumb and dashed it upon her, some splashing into her mouth. Her shrieking shifted to little disoriented mewling noises. One hand weakly grasped the base of the stake while the other flailed pitifully over the dusty ground as she stared upwards. Her body took on the rippling, flickering effect as if she might blink out of existence, yet she remained solid matter. Her claws reverted to small, feminine hands, and the ink in her eyes bled back as if the monstrous side of her were coming undone, and she struggled to hold onto it.

Becker crawled back from her, got his feet under him started to rise. *A seizure*, he realized in the briefness he had to analyze it. It was the equivalent of a seizure. Everything had happened so fast he had not had a second to track Genevieve, but her angry, inhuman shout gave her away as she came in from somewhere behind him.

"Noooooooooo!"

In grabbing the second vial of holy water, his hand had also brushed his cross. He fished for it as he spun around, knees straining under him to get into a full stand and face the incoming threat. Genevieve struck him like a battering ram, pushing him backward and pinning him against the support on the bakery corner. A stabbing pain erupted in his lower side, forcing a raucous cry out of him.

Before him, Genevieve's face, lovely and porcelain, had transformed into a twisted, ugly thing with its black eyes and snarl. Tiny glints of moonlight, penetrating the haze, defined long canines dripping with saliva. Her delicate brow had sunken into a vicious glare, but it didn't last long.

Becker's hand was firmly pressed against her chest, keeping her from plunging her fangs into his throat. In the pause, he looked down to see that she'd stabbed him with her claws. With her fingers spread, she'd penetrated his side torso up to her first knuckles while the razor-thin tips of her nails reached deeper. The wounds were inflicted on soft tissue, he readily estimated, but they still hurt like hell.

He realized it was the contact with his blood that had stopped her from stabbing deeper. The grimace of rage on her face turned to shock. The shuddering effect took hold of her, and Becker seized that moment to pull the cross from his pocket and present it directly to her face.

She let out a sharp gasp and stepped back, jerking her hand free from his body in the same motion. She gaped down at her bloody fingers and then up again. Becker clamped his other hand over his side, compressing the four minor stab wounds as best he could, given the situation, and held the cross out in the air.

Nora continued to shudder and seize on the ground nearby while Genevieve held herself together, looking down at her lover with worry.

"You ladies do love to tempt fate, don't you?" he said.

Lucinda heard the distant grappling in the front room as she came around, last recalling that in fleeing into the furthest back rooms of the vaults, she'd pulled over anything she could to hinder her path. She'd torn through old paper mâché props from long ago productions, ripped down costume racks of musty clothes, shelves of tools, and finally, in the deepest room, planks and pieces of disassembled platform used for outdoor presentations. For every obstacle she sent crashing to the ground behind her, August dodged it with ease until he was upon her.

There were four of these rooms in all, the doorways forming one long opening through which the now distant light of the dressing room showed. When she reached the fourth and final room, her thoughts spun for defensive options she did not have.

"August, please, stop!" she cried as his arms wrapped around her from behind, pulled her backward into a tight embrace. He grabbed her wrists and pinned them across her chest while she stared outward into the dark, the shapes of more stage pieces and two presentation podiums before her as well as the last wall at the very back of the vaults. Now she was cornered, and her heart raced to a dizzying height.

"Lucinda, calm down," he whispered in her ear. "It is not as bad as you think. I promise. You're scared now, and I understand that. The pestilence also makes you reactionary, instinctive. That will pass once you're blooded and have more control. You'll see."

"I don't want to be *blooded!*" She resorted to one of her brother's tactics. Prying one hand free, she brought her elbow back into his ribs as hard as she could muster. Like his shin, his ribs proved as sensitive as they would be for any human man. She scrambled free and reached for one of the podiums, felt him grasp at her again.

"Get away from me!" she shouted and gripped the edges of the narrow wooden block with its slant top, then pulled it forward as she side-stepped. She was wearing down, she knew. While a bizarre cold filled her middle, on the surface, she broke out in a sweat.

"Lucinda!" Jesse's voice called from the front room under the stage, and she spun around, freezing in place.

August, too, stopped in his next advance and straightened, head tilted. "Well," he said in a low, hungry rasp, "if it isn't the man of the hour." He turned and took a step toward the opening to head back toward the dressing room.

"Jesse!" she shouted and ran forward to grab August's arm, to stall him. "Jesse, he's coming!"

Before she could do anything more, August spun and shoved her back, sent her colliding with a collection of oak planks stored against the left wall. She heard the planks topple around her right before the back of her head hit the brick, and she slid down. Sparks danced behind her eyes as she lost her breath and tilted over, caught herself on her elbow as her hearing suddenly took on a strange underwater effect. Her mouth bobbed open, fighting to pull in a breath, and for an instant, she blinked out. Everything went dark... hearing, seeing, feeling.

Then it all exploded back into place, and she gasped, pulled in a deep lungful of musty air and coughed it back out. Above her, the boards of the main floor and the joists creaked from movement, and she heard muffled voices, one that might even be her father speaking, but the noises in the vaults drew her attention far more.

A struggle was happening in the dressing room, and she realized she'd been out for a handful of minutes, enough for August to do more damage. She heard Jesse let out a heart-rending scream of pain and murmured, 'No... no... no...' as she staggered to her feet, paused to hold a hand to the back of her sore head. She put one foot in front of the other and leaned into it as she passed through one opening, wove back through her prior path where a giant paper maché dog lay busted in the middle of the floor. The light grew closer, and then she had only one more room to clear. Ahead lay the first costume rack she'd overturned in her flight, and when she reached that door, braced the old brick edge of the opening, she feared she would find Jesse already dead. Perhaps he would be a mangled mess that August had fed upon. Maybe his neck would be broken. Maybe...

He was on his knees.

Lucinda caught a breath of bittersweet relief to see that he was not dead but hunched over, catching his breath as August stood over him straight and strong, domineering.

"Get up, dog," August spat bitterly.

They were both facing away from her, leaving her to wonder what exactly she'd missed, but it was to her greatest shock when Jesse slowly rose to his feet, straightened, and turned around to face August with a blank stare in his eyes. Blood leaked from the corner of his mouth, marbled with spit as it slid down to his chin, and some appeared caked around the edges of his nostrils.

"Jesse?" she uttered.

His gaze did not shift to look at her. His brow did not furrow at the sound of his name, nor did any other line deepen in his face indicating some acknowledgment.

August turned to her, those black eyes angled in such a way as to look devious, especially with the slight upward curl to his sculpted lips. "I saved him for you, Lucinda. Jesse will make a fine addition to our household staff." He chuckled as if he thought himself so clever. "Think of his life as a wedding present."

Lucinda stepped from the doorway, eased carefully around the heaps of costumes, but one snagged her foot and caused her to trip while she still fought through the wooziness of knocking her head on brick. So, this was to be it? Was August going to use Jesse somehow as an enthralled hostage?

August caught her under the arms, hefted her to her feet and held her steady. "Don't worry. He's right as rain now." He pulled her into him, arms holding her tighter. She tolerated his light little kisses while she stared past his shoulder at the figure who seemed utterly vacant.

"What did you do to him?" she whispered.

"I've healed him," August said gently, dropped another kiss along the angle of her cheek as he worked his way to her lips. "I've given his life a *real* purpose."

It was all Lucinda could do not to weep, to mourn Jesse even as he stood there alive, dusty and worn.

"He'll protect us," August said softly and guided her to sit on the edge of the chaise lounge again. "Protect you."

It was the last thing she wanted, and she feared for Jesse's life—and his mind—more than ever. She'd seen what longevity had done to Jasper O'Brian, what a husk it had left of him once he was cast aside. Further, she feared what August might do if she didn't cooperate. *This* Jesse, rendered vacant and dumb, would stand by and take any amount of abuse, only to be healed by August's blood to start over again.

She surrendered as he laid her back down and stretched himself upon her. He dropped light kisses along the crook of her neck. The sensations were not without their appeal, soft, little damp butterflies dancing their way over her collar bone to the swell above her bodice. All the while, she watched Jesse stare at nothing.

"I've never wanted anything as much as I want you, Lucinda," August whispered. He was back to her ear now, nuzzling her lobe. "I promise you an eternity of roses."

Why? she asked herself. Oh, *why* had she pitted them against each other? She'd been so bored in the Bend, wanted culture and excitement. When it came along, she'd played up to it, pursued it, presented everything she knew about art and theater to August to impress him when she was just a simple girl, grieving and desperate and feeling trapped. August embodied everything she'd dreamed of seeing beyond the borders of her wilting little town, the escape she thought she wanted. But then she'd used that to try to force some culture on Jesse, to unfairly change him into something he was not, and utmost she'd relished their competing attentions. It was more wretched unfairness she'd put Jesse through, testing him to see how far he'd go.

And here he was, caught up in it, lost, and it was all her fault.

She felt August's cool hand carefully push up her skirt as it maneuvered along the side of her leg, fingers spidering into her junction, the pad of his thumb beginning to circle hard against the cotton of her pantalets. Were the circumstances different and she felt the same passion for him, it would have sent waves of pleasure up through her, hardened her nipples against the inside of her bodice. A few days ago, she would have tipped head-on into it, embraced him back, but now his true intent glared blatantly. Looking over his shoulder, she braced when she saw how Jesse's brow furrowed just slightly, the first sign of any emotion or resistance in him.

August was making him *watch* this, torturing him, she realized, and tears welled up fresh, spilled over. Her cruel new lover-to-be did not notice as his face remained buried in her neck, lips nipping at her ear.

"I'm sorry," she whispered. "I'm so sorry." Then she closed her eyes and shut out everything, let the heavy sinking feeling in her chest pull her toward a state of numbness. That was where she'd stay, no matter what August did. He could blood her all he wanted, and that might force a new way of life upon her that she'd not asked for, but she would never give in and return his passion. Maybe, in time, he'd see that he'd killed her inside, too.

But she doubted it.

Men like August, she knew now, would never recognize their own horrible flaws or what they did to other people. The creature, the *vampire*, had nothing to do with that.

All she felt were her tears spilling over, running down her temples into her hair, flooding her ears, and she thought she heard her heartbeat slowing down, while August's boomed from his desire, vibrating from his chest into hers, and nearby, there was Jesse's, steady, unfazed.

Was this what her father felt, with the pestilence raging through him?

She drifted, burrowing deeper into that self-drugged place in her mind where August couldn't reach her, but then something else did. The third heartbeat in the room, Jesse's, rose ever so. She thought at first that she was fooling herself, but then the space between one beat and the next closed tighter and tighter until the beats hammered more rapidly than they were a minute ago.

It was as she started to drag her bleary eyes back open that she saw the shadow move, almost silently, except for the minuscule scuff of a boot on the floor, and then August was grabbed from behind and hauled off of her with tremendous strength and force. The immediate absence of his weight upon her felt like a slab lifting, giving her breath back. At the same moment, she glimpsed his arms and legs flailing as he arced up, out of view.

Lucinda lifted her head in time to see Jesse spin August around and slam him into the top of the nearest vanity. The mirror cracked with a *spack* and spider-webbed out from August's shoulders, the shards clinging like puzzle pieces in the frame. The oil lamp next to them toppled over, and the hurricane shattered. Oil leaked out of the reservoir down through the wick and immediately sent a pool of flame over the other end of the table, catching on pots of makeup and wigs that went up with an immediate burst of light.

August roared at the interruption and swatted at Jesse, pushed back at him, but Jesse seemed infused with as great a strength of his own as he kept the thrashing vampire pinned, both men remaining dangerously close to the growing flames that were eating up the corner of the vanity and climbing the mirror's wood frame. Above, the heat singed a dark spot in the joists under the stage. Soon the blaze would eat a hole through the floor above.

Lucinda scrambled into a sit, got her feet back over the edge of the lounge and looked around desperately for a means to help. In the brilliance of the dancing flames, one thing caught her eye as it reflected the amber light in its broadside: the sword. The same one she'd seen Morgan Reed use to threaten her brother and sister. The blade rested half-snagged in the fabric of one of the chairs, which had a busted arm, while the handle dipped toward the floor. She had not witnessed how it had gotten there, but August hadn't seen fit to retrieve it or do anything else with it. She knelt to grab the handle, gasped to realize how heavy the thing was. She slid the blade free of the upholstery but then wavered off balance and had to get her forearm along the handle to give it enough support. That allowed her to seesaw the blade upward before it clattered on the floor.

The struggle on the vanity continued with August pushing back, his eyes black again, his face warped into a mask of rage and insult.

"You can't fight me, dog," he sneered at Jesse, who coolly said nothing as he fought to keep his nemesis pinned. "I'm your master." Then in a burst of strength, he worked his clawed hands between his body and Jesse's and dug in. Jesse let out a strained cry and involuntarily backed up as the claws ripped through his shirt and into his chest. The space was enough for August to shove him away from the vanity, and both careened over, two sets of feet losing purchase as they hit the floor amid the prone costume rack and its scattered contents.

Lucinda blinked at a strange sharpness that tracked readily with their movement, and for a moment, the sword did not feel quite so heavy.

August rose into the air, dragging Jesse with him as the ranch hand threw repeated punches at him, pouring in every ounce of bodily leverage that he could muster. They clung to each other for a matter of seconds before separating and plunging back to the floor. While August landed in a more experienced crouch, graceful and ready to lunge again, Jesse came down hard on one knee but kept his other foot planted, prepared to rise against the next attack.

By now, the flames in the corner of the room had climbed and caught on the joists. Smoke built up and crawled across the ceiling, growing thicker and lower.

The combatants stared at each other, Jesse's face still an unreadable mask, while August's mouth drew into a sneer, made all the worse by his black eyes as they stared at each other for a moment.

"You've got balls," August said, "I'll grant you that, but that will only make it all the more thrilling to break you over and over again."

Jesse didn't take his intense eyes off his opponent while his hand reached down into the top of his boot and drew out a ten or so inch length of wood with the end broken off into a sharp, splintery point. He flipped it around in his hand, held like a knife.

Lucinda was not sure what happened next with her senses, only that an acute awareness struck her. Time slowed, and her vision telescoped forward to note every visible muscle bracing in each man. Their jaws clenched in preparation, and each drew back two to three inches before launching at the other, arms reaching savagely. She lunged at the same time, raising the sword in both hands, unable to get the end of the blade much higher than her waist as she thrust it forward, instinct calculating and aiming at a small space of empty air that filled less than a second later as her target plunged into her path.

August roared as the tip of the blade pierced his side, below the ribs, up to at least four inches, and shoved him off course. It was more of a diversion than anything, but it was enough as he lost his forward momentum, and his focus on attacking Jesse turned to surprise. Jesse readily followed the shift, brought the stake back in his grip and pivoted the entire side of his body forward, driving it into the front of August's belly, angled upward to get under his ribs.

The vampire screamed and fell over backward, sliding off the end of the sword. Jesse went over right on top of him, straddled and pinned him, continued to shove the stake in, just enough to make the hole a little bigger, to drive a path through the flesh and beneath the rib cage.

Lucinda, meanwhile, adjusted her grip on the sword to go at August again. This time, she didn't thrust. She aligned herself, found the strength to raise the blade not just level with the floor but up high, going above her head. All the while, at her back, the flames roared. The tip of the blade reached high enough to swirl through the thickening layer of smoke.

The rest happened in only seconds, drawn out by August's horrific screams. His mouth gaped wide, his canine teeth and the incisors next to them extended into long, narrow fangs slathered in saliva. Jesse withdrew the stake, then, fingers pinched together, he shoved his entire hand into the hole, dug and pushed, flesh closing around his forearm. August swiped up at him, grazed his cheek and bowed to try to buck Jesse off, but that ceased when Lucinda brought the edge of the blade arcing down, aligned surprisingly—perfectly—with August's neck.

The cut was anything but neat. The edge clipped off the bottom of August's finely shaped chin and, with a wet crunch, severed vocal cords, effectively stopped the screaming and then lodged right at the line of vertebrae. Blood spurted out of his open mouth and began to spread around his head.

At the same time that August's head was almost cleaved free, Jesse found what he was going after and jerked back his elbow. His hand emerged from beneath August's ribs, tearing with it the bloody, tightly gripped mass of his heart. This, too, was not a neat severing. Tendons and skin trailed with it. The opening closed slightly back up while blood flooded out, and August lay still, his partially attached head staring up at the ceiling, mouth still forced open by the lengthy fangs. It looked like there might still be some awareness behind those inky eyes, enough consciousness lingering to experience shock at how things had turned, but no more was he the beautiful young man who had enraptured Lucinda upon first sight.

Jesse, holding the pulpy heart in his hand, hoisted himself off August's body but remained on one knee, unsteady, shaking.

"Jesse?" Lucinda gasped. She looked down at the handle of the sword, still gripped in her hands which seemed so small holding it, and she allowed herself a briefness to marvel at what she'd done. Then she dropped it. The handle and crossguard rattled on the floor while the edge of the blade remained cradled in the deep fissure of August's throat.

Somehow, the gore no longer alarmed her. She hurried around the body, knelt next to Jesse, ignoring that her knee came down in a spreading pool of blood, and pulled his neck into a tight hug. All the while, he gasped, caught his breath while the blood in his mouth oozed over his lips, and his right hand still gripped August's heart like a grizzly trophy.

"I'm right as…" he coughed, gurgling a little as he mocked August's words. "Right as rain."

He sounded so exhausted, still focused on shaking August's hold. It was all Lucinda could do not to break into a full sob for his sake. Instead, she allowed herself a few tears of joy to hear his voice, even if it was a little off. Part of her recognized the greatest irony of the situation. In attempting to enslave Jesse with his blood, August had given him the strength to fight back. How long it would last was the question.

Behind them, the flames consumed most of the vanity table. Sparks carried them to the lounging area, where they caught on the upholstery and thrived. Lucinda was the first to get to her feet, her arms around Jesse's middle as she tried to guide him up. He wavered, dazed, and stared down to locate the Colt her father had given him. He grabbed it with his free hand and fumbled it back into the holster, then worked up the momentum to stand.

The flames were still out of range but spreading and forcing her to raise her voice. "What do we do?" she said, anxiously pulling him toward the steps.

Jesse stared at the blaze, unconcerned. "Fire purifies," he said distantly and then looked down at the heart, his hand so bloodied as to appear melded with the meaty lump, fingers curled tightly around it as if to keep it from escaping. "I need to get this to Pastor Becker." His eyes swept down over them both from her dress now covered in blood to his own clothes, and then, finally, she felt the slick touch of his fingers on her neck at the area of the punctures. "I think we both need that cure now."

CHAPTER THIRTY-THREE

Caleb had run with Ellie in his arms even as the dust rolled in. With their heads tucked together and eyes squeezed shut, noses covered as best they could, they'd stayed in motion as if his legs had a mind of their own. All he could do was keep the sense of a straight line as he ran toward the opera house. The waves rolling in, pushing him from all sides, drove him off course, but when he could finally open his eyes, he made out Teddy's rump trotting head-on into the haze. Horses were far more adapted to the outdoors and hazardous conditions, but at least the storm had slowed the gelding down.

He thought it had slowed Morgan Reed down as well, but then he dared to look back and saw the man bleed out of the dust, still in pursuit, a crazed look in his dark eyes.

"Caweb he's stiw thew!" Ellie yelled in his ear.

Caleb leaned into it, coughed as the dust veil sucked in and scathed his throat. Then he didn't lift a foot high enough and tripped himself. He managed not to go tumbling entirely forward, but Ellie tipped out of his arms, screaming again. He stopped her from landing on anything worse than her knees, gripped her forearms and pulled her up as he continued running, slower now. So damned slow now.

"Run," he rasped, unable to get his voice louder than that. "Just run, Ellie."

"Caleb!" Pastor Becker's voice called from ahead. "Ellie! Over here!"

Caleb thought he could make out the man's shape ahead, an arm high and waving to them, and started for him, but then suddenly the pastor was gone, swept away as if a giant broom had come through. Something too fast to define parted the dust, slammed into him, and carried him across the thoroughfare to the other side. What followed was a scuffle with the growls of a wildcat over top Becker's grunts and groans, and Caleb's heart sank. The man couldn't defend them if he was busy defending himself. So Caleb kept running, dragging Ellie until, just at the front of the Palace, her hand tore free from his, and she veered away.

Caleb frantically turned to look after her, saw that she was scrambling for the hole in the front panel of the higher boardwalk, the one that Uncle Silas' horse had kicked in.

"Ellie, not there!" he shouted, but already she had dropped to her knees and wiggled into the hole, probably oblivious to the fact her brother was far too big to get in there, too, or that cornering oneself was not a great idea either. *"Elllllie!"* he called in further frustration.

Far more terrifying was that Morgan Reed went right for her.

"Shit," Caleb coughed. "Hey!" he yelled. Coughed again. "Over here!"

From deep within the hidey-hole she'd chosen, Ellie started screaming as Reed dropped to his knees and, disregarding the size of the hole, grabbed its edges with his big hands and began to rip out chunks of the brittle wood.

"Leave her alone!" Caleb screamed. His mind raced for a solution. Reed would strangle him if he tried to dive on him, and Ellie sounded decently lodged under there. The underside of the boardwalk ended where the front wall of the saloon began, so she couldn't go further than that, but maybe it was enough to buy Caleb time. He turned and bolted past the hotel and toward Fraleigh's Mercantile. By now, the haze had thinned, settling enough to allow in more moonlight, though Caleb's throat burned, and he knew shouting for help was no longer possible. He reached the front of the store and stopped, still hearing Ellie's muted screams.

The solution, scary as hell, seemed simple enough then.

If he couldn't lure Morgan Reed away from his sister, he'd take the battle back to Morgan Reed.

Stepping up onto the shorter boardwalk in front of the mercantile, he boosted up on the balls of his feet and pulled a lantern down from the underhang, covered his eyes with one elbow, then threw the entire lantern, base first, furiously at the front window on the left. Shattering glass pierced his ears and rained down. He lowered his arm and scrambled over the sill, cutting his hands as he went, and turned to the left wall where Mr. Fraleigh had always displayed the farm tools, among which was an ax that Caleb had had his eyes on for some time.

"Why do you need that when we've got a perfectly good ax in the barn?" Papa had said. "You already killed a rattler with it just fine."

Caleb didn't remember the incident with the rattler quite so well, only that it had almost gotten him chewed out. Didn't matter. Mr. Fraleigh's display was up too high, meant to be out of reach for kids like Caleb with their curiosity and determination. Caleb had the latter in spades. He had to step up on a crate to reach the ax, but in moments it was in his hands, and he was clambering back over the windowsill.

Ellie's screams persisted, a beacon through the haze. By the time Caleb returned, Reed's lower body protruded out of the hole from the hips down.

"Come here, you little shit!" the man's angry shout came from under the boards along with some thumping around. There was no telling what was going on under there except that Ellie was probably kicking with her screaming. Then abruptly, Morgan Reed started screaming, too. It was not an expression of rage but a startled cry of pain. The man's lower half bucked and squirmed, began to shift backward as he started extracting himself from the hole.

Caleb didn't care why the turn of events. He barely had time to see that something was crawling on Reed's back before he raised the ax high and brought it down on the man's spine below the shoulder blades.

A sickening wet crunch sounded, and blood splattered up the wedge of the ax's blade. Reed's scream reached a crescendo. Caleb wrenched the ax free, raised it, brought it down again with a fire in his head that told him not to stop until the bad man stopped moving. Hot tears streamed from his eyes, rinsing the dust free, making rivulets down his cheeks. He gritted his teeth and found his voice again, even if it made his throat feel like he'd swallowed razor blades.

"Get!"

Crunch.

"Away!"

Crunch.

"From!"

Crunch.

"My!"

Crunch.

"Sister!"

By now, the screaming had stopped. Reed's back was a bloody mess of ripped shirt, pulped skin and chunked vertebrae, and he lay still on his belly, though one leg twitched.

Caleb raised the ax one more time, only to find a gentle hand on his arm.

"Caleb, stop," Pastor Becker's voice broke through the tunnel down which his senses had traveled, fixed like a train on tracks. "He's dead, boy! You can stop now!"

Snot flooded from his nose as Caleb broke into a full sob. "I killed him," he said under his ragged breath. "I *killed* him." The gross, disturbing act of it caught up with him. He had taken a man's life, even a man who…

… *was disintegrating.*

Caleb shouted and backed away as he watched Morgan Reed's corpse turn from flesh-toned to gray and withered before it collapsed with a whoosh of dust, and his clothes fell in. A bloom of small scorpions ran out from the settling cloud.

He shuddered and dropped the ax, still shaking off the sensation of feeling the blade hack through skin and bone. He looked up at the pastor and saw that he was holding out his cross, keeping the red-haired vampiress at bay as she threatened to approach one moment then retreated the next, her teeth bared, a low growl issuing from her throat.

"Ellie?" Caleb called hoarsely. "You okay?"

"Yeah," her voice answered with a tremble.

"Stay there an' be still." If what he'd just seen was any indication, there was a scorpion nest under there with her. Still, it was better to deal with that than to have Cage Edwards or one of his goons eating her neck.

"You okay, son?" Pastor Becker asked, not taking his eyes off the woman.

"Y-yeah," Caleb said and coughed again.

A loud bang sounded from the area of the opera house. The dust haze had settled enough that he could see the figure of a man thrown out onto the street, tumbling several feet, a long coat flapping with each roll until he came to a stop face down, sprawled and still.

Caleb's breath hitched, and new dread gripped him.

It was his father.

*
**

Hiram blinked and, with a jolt, found himself lying on the floor of the opera house, a heavy knee still on his chest. His stomach flipped as the memory of that night in the jail settled into its proper space in the puzzle of his mind.

Cage, cool as ice, smiled like a brother who had just come home from a long holiday. "I kept watching you that night," he added. "From the pinnacle of the saloon, I tracked you, crouched and curious to see what would happen. Even after the volition it took for me to suppress your memory, you still fought it. You thought you were about to have a breakdown when you stopped outside the saloon, but it was only your instinct telling you something was wrong. You knew you had an unprecedented gap in your mind, and you were desperate to fill it. Hell, you even broke my command. You were supposed to go home and sleep, but you fell upon your friend's doorstep."

"You were in my head," Hiram said through his teeth, new rage bubbling up at the very idea of the violation.

"Hardly. Your doors were shut tight. I just slipped a letter through the crack, and you read it."

With a shout and a new surge of strength, Hiram grabbed onto Cage's knee and rolled sideways, dumping the other man's weight off and throwing him over. Cage turned the off-balance maneuver into a graceful roll and recovered as he came up, back into another kneel before he rose and turned back around.

Hiram got to his knees, looked across the floor where his Colt had come to rest near a bank of folded chairs. Bullets, even blessed ones, might not kill a vampire, but if he could get at least one lodged in Cage's body, maybe the disruption would gain him an upper hand.

But Cage had already followed Hiram's gaze, so when the marshal moved, the vampire moved, too. Hiram scrambled to his feet, cleared several paces and dove toward the Colt, but just as he slid toward it, his hand opened and closing in, a foot kicked it away. Cage reached down and flipped him over, grabbed him by the lapels, and hoisted him to his feet.

"My patience is wearing thin, Marshal," he said and drew back a fist, slammed it across Hiram's jaw, whipping his head sideways.

366

The real pain of it exploded in Hiram's mouth as he bit his tongue, but he shuddered more as the taste of blood welled up. It might be his own, but the gnawing in his core rose to meet it. He groaned as he weakly pivoted his head back around and found Cage staring with ink-black eyes.

"Tell me something, Cage," he said, dribbling a combination of blood and spit. He gulped the blood down, but it only made his stomach lurch all the more. Oh God, he wanted *more*. "Are you still a man… or just a monster?"

Cage paused, clearly taken aback by the question. "Why do you ask *that*?" His lips curled back, revealing gritted teeth with the canines now long and sharp.

"Because if you're a man, I can still do this." Hiram gave his body a little blunt but precise twist as he brought up his knee and connected it strongly with Cage's groin.

Cage cried out and let go, but he hardly doubled over the way an ordinary human man would having his balls kicked. The distraction, however, served its purpose. Hiram reached beneath his coat, found the blunt end of the chair leg that he'd tucked into his belt at the small of his back, and withdrew it.

He flipped it in his hand and shoved the pointed end up, planning to plunge it into Cage's belly at an angle that would slip just beneath the fence of his rib cage and into his heart chamber. The tip only made it perhaps an inch in before Cage gripped the makeshift stake, gave a jerk and pulled it free. A bloom of red appeared on his shirt but didn't grow very much. With little effort, he ripped the stake from Hiram's hand.

"That was cheap," the vampire snarled.

The next thing Hiram knew, he and Cage both rose into the air as Cage leaped, hauling him along. He felt the dizzying rapid climb, saw the ceiling and the glittering edge of the chandelier's sharp crystal points growing closer, then a disorienting pause midair before the plunge came. They came down on the stage, on the pallet of soil that served as a false cemetery. Hiram's head bounced in the pile, and a spray of the dirt shot out from under him, but he recovered just in time to grab and stop the stake from coming down directly into his own heart.

Cage snarled at him and leaned hard on the blunt end, pushing the point down until it connected with the exact spot where Hiram had almost been pierced by the one Jasper O'Brian had employed to kill Silas. It stung as it dug through the scab and thin layer of skin and ground against his sternum. Then to his horror and pain, he felt the platform of bone cave slightly with a dull crack.

Hiram screamed and pushed back. Somewhere beneath him, under the stage, he thought he heard another scream, a shriek, a scuffle, but his greater attention remained on the deadly tip of the stake. How fitting that it should be used on him instead of its intended target. He realized that Cage had paused, held the stake in place right where the agony worsened, and Hiram's heartbeat thundered.

"You can't beat me, Marshal. You can take hits, and you may be recovering faster, but you'll never be strong enough to stop *me*. You haven't even fed for the first time."

Hiram tried to rock sideways to throw the weight off, turned his head and looked around for something to grab that might aid him. He glimpsed a prop skull sitting at the base of one of the fake tombstones, staring at him through dark sockets, like real death grinning in amusement. Then he was forced to apply all of his attention to Cage again. The slow, descending pressure caused the stake not to break completely through but to press his entire sternum in, gradually tearing the cartilage and muscle connecting his ribs. He threw his head back, eyes squeezed shut and tears streaming as, for a fleeting moment, he visualized the entire bone plate tearing free and caving in.

Humanly impossible if you ask me.

Becker's words about the Evans brothers' bodies and their twisted-off heads came to him, and he knew then that Cage spoke the truth. He could not beat something that could move so fast, remove a man's head with bare hands, that could dig up into a chest past belly and liver without a knife and rip out a heart. And, most of all, he could not defeat a being that could command the elements of earth and wind to a life of their own and wall off an entire town.

"Just... don't," Hiram pleaded through his teeth, "don't hurt my family... please." The torture of it cut him off. He braced for the final thrust of wood and broken bone down into his heart.

It never came.

Cage paused, suddenly sniffed the air and then eased off, pulled the stake free. His frown seemed to redirect from Hiram to something else.

Hiram drew in a breath and smelled it, too.

Smoke.

It seeped up between the cracks in the stage floor from somewhere over in the corner beneath a panel that served as a castle wall. He heard the boards there warping, the sound of flames licking and building, and layered somewhere beneath that, someone was screaming horribly, and Hiram's senses could no longer separate who it might be.

Cage stood up over him, the stake still in his hand. "Here's the thing. I don't wish to kill you, not really, and not if my hunch is correct. I will if I have to, though."

Gasping for breath, astonished, Hiram winced and shuddered. "Hunch?" The pain lingered on the surface around his sternum then faded, but the churning in his middle remained, niggling and teasing him.

Cage walked over to the other end of the stage and collected his coat. He cocked an ear, listened, drew in a long breath that he analyzed, eyes narrowed. "Hmmm," he murmured and looked toward the door that led down to the vaults. "I sense that Mr. Chandler has shuffled off his immortal coil."

Hiram thought of his daughter down there, along with Jesse, and needed to know if they were all right. What was happening? Were they clear of the fire? He rolled off the stage, legs folding forward, and landed in a crouch before springing up and running toward the vault door. "Lucinda!" he shouted. "Jesse!"

Before he reached the opening, Cage appeared before him, already pivoting a hard swing with the back of a fist that cracked on his jaw and sent him flying back. He reeled but recovered, and in a new rage, dove at Cage with his arms forward, aiming to tackle him and throw him back.

But Cage was gone, already a blur, and Hiram could only turn, trying to follow, losing track of him. If he'd had time to think about each move and how his opponent had resorted to maneuvers of a virtually untouchable nature, he'd have understood that Cage was attempting to wear him down. He'd have recognized that all bets were off, and the vampire was tired of playing if that was what he'd been doing.

For every attack Hiram now tried, there was an evasion so fast and clever that he only grew more frustrated, more stupid until all he could hear was the blood racing in his veins, and all he hit was empty air. Brighter light flickered in the far corner of the stage as the fire ate its way through, and in seconds began to consume the backdrop and the wall panel.

Hiram was near the doors now, Cage stalking toward him, when he was distracted to see two shapes emerge from the doorway on the far left of the stage, both familiar, both dear, and the moment of relief he felt cost him the attention he should have been paying to Cage. The vampire rushed in with a hard slam to Hiram's middle that sent him crashing out through the doors and into the night.

He hit the ground and tumbled over and over until stopping, belly down. He groaned and lay still for a few seconds before getting an elbow under him to at least push his face up from the ground, head hanging. Everything hurt. There were no longer isolated pains from taking punches, no singular stings from the slashes Cage's claws had delivered. His skin hummed with a disorienting soreness; his veins felt like stiff wires strung around his bones.

Slowly, he got his bearing and looked up through the settling haze and the muted effect it created in the air. The night sky cleared around it, deep blue-black and glittering with stars and the patches of the Milky Way arcing over the half-moon that was so bright, Hiram had to look back down and blink away the glaring white spots trapped in his eyes.

"Papa!" Caleb called, and Hiram's head shot up. New questions shot through his mind. Why wasn't Caleb in the church? Where was Ellie? Why was Teddy standing over him, looking at him like he was a damned fool?

The horse snorted, and Hiram winced as he flipped himself over to sit up. With the opera house straight in front of him, he found to his left, Nora Long lay still in the street, a pale, limp form in a bloodied, gauzy dress, while on the other side, near the Palace, Becker stood holding Genevieve Blakely at bay with a cross while keeping Caleb shielded behind him.

All of them were a reasonable distance apart, but his vision picked them out easily enough. The two vampiresses, like their leader, had no appeal, but Hiram shuddered to realize he could smell Becker's blood from here, and Caleb's and even his horse's, and it made his body hurt all the more, especially down in his needling core.

Cage stepped into the opening of the opera house, backlit by the growing flicker of the fire. He'd pulled on his coat and now stepped out into the street, advancing on Hiram with a hitch in his shoulders as if ready to attack, then he paused to look around as well, surveying the situation.

All Hiram could muster, for that moment, was to stay on his ass, propped up on his hands, knees bent and ready to back crawl because he wasn't sure he could stand anymore.

Genevieve had taken her eyes off of Becker and Caleb, looked at her leader for advice as her body shuddered and blinked, solid one moment, illusion the next, and she seemed trapped in that state, unable to make a move.

As quickly as his dander had raised, Cage calmed and gave a jerk of his head. "Genevieve, stand down," he said. "See to Nora."

She backed away from Becker, the distance strengthening her again as the shuddering, flickering effect stabilized, though her hand hung awkwardly at her side, and Hiram made out dark sheaths of blood on her fingers. "We aren't finished here," she said in a throaty growl.

"We are," Cage said shortly. "Take her and leave. *Now.*"

"But, Cage—"

"*Leave!*"

She blurred at the enraged command, her motion in the air stirring around Hiram. He heard hoof clops and equine grumbles and realized that the other two horses were also out of the cemetery and milling around the thoroughfare. Up near the bakery, Genevieve materialized in a kneel over Nora. There was a wet crunch as the stake came free and, a moment later, a hoarse gasp.

Hiram followed the sounds, saw how Genevieve cradled Nora's body tenderly, a thick sense of relief hovering in the air around them as Genevieve kissed the other woman's face repeatedly, murmuring to her. Then in a gust of wind and mist, they were both simply… *gone.*

The way these creatures could move so fast as to be a mere blur, and now this apparent ability to turn to mist, only now caught up with him how Cage had seemed able to show up out of nowhere, just on the edge of sunset. Hiram had thought the crazy actor was walking everywhere he went rather than ride any of the horses available to him, which O'Brian and Reed had both used for their own transportation. But now he saw those sudden appearances and timings for what they were, carefully crafted deceptions to throw off human perception. Every step, every appearance, played on the habit of assumption.

He looked back toward Cage, whose eyes appeared to be tracking the women's departure, seeing something that everyone else present could not as his gaze swept upward and toward the northeast away from town. Behind the tall vampire, Lucinda and Jesse appeared in the doorway of the opera house and stepped out.

Thank God, he thought. For them to both be standing there meant that August Chandler had been defeated, somehow. The difficulty of the task was particularly etched on Jesse's face. He next noticed that the kid held, in one hand, the bloody mass of a heart—hell, he could smell that, too, but it was nowhere as appetizing as the thought of the fresh human blood around him. Jesse's other hand, Hiram saw, gripped Lucinda's tightly. That sight made his own heart feel good, at least. His daughter had made her choice, the right one, and then it occurred to him how Cage had seemed relatively calm about losing a member of his troupe. August Chandler had apparently failed to endear himself to his leader, and there was something sad in that, though Hiram didn't plan to waste any tears on it.

Cage, for his part, made no further move, only stood over Hiram as his gaze circled back around to the marshal sprawled on the ground before him.

The night breeze distributing the last of the dust stirred his coat and hair. His eyes, restored from black to gray again, refocused, intent, no sign of fear whatsoever. He was not alone, certainly. He'd dismissed Genevieve and Nora for reasons that remained a mystery in the eerie quiet that descended, but Hiram had no doubt he could call them back.

The now-familiar chill in Hiram pulsed, and the night around him fell into a totality for merely a second before he shook it off, groaning as the hunger churned. He looked toward Becker, who had lowered his cross and approached slowly but kept a reasonable distance. Caleb edged behind him, curious and scared at the same time.

"It's closing in on you, Marshal," Cage said. "You don't have much time left. Why don't we take this elsewhere? I believe you know where to find me."

With that, he spread his arms out and transformed. The whole of his body condensed into a black fog, shrunk slightly, and then shaped out into something winged that flapped and hovered briefly in the air over Hiram before veering away and rising on the winds. It sailed toward the northwestern side of town, moonlight catching on its silent feathers.

Hiram gaped and, despite all of the discomfort wracking his body, turned himself over to get on his knees and push to his feet. "An owl," he said under his breath. "He turned into an owl." He remembered *that* owl, similar to a screech owl with its bars and horn-like tips, but far too large, far too dark, and its eyes the glossy-ink spheres that Cage's had become during their brawl. "Fuck," he rasped and glared after the disappearing shadow. "He's been watching me this entire time." Hadn't the restoration of his memory from the jail incident proven that?

"Family *strigidae*," the pastor said, "the Greeks had their form of vampire called the *strix*. It took owl form." Again, presenting more of the bizarre arcane knowledge he'd been hiding in that head of his.

"Well, I've seen that same goddamned owl," Hiram spat. "It was watching me out at the Hanson farm nearly two weeks ago." He recalled the bizarre bird, unlike any owl he'd ever seen in all of his desert living, and how it watched him, and he, in an attempt at humor, had tipped his hat to it. "This started there," he said, thinking out loud. "At least, Cage's interest in *me* did."

"He's luring you out alone," Becker said as Jesse and Lucinda stepped up to his side.

"And I have to go," Hiram concluded, looking at his daughter, who stared back with her large brown eyes, so like her mother, and he thought his heart was going to break all over again. "Somehow, this all ended up between him and me. I don't know how or why, but he called me out."

Caleb came running up behind them, and a moment later, Ellie, too. Hiram didn't see where she'd come from, but she scrambled into him, and he fought the pounding temptation that dug into him with every little beat of her heart and the sweet smell of her.

"God," he whispered.

"Papa?" Lucinda uttered, the quiver in her voice indicating she knew the truth. After everything she'd been through, she had grown up by years within the space of a few days. Still, there was enough hope in her to ask, "Can't you just try the cure?"

He wished it were possible but, somehow, he believed Jasper's and Cage's claim. What he felt coursing inside him would not respond to holy water or the ash of August's heart or some herb Becker had grown with tender care in his garden. "I think we can all agree this is it." He gripped a hand over his belly, winced, and again pushed back patches of darkness, blinked to find his children all had tears in their eyes, and so did Becker and Jesse. "I'll say it again. I love you all so much. Between your mother and you, you all saved *me* far more than you'll ever know, but I've got to finish this, or Cage and his kind will be a plague on the world forever."

Becker nodded. "I know." He indicated the heart in Jesse's hand. "And I have work to do here."

Hiram nodded and started to back away from them, aching with every step.

Caleb had shed tears once and now again, but there were no objections except from Ellie, whom he had to pry free. He hugged her and kissed the top of her head, then he turned and approached Teddy, whose ears pricked forward curiously.

He stroked the gelding's blaze, scratched under the angles of his jaw. "Well, Theodore," he said pointedly. "One more good ride, boy?"

A snuffle answered him, and then Hiram climbed into the saddle and reined the horse into a mad race into the night.

CHAPTER THIRTY-FOUR

He didn't look at his home as he raced by, tried not to think about how hard he was driving his horse—faithful, stubborn Teddy, whom Lucinda had named when she was eleven years old—whose breath chuffed ruggedly. Outside of town, the boundary of the dust storm became apparent in the swept pattern across the road, and the last of the sediment hanging in a low layer stirred up as he passed through.

Although the landscape ahead appeared clearly and silver-lit to his vision, cloudy black tendrils were closing in around the edges, creating a tunnel in his head. With each hoof-pounding stride forward, he outpaced that crawling darkness just enough, forced it behind him, but it made the dash for Pit Creek seem far longer than the many times in the past he'd made the trip at a casual trot.

He reached the old, twisted mesquite tree that served as a signpost for the Hanson farm before Teddy had enough and whinnied as he skidded to a bucking halt, done with his rider and maybe the whole goddamned situation.

Hiram drew in the reins hard with a *"Whooooa, boy!"* He swayed and balanced until there was just enough of an ebb for him to kick a leg over and boost himself safely out of the saddle and plant both feet without falling over. He let go of the reins and gave Teddy his head to trot off to a safer range.

There, outside the fence into the Hanson yard, he paused, listened, and heard the heartbeat steadily calling him forward. He walked past the house and the lean-to over the wall of unused firewood. Then he proceeded into the barnyard that was so similar to his own, and movement caught his eye.

Cage stepped from the shadows around the nearer side of the barn, materializing with a shit-eating grin that made Hiram want to kill him even more.

"You recite that tomorrow and tomorrow crap again, I'll beat you where you stand," Hiram griped even though that likelihood remained slim. Then he winced as the cold lightning shot through him, leaving a prickling sensation. He raised his hands and looked down at them as the skin tightened, black veins crawling beneath.

"Told you, you don't have much time left," Cage said soberly. "Soon, that brilliant mind in there will die, Marshal, and you'll go the way of your friend."

"Don't talk about him like that," Hiram said, thinking about how fast the disease had taken Silas. Overnight, with no understanding of what was happening. Silas had been unconscious from the moment he bled out, having no idea that something vile and dark was taking over his body, what it was turning him into. The greatest pain of it was that Hiram had not been able to say goodbye.

"I'm sorry for what happened with Mr. LeBlanc," Cage said. "I rather liked him. Not that it will make you feel any better, but I put down the remaining coyotes before they could spread it further." To Hiram's disturbed expression, he added, "Oh yes, there were more of them. There are always *more* when the pestilence finds a home in a wild animal."

"More?" A sour taste rose in Hiram's mouth.

"It spreads so easily, creating mindless revenants like Silas became, or like that coyote that innocently scavenged remains that had not been cleansed. All revenants, human or animal, are savage creatures. They kill and feed without strategy, cause wasteful epidemics and chaos, and they can rage easily out of control if not prevented. We must always clean up our messes thoroughly. Sometimes it requires a little help, such as employing thralls like Jasper."

"That's why you burn the bodies of your victims," Hiram stated, though it had all become quite clear already.

"*Marks*. We call them marks. It takes a lot of blood to feed ourselves *and* keep a couple of thralls. Fully transmuted blood is the *elixir* capable of sustaining them for as long as they feed directly from us. Jasper failed to earn his when he left an entire arm intact for predators to find."

The numbers added up in Hiram's head, a struggle no less than keeping the rest of his focus. He thought about how many folks were left in and around Mica Bend since the decline began. He'd seen no more than fifty at the troupe's performance. Four vampires and two thralls meant at least six people a night. That wiped out most of that near-fifty in less than eight nights.

Six marks a night, maybe seven. His throat tightened at the idea of all those lives slipping away right out from under his watch.

I think you can back off yourself, Becker had said. *No one, not even the great Sheriff Slaughter, could imagine something like this happening.*

That still did not make Hiram feel any better.

Cage turned, strolled toward the old barn, gestured casually at the corral and the open doors as if giving a tour. "I've often needed a place for solitude when traveling with a kith. We came upon this farm nearly four weeks ago, our first hit. I found the hidden passage between the house and the barn. It's been my day haven for most of this time, along with some of the caverns up in the mountains. So, imagine my surprise when, upon preparing to go out one evening, I encountered the cellar door in the barn opening and a voice calling hello. *Your* voice. I was ready to kill and feed then and there, save myself a hunt, but you did not investigate any further."

"Four weeks?" Mortified, Hiram stared. It wasn't that he'd come so close to Cage by accident that disturbed him but that the troupe had been here, right under his nose, for much longer than he had estimated. Time enough to get rid of the wagon Zach kept around back, cover the furniture in the house, and make the place look legitimately abandoned. They had probably done the same to countless other homes out on the ranges, families and places he could never have kept up with because living out here was so naturally disconnected.

Then Cage confirmed that himself. "We came through, picked off the surrounding farms, then moved toward the town, meeting our schedule via the arrangement I made with your mayor. After a point, we isolated the region. No one went in, no one got out, like your deputy."

Hiram had known the moment he'd seen Nathan's horses roll in with the buckboard, frothy and huffing, that his deputy had to be dead. Even while he planned a search, he'd known he'd come up with nothing. His throat tightened at the thought of Nathan dying out in the desert night alone, frightened. "Please say it was quick," was all he could get out.

"Oh, I'm sure it was. Genevieve does not toy with her food. Pardon me for putting it that way. I know it offends your sensibilities." Cage turned back around to face him, sniffing indifferently.

Hiram's left hand absently felt around his holster, expecting to tap on the grip of his Colt, only to find it wasn't there.

Idiot!

He'd drawn on Cage at the opera house and lost the gun in their struggle, never to recover it. How had he forgotten that? Interminable memory—images, faces, places, things said and done—had plagued him since birth, driven him at one point to seek refuge in an opium pipe, and yet he would do anything to keep it now, to remain so sharp and centered. He'd figured on getting at least one blessed bullet into his nemesis, to disrupt Cage's abilities as much as possible and gain an edge, enough to decapitate him, stake his heart, then he'd put the barrel in his own mouth and let the sun do the rest come morning.

Can't eat a bullet without a gun.

Cage must have seen the alarm in his eyes. "You're fading, Marshal," he said. "You've been pushed to your limits. Your body and mind are probably the most stubborn I've encountered in an infected individual. You've fought it well, but the pestilence will always win as it has for hundreds of thousands of years."

Hundreds of thousands? Hiram almost couldn't comprehend such numbers on a scale of time and history. He knew what he knew from book learning as a boy and the events of his own life, not some vague notion of a nearly infinite past. Just thinking about it brought forward the blackness, bleeding around his vision, and the churning, violent urge rose, primordial and annihilatory. For an intense second, the instinct seized him to go for Cage's throat, tear it out, whether with his hands or his teeth. He'd rip the pretty, tall actor apart and never feel a single regret, never feel anything again but this wrenching hunger humming under his skin. With winding tension and a groan, he pushed it back down.

"Just tell me why?" he asked. "Why wipe out an entire town?"

Cage sounded happy to oblige. "A spree like this is like a holiday for us, a chance at easy pickings. No one will miss that town when it's gone. No one questions where everyone went, given the train no longer stops there or the post office is closing. A town like the Bend sits for a decade, maybe a little more, with the mines poisoning the land and inspiring false hope before there are no more resources. Then everyone moves on to the next opportunity to bleed it dry, too, leaving one old timber ruin after another. Not much difference between you and us, is there?"

"That town was my home!" the rage burst from him, and in a renewed flash of speed, he found himself in front of Cage, fist swinging right for the jaw. There was a loud *crack,* and Hiram felt a shock in his knuckles vibrate down through the back of his hand.

The vampire took the hit, head snapping sideways, though his body barely budged. He calmly turned back just as Hiram tried again. In a split second, he caught the incoming fist, blanketing it in his broad grip. Hiram undulated his wrist to try to pull free.

"That town was your *prison,*" Cage said through his teeth as he stared steadily at the struggling man. "The place where you buried your wife, where you were determined to keep your children until all hope of a future faded from their eyes, all for you and your grief. Look at you, not even forty and already past your prime with that wrecked spine, and you would pull them down with you."

The words bore truth, provoking little stabs of shame and regret. The black closed a little tighter. A strange sense of emptiness washed through him, Marshal Hiram Wells there one moment, gone the next, then back, as if he'd dropped off into a doze where he stood. Then the agony reached its peak. The sensation of a million razors tore through him. Hiram's teeth gritted so hard his jaw creaked. He dropped to a knee, and Cage let his hand go.

So, this was how it would end, with him on the ground, his consciousness blinking in and out until it went out for good, leaving a mindless thing to scuttle across the land looking to kill anything it could get its clutches on. He looked down at his hands again, saw how ashen his flesh had turned, how his fingernails looked longer, sharper. He'd force himself to stand and tear into Cage with those nails if he could just *will* his legs to *move.*

"Believe it or not, we have a common goal," Cage said. "There is a war among my kind, a conflict that affects the human world, too. I said before that you would be a worthy ally. It would be such a waste to have to kill you when I could use a man of your instincts and focus. There is no time for me to explain it now, but if you come with me, you will learn everything."

"War?" Hiram gasped, struggling to remember the word. "Ah!" he shouted and doubled over, gripping his belly. "God!"

"No," Cage said. "No God here. I'm your savior now." He presented his wrist before Hiram's eyes, and a long, pointed nail slid across it, opened it up and released a flow of brilliant red. The rich, coppery aroma of it curled around Hiram as it dripped to the ground, enticing as warm honey. "Take it!" Cage insisted. "If my blood is your first, you'll be spared. You'll become a noble like me. You'll have immortality, a fresh start, no regrets."

He convulsed as another—this time nauseating—surge of darkness closed in and out, buffeting him like those waves he'd experienced as a boy nearly carried out to sea, and Silas' words came to him in a gut punch.

You're the one man I know who can walk through that kind of darkness with the absolute knowledge that he will not fall in, and you will get to that light.

Silas had known him better than anyone else, perhaps even Rachel, but there was no light ahead of him, not with where he was going. Still, he appreciated the sentiment.

Rachel's cross, he knew, was the only leverage he had in this situation. Small though it was, it might do against Cage. He could shove it into the smug bastard's mouth, and that might distract, disrupt his equilibrium and strength, but what then? To kill Cage would mean to still die himself. Perhaps worse. He might kill Cage but then spend the rest of his days roaming the desert, a mindless killing thing that found its way back to town, back to his children the way the coyote had tracked Nathan's horses.

But what if, ironically, Cage's blood could be that light Silas spoke of? He would lose his family either way, but they were safe now so long as he did not come creeping after them to feed like the creatures of Becker's village folklore.

And then his own words flooded his mind, a small triumph considering it was growing so hard to hold on, what he had said to Becker as they sat reconciling under that oak tree when he realized he was going to die of this.

I want to find them all, Becker, these things… vampires…whatever the hell they are. I want to burn them out of this world, the way they've been burning out our town.

Cage's blood could give him that opportunity, a chance to find more of *them*, to have the strength to fight them and burn them from within their ranks, to cut the disease out at its root. The only question remaining was could he hold on to who he was even as he embraced the existence of a creature that survived on human life?

I'll say it again… you can walk through that darkness and not fall in… Silas' voice repeated from somewhere in his mind.

It felt so *real*, not his imagination, speaking to him from across the unknown space between Heaven and Hell if there were such a place.

Silas?

Yeah, H. I'm here. You won't be alone, I promise.

Hiram closed his eyes, pushed out streams of chilled tears, and with one last shiver, whispered, "Alright… but I'll *keep* my regrets."

He grabbed Cage's wrist and locked his mouth over it. Above him, Cage sighed as if with relief as Hiram drew in a mouthful, savored it like sweet water after a drought, and gulped repeatedly. He forced his tongue into the cut to keep it open, heard himself moan as the blood soothed his stomach, dissolved the razor blades and ramified out in his veins, soaked into his skin from the inside out.

He was just beginning to feel sated when Cage withdrew his wrist. "That'll do."

That was when things seemed to go from bad to worse. The consuming pain may have departed, but Hiram found himself still blinking in and out, his body numb and heavy, his extremities not responding. He started to fall over backward, unable to move at all, but Cage caught him around the shoulders and the back of his head, lowered him gently to the ground. He stared up into the starry sky with Cage's face, framed in its golden halo, hovering over him.

"What's h… hap…pening…" he uttered before he found he couldn't draw another breath.

"Do not worry," Cage said. "It's only temporary death."

He clung to consciousness for one more fleeting moment, then the last thing Hiram Wells saw were fingertips coming down to brush over his eyelids and close them.

They did not watch the marshal's figure dwindle into the distance for long. To do so would waste precious time and dig the grief of the Wells children in deeper, dimming their focus on the crucial task at hand.

"He's not going to stop, is he?" Lucinda asked, her voice thick with that grief.

Becker turned to her, noted the twin punctures at the junction of her neck and shoulder. He wished he could be shocked it had happened. Dark hollows already formed under her eyes, which pleaded with him silently somehow. "And neither are we," he said.

Then he set about getting the cure ready. "Caleb, fetch a lantern from the boardwalk in case I need the kerosene." He turned to Jesse, halted as he got a better look at the young man, whose eyes bore an eerie dullness.

From his nostrils down over his chin, drying blood coated Jesse's face. As if he knew what Becker was about to ask, he said with gravel in his voice and a sorrowful glitter in his eyes, "It's August's. He made me drink it."

Becker nodded, angry for the young man's sake. "Jesse," he said more gently, "hunt up a tin pan for that heart. Try the mercantile. Caleb already busted the window in for you."

Lucinda stood with Ellie in front, hands on her little sister's shoulders, to briefly watch the light flicker in the opera house doors where wisps of smoke started to curl out and trail heavenward. Even Ellie's tears had stopped, dried up by dust and exhaustion but, somehow, she'd climbed from beneath the Palace boardwalk without a single sting from the scorpion nest she and Morgan Reed had disturbed.

Becker stepped up to watch with them for a moment. The flicker grew brighter as the fire ate its way closer to the doors. Soon the flames would penetrate the roof, and the insides would start to fall in, a fitting end, he felt, for the place that had become the nexus for the town's doom.

"Got it," Jesse called, and they all turned to go join him.

Crouched in a circle outside the Palace and around a blue enameled wash pan, they all watched Becker hastily crunch up some of the dried vervain as kindling around the heart. He tried to light it without the need of an accelerant and was pleased when August's little black heart went up almost immediately without any need for kerosene. If sunlight had such an immediate effect, it stood to reason that fire would be as efficient. As the flames burned down quickly, leaving a pile of glittering ash, he added more crushed vervain, mixed it in, and then swirled in the holy water one vial at a time. This supernatural recipe did not come with any other instructions, no measurements as the pharmacist in him was used to following, so he hoped there were no rules to the combination. When the mixture seemed tolerable enough, less thick, easily drinkable, the pan was passed to Jesse and Lucinda.

Both held their breath and looked dubiously at Becker.

"Shouldn't be any worse than taking charcoal for a bellyache," he told them. "Eh, the vervain might make you have to pee a lot."

That side effect deemed not too frightening, each took huge gulps from the rim, looked at each other with wide, curious eyes. Becker didn't know what they'd been through down in those vaults, but their faces spoke of a bond now formed that went beyond teenage affection.

"Do you feel any different?" Lucinda asked.

"Not yet."

"Me neith—" She doubled over, clamped a hand to her belly and coughed.

A second later, Jesse joined her, and both dropped to their knees.

"Ah, God… it's like fire in my veins," she gasped.

"I just wanna puke," Jesse declared, and a moment later, he did. Holy water, swirled with the black of the ash and a dark red substance—which Becker assumed was an undigested quantity of August's blood—came spewing out of him and splashed upon the street.

There wasn't much Becker could do but let the mix run its course. He tilted the pan and took a swig himself just in case since Genevieve had driven her claws into his side and Nora had grazed his face. The side wound, particularly, still hurt like a sonofabitch, but he would live. The ashes left a fine grit between his teeth but merely tasted like burnt meat mingled with the herbiness of the vervain. He took another gulp.

"Caleb, I think you and Ellie should, too…" he said, looking up. Ellie still stood within the circle, watching her sister, but Caleb was gone.

"Caleb?" He looked around, gasped to see the boy's figure disappear through the doors into the opera house, a silhouette engulfed by the growing smoke. "Caleb!" He set down the pan and started for the church.

Though in discomfort, Lucinda lifted her head to see where the pastor was going. "Caleb?" she gasped and got to her feet to come running after. "Caleb!"

Soon Ellie's voice echoed them, high pitched and determined as always, and Becker heard her running behind as well, but before they reached the doors, Caleb emerged again, wiping the sting of the smoke from his eyes and holding something in his hand.

"Caleb!" Lucinda rushed ahead of Becker, grabbed her brother by the shoulders, and gave him a firm shake. "You don't run into a burning building, you little idiot!"

"I just… realized something," he said through a new round of coughs.

"It's Papa's gun. He didn't have it." He held up the Colt Peacemaker.

"Oh," Lucinda said, her brother's careless stunt forgotten. "Oh, no."

Becker's heart sank, and the ash water churned in his belly. *"Scheisse,"* he murmured.

From within the opera house came a crash as the stage, just visible straight through the doors, caved in on one side and pushed out a wave of hot air and smoke. Becker grabbed Caleb's shoulder and steered him away, herded them all away as he took the gun, and they all rushed back to Jesse, who was on his knees, looking the worse for wear but alert.

"The marshal doesn't have his gun," Becker informed him. "He can't beat Cage without at least that."

"Then I'll take it to him," Jesse said and forced himself to stand.

"I'll go with you," Becker insisted. It was worth it for the marshal to at least try the cure as well. Becker poured some of it into one of the emptied bottles and pocketed it.

They rounded up Peso and the roan, who were none too pleased to be pulled back into the middle of the thoroughfare, snorting and snuffling and stamping with agitation.

"Be careful," Lucinda said as she watched the pastor and Jesse mount up.

"Get into the church again," Becker said to her. "Take as much more of that mixture as you can stand and *stay* in there." He remained too aware that Genevieve and Nora were out there somewhere, even if their departure at Cage's order had *seemed* final.

She nodded, then her eyes met Jesse's. "I love you," she said.

For the first time since they'd emerged from the opera house, bedraggled and tapped, Becker saw the kid's eyes regain some life. Real *life*. Even in the half-dark of moonglow, they gleamed with hope.

"I love you, too," he said.

She stepped back, guiding her brother and sister with her, and gathered up the pan to take back toward the church.

Then Becker and Jesse rode, hellbent, following the same shallow scuffs of hoof prints Hiram's horse had beaten into the road. They passed out of the north bend, past the dark hollow of the former Wagon Town and the Wells house.

Pit Creek had never seemed so far away. Becker had only made a couple of house calls out to the Hanson farm in past years, so he was less familiar with the route and thus let Jesse lead.

Over the miles they raced, he caught glimpses of the kid's scowling face. By the time they turned southward off the main road and approached the Hansons' lands, the moon had dipped lower to take on a more brilliant, creamy illumination that lengthened the shadows, indicating that dawn could not be too far away.

Jesse nodded ahead, shouted over the pound of hooves and the wind in their ears, "There's his horse!"

Becker squinted ahead, saw that the chestnut gelding was standing out in the middle of the path, ears pricked up, glancing at them and then into the barnyard past the house and back again. He wandered out of their way as they rushed in and halted at the twisted mesquite remains that served as a signpost. Both horses were winded and agitated, refusing to go past the fence line into the yard.

Becker suppressed a curse and climbed down, noticing that a breeze was picking up, the dust around them stirring again though not nearly as fearsome as when the storm had walled off the town.

Jesse hesitated then finally hoisted a leg over. He held his forearm against his body now, and Becker made a note in his mind to check what was happening with that, but first, they walked forward, looking for the marshal.

Chills bloomed in Becker's middle, tingled on the backs of his arms when he saw the shape of a man kneeling some twenty yards away, broad shoulders, flowing crown of pale hair that stood out amidst the monochrome landscape and structures within the yard. He faced away from them, but Becker made out a pair of sprawled legs on one side on the ground, part of a head of light brown hair on the other.

"No," Jesse said with broken desperation as he rushed forward, drawing his Colt awkwardly and firing, hitting nothing as he'd attempted to fire with his left hand.

The figure leaned steeply forward, away from them, then rose with natural grace, bringing what lay on the ground with it, and Cage Edwards turned around to face them. Hiram Wells' body hung limp in his arms, head thrown back, arms slack, purely dead weight that Cage carried effortlessly.

"No… no… no…" Jesse said, the gun still aimed, shaking in his hand. He clearly feared taking a shot and hitting the wrong target now.

Becker reached into his coat and withdrew the marshal's Peacemaker, wavered as a sickening wave washed through him. The wind rose further, sweeping up a surge of dust, and the last thing he made out was that Cage appeared to be smiling back, wickedly satisfied.

Too late, he thought. *Too late...*

The dust cloud engulfed the vampire and his cargo, clearing only a few seconds later to reveal nothing there.

Both had vanished like a mirage on the horizon.

"Why did he take the marshal's body?" Jesse rasped through a building sob.

Becker swallowed down a hard lump. "I don't know," he said hollowly. One reason would simply be for disposal, but he had another idea why Cage might spirit Hiram Wells away that he was not about to share for its disturbing possibility.

"What am I going to tell Lucinda?"

"Jesse, go get the horses. Get the marshal's, too." He tried to get the young man focused while he walked forward a few paces, looking out at the shadowed scrub, but there were no signs of Cage Edwards or the marshal, not even a wisp of a black mist moving against the sky or the large uncanny owl that Cage had transformed into in town.

The eastern sky had gone from blue to muddy, but dawn light was still a long way from reaching the Hanson farm. So much had happened so fast, it was hard to believe almost an entire night had passed.

He could hear Jesse's sobbing as he strode back out to the road and gathered the reins of the three milling horses.

Becker took a moment to recall precisely what he'd just seen. The marshal indeed appeared dead, his skin still cast in a grayish hue, but there had been a stain on his lips, a slight tinge of crimson sparkling like a dark ruby, and Becker took a breath as he wondered if Marshal Hiram Wells had somehow made a last-ditch deal with the devil.

CHAPTER THIRTY-FIVE

The Raskin family left Mica Bend two days after the events that marked the town's final hours. Becker and the Wells children said goodbye to them, and their covered wagon rolled out on a crisp morning. They chose to go east into New Mexico.

Becker watched them go like a quiet last breath leaving the body of the town. That would be him, soon, along with his new little family. Plans were in the works, preparations. His old luggage had been pulled out of the church basement and was being meticulously packed with all his books and medical supplies while Lucinda and Jesse oversaw things at the Wells house.

Since returning from the Hanson farm with nothing but more questions, he and Jesse had tried to find other survivors. They came up with a handful, but there were no others within the town limits, and Titus Watkins, last seen in a half-responsive state, had also gone missing. Brice Tucker's ranch seemed to have been spared for the most part but for the hands who had disappeared on their nights off. Jesse had only gone back there to give notice and clean out his locker.

With Jesse's help, Becker had gone carefully through the burnt interior of the Spanish mission chapel and located what was left of Father Ramirez and Izabel and buried their remains in the Catholic cemetery, respecting their branch of the faith as much as he knew how.

Then they systematically burned the jail, the Palace, and the Simpson house, watched all three go up in black smoke. Only the jail fire had spread—an expected risk with any timber structures—and, ironically, taken the mayor's office with it. Two horses were removed from the livery, including Silas' ornery Saddlebred, Arsenic, and the troupe's massive hauling horses were brought into town to be temporarily homed in the Wells barn.

In the early evening of the fourth night, he ate again at the Wells house, savoring another round of Lucinda's chicken and dumplings. Since she'd only found three of the escaped hens, she had decided it was better to butcher and cook them as well as use up the last of the kitchen supplies.

Suppers thus far had been spent in quiet, heads mostly down—even little Ellie, for all her normal rambunctiousness, held her piece—though more plans occasionally came up, and Becker counseled the grieving children when necessary.

"You want an escort back up the thoroughfare?" Jesse asked him when his belly was full, and it was time to go.

He looked at the young man's right arm, secured in a sling and confining him to left-handedness for a while, and his tired face. Jesse's right cheek now bore a long seam of stitches where Becker had attempted reconstructive surgery.

"No, *danke*, I think I'll be fine, Jesse," he said as he patted his coat pocket where his trusty cross had ridden around with him ever since that night. He'd also taken to tossing back vials of holy water as darkness fell, a practice he was sure his superiors in the Lutheran hierarchy would frown upon if they found out. They would never comprehend his reasons, so he never intended upon them finding out.

The rosy-hued sky in the west cast a sense of peace upon the Bend as he walked back to the church, but the charred husk of the Orleans Palace stirred the sadness that lingered in him as it did in the Wells children. The smell was purely burned timber, earthy and sharp, void of the subtle rotten smell that accompanied the bones the marshal had found in the desert. He'd buried those as well, all of them, in the cemetery, blessed them and hoped that those people's souls, whoever they were, were at peace.

He passed the brick hull of the opera house and then the jail. Like the Palace, some timbers and wall panels still stood, though blackened and half-collapsed. The roof had fallen in and left a chaotic pile over the hole where a floor had been. The safe was still intact but on its side, as were the iron cell panels.

He didn't pay any attention to the pile that had been Watkins' office as he rounded that and crossed the handful of yards to the church, going toward the back to let himself into the rectory.

Ahead, he swore he saw a shadow move within the cemetery, and tried to blink it away, sure it was simply a branch from the old oak swaying as a breeze stirred.

But it did not simply blink away.

Becker braced himself, his hand sliding into his pocket to grip the end of the cross, and he stepped up until he reached the edge of the picket fence and looked in, under the deeper shadows of the oak, to see a man in a long black coat kneeling over two particular graves, head bowed.

Becker's heart leaped into his throat, and his thoughts teetered between disbelief and alleviation. "I didn't know if I would ever see you again," he said hoarsely. "How is it that you're on holy ground?"

"I don't know." Hiram Wells said, then stood up and turned to walk closer, his face easing into the more open light, and Becker took a breath.

The marshal looked younger, somehow. He stood straighter, showing no signs of back pain. The lines that had been etched in his face, shallow though they had been, were gone completely. Where he'd typically sported the shadow of thick stubble, his face was as clean and smooth as marble, free of the ashen tone or the crawl of black veins that had signaled his deterioration days ago. The blue showed clearly in eyes that had not looked so alive in a long time. Indeed, where standing in that cemetery would undoubtedly have caused any of the others to ripple and blink, energies disrupting or weakening them, he looked vibrant.

"I came to say goodbye and had to test my boundaries. See this?" He reached into his pocket and drew out a tiny silver cross—Becker recognized it as Rachel's—and held it up, dangling over the back of his hand by the chain. "This doesn't affect me either."

"But how... I... what..." Becker couldn't find the words.

"You put Silas next to her," he said, undaunted by the pastor's confusion. "Thank you for that."

Becker finally got a hold of himself, nodded. "It was only proper. Silas never attended church, but I wanted him to be at rest."

"I can't say if he is," Wells said, "I mean..." He looked away, the wind stirring his hair that also looked fuller, no longer matted with the oil and grime that accumulated in it before. "It's complicated. It's all *so* complicated, Becker." He looked back at the graves. "And *that* memorial stone," he indicated the other side of Rachel's plot. "Really?"

"That one's for your children," Becker said firmly. "It was all I could do to give them some kind of closure."

"You put anything there?"

"Your gun. It's buried in your place." On the visitor's quiet nod, he asked, "What now, then?"

"One step at a time. I'm going with him, wherever that is. It's like Jasper O'Brian said. Cage is looking for something, and he was interested in me particularly. I don't know why. He mentioned a war among his kind, something that affects the normal world as well. The human world. That alone is reason enough for my involvement, even if it means being this *thing*."

Normal world, Becker echoed that in his mind. Such irony to hear it from a man who was no longer human, at least not bodily.

"All I know is this is my chance to do what I can from the inside." He was trying to defend his choice, though there had not been much of a choice at all the way Becker saw it.

"So, you're still *you* then?" Becker narrowed his gaze, examined the weirdly younger face, searched the eyes for a clear sign that it was indeed the marshal standing here, speaking to him. *But of course, it is*, he chastised himself. The man could still walk on holy ground unaffected. That had to be a sign, possibly some omen among vampires.

"Mostly."

"You'll have to kill to survive."

"I know." He stepped to the gate and let himself out, a motion that—despite the proof of goodwill presented—made Becker's back muscles recoil and his nerves prickle. "I can only try to make careful choices in that regard, perhaps even steer Cage while I learn more about him and the others. He'll do his damnedest to corrupt me, I'm sure. I can only fight to stay on course, and someday, when the time is right, I *will* kill the sonofabitch, Becker."

"What can I do?"

"First, don't tell the kids you saw me. I don't want them trying to look for me." He reached into his other coat pocket, drew out two vials and presented them. They were full of thick red liquid.

Blood, Becker realized. *Noble vampire blood.* It would go a lot further toward study than the bits of Silas's blood he'd scraped off the clinic floor and spooned, splinters and stains together, into glass bottles along with the precaution of a few crumbs of communion bread.

"It's mine," Wells said. On Becker's wide-eyed, alarmed look, he added, "Forgive me, but I was already in the rectory raiding your glass supplies."

Becker reached out, took them as gingerly as if they were crown jewels.

"Study it, just don't expose the vials to sunlight all at once, don't let the blood touch a cut or taste it. Just make it last and burn it when you're done."

"I believe I already have that part figured out," Becker griped.

"I don't know when I can get more to you."

He nodded. "How did this happen? How did he save you?"

"He fed me his blood directly. It's like the disease is the first stage, the thing that starts changing the body. They always call it the *pestilence*. But noble blood is like a stabilizer, like…"

"An inoculation," Becker concluded, "but it still elicits a change."

"Right, the *elixir*, but the disease has to be present first through a bite. Then there's a… a sort of *death* phase… or a coma, or something, while that change happens. I was out for three days before I woke."

"Huh," Becker murmured. *And on the third day, he rose from the dead.* The irony of that did not escape him—gave him chills—but he appreciated that the marshal had already collected enough interesting information for him to ponder.

"It's what makes the difference between creating a noble versus a thrall. I get the impression it's a pretty thin line. Thralls still eat normal food, too, but they need a regular dose of noble blood. They can survive for centuries as long as they're maintained."

"Hence how Jasper O'Brian came into possession of a broadsword? May have been from his previous life."

Wells shrugged. "I suppose, but maybe, if there's a cure for the early stages, there's still a cure for even the likes of me." His gaze dropped, a brief look of sadness withering his otherwise perfect features. "How are my children? Is Lucinda cured? And Jesse?"

"They're as well as can be expected. Ja, the cure worked. Lucinda is fine. Jesse had a hard time of it. Once the effect of August's blood wore off, I had to reset his broken wrist, and he'll have a scar on his cheek the rest of his life. August seriously got inside his head, so he may be the worst affected of them all. Only time will tell, but he's proposed to

Lucinda, and she's accepted. They're still young, so marriage will be a while coming."

The news only elicited a vacant, unsurprised nod. "They have my blessing, such as it is. You be the judge of when they're ready." The blue eyes roamed over Becker's face. "And *your* scars?" It was the gentlest, truly concerned question he had ever asked of the pastor's wellbeing.

Becker absently raised fingers to brush over the three long, scabbed slashes Nora had inflicted on his right temple and cheek, barely missing his eye. There were the others somewhat hidden in his hairline, but they were minimal. "Healing fine with a little comfrey balm." He dared a step closer. "The Raskins left. Oh, the Kranes and Terry Wilkes were fine. The Kranes just hadn't been social, and Terry was tucked at home sick after drinking some bad milk. They're all moving on, too.

"I assume the telegraph lines are fixed now, but I don't know how to send one. In two days, we'll be going to Tucson. Jesse will sell the horses there for funds, and then I'll telegraph James to make arrangements for our arrival in Philadelphia."

"You're going, too, then. Good..." he whispered it. "Good." It sounded like relief. He looked up and past Becker, toward the horizon and the wash of gold against the rising stars. "I can't see my children grow up, but at least I can still see sunsets," he mused, more to himself than the pastor. "That sky... it is amazing. I can even hear it sing."

Becker could only imagine what that sky must look and sound like now to a man whose perspective had changed so much. Cold comfort, perhaps, but something.

"There may come a day soon I'll need a holy man at my side in this war."

"I'll be there," Becker confirmed.

"I should be going. I don't sense Cage near, but I can't be too careful. He was making some final arrangement for our departure."

"How will I find you?"

"Don't worry about it. I'll find y—"

Before he could help himself, Becker reached out and pulled the man into a bear hug. Hiram Wells' body tensed at the unexpected embrace, then slowly acquiesced and uncoiled. Becker could feel that he radiated a cool aura, though he no longer shivered as he had in his previous state. Slowly a hand rose to pat Becker's shoulder awkwardly.

"Godspeed, Marshal," he whispered as tears warmed his eyes.

"I'm not a marshal anymore," the other replied dully.

Becker drew back, looked him in the eyes and saw nothing but the man with whom he had been through so much sorrow and pain, ridden and fought no ordinary enemy, and whom he'd always call a friend no matter what. "Ja," he said habitually, then cleared his throat.

"Yes," he repeated. "Yes, you *are*."

Cage had told him that his new abilities would come naturally to him as if born to them, and they did, just as his senses had served him even before his blooding.

Transformation, giving him the ability to fly, was the first and the strangest, but he had taken to it far easier than expected and quickly learned not to try to explain how it worked. It was not merely his body that transformed, but his clothing, too. He'd seen that example when Cage had changed in front of him for the first time. In life, he had never thought magic was real, at least not on such a grand scale. What he had felt for Rachel—their meeting, falling in love—that had been magic, natural and believable.

Below him, the desert swept by, soon to be consumed by intolerable, deadly sunlight as the eastern horizon lightened to hues that were already brighter and richer to his wholly altered vision. All of his heightened senses were balanced now, unlike when they came and went in disorienting bouts when he was merely infected. His flight was silent, but he felt wind under wings, dipped and soared toward a rendezvous point on the road north of the Arduous Range.

Those mountains now represented both his tomb and the womb in the earth from which he'd been newly birthed. He'd awakened in a cavern there, tasted more of Cage's blood—*bottle feeding*, Cage called it—until his training could begin. He'd sworn to himself that he would pick off only the lowlifes, the Frank Evanses of the world, though he expected Cage to make that difficult at times.

He soared on, cutting the time hazardously close to dawn, and spotted the black coach below. Its signage had been painted over, and the team of black Saddlebreds was hitched and ready. Cage had said nothing about it but given the adjustments to the coach and the abandoned freighter, the ruse of a traveling act was over.

Hiram dove steeply toward the coach, then banked and swept back upward before he came too close to the ground. It presented an exhilarating sensation in his belly, a thrill in his head. He hovered with the beat of silent wings and then felt his body dissolve into a misty state as it shifted from avian to human. Then he stood firmly on two legs, clothing threaded back together, a breeze stirring his hair and coat. He heard Cage's heartbeat as the noble approached and a second one from somewhere on the other side of the coach.

"Have you said your goodbyes to the Bend?" Cage asked.

Hiram nodded.

Cage only *tsked,* then opened the door of the coach and gestured for Hiram to climb in. "Don't worry. We'll be safe. As you've figured out, traveling during the day perpetuates the deception even with the lack of windows. Besides, this coach is reinforced, a vault that no one may break into no matter what our circumstances."

Hiram had already been informed that Genevieve and Nora would not be joining them. They had been dismissed to go their own way, though they might turn up later at one of the kith's regular haunts wherever that might be.

He looked from the open door to the front and down the line of horses. "Who is going to drive it?" The other heartbeat thrummed steadily as it came around the back end of the coach.

As if to answer his question, none other than Titus Watkins appeared. He did not look nearly as groomed as before but now sported the uniform of his predecessors, Jasper O'Brian and Morgan Reed, the long black coat and a wide-brimmed black hat. In his gloved hand was a coiled whip. Gone was the cane that he used to emphasize his bombastic speeches. Gone was the dapper derby and pomade, the smug ambition and ignorance that had unwittingly led Mica Bend to its ruin. The town had already been going ghost, that was true, but Watkins had helped it into an early grave.

"Hiram," he greeted with a nod, his tone far less commanding than it had been in his career as mayor. "I know this is quite a surprise for you."

"No shit." But he could see in the man's eyes a defeat worse than the death Cage might have given him. An uncertain future in service to blood and darkness was far worse, and Hiram did not give two damns.

The punishment, he thought, *fits the crime.*

Watkins seemed to pick up on the apathy, and he lowered his head in what might be shame, hid his eyes under the brim of the hat. "Yes, well, I'll be getting you gentlemen to Phoenix."

"Thank you, Titus," Cage said.

"You're welcome, Mr. Edwards," the new thrall replied and proceeded to climb up into the driver's seat at the front.

Cage climbed into the compartment and leaned into the doorway to gesture for Hiram to follow. "Come along. Your greatest enemy now is the sun."

Hiram looked past the rear of the coach and toward the mountains in the distance, feeling a strange bereavement at the idea of leaving them.

Cage followed his gaze then nodded with understanding. "You will still feel drawn here," he explained. "We always feel connected to the place of our burial. That was your tomb out there in those mountains, the only place that we could safely take haven at such short notice."

Haven, Hiram thought, another term filed away for regular use now. He'd already learned *pestilence, elixir, kith, noble, revenant, sire, blooded*, but Cage assured him of a greater lexicon to come. There was so much more to learn now, and he'd be briefed as they finally wheeled on into the uncertain future. With a deep breath, he climbed into the coach. Cage shut the door and slid a large bolt into place. The opposite door had its own bolt. Hiram's vision did not perceive the darkness around him. He could still see the details of the compartment's seats and steel fittings that revealed some of the reinforcement, and then there was Cage sitting opposite him, relaxed and confident.

"Where are you drawn to?" Hiram asked. "Where was your tomb?"

Cage only gave a slight smirk to that, humored by the question, but he was far from revealing any personal details or history.

Hiram would acquire the information eventually. Somehow. It might prove important for his mission. He feigned acceptance and tried to lean back, relax into the seat. "Will I meet others?" he asked.

"Yes. Eventually." The smirk drew in again and, after a moment of consideration, he then said frigidly, "Look, I know I'm a long way from earning your trust, but be assured, I do not entirely trust *you*, either. You accepted my blood out of desperation, so we still have a long path ahead of us, don't we?"

A little jab of paranoia made him wonder if Cage had followed him into town, watched him have that discussion with Becker, watched him walk, *unflinching*, on holy ground. But surely not. He had left the cavern certain that his sire had gone his own way because Cage had to feed three times over to support his new apprentice *and* a thrall for a few nights more. More innocent people were dying out there for his mission, a thought that still unsettled Hiram despite his new nature. He had not sensed or smelled the elder vampire anywhere near enough to listen in, and even if Cage had, Hiram had no doubt he was the kind of man who would have confronted him over it immediately.

"Fair enough." He nodded it all off and attempted another approach. "You kept your promise." He tried to sound sincere, appreciative. "You said you wouldn't harm my family, and you didn't."

"I always keep my promises." The leather seat shifted under him as he sat up and forward, propped on a knee, and angled his head in an eerily animalistic gesture, an old wolf examining a pup. "And I promise you this. Betray me, and I will make this existence an eternal hell for you."

Hiram did not doubt Cage's veracity. In the end, all he could do was give another submissive nod and play along.

Sitting next to Cage, the vague image of Silas cut his jade eyes from one to the other as he sat back, one leg crossed casually over the other, sporting the same fine clothing he'd worn in life. He looked deeply amused, but then the southerner had often resorted to humor, even in some of the darkest situations.

"You've always been a crazy bastard, H. I know you didn't have much choice, but this takes the cake."

Hiram fought the urge to speak out loud, resorted to a thought. *Whatever it takes.*

Then swiftly, Cage's demeanor changed, going from warning growl to grins and delight now that his grim promise had been made. "Ah, but I think you will come around and adapt well once you see what else is out there besides *us.*

"The things you will see in this world, Hiram. The *things* you will see…"

EPILOGUE

Late afternoon light shined from the west upon the city of brotherly love as the train sped eastward across the Schuylkill River, nearing its destination. Becker and Jesse sat together and stared out the window from one side of their berth while Lucinda sat between Caleb and Ellie on the other, her arms protectively around them. They all shook off an afternoon doze as they finally approached their destination. Once the river was behind them, they watched, in heavy silence, as packed neighborhoods of old, federal and colonial-style structures sped by, and only the click of the wheels on the track, the distant chug of the engine and whistle breeched the compartment.

The train slowed and began to rise onto an elevated track, putting the streets into greater perspective with their almost perfectly platted blocks. A radius of black soot had coated those houses and businesses closest to the tracks and beneath the bridge, easily noticeable as golden sun cast upon the western faces, twinkled off windows.

"Never thought I'd be happy to live in such a crowded place," Jesse said softly. "Is that strange?"

"Not at all," Becker said. "I came through here many years ago when I came over from Germany. Came through New York, then down through Philadelphia, before I went west."

"So, this is like backtracking for you," Jesse said. His arm still rested in a sling, and he looked exhausted. Becker knew the young man had been losing much sleep, even long after they'd left Arizona territory behind. At least, his cheek seemed to be healing well enough that the stitches had been removed, and his cheekbone did not appear too skewed, but he was still in pain.

Becker watched, with an undercurrent of dread, as Jesse withdrew a bottle of laudanum from his jacket pocket and awkwardly twisted off the cap with his left hand alone before sipping it. Somewhere back down the line, days ago, Becker had begun counting sips—until he lost count, and a new bottle came into Jesse's possession at their stop in Baltimore—and was preparing himself for an intervention once the binding came off that wrist.

"I haven't seen it since I was a tiny child," Lucinda joined in. "Can't really remember it."

Becker smiled wistfully to himself. "It will be very different for all of us."

The train slowed further until the huffs from the smokestack were far apart, and the last whistle sounded as it came to a stop on the platform.

After recovering their more immediate items from the racks over the seats, they shrugged into their coats. Lucinda buttoned up hers and then Ellie's while Becker assisted Jesse with his, then they led the way and filed out into the corridor. Lucinda held her floral bag in one hand and Ellie's hand tightly in the other while Caleb and Jesse managed their own hand luggage.

Becker, as always, carried his Gladstone. He had barely let it out of his sight over the course of the journey, his mind often drifting to the hidden compartment he'd rigged in the bottom to cushion the precious samples of Hiram Wells' blood.

Upon the platform, a fall breeze—far chillier than those in southern Arizona—met them as they wove their way toward the baggage car to await their trunks.

Becker watched two uniformed porters unload and group pieces of luggage together, feeling, as anyone would, the twinge of concern that all of his other supplies had made it safely.

"Papa?" Ellie suddenly gasped.

"No, Ellie, that's Uncle James," Lucinda corrected her.

"I'll be damned," Jesse said.

"What?" Becker turned, wondering what had started all of that, and then froze as his gaze landed on the man approaching them. "Marshal?" he said under his breath, but the face he was observing was far friendlier than Hiram Wells' had ever been. It was the same down to the angle of the cheeks, the blue of the eyes, except that it sported a perfectly groomed mustache. The man wore a derby hat over neatly clipped hair and a crisp suit and coat that no one would ever be able to imagine on the town marshal of Mica Bend. Not only that, but he was slightly taller than the marshal, perhaps sturdier.

"Uncle James!" Lucinda's voice lifted in relief. She pulled her sister with her and fell into the man's arms while Ellie hesitated, face set in harsh scrutiny.

"Lucy-Belle, it's so wonderful to see you, sweetheart! It's been what? Eight years? You've doubled in height! Oh, my word, and… Caleb?"

"Yessir." Caleb maintained an uncomfortable stiffness looking at this *almost* perfect likeness of his father.

"You were only four last time you saw me, probably don't remember that exactly."

"A little, Sir," Caleb said, eyes cast downward. "Thank you for the stories you've been sending. I hope there will be more."

"Of course, there will. Perhaps you can even help my writers come up with new directions for the story."

This proposal did not seem to thrill Caleb as it was probably intended to. He nodded along with it, but Becker noted the glaze that formed in his eyes, indicating that he was not quite ready, while his uncle could not possibly have understood the lack of enthusiasm.

"Ellie, say hello to your uncle," Lucinda coaxed her little sister.

"Why do you wook wike Papa?" was all the six-year-old asked.

The smile melted, and a little wash of sadness passed through his eyes. "I know it will take some getting used to." He looked up from the disapproving little girl, and his gaze finally met Becker's. "Pastor Becker?" He came forward with an arm warmly draped around Lucinda, who now had to drag her sister along. "I'm James Wells, Hiram's brother." He let go of his niece to reach out his hand.

"Twins?" Becker said.

A seriousness washed through James' eyes as they darted over Becker's face, traced the thin, pink lines of the scars that ran from his temple. Then the smile returned beneath the mustache as he refrained from asking about them. "I could tell by the look on your faces that he never said anything."

"No, he did not. I always got the impression that you were older."

"Well, I am, by three hours." James turned then to Jesse. "And you must be Jesse. I understand you're engaged to our lovely Lucinda?"

"Yessir," the young man replied, winced as he started to maneuver his right hand then and resorted to the left. "Pardon me, as you can see, my wing's clipped a bit."

"Understood."

"Three hours?" Becker burst out. "That *can't* be."

"Oh, a day if you count that I was born on Saturday night, and he followed after midnight on Sunday. Our poor mother. That was hard on her, but when he finally emerged, he was a force, wouldn't you say?"

"And the puny one at that," Becker commented absently, still observing the size difference between the two men. For a long moment, he could not simply wrap his head around that. Twins born more than thirty minutes apart usually meant a stillbirth of the second one as it was smothered in the womb.

"Yes, Pastor," James said more soberly, "my brother was a miracle. I understand you're a doctor, too, hence the speculation."

"Ja, I…" Becker cleared his throat and realized he had yet to accept the man's handshake. He reached out, felt the firm grip. "I'm sorry about your brother. In the end, he was very sick, and there was nothing more I could do for him. I have a letter he penned to you."

James nodded, eyes glittering, picking up a spark of orange from the sunset. The tears remained suppressed. "All in good time." He took a breath. "You ever notice that memory of his?"

Becker's brows shot up. "Ja, remarkable."

"Yes, the whole family loved to test him when he was young. He hated it."

And no wonder he ran away, Becker thought with amusement. "Well, it served him well later," he said.

"Right, well. Let's see about getting you all home and a hot meal. I'll bet you're well tired of traveling food." James craned up his head to look across the platform. "Porter!" he called to the young man who stood near a doorway in the station lobby.

While James went to arrange some assistance with the luggage, Becker chewed relentlessly on what he'd just learned.

The man should have died as an infant, he thought. He should have died, yet he lived and bore the curse of Mnemosyne. Not only that, but now he could still walk freely on holy ground and grasp sacred objects despite what he'd become.

Miracle, indeed.

Godspeed, Marshal, he thought again as he looked toward the west and the spread of golden light with the disk of the sun hovering there.

"I know there's more," Caleb's voice suddenly said next to Becker.

He startled and turned to look at the boy, eyes wide. "What do you mean?"

"You and Jesse saw something, didn't you?" It was more accusative than Becker would have expected. More shocking that it came out now, over two weeks after the night that changed their lives forever.

He looked around, saw that James and the others were distracted with getting the chests onto a dolly for removal.

The boy's eyes bored into him, and Becker could see his father in there, observant, critical.

"I'll find out, Pastor Becker," he said. "You might not tell me now, but you will. Someday, I will know everything."

Becker caught himself from caving to a nod at that intense stare. He had no doubt. Yes, he would tell Caleb everything, somehow, somewhen.

But for now, he was relieved to keep the marshal's secret safe a little longer.

EASTER EGGS

Besides the new series title *Mythic Wild West*, going forward, every book will wrap with *Easter Eggs*, a little extra fun intel on my use of historical or mythological details that I hope readers will enjoy. While I may not tackle every one, I'll certainly address some of those that stand out.

Arbuckles' Coffee – The big deal Hiram makes over his Arbuckles' is no joke. Before Arbuckles', cooks on chuck wagons ordered green coffee beans and had to roast the beans themselves before brewing because pre-roasted beans tended to mold or go stale in transportation. In the 1860s, John Arbuckle III, a Scottish immigrant, patented a method of roasting that used an egg white glaze (and later sugar) that kept coffee beans fresh. John and his brother Charles created the *Arbuckle Brothers Company* in New York City in 1871. Their product spread like wildfire and became a staple out west under the *Ariosa* brand. However, over time, other coffee companies caught on to the technique and created their own brands, but many people in the west were so used to calling coffee "Arbuckles'" that they automatically called all coffees by the same name. Today, Arbuckles' Coffee is still produced and sold in Tucson, AZ, and it is some pretty fantastic coffee. Traditionally, the Arbuckle brothers included coupons for other products in their coffee bags as well as a peppermint stick for an extra treat. The company still includes the peppermint stick in its coffee bags today.

Mention of the Earp Brothers Vendetta Ride – The legendary showdown at the OK Corral happened in Tombstone, AZ on October

26, 1881, seven years before the events of The Bend. Multiple conflicts between the Earps and the Cowboy gang (by the way they were not really called "Cowboys" as modern movies portray) led to the assassination of Morgan Earp in December of the same year. This resulted in Wyatt Earp leading the infamous Vendetta Ride that included his brother Warren, Doc Holiday, Turkey Creek Jack Johnson, and ex-outlaw Sherman MacMaster among others. That this posse would have ridden through a small town like The Bend, within easy range of Tombstone, would be quite possible. Wyatt Earp sought refuge in towns and on ranches throughout the territory, sometimes being turned away by those who didn't want the Earps' troubles to spill into their own backyards.

Carrying Guns in Town – The Bend portrays many characters besides Hiram as carrying handguns in town. This was, technically, illegal if you weren't law enforcement, but it was a hard ordinance to uphold, and a town marshal might well turn a blind eye to folks he trusted carrying in town.

Silas Using Chicory in the Coffee – This little detail stems from Silas' origins in New Orleans. Chicory did not become a popular addition to coffee because of taste. Historically, it had been used as a substitute for coffee during Napoleon's Continental Blockade, a practice which spread to the French colonies like New Orleans. It was used both as a substitute—albeit without any caffeine—or in coffee blends to make the coffee go further, and this created a natural tradition. Silas would be no stranger to stretching the Arbuckles' in stock to make it last.

Shakespeare in the Old West – One of the things about the Frontier that many don't realize is the love of culture. People of all walks and social statuses missed seeing plays and other such entertainment as they had back east, so when a thespian troupe came to town, it was a reason to get excited. People loved stimulation from the creative arts and would go out of their way for it. If a town lacked a proper theater to boast it at least had a small stage in the city hall that could serve the purpose. Variety shows were popular and one honorable mention in The Bend is actor Eddy Foy, who toured widely and even met Wyatt Earp, Doc Holiday, and Bat Masterson in Dodge City.

Dime Novels and Penny Dreadfuls – Caleb's reading material already had a long and rich history before 1888. Printed on cheap newsprint and sold for mere cents, these serial tales were affordable and captivating as they always ended with a cliffhanger to bring readers back for more. While dime novels are primarily considered American and penny dreadfuls English, the term "penny dreadful" made its way to US shores denoting stories derived more from Gothic tales of horror. Dime novels focused more on the adventures of famous gunslingers and detectives and could be a one-shot or a long serial. As serials, both genres could drag on for years, such as the famous *Varney the Vampire* series in England, which inspired the Lord Covington of Caleb's pages.

Cleaning up the Town – It may come as a surprise to some readers when Mayor Watkins demands that Hiram keep the town clean. Historically a sheriff's or marshal's job was not just fighting crime and keeping out the riff-raff. It was literally taking out the trash.

Hiram's Memory – Hiram is gifted (or cursed) with an eidetic memory, which means he has total recall of events including visual and audio without use of a mnemonic device. Unlike photographic memory, which focuses on purely visual recall like photos and text, eidetic memory is described as so vivid as to be projective like reliving the event. On top of this, Hiram has the skill of visually filling in the blanks such as looking at a black and white sketch or photo and seeing it in real life color. In 1888, there were no terms for such a skill. It would simply be "that weird memory of his/hers" to anyone witnessing it in use. However, today, claims of the actual existence of eidetic memory are unverified by science.

Becker's Knowledge of Vampires – Augustin Calmet and Gerard van Swieten are real historical figures whom Becker cites in his research. Calmet, a French abbot, wrote a dissertation on supernatural entities that was broadly known and even used as a source by Voltaire. In 1755, under the order of Austro-Hungarian Empress Maria Theresa, van Swieten investigated claims of vampire activity in Serbia in attempts to abolish superstitious practices among the peasantry. Becker, an immigrant of Old Europe, states that his father had an interest in the occult. It would not be surprising that these works would turn up in his library, even if just items of curiosity.

ABOUT THE AUTHOR

J.H. Kimbrell penned the award-winning short film *Viridescent*, which had its world premiere at the TLC Chinese Theater in the Beverly Hills Film Fest. Among her other past works are her first book *The Kinship of Stars* (an out of print space opera), *Afterlife: The Arcadia Chronicles* (as J.K. Ishaya) co-written with Kenneth Mader, and *Corvus Rex: The Substance of Darkness*, the first of a Lovecraftian historical fantasy series.

A graduate of UNC-Asheville, she has also studied abroad at Oxford, England. She has lived on both coasts and in between, but now happily resides in her hometown near Asheville, North Carolina. She is an admitted crazy cat lady with three fur babies, a coffee obsession, and a love of the outdoors and travel.

MYTHIC WILD WEST

Vampires, fallen angels, pagan gods and other otherworldly entities. They've been among us from the beginning of time, and they roam the American Old West. Now former town marshal, Hiram Wells, a man gifted - or cursed - with a preternatural memory, walks among them, and justice is still being served.

Hiram's adventures continue in...

RAGING ANGELS

MYTHIC WILD WEST

Book 2

Coming Fall of 2025

Seth Raines' destiny was carved out for him from the moment he was born. Descended from fallen angels, he and his kind are in a secret war with an ancient enemy that seeks to use them to reshape all of creation.

But Seth has personal demons to conquer before he can save his people, and it will take the help of a vampire, former town marshal Hiram Wells, to shake him out of his mental prison.

PROLOGUE

Phoenix, Arizona Territory
November, 1888

He watched George Mason from the bar. Watched with more than his eyes. He'd ruled out as many heartbeats in the room as possible and focused purely on that single, thrumming beacon, and while it was impossible to ignore all the scents—potent or subtle—around him, he managed to sieve attention down to Mason's particular odor, hanging over the man like a putrid veil. Only the coppery, warm scent pulsing beneath stale sweat kept the watcher from wanting to gag. That and knowledge of Mason's deeds, which fueled the sense of rightness in what was about to happen.

Mason guffawed with some of his pals in a corner nook, playing poker while he drank beer that was one notch up from horse piss to Hiram Wells' new senses. The kerosene lamps burning in the dingy saloon created a perimeter of bright halos that Hiram squinted past to see his mark finally get up, slap one of his companions on the back, and meander toward the bat-wing doors.

"Time ta drain tha snake 'for ya clean me out, Carson!" the man's gravelly voice announced before he gave a watery burp. "Ma room's prolly ready b'now anyway."

Hiram gave him a minute's lead before pushing away from the bar, leaving behind a glass of beer that he'd ordered for the sake of appearances, drained by gradually spilling at little at a time behind the bar counter when no one was looking.

Out on the thoroughfare, he paused to wait as a horse-drawn streetcar clomped by, the grease on the wheel hubs gleaming in the flicker of gas lamps. Other horse traffic trotted by and a group of young men on bicycles pedaled past. Hiram sniffed the air, locating Mason's trail in seconds.

Across the street, a man in a long black coat and a broad-brimmed black hat stood staring back at him from the front of one of Phoenix's many adobe structures. Hiram gave a clip of a nod then turned and followed Mason's scent up Washington Street. It wasn't that late, only a couple hours past sunset, and Phoenix's weekend night life was only beginning to bloom as cowboys and other ranch hands came into town to spend their pay, and entertainment of all varieties could be had despite the cold snap of early November.

He strolled past other saloons, where the clanking notes of poorly tuned pianos poured out, and specialty shops. The acrid scent of leather dye from a tanner enveloped him for a moment before swirling away, replaced by the reek of cigar smoke. Hiram held his breath until the odor passed, then went back to sniffing his way along. He listened to the clomp of hooves and suddenly missed his horse. He missed a lot of things, but this was his existence now, and there was no helping it except in small ways. Upon first reaching Phoenix, he'd been given a budget for new clothes. He'd traded in his heavy black wool coat for a new duster and a Stetson in his favored cavalry style. The petite silver cross that had belonged to his wife, Rachel, was transferred into a hidden pocket inside the duster and secured there well out of sight and suspicion, and he could only hope that Cage never sensed it.

On the other side of the street, the shadowy man followed. Hiram ducked down an alleyway, following Mason's trail from Washington toward Jefferson, but stopped halfway. The trail condensed at the entrance to a smaller, dirtier saloon with a sloppily hand-painted sign out front that read *Rooms By the Hour* on it. He pushed open the bat-wing doors and waded back into the smell of piss for beer, the lanterns in here more scattered and dimmer than the last place. The ceiling was low and creaked as footsteps moved on the floor above. A few shaggy heads lifted from their beer mugs then dipped again with disinterest. The bar tender, who had a lazy eye, chewed on a cold cheroot as he looked up. Hiram's gaze swept the room, committing every detail to memory, filing it away in case of later need.

What a joke, he thought. There would be no need to remember this place, but his mind would do it anyway like it always had. Tonight was his last night in Phoenix for what he guessed would be a long while. Cage had said as much, though Hiram did not yet have the details on where they would be headed next. He had learned the basics of survival. Now it was time to up the ante.

Hiram locked eyes with the bartender, who only gave a small frown, then he tapped the brim of his hat and followed his nose to a rickety stairwell that led to the second floor. The narrow corridor was lit by one faint oil lamp in a sconce, a fire hazard for sure which gave him notions of simply burning the joint down when he was done. That would cover his tracks and prevent other problems, but there were procedures to follow. Mason's scent ended at the furthest door. Good. That meant he wasn't in one of the rooms directly over the saloon so possible clomping, struggling foot falls shouldn't draw much attention from the already unenthused patrons.

Briefly he cocked an ear and listened to the heartbeat on the other side, only to be surprised by the addition of a second beat, smaller, faster… *frightened.*

He gave the doorknob a gentle twist to see if it was locked—it was— then without further hesitation, he gripped harder and turned sharply, preternatural strength breaking the lock before he flung the door open and let it crash against the wall.

George Mason was just unbuttoning his trousers in front of a young lady who was sitting on the bed in the dingy room with its simple furnishings. In the moment that he moved in, time slowed and Hiram took in the entire scene in detail: the look of hesitation and shame on the girl's face as she braced herself for an unsavory time with Mason, her slender frame clothed in a thin chemise, lacy open drawers, and a corset cinched tight into an hourglass, squeezing her small bosom to look larger than it was. She couldn't yet be eighteen with that soft pretty face and carefully shaped chestnut ringlets falling around her shoulders. Then Hiram blinked and time shifted back to normal.

The girl screamed at the sudden entry while Mason startled and spun, rangy brows knitting into an ugly frown that made his weasel-dark eyes seem all the meaner. "Who the hell'r you?"

Hiram paused in the doorway, looking at his quarry calmly as he reached into his vest to pull out a wanted ad which he unfolded and held up, pretended to compare the sketch portrait on it to the man in the room. He'd already confirmed it was Mason, but being around Cage for a week seemed to have infused him with a sense of drama. "Yep, that's you, isn't it, Mason?" He flipped the ad around.

The man's lips pursed as if whispering, *Oops*. "That ain't me. Just some feller looks like me." Weasel eyes darted around the room looking for some way out other than the door. There was one small window that faced the back of the building, but it was latched and there was no way any man could get that opened and scramble out before Hiram could stop him.

Hiram set the ad down on the side table, removed his coat and draped it over the chair, then his hat. It made for more dramatics, but he also didn't want to mess up his new, good duster so soon. "You realize that you still responded to the name Mason?" Only a dumbfounded stare answered him. "Says here you killed a man in Tip Top. That's only fifty miles away. You've either got balls of stone or stone for brains to still be sporting around here."

Mason shifted on his feet. "You're just a low-life bounty hunter ain't'cha?"

Hiram shrugged. "Something like that."

"Don't see no gun on ya."

Between their exchange, he could hear the girl's breath catch and release as if with relief.

Hiram sighed. Yeah. He missed his gun, too. That would at least give more of the impression that he *was* a bounty hunter. He held up a hand to count off Mason's other crimes, those not listed but which he'd heard on the wind while listening outside the Maricopa County sheriff's office all week as he'd carefully picked each mark, assuming they were in town. He'd had two successful hunts in four days using the method. Not bad. "Horse thieving." He uncurled a finger. "Rustling." Another finger. "Uh more rustling." He lowered his hand and sobered to deadly seriousness. "You also raped a sixteen-year-old girl, George." He barely suppressed the growl that wanted to creep out in his voice.

By now Mason's heartbeat had become a loud drum in Hiram's ears, picking up pace with each second he remained cornered. "Yeah, well, sixteen's nice'n tender. Good age to teach a girl to be a woman. Like this here lil filly. Purty, ain't she?"

That did it.

Hiram shot across the room in a blur and had grabbed Mason by the arm, yanked him close in a violent, jarring motion. Mason managed a yelp and his free arm flailed to try to get in a punch before Hiram spun the man, who was not much smaller than him, to the side, gripped him by the throat, lifted and tipped him in a backward arc. At the same moment, Hiram brought up a knee, meeting the middle of Mason's back like breaking a piece of kindling. A satisfying crunch sounded deep inside the bone and tissue. Mason gaped in shock, unable to get another cry out. His mouth bobbed open like a fish as Hiram held his upper body by the shoulders. His legs went instantly limp, but his arms spasmed as if shot with lightning.

Hiram looked up coolly at the girl, not sure how much longer he could control himself. She was cringing against the wall, knees drawn to her chest. Eyes wide and mouth gaping to summon a scream that would not come.

"Go," he said lowly. "Now."

Without a word, only gasps and a frightened, bobbling nod, she scrambled off the bed and hurried past him, out the door, her bare footsteps padding down the hall.

Satisfied that she was gone, Hiram leaned over his mark and felt a sore grinding in his upper jaw as his canines lengthened into sharp fangs, forcing him to open his mouth before the tips cut into his lower gums. "My daughter is sixteen, you piece of shit," he snarled before he gripped a handful of Mason's greasy hair and forced his head to the side to expose a dirt-streaked, sweaty neck. He winced at the initial sour taste of Mason's skin as he spread his mouth open over the man's carotid, and then his fangs plunged in, popping the surface before retracting, leaving too perfect holes which filled his mouth with blood. Mason's upper body stiffened with more shock and confusion as he no doubt wondered what exactly was happening to him or maybe how his assailant had moved so fast. Hiram gulped down one fresh draw after another. For a small eternity all he knew was the satiating taste of copper and salt, the warmth that filled his belly and coursed out into his own veins. His hearing homed in on Mason's heartbeat, now booming with an underwater effect in Hiram's ears as it began to slow to a stop.

Boom.

Hiram moaned as he felt a pleasurable flush come to his skin.

Boom.

He drank faster, each draw dwindling, each space between beats growing longer.

Boom.

Until nothing, and Hiram still drank, pulled hard to get out every last drop he could, to spill absolutely none of it, to sense and feel that the veins had collapsed. When the taste of blood turned back into sour flesh, he rejoined his wits and released his mark, dropped the body to the floor and stared down at it.

Mason's weasel eyes were not so weaselly now, rolled back in his head, his mouth hung open and slack. Already, a thin web of black veins was showing through the skin around the bite area.

"I have to say, H, this is beyond disturbing. There's brutal and then there's…" Silas appeared to lean in the open doorway as if he'd been there the entire time. "This," he finished.

Hiram licked his lips, ran his tongue over his gums, swallowed to clear his mouth of the last remnants of his grizzly meal. "You heard the man," he said to the ghost. "Sixteen is tender," he repeated Mason's words. "I couldn't make it easy for him."

"I know you couldn't," Silas replied. "Not like you have a choice now."

Hiram started to look at him again, but the phantasm of a Creole gentleman of forty in a maroon satin vest and frilled shirt had already vanished. He grabbed his coat and hat, put them both back on and straightened himself up, then he took the wanted ad in one hand and reached down and grabbed Mason by the grubby front of his shirt, used it as a handle to hoist the body and drag it unceremoniously from the room and down the hallway, paying no mind when the head incidentally thumped against a wall like a melon.

At the bottom of the stairwell, two of the saloon's patrons and the lazy-eyed bartender had gathered to look up. The girl was not among them, so Hiram assumed they'd witnessed her fleeing and perhaps they'd heard some of the scuffling upstairs. Hiram didn't give them time to examine that his cargo was stone-cold dead. For all they knew Mason was simply unconscious. He waved the ad at them as he descended the steps, dragging the body with little effort.

"Pardon me gentlemen, I'm just here to collect this bounty," he announced as he stepped down. God, he really did miss his gun, but unlike Mason, they didn't notice that he wasn't carrying. They scrambled back and squinted at the paper. Then, satisfied, the two patrons started to go back to their tables.

"He was booked two whole nights," the bartender commented, unfazed. This all seemed normal for him.

"Meh." Hiram adjusted for a better grip on his *bounty*. "Use the extra to give that room a good cleaning after this filth." With that he bent over and effortlessly hauled Mason's body over his shoulder, remembering to stagger just so to make it appear there was at least a little effort. He swung his way out through the doors and quickly spirited his load off the boardwalk and around the side of the building into the alleyway. The darkness here was a comfort to his sensitive eyes, every detail still clear, still forming a string of photographs in his mind that he had no choice but to accept and keep filing away. An eternity of this was going to get tiring, but he had to do what he had to do.

The shadow of the man in black stood halfway down the passage, pale face standing out from under the brim of his hat and the high rise of his coat collar. "That was fast. You're getting very good at this."

"Thank you, Titus," Hiram replied tritely to the former mayor of Mica Bend. In the last week since the town's demise, and since departing with his new companions, Hiram had been nothing short of cold toward the thrall. He'd watched Cage return from a hunt gorged with blood, half of which he then fed to Titus to keep him wound up and moving, the elixir imparting similar strength and healing abilities to that of the two noble vampires whom Titus now served without question. Hiram cringed at the thought that one day he might need to create a thrall of his own, but for now he was considered a baby by vampire standards, a fledgling that had just learned to hunt and survive.

"I'll handle the rest, Hiram. You go on back to the hotel. Cage is making plans."

"Of course he is." Hiram handed off his load and in moments Titus Watkins had disappeared into the night with it. Somewhere away from town, the body would be dismembered and burned.

The former marshal of Mica Bend turned and left the alley, went back to Washington Street and proceeded east toward the Lemon Hotel at the corner of Washington and Pima. The crowds remained thick, but now that he'd fed, every pulse and heartbeat no longer called to the hungry thing inside him.

A week now since leaving Mica Bend to be claimed by the desert. A

week now since letting his children go to Philadelphia with the good
Pastor Norman Becker, who had aided him in the losing war against Cage
and the other vampires who had chosen the already dying town as a
buffet to pick over.

You had no choice, Silas constantly reminded him.

Upon being infected with the initial disease that began to slowly
change him into a mindless revenant, Hiram had expected to go down
fighting to his last human breath and die heroically for his family, but bad
luck and not enough knowledge of his enemy had changed all of that.
When Micajah "Cage" Edwards offered him noble blood as a means to
survive and become a whole, thinking creature and not merely a savage,
violent husk, he'd taken it. Maybe, he had thought, he would be able to
use it to his advantage, appear to turn and join the ranks of Cage's kind,
burn them from the inside out. It would take patience and observation,
self-discipline not to give himself away asking too many eager questions,
wondering when Cage would get the beginnings of this new kith out of
Phoenix and introduce Hiram to a deeper realm of vampire society.

Merely a week later, he found it growing ever so slightly harder to
hang on to that goal. Already his new instincts occasionally overrode his
reason. He tried to choose the vilest marks, like Mason, as he could find
by haunting the dives, watching and listening for the most unsavory
discussions that told him he'd found a bad man who deserved the death
he had to deliver. He lurked around the sheriff's and marshal's offices
collecting wanted ads in his mind, and this was his plan for wherever he
should go, following Cage, hoping to gain the damnable creature's trust
while walking the razor's edge of this damnable game.

But there was a part of him that didn't want to care about human
innocence and simply feed. It belonged to the beast that wanted only to
survive and had been there almost from the moment he'd awakened from
the death sleep that completed his transformation. At least Cage had
honored his agreement to let Hiram's children go. They were safe, under
the watch of Becker and by now on their way back east, moving on to a
new life that Hiram had been unable to give them. The rest of the whole
ordeal felt so distant as he stood on dusty Washington Street,
acknowledging how different the chill of night felt now, looking up into a
vault of stars that was ten times more brilliant to his vision than before,
and if he focused his hearing, he detected ethereal hums and pulses. He
might be a supernatural creature discovering abilities beyond his

imagination, but this, at least, reminded him that he was still a small thing under that vast, singing sky. It was a very grounding thought that made the beast be quiet.

"Hiram," Cage's smooth as honey but deep voice said behind him.

He suppressed a startle and gritted his teeth for a second. *Dammit.*

"I know your new senses pick up a lot of beautiful things now, but never allow yourself to be so distracted," the noble said as he stepped into view next to his creation. Irate though his tone, he became more so as he looked Hiram up and down. "Seriously, I gave you plenty of money and you still strive to look like the lawman you were."

"I like dusters."

"Well, I suppose they do blend in anywhere." Cage had a fold of paper in his hand, a telegram slip.

"What's that?"

"Our new orders. We will be leaving for Bodie tonight, as soon as Titus is finished with clean up."

"What the hell's in Bodie?" He'd been through the gold town in California nearly two decades ago when it was still a developing mining camp, when he and Silas were young, adventurous and stupid, played at every card table, laid down in every brothel, and vampires were only a thing found in serial pulp like his son's penny dreadfuls.

"For one, I have a meeting to keep. For another, it's the perfect place to winter." On Hiram's confused frown he elaborated merrily. "I know, it's in the middle of nowhere, but like your old town, that makes it easier to feed and clean there, and when the snows hit and block the roads in…" His mouth twitched in the wickedest of smirks. "People disappear there, naturally."

"Naturally," Hiram echoed dryly.

"And those disappearances are easily explained away," he finished. "Besides, there will be some surprises for you."

"Oh?" Hiram raised a brow, immediately uncomfortable with the idea of any more surprises. "You mean your kith arriving in my town wasn't enough?"

Cage chuckled lowly then gave Hiram a slap on the shoulder, the gesture too friendly, too familiar. Too intrusive. "I promised to show you a new world, didn't I? Come now, we have to prepare." He started walking toward the Lemon Hotel, tucking the telegram into the vest beneath his great coat.

Hiram wanted, for the most fleeting of seconds, to bash his sire's head in, beat him to a bloody pulp and dump his remains to burn in the morning sun. But firstly, that was impossible. Secondly, Cage was a means to an end to all of this madness.

Patience, he reminded himself and the thrum of his heart remained slow and steady, betraying nothing of the angry flare in his mind or how much he would always hate Cage Edwards. Then Hiram took a new breath and followed, listening to the stars.

CHAPTER ONE

Mica Bend, Arizona Territory
Three Weeks Ago

A shrill cry like that of a hawk bounded beyond the jagged teeth of a newborn mountain range to echo in the valley below. It was accompanied by the steel-like ring of one power clashing against another and then a feathery glowing luminance danced across the sky. Thunder clapped as mighty wings beat the air and stirred smoky-black clouds that formed a patchwork across a red-gold horizon dotted with swarms of raging angels.

In moments the clouds condensed into a black blanket and gushed curtains of rain that collected on the earth below. Mere puddles became ponds, then lakes, and finally there was no land but the surrounding mountains.

He watched the event from a rocky outcropping on one of the lofty peaks, perched like an indignant bird as the waters rose below. Bloated bodies drifted on the surface, and he could do nothing about it. Occasionally they snagged each other. Someone's toes tangled in someone else's hair over here, or curled fingers hooked into the seam of a tattered dress over there, until they'd formed a chain of grisly fish food.

"There ain't no hell, Raines, this is it," Sergeant Danny Connor's raspy, weakening voice said next to him before a loud screech of iron grinding on iron startled him.

Seth Raines' eyes snapped open to stare at the ceiling of the jail cell from where he lay on the hard bunk, brilliant light streaming in from the Venetian blinds over the front windows. The noise of the dream slowly faded from inside his skull and, as always upon awakening, he felt a numb tingle pass through the entirety of his skin, especially over his head and face. It settled with a tight, stifling feeling that he'd grown used to over the course of his life. A stabbing pain gripped his temples, and he burped up the taste of whiskey and bile before swallowing it back down. Taking a breath, he rolled his eyes to behold Marshal Hiram Wells standing back from the opening in the cell while another, all too familiar figure stood waiting.

"He's all yours," Wells said to the newcomer, who unbuckled a heavy, dusty buckskin coat and removed a pair of tinted spectacles.

"You let anyone in this town anymore, don't you Marshal?" Seth grated out. "Thought you were more cautious than that."

"My judgment's been slipping since I let you in, Raines," Wells responded almost jovially. That was something, considering the constant dark cloud that had followed the man around since his wife's death in the spring. Seth's gaze shifted to the figure of his brother entering the cell. Wells stepped out of the way and went over to the safe where he busied himself with the dial on the lock.

Ben looked virtually the same, suspended somewhere in his early thirties despite being fifty-one. His hair had been cut short in back since the last time Seth had seen him but left a long sweep of fringing bangs in the front. His face was covered in a thin mask of road dust while the hollows of his eyes were somewhat spared via the spectacles. His dark eyes drifted around the cell, found nothing much to look at, then settled on Seth. "God, it gets worse every time I see you," he said. "This your permanent residence?"

"Ha," Seth burped again. "Yeah, what would Mama say, eh?"

"Mama's the reason I'm here." Ben approached and bent over to try to prod him to get up. Seth smirked and refused to cooperate as Ben gripped the younger man's shoulders and wrenched Seth up into at least a sitting position. "Oh damn, that breath, brother." Ben almost turned green. "Blow a buzzard off a shit wagon."

"S'jus' whiskey," Seth said as he staunched the bizarre clash of emotions over seeing his big brother for the first in a long while. He wanted to ask more specifically *why* Ben had shown up, but there were other ears in the room, and while their kind had their own language, the last thing he needed was Marshal Wells' generous sense of curiosity digging in his business asking for a translation, please.

"Time for food and maybe a bucket of cold water," Ben suggested.

By now, Wells had the safe open and Seth's confiscated—not for the first time—Colt Army revolver settled in his hands as he stared at it for a moment longer as if in love with the thing. Seth had to grin a bit at that; he himself was partial to the piece for reasons. Then Wells chimed in helpfully, "Pump's around the side. Well water's nice and cold."

"Fuck you, Marshal," Seth griped as his brother finally guided one of his arms over a shoulder and hauled Seth to his feet. The sudden motion sent his stomach flipping and, contrary to his spiteful sentiment toward the marshal, a visit to said pump sounded perfect. He pulled away from Ben, got his balance, and stumbled from the cell with a grunt under his breath of, "I can do it." With that he leaned into some forward momentum and wove his way around the front marshal's and deputy's desks and right for the door, leaving Ben to finalize things with Wells.

He flung the door open, wincing at the afternoon light that accosted him, and stumbled out from the jail house boardwalk into the wide, dusty street. Wells' horse was tethered to the hitch next to a dappled gray mare which Seth assumed was his brother's. Both animals let out tiny squeals and grumbles at Seth's abrupt emergence. From there he turned on a heel and headed around the side of the building to the left, into the space between the jail and the mayor's office that stood not far off. He began to furiously pump the water, cupped it in his hands and splashed his face, gulped it down to clear the acid from his throat. He heard the soft approach of hooves as Ben had retrieved his horse from the hitch before following.

"Thank the Presence," Ben's voice said behind him. "I thought I'd have to do that for you." He stroked the mare's soft lavender-gray nostrils and watched the haphazard attempt at a bath.

Seth stuck a finger in his mouth and ran it over his teeth, scraping away grit and plaque with a fingernail. "Hell'er you doin' in the Bend?" He noticed Ben now had the Colt Army, its belt and ammo pouch gripped in his hand. "Can I have my gun back?"

"Why hello, brother, how you been?" Ben said snidely. "How long has it been and not even a telegram?" Ben coughed and dropped the sarcasm. "Not yet," he said about the gun as he turned and tucked the bundle into a saddle bag and secured it, "not until I'm sure you won't end up right back in that cell. I see you've been here long enough to ingratiate yourself with the locals." He looked up and scanned the horizon south toward the schoolhouse and the hazy rise of the Arduous range in the distance then back around to Seth, who had dunked his entire head under the flow of the water. "Looks like a good place to drop out of the world for a while. But then, you were always good at that." He leveled his gaze.

Seth massaged his scalp and temples, savored the cool drip around his pounding head. "Get off it. You know it's more complicated than that."

He stood, wringing out a long, thick twist of dark hair that he settled back on his shoulders where it continued to drip onto his yellow-stained undershirt. Already the southern Arizona climate dried both shirt and hair at a rapid rate. For a moment he listened, heard the softer clomp of Wells' boots on the boardwalk, then the jail house door closing, the creak of leather as the marshal mounted up on his horse and rode off, hoof beats fading toward the northwest end of town.

Then Seth started walking, taking the back route around the jail and toward the old cribs that miners and prostitutes alike rented and toward the old Chinese laundry, where a sheet wall hung. He could hear the last few celestials chattering distantly as they worked, not that they had much work anymore—probably only Silas LeBlanc's dandy wear—and Seth had never given them any of his business. Right now, he wanted to avoid crossing paths with Terry Wilkes, because it was his barber pole that Seth had almost, accidentally-on-purpose, shot at earlier today. Seth couldn't even remember why or what triggered such an urge now, only that cheap whiskey had been involved.

"*A Aran gil de camliax nonca,*" Ben called out behind him in the Tongue.

Seth stopped in his tracks for a moment to switch to vocabulary and grammar he hadn't needed for some time.

A Aran meant "the elder" but in this case it was used to mean a certain title, *The Sage,* and while it sounded singular, it was plural, a conglomerate of clan elders mystically linked and working together.

With a deep breath, Seth spoke dismissively back in the same tongue, "The Sage *always* wants to speak with me." With that he kept walking.

"Seth, come on, brother," Ben switched back to English. "It wouldn't hurt you to pay a visit."

Seth turned around. "So Mama sent you, huh?" He gave an incriminating arch of his brow. Their mother, Abigail Raines, pretty much went along quietly with their father on everything related to Seth even if she didn't seem to approve. *Mama sent me* was more like code for, *Shit's going down at home and we would like for you to address it.*

"Absolutely," Ben said, going along. "She misses you terribly." He smirked then, and the last few minutes' tension between them dissolved.

A slow smile spread across Seth's lips and he opened his arms. "It's good to see you, brother."

Ben embraced him to be met with a hard slap on the back. "*Oof,* you still don't know your own strength, you little shit." He gave a solid slap of his own but stopped there—anymore and the nice reunion would degrade into a wrestling match—before they broke apart. "You still need to do something about your breath."

Seth grinned, intentionally huffed a gust of said nasty breath right in Ben's face—the resultant cringe completely worth it—and turned to proceed along the back way, Ben beside him leading the mare. Seth switched back to their mother tongue out of general precaution. *"Par donsregn nonci."*

They sent you.

That was the closest translation, anyway. A literal use would be more like, *They delivered you.*

Ben never could lie, so he didn't even try. *"Noib."*

Yes.

He continued, still in the tongue, "I told them I'd check on you, but I didn't tell them where I was going. I promise you that."

"I know." Seth nodded, certain that Ben had kept his word that he would never lead The Sage to the subject of their long-held obsession. At least one member of his damn big family showed him some respect after the life he'd been forced into from birth.

They passed the back of the Orleans Palace Saloon, owned by LeBlanc, who was known to be Marshal Wells' best friend. Tonight, Seth figured he'd be patronizing that great establishment and asking himself why he'd ever let Ben know where he was, even if he did love his brother. He loved his entire clan, even if they were right pricks. That was why they sent Ben, because out of all six of his older brothers, Ben was the one he trusted the most. The one who could show up without causing Seth to spook and run like he had when Dane, the oldest, confronted him in Barstow years ago. Dane's method of reeling in his runaway baby brother was pretty much straight up arrest, manacles at the ready, but if there was one thing his family had gifted Seth that came in most handy, it was the skill of slipperiness.

He smiled smugly to himself pondering that last escape. He was probably already in Los Angeles before Dane even realized he'd fled.

"What?" Ben asked, flipping back to English.

Seth blinked. "What?"

"What are you grinning about?"

"Nothin'." He perked up to the distant sound of heavy hooves and multiple wheels grinding in the packed sand on the main street and his attention drifted elsewhere. "Hey, what is that?" Curious, he slipped down the alleyway between the Palace and the Raskin Hotel, just in time to see the approach of a huge black freight wagon pulled by a team of six black draft horses. The driver, hunched high in the seat, was covered in a heavy black woolen coat with a wide brimmed hat tipped forward to hide most of his pale face from view and shade his eyes. The side of the coach was painted with garish red and gold letters reading: *The Chamberlain Players.*

An acting troupe, it seemed. But a certain smell wafted from the entire beast of a vehicle, familiar and disturbing and Seth immediately backed up against the alley wall, keeping out of sight as the freighter passed. Ben, who had left his horse at the rear of the alley and followed, did the same. Both of them knew what that uniform meant, and even more by the next vehicle to come along, an elegant black coach that was clearly sealed up, no windows to speak of, drawn by a team of Saddlebreds that were as pure black as the draft team. The same red and gold letters decorated the sides.

Seth didn't have to guess who the passengers were. They were here to entertain and seduce the town, what was left of it, distract the locals. "Shit," he hissed. "That's Micajah Edwards' kith."

"I'm a little concerned you even know his name," Ben whispered.

"Saw their shit show in Prescott, made me wanna puke."

"Charming." Ben only put on an air of patience as the troupe wagons passed, but Seth remained wound up.

"They're here for only one reason, Ben," he said sharply under his breath. "The Bend's barely hanging on. Mines are dead, people are moving out. Edwards is gonna bleed what's left of it."

"And there's nothing we can do about that, Seth."

"I've gotta warn the marshal." He started to boost away from the wall only to have Ben grab his arm firmly and pull him back with a hard thump against the wood that nearly jarred the breath out of him.

Ben spun to face him, pinning his shoulders, ready to shake sense into him. "You'll do no such thing." His brown eyes turned almost black as he spoke through his teeth. "That's breaking the agreement, Seth." Ben's voice had gone from that of a loving brother to deadly serious. "You can't touch Edwards or anyone else in his kith."

Seth cursed under his breath and swallowed down a lump of hopelessness as the sound of the wheels ground on down the street. He shoved his brother back, stepped away from the wall and paced, feeling bolts of nervy energy streak through him. And anger. So much anger. "Shit."

"Pretty much." Ben turned and went back to collect his horse and returned. "Let it go."

Seth's jaw clenched as he considered the town's fate. Truth was, he liked most of the people here, and he liked the marshal. He'd watched the man grieve the loss of his wife this past spring. Her name was Rachel—a name that already carried a powerful hold over Seth's emotions—and she had been one of the loveliest, kindest people Seth had ever met. She'd even managed to calm him one morning when she was strolling into town from the Wells house and found him sitting outside the now defunct Grand Saloon, hungover, on his ass on the edge of the boardwalk because the last nightmare to plague him kept flashing through his skull and he didn't know what to do about it. Clearly, no amount of booze had done any good, and he couldn't tell anyone what he saw in his head. They could never understand because the reasons behind it were too far beyond the box of human scope.

Rachel Wells respectfully did not try to pry answers from him, only looked at him and smiled softly. "What's wrong, Seth?"

"Nothin', Ma'am, just another bad night." He wiped warm snot out from under his nose.

Another soft smile. "I see." She had a basket under her arm, and she was wearing a faded pink dress that might have seen better days, but she'd kept it mended and neat, and her blonde hair made a soft halo against the sun. "Here…" She reached into the basket beneath a cloth and pulled out a neatly cut square of dried fruit pie. "It won't make a bad night totally go away, but it'll help you see the morning light."

Seth realized she was probably delivering some breakfast to her husband at the jail, and he hoped the marshal wouldn't mind the portion being a bit smaller. He could still taste that exquisite pie, packed with dried cherries and dates bound in batter flavored just slightly with vanilla and cinnamon. Then he remembered the morning he'd heard the news of her death. She'd come down sick with typhoid, and for days the town was deathly quiet. When Hiram Wells appeared again after her funeral, it was to bury himself in his work at the jail, or at the Palace, or anywhere that kept him from staying too long at home, even with his three children there. Unknown to him, Seth had wept, too, quietly and alone out at his camp at the foot of the Arduous Range.

"Seth…" Ben's voice reached through the clouds in his ears. "Seth, come on. Let's go. I'll get you supper. I'll even pay for a visit to the bathhouse. That pump ain't nearly enough."

Seth stared at the late afternoon glare of sun on the sand, turning it slightly golden, and the tracks the newcomers had left up the thoroughfare.

This time, Ben's hand on his arm was gentler, guiding. "Please."

"Yeah," Seth muttered and sniffled. Then he surrendered and let his brother take the lead, just for a little while.